VAMPIRE'S KISS

MAFIA MONSTERS SERIES BOOK ONE

ATLAS ROSE

KIM FAULKS

He captured my wrist, smooth black leather against my skin. The kiss was hungry, and urgent. His hard chest pressed me against the bricks and before I knew it, my hand rising to meet the wall.

He had me. Gloved hand pinning my wrists above me. His finger at my temple.

And his lips taking...taking...taking.

The Hidden, we call them. Four Vampires who run this city west of the river.
And my family runs the east.

They're immortal *beasts*...more dangerous than my family, the Costello's.

Only my dying dad has left behind a fuck load of trouble.

One of them, a deal with these fanged beasts...*a deal that's now gone south.*

Threats on my windshield, and a dead rat impaled on my door makes me confront these monsters.

Elithien, the leader of the Vampire Clan wants to tell me the truth.

Only it's a truth I don't want to believe.

But somehow I always return to them.

These Vampires invade my mind...and leave me craving their touch.

Hurrow, Justice and Rule are possessive, and jealous and every bit the bloodthirsty hunters I knew them to be.

I *will* fight the lies they tell me. I will hold on to the last traces of my sanity.

I won't become a monster like them...not even for love.

BE THE FIRST TO KNOW OF A NEW RELEASE!
Click here to signup for my newsletter.
Like my Facebook Page
Join my Facebook Group

"You gonna cry?"

Shadows moved against the sun. Chubby fingers clenched around my wrist and shoved hard against the concrete walk. We were alone here, out of sight from the house, where no one would hear me scream.

"Go on...cry."

Another's hand over my chest, until I couldn't breathe. His fingers searched, pinching the tiny pink nub as he licked his lips and sneered.

Daddy, where are you?

But no one was here to save me. No one but me.

I swallowed the pain. They'd caught me off guard. Next time I'll know better.

"You tell no one, *got it?*" He pinched harder.

But I didn't nod, not even when the tears came. They were supposed to be family. Supposed to be *my* friend.

Next time, I won't be so powerless. I'll run...I'll fight...
I'll survive.

Next time, I'll save myself.
Maybe then I'll win.

L aughter filled the back room of the Jewel.

Deep, growling, raucous laughter that boomed from almost every seat at the table in the most exclusive bar this side of the river.

Crystal sparkled and champagne flowed.

There were mostly men, apart from the odd sparkling handbag; women who served no other purpose than to hang off the arm of their boyfriend, or *gentleman friend* for the night, and smile.

The women were few and far between, and they never stayed long. Long enough to show off their brand new breasts and sparkling Cartier, before they were gone, waltzing through the bar, with the doors closing behind them as the men stayed here.

Then there were no more women…*except for me.*

The rich were here…but that wasn't what got them an invite. Power was the commodity these men traded. Power, money, drugs, and women. These were *powerful men*. I winced at the roar, and they were also fucking loud.

I singled out Dad's laughter; deeper than the others, as though a single tone could epitomize the man. He *was* deeper, like a river carved through the belly of this city, stronger, and more powerful than any other man sitting here—and they all knew it.

Secret smiles for him. A nod of the head, first draw of the fat Cohiba Behike cigar while they all watched, eyes alight with ravenous hunger.

I glanced at the other side of the room, to the empty tables waiting for the other half of Crown City's most elite, and felt my stomach clench. The ones who ran the 'other side' of the river.

The other side.

The words lingered as I stared at the three tables; three tables with six seats each. One for the Wolves, one for the Unseelies, and one for the Vampires. I'd heard that there were only three heads of each of the Immortal Mafia. The name made me wince, the *M word.* We didn't say it in our house, not *gang,* or *Crime Syndicate.* Nothing that *trashy.*

We were businessmen—I glanced around the testosterone-drenched room—*and woman.*

I stared at the empty tables. Three heads of each *breed* and three other chairs. I thought they'd show. Thought they'd grace us mere mortals with their presence. Thought I'd get my first look at those monsters in the dark.

Maybe our whiskey wasn't good enough for them... maybe our blood a little too tempting?

My stomach tightened and my blood ran cold as Dad threw his head backwards and clutched the white napkin. Something Irish said made him shake with a pent-up roar, like a volcano ready to erupt. And he did, spitting out small white plumes of the vile cigar smoke, until the laughter turned into something else.

A dry hacking cough gripped him, turning his face redder than laughter ever could, until he fought for a gasp of breath.

"You okay?" Sol called across the table.

"Hey!" Irish's sparkling green eyes darkened with fear as he stood and slapped Dad on the back. "Denny? You all good?"

It was the same savage cough I'd been hearing for weeks now. The same one I'd fought with him over, making appointment after appointment with the doctor, only for him to have some lackey call behind my back and cancel.

He nodded, tears streaming down his cheeks as Irish gave him another *thump* on the back, shaking whatever shit was inside him loose.

Dad gulped in air and nodded, blue eyes sparkling as he looked at me. His hand rose from the table, fingers splayed as he patted the air. *I'm okay, don't call a fucking ambulance, kid. I'm okay.*

His words rang inside my head as clearly as though he was standing next to me. My heart hammered, hands clenched around the end of the bar.

I watched them, *had spent my entire fucking life watching them, actually…*my focus mostly on Dad as he tried to follow that gulp of air with another and glanced at me once more with a nod. *I'm okay, Ruthy.*

The good ol' boys' club. If you wanted to take the crime rate down a notch in Crown City, then this was the place to bomb…on a night like tonight.

I hated the hacking sound, hated the laughter, really. I

liked the quiet, and the cold. I liked it when I could fucking think. A smile in place of a wince. I gave a nod as every now and then someone at the table glanced my way.

I stood here as Ruth Costello, daughter of the most powerful man in Crown City. But no one really knew me. No one knew the woman screaming to get out, to be free, to be anything but the ball-busting, cold-hearted bitch they saw.

I was a product of my environment, a leather-leashed dog in the most vicious, vindictive dogfight this city has ever seen. I just needed to keep on fighting, keep on being the bitch they all saw.

"Another?" the bartender slid a tumbler my way.

Amber sparkled at the bottom, inviting. "Why the hell not," I muttered, and grabbed the glass, downing the contents in one swallow and held it out once more. "Another…on second thought." I lifted my gaze to the good-looking guy. "Leave the bottle."

One slow nod. He glanced toward the table, then back to me. "You waiting?" He jerked a glance toward them. "They might be a while."

His gaze slipped to the plunging neckline on my top. *Cocky bastard.* "Yeah, I'm waiting." *Waiting for my fucking turn at the table. Did that count?*

"So, are you exclusive? I mean, escort-wise?" His gaze skimmed the tops of my breasts, I was bare under the shimmering material, bare and raw and *savage.*

The sonofabitch thought I was a hooker? He must be goddamn new. I leaned forward, grasped the bottle, showing him just a little more. "Depends on what you mean by exclusive?"

Chairs scraped behind me. There was a grunt, and a joke…*a vile fucking joke.* Still, I never turned away from the delicious morsel in front of me.

"What I mean is," he smiled, showing me perfect white teeth, and gripped the bar with both hands, arms flexing, showing me the power I could enjoy with a simple, *do you want to fuck me?*

A hard, full-handed *slap* tore along my ass, stinging and burning.

"Get us two more, will you, love?" Underland never waited for an answer, just gave me a greasy smirk, showing nicotine-stained teeth, then a wink with his beady black eyes. "That's a good girl."

Anger plunged deep, swallowing the burn of my ass with a frigid touch. I rose, looked at the foul, fucking lackey who made every fucking attempt to put me down and met his stare. "How about you *get your own fucking drink?* Or I'm gonna take this bottle, smash the end, and glass your goddamn face. How 'bout that?"

He froze, and the roar of laugher inside the room quieted. I didn't have to turn my head to see all eyes were on me. *Ice cold cunt. Fucking frigid queen.* I knew the names they called me. If not them, then the men under their rule, the ones they allowed to spread the hateful names.

Underland's little black eyes widened. The hitch in his breath trembled the jowl of fat that hung under his chin. "Jesus Christ, Ruthy. I was only making a fucking joke." One glance behind him and a jerk of his head my way, and the room rocked with howls and hoots of laughter once more.

Only this time, a little louder. I shifted my glance to

my father. He never laughed, only smiled. A secret smile. One just for me, as he nodded his head and turned back to them.

The powerful.

The elite.

"Just a joke, Ruthy." Underland turned to me once more and smiled his greedy fucking smile.

It was always *just a joke.* Always *just a brush of the hand.* Always *just a boys' club, and if you want to fit in...then do what we say.*

I glanced at the barman. His eyes were wide and he was no longer smiling. Now he just looked at me like every other asshole in the city did—with fear.

"I'm s-sorry," he stammered, and swallowed hard. "Didn't realize you were..."

Didn't realize I was what exactly? A woman. One who deserves a little goddamn respect, regardless of her profession? "Forget it." I looked away and grabbed the bottle once more.

Two glasses hit the bar. Gin splashed the bottoms.

"What is this, a fucking AA meeting?" Underland snapped at the barman and jerked his head toward the glasses. "Fill 'em up, dipshit."

I left them then, left them floundering, one asshole nursing his stinking fucking pride, and the other a desperate need to keep his goddamn job. I grabbed my glass and my bottle and headed for one of the empty tables.

The Wolves weren't using them, so why the hell not?

Fucking Wolves. I can't believe they wanted them here. I'd been asking the same damn questions since I arrived, and all I got in return was tight smiles and a pat on the back of my hand. I looked to Dad, sitting there amongst his followers, smile wide, blue eyes shining. But I could tell it was a lie. Something was up, something he didn't like.

Something he wasn't telling me.

The door to the private room opened.

"Sir, you're not permitted back here!" growled a guard from the door.

The Jewel was glamor, and prestige. The most exclusive bar this side of the river, you didn't pay to get into a place like this...*you earned.* Earned a name. Earned a reputation, and I wasn't talking street-level though, with a Glock against his palm like it was a second cock. I meant dealings, power play. I meant the kind of acquisitions one makes with a simple nod.

Yeah, shit like that went down in the Jewel on a weekly basis. This place was more than velvet-backed chairs and the finest liquor you can buy. It was sacred...and also known to every two-bit gangsta thug who thought he was *entitled* to a piece of the damn pie.

All heads turned toward the commotion. Movement came from the side, from the row of tables set aside for the muscle. Hands went to hips, some were already lifting their hands, muzzles carving through the air.

Trouble would be one of them, one with his gun in hand. One stepping to the forefront, not giving a shit who he had to shoot in his way. I swallowed and searched the room for him.

There he was, quick brown eyes, muscled physique under his open jacket. He relaxed a little when he saw his opponent…or *opponents.* Five of them entered, dressed in baggy jeans with the crotch hanging somewhere near their knees. White, black, Hispanic, it didn't matter. They weren't one of *us.*

They weren't born into it, didn't forge it out of mud and blood with their bare hands. They were the babies of this pyramid of power. Infants still sucking on their momma's tit.

The leader jumped and danced with a swagger that reminded me of someone with a disability, then pushed his way into the room.

"Sorry I'm late, *Pops.*" He glared at Dad when he said it. "But I seem to have missed *my* fucking invite."

Movement came from the side again. Trouble, pushing forward. One wave of Dad's hand stopped him. The napkin was set down in front of him, and Dad carefully rose to stand.

Power rippled around the room…*deadly power.* I could almost hear the hiss. I lowered my hand, fingers curled, sliding it under the rim of the table in front of me.

"You didn't get your invite because there was none sent," Dad answered.

The thug snorted laughter, looked behind him to his little harem of fuckboys and hangers-on, and shook his head. "I don't think you understand who you're talkin' to, old man."

"I know *exactly* who I'm talking to, Nathaniel Lorcrombe." Dad's tone lowered, cold steel, cutting edge.

The kid flinched at the name, the smile disappearing from his lips. There was a spark in his eye as his hand rose, fingers dancing near the waistband of his jeans. One wrong fucking move and the room would light up like the

Fourth of July. "No one calls me that 'round here. I'm Skull. I run these streets."

"You *run* what we *allow* you to run," Dad answered coldly. "Remember that."

I reached a little further under the table, until the cold steel kissed the tips of my fingers. The movement drew the thug's focus. His gaze slipped from my father's as he turned toward me. "There's spare seats there," he said, dark eyes shining with the curl of his lips.

I swallowed a shudder of revulsion as his gaze skimmed my body, lingering at the open neckline of my top. "Plenty of seats. That bitch don't need to be here. *Move, bitch.*"

Shadows shifted behind him. Soft, heavy steps echoed, blurring all around me as I crept my fingers along the gun. My heart thundered as a deep, guttural snarl came from behind the piece of shit. "Exactly what I was thinking, *move, bitch.*"

Fear crept along my spine as those shadows moved closer. Silver eyes glinted from the darkness. But it wasn't me the Wolf was looking at. It wasn't me his words were meant for. The mammoth male stepped closer, looming over the thug, curled lips revealing long, thick fangs.

The Wolves.

Two more stepped closer, flanking either side. They were just as big, hulking muscles straining the buttoned-up shirts they wore. Their hands were by their sides. I was gripped by the sight of the thick, calloused, curled fingers, and perfectly trimmed nails.

Were their claws just waiting? One thought and they'd shift into beasts and tear this entire room apart?

Panic seized me, tearing through my nerves.

Immortals.

I caught the whisper from my uncle to my dad, and pieced together the careful glances and quiet nods. They'd invited them here, those *monsters.* Vampires, Fae…Wolves. I'd seen those silver-eyed beasts only once, years ago as I waited in the back seat of dad's car. I shivered now just as I'd shivered then, staring at the hulking shadows, too terrified to move.

"You want me to ask twice?" the Alpha sneered, and leaned closer to the mouthy piece of shit. "I never ask twice."

"Phantom's right, he never asks twice," one of the other Wolves explained, then lifted his hand to stare at his nails. "Usually just rips your head off and throws it across the room."

"He has a temper," the other Wolf added.

Jesus, it was hard to tell them apart at first. The middle one, the *Alpha* of the three, had a scar that ran down the length of his cheek and cold dark eyes that shone with silver when they moved.

He was gorgeous, and totally not my type. Too…*Wolfy.*

And as though he heard my thoughts, he lifted his head and directed his cold, calculating gaze my way. The kid shrank from the beast's presence, jerking a panicked gaze around the room as a deep, rolling, chilling sound reverberated from the men.

"Now…," Phantom snarled, and glanced at the thug once more. "You going to make me ask again, or do you want to lose your fucking head?"

There was a whimper, and then a shuffle. But no swagger, not anymore, as the thug stumbled out of the Wolves' way and scurried for the door.

"That's what I figured," the Alpha snarled, his hungry gaze finding me again, as they turned to the real reason they were here—Crown City's most powerful men.

2

There was no *'sorry I'm late'.*

Just a nod.

A simple fucking nod, before the Alpha with the scarred face strode toward me, heaving all two hundred and twenty pounds of pure muscle my way. My finger danced near the trigger of the gun strapped under the table. Cold steel was all I felt. Cold steel and a healthy dose of fear.

He was tall, they all were six-three at least, muscles bunched around their shoulders like a second fucking coat. I tore my gaze from the scar on the Alpha's cheek to the blue eyes and shaggy brown hair of his second. Heat spilled through me, making that nerve in my temple bite like a bitch.

"This table for us?" Phantom muttered.

He knew damn well it was. I felt Dad's gaze on the side of my face as I gave a small nod and eased backwards, finger slipping from around the trigger guard.

"'Bout fucking time you showed up." Diggery stepped

closer, bottle and glasses clinking in his hand. "People were starting to think you guys were nothing more than a goddamn fairytale." He turned his head to the others at the table when he said the last part.

Laughter followed.

The Alpha's scar buckled with the wince, as he turned his gaze to Diggery, the dumb fuck. He was one of Dad's friends, but that didn't mean I had to like him. It just meant I couldn't call him a dumb fuck to his face.

The Alpha's second turned to the bumbling idiot and smiled, showing all white teeth and fangs. "*Fairy-tale*. I get it. Although, no offense taken, seeing as how Church over here likes dick."

A savage snarl came from the Wolf behind him. But Diggery's eyes widened and the smile slipped from his mouth like he was a wax doll left far too close to a fire.

And these Wolves were all fire, all heat. I rose carefully, feeling that pounding in my temple spear its way across my head.

"I d-didn't m-mean…" Diggery stuttered.

"Forget it." The blue-eyed beast stepped closer, looming over the fool, and snatched the bottle in one movement, leaving the glasses behind. "One bottle…is that all? We share some things, Diggery…but alcohol isn't one of them."

He just blubbered and stuttered, something about the best whiskey…five hundred dollars a bottle. But the Wolf had zero fucks to give, just strangled the neck of the bottle and lifted the rim to his lips.

One draw and he lowered his hand and gave a contented sigh. "Fuck, that shit *is* good."

Dad gave a wave of his hand, shooing Diggery away, still clutching the glasses.

More bottles came as I gripped my own and reached for my glass, ready to move.

"Stay if you want." The Alpha stepped closer and his dark, hungry gaze skimmed over me. But not like I was tits and ass for his attention, like I was dangerous…just as dangerous as the men—I kinda liked that. "Our other guests decided not to attend tonight."

"Your captives, you mean?" The words just spilled from my mouth without thought. Now I sounded like the damn fool.

Only there was no stutter, no weaseling my way back from the fucking ledge. Instead, the Wolf leaned in, nostrils flaring. *He's inhaling my damn scent.* The thought of that chilled me to the bone. Still, I refused to let the hairy bastard rattle my cage.

"No," Phantom gave a chuckle. "Our accountant, and chief of production."

"Chief of Production…hmmm, such a classy title. I prefer to call him what he is *your pimp.*"

The room stilled. It was an unspoken rule, we *never* discussed specifics of our operations…and never so crudely. That wasn't how we ran our business. But I hated it. I *fucking hated it.* I hated the thought of all those women being forced onto their backs. Hated the money just rolling into their pockets.

"That is what you run, right?" I glanced at the second as he took another swig from the bottle. "You run the women, the Dark Fae run the power…and the Vampires… the Vampires run the money."

There was a spark in the Wolf's gaze, a flare of *interest.* My pulse raced as that voice inside my head whispered *'you run your goddamn mouth, Ruth.'*

Still, I clenched my jaw and gave him my best murderous smile. I'd give him interest. Kick him right in the balls. But Jesus, those eyes…that hair, wavy and thick. He was all animal…all *beast.* It was hard not to be affected my him.

A fantasy came to life in my mind. The beast naked in front of me, all rippling muscles and ravenous hunger. I bet he'd have stamina, too…*I'd bet he'd fuck all night.*

My breaths deepened, desire flared for one fucking second…

What the hell am I doing?

I flinched and caught the Wolf's lips twitch with a smile. He knew…he knew what I was thinking. *Jesus…Jesus, no…*

"All legitimate businesses," Dad countered behind me. "And there's always a chance for Governor with the election coming up."

I flinched at his careful tone and jerked my gaze toward him. I'd lost myself there for a second, let the mask slip. I'd let plenty slip. But *Governor? Election?* What the hell did that have to do with any of this?

I caught a look that passed from Dad to the Alpha behind me…seemed like it had a helluva lot to do with it.

"Which is why we're here, isn't it? To discuss more important matters."

A sting raced along my arm, then swept through my body. I sucked in a hard breath with the pain and turned my head. Black, that was all I saw. Midnight eyes, pale skin…black leather and long, thick, black hair that dropped over their shoulders as three of the most lethal-looking men I'd ever seen stepped into the room.

"Car trouble," the center male muttered and glanced from the Alpha Wolf to me.

I felt myself cringe as they stepped closer, and the shadows of the room seemed to pull tighter like a cloak they wore.

"We interrupting something?" the taller Fae moved close, and snatched the bottle from the Wolf's hand.

A savage snarl echoed, "Hey, I was fucking drinking that."

"There's plenty enough to go 'round," Dad muttered and hurried the bartender forward. "Although now, I'm starting to think I underestimated your…*thirst.*"

The empty-handed Wolf gave a shrug. "Not the first thing you've underestimated about us."

But I knew the words were meant for me. They crowded the table, all six of them. And suddenly I felt this place wasn't big enough for even one of them…let alone all six.

Air seemed to well in my throat, but no matter how hard my muscles worked to draw it deeper, the bubble was stuck. "I think I need a little air."

I stepped away, taking my bottle and my glass. I didn't know what came over me, blurting out like that. Making a fool of myself…and Dad.

I glanced his way as the asshole bartender stumbled forward carrying a tray laden with bottles. Glass bottoms smacked the tables as the Wolves and the Fae stepped further into the room.

The conversation seemed to settle, before a chuckle echoed from one of the men, and it was followed with another. Dad stepped closer, and reached out, offering his hand to each of the Wolves, and then the Unseelie Fae.

They shook his hand. One even drew him into a hug which was little more than a slap on the back. It shocked me how well he knew them. It wasn't that long ago I'd never even known they existed…and now…*here we were.*

Wolves.

Unseelie Fae…

And Vampires.

I looked around the room, and froze as the door opened and a male dressed in an expensive suit stepped in. I scanned the neatly buttoned double-breasted jacket, then lifted my gaze.

But there was no shadow, no darkness spilling across the floor. Nothing that gave them away. There was just silence…and *them.*

The last Immortals to arrive.

The fucking Vampires.

My pulse spiked, ramming that needle of agony through my temples. I never waited for the rest of his clan, or coven…or whatever the fuck they called themselves, only stepped around the chairs and went to the bar. I had to get out of here, had to find some goddamn air.

I slid the glass along the bar, and took the bottle with me. The sharp roar of laughter filled the room, and before I'd even hit the end of the hallway to the rear of the Jewel, the room returned to its deafening, jovial state.

It was all too much.

Too much laughter.

Too much *male.*

"Hey Ruthy, where're you going?" some asshole called out. "Ruth...*Ruth Costello."*

I strode along the hallway and headed for the service exit. A sign called me forward, one marked *Employees Only!* I didn't care, nor did I slow, only shoved against the steel bar across the door and felt it give way.

The cold midnight air hit me like a slap across the face. I closed my eyes for a moment and stepped into the dead-end alley. Still the roar of laughter spilled out behind me. "God fucking save me."

My stilettos clattered on the uneven pavers as I opened my eyes and stepped forward, letting the door slam closed behind me.

A shiver crept across my skin. In hindsight, the flimsy silver top may not have been the best decision. But I wanted to stand out, to be seen, and not just as a pair of tits and an ass, but as someone powerful, someone able to stand head to head with those in that room.

Someone who one day might be sitting at *the seat* on the executive table.

A shudder raced through me, reaching a little deeper than the tremor of cold.

I wanted it. Not now, of course. But one day. I wanted to be the Costello others looked to, the one who caught the secret smiles...the one with all the money...*and power.*

A whisper of movement caught my eye. Just a brush of fabric, *or maybe it was a breath?*

My pulse spiked. Pain rammed through my head, tearing a whimper from my chest. My fingers danced in the air before I pressed them against the bulging vein.

"Sorry to startle you," came a deep murmur in the shadows.

I winced, pressing my fingers a little harder, and felt myself step backwards toward the door.

"Don't leave," he commanded, taking a step into the soft moonlight that owned a sliver of the alley. "Not on my account, at least."

I stared as the long shadow fell across the jutting moss-covered pavers, and lifted my head. Pale skin peeked out as his shirt sleeve rode up. But it was the gloves he wore which caught my attention. I couldn't get a good look at him. He was tall and broad shouldered, his spine stiff.

"You can smoke inside, you know. Second-hand smoke be damned," I muttered, fishing.

"I don't smoke. Just the scent of *them,* in there, you know...."

He hated them. The Vampires and the Wolves, and every other damn Immortal that remained hidden. I felt myself ease a little and stepped back into the alley. Looks like we had that in common. "I know exactly what you mean. I didn't even know they existed until three years ago, and here we all are sitting at the same fucking table, go figure."

He never said a word. Shadows clung to him. I couldn't get a read on him...couldn't find his eyes. All I felt was the washing machine of emotions. Hate lashed the air, unbridled rage, swallowed like poison, taking it down...down...*down.* I swallowed the sting, shaking that illusion free...*get it together, Ruth.*

But for some strange reason, a thought surfaced...*that hate's not mine.*

21

Pain cleaved my head. I gripped the bottle and dug the fingers of my other hand into the frantic vein.

"You're in pain," he took a step closer. "I can help with that."

I gave a soft bark of laughter as he came close…a little *too* close. I stepped backwards as black leather gloves reached through the light.

"Hey…*don't.*" I hit the brick wall and stopped, spine flattening, the bottle firm in my hand. "I know karate."

It was a lie. I didn't know the first thing about self-defense.

The only defense I carried…was my fucking name.

"I'm not going to hurt you, I promise."

Smooth leather touched my temple. I flinched from his touch, eyes searching the darkness. Short midnight hair and pale skin, jutting cheekbones…I could just make out his lips, full and lush. My God, they were beautiful.

He towered over me, leaning in to press his fingers against my temple. Soft circling motion followed, massaging over and over again. I wasn't giving into him. Not for one second. I ground my teeth, muscles flaring.

"You're not like them…in there…*are you?*" he asked.

But the motion on my temples seemed to take over. I tried to find the sharp retort to answer. But I was sucked into that touch, stolen and captivated, and before it fully registered, I was sinking into that feeling. The tension inside trembled, desperate to let go.

"No, I don't think you're like them at all," he whispered.

My shoulders sank, and a pent-up breath escaped. I closed my eyes, feeling his fingers going around and around…*and around.*

I could hear sirens in the distance, feel the cold, damp moss at my back, feel his hands, his breath against my cheek. I tilted my head as he pressed his lips to mine, then pulled away.

It was just a brush...just a perfect brush. This wasn't me, not in the slightest. In there, to *them,* was the bitch, the hard-ass. But just once, just for a second, I needed to be the real me, the one desperate to feel something other than the constant need to be on guard. I opened my eyes, finding him in the shadows. My grip slipped, and the bottle clattered to the ground with a *clunk*. I wasn't guarded here, in this moment...*I wasn't me.*

"Are you a bartender?" I questioned.

He didn't answer, only leaned closer, and this time, I opened my mouth, taking the kiss deeper.

Still his fingers kneaded that vein on the side of my head, stealing the pain with the motion of his hand, and my breath with his lips.

Cold licked my nipples through my top, tightening, puckering as he pressed against me. I lifted my other hand, reaching for the back of his head. But he captured my fingers, smooth black leather against my hand.

The kiss was hungry, and urgent. His hard chest pressed me against the bricks and before I knew it, my hand was rising to meet the wall.

He had me.

Hand high on the wall beside me.

His finger at my temple.

And his lips taking...taking...*taking.*

A moan welled in the back of my throat. Without saying a word, I knew the things he'd do to me—here in the filthy service alley—and my knees weakened.

I arched my spine, hips thrusting forward. I'd let him, let him do anything he wanted. The back of a finger skimmed the tight peak of my breast.

I hadn't felt him move, hadn't felt anything at all. His tongue darted into my mouth, teasing mine before it was gone again, as the touch danced across my breast once more.

His lips left mine, breaking the connection. I licked the ache, and dragged my teeth across soft flesh. "More," I whispered, my gaze boring through the dark.

I liked not seeing him...liked the mystery. *I liked not caring.*

The back of his finger grazed my breast once more, only this time it was slower. The leather was cold through the flimsy material of my top.

My body shuddered and my knees trembled. Still he pinned my hand against the wall as his finger slipped into the neckline of my top. "Kiss me," I sighed as I thrust my hips toward him.

Slow. *God, he was excruciatingly slow.*

Like he had all the time in the world...all the time to explore my body. His finger brushed bare skin, reaching deeper. Leather cold against sensitive flesh, teasing, dancing, rolling around the edges before brushing feather-light against the tip.

Like he had all the time to...my moan deepened, eyes fluttering closed as he rolled my nipple between his fingers.

I was trapped by the sensation of leather, smooth and cold against the fire that built inside. I opened my eyes and looked down as he swept the neckline aside, exposing my breast for anyone to see.

A surge of excitement tore through me, and heat followed, welling between my thighs. Black leather against my pale breast was breathtaking and his finger never stopped, sliding lower…and lower, past my navel, until it dropped to sweep one finger upwards between my thighs.

"Holy fuck," I whispered.

My knees shook harder. I was either going to collapse or cum. Cold kissed my nipple, the dusty pink darkening as he reached lower, delving deeper along my crease. I lost sight of the leather, the black melding into the color of my slacks. Now I wished I'd worn white.

I needed more, needed *something*. I jerked my gaze to the shadows, searching for his eyes as he slid his hand lower, finger pressed against my core. "Tell me your name."

Silence…goddamn silence. *Did he know who I was? Did he know what was going on inside that bar?* They were taking over the fucking city.

"Give me something," I whimpered as he slid his finger higher and circled my clit with the same motion he used on my temple.

Oh God.

Around and around, just the right pressure…just the right—a quake tore free, spilling outwards. I dragged teeth along my lips once more. "Just kiss me, *for fuck's sake.*"

There was a soft chuckle, a hint of *something*, as he alternated hard with soft, and slid lower to press against my damp core. "I want you. Jesus Christ, *I want you.*" I moaned.

"Do you?" he asked, his voice deep and dangerous. "Tell me…Ruth Costello…*how much do you want me?*"

Fear plunged through my veins at the same time as my climax tore free. He pressed his fingers harder. Black leather shone between my thighs, glistening like an oil slick. I gripped his hand high up on the wall and felt my entire world shake.

He'd not even fucked me.

Not pushed his head between my thighs.

Not sheathed his cock inside the slickness of my need.

A cry tore from my lips. I slammed open my eyes as he moved closer, those perfect lips slipping into the beam of moonlight…and *he smiled.*

Hard panting breaths took over as the pressure of his hand eased on mine. I was trembling, unhinged, and unhooked. Soft and warm in the middle.

"You know my name," I gasped. "Now how 'bout you tell me yours?"

There was that guttural chuckle as he reached for my top, sliding it in place to cover my breast.

So he was a goddamn gentleman as well?

His shoes scuffed the pavers as he stepped backwards. He was leaving me…leaving me in the wake of the most intense orgasm of my life.

And I didn't even know who he was.

His hand slid from between my legs, nice and slow. "How's the headache now?"

"Fuck the headache," I growled. "I want more."

I was a greedy bitch, and it was also the best *nonsex*-sex I'd ever had.

"As do I," he answered, then turned his back on me. "It was nice meeting you, Ruth Costello…*very nice indeed.*"

And in one frantic booming heartbeat…he was gone, striding through the shadows and along the alley. Leaving me alone…desperate to know who the hell he was.

3

Footsteps carried along the alley. He was nothing more than a ghost in the shadows…one who'd almost brought me to my knees with desire.

Until in a heartbeat, he was gone.

I swallowed hard, trying to work enough feeling into my hand to push myself from the mossy brick wall.

God, this place was filthy.

Filled trashcans were stacked on one another like some god-awful rendition of the Leaning Tower of Pisa. Every time I thought that name, I thought of pizza…and now I was just damn hungry.

Great.

I brushed moss from the back of my hand and waited for my damn knees to stop shaking. It was the most exhilarating thing I'd ever done. Sex…in public. Not just sex, but goddamn delicious hand between my thighs, tongue in my mouth, exposing my breast sex.

I felt him there, in the ache…in the hunger. I pressed

my tongue against the roof of my mouth as footsteps echoed once more.

My lips curled as I shoved myself forward, forcing my knees to lock in place. "I knew you'd be back. I knew you wanted…"

More footsteps. He had friends.

I jerked my gaze upwards as they spilled into the alley. Only it wasn't my gloved lover…it was the party-crashing thug and his gang.

My blood turned cold as they invaded like a rumor, spilling out and around.

"Well, *looky here,* rich bitch is waiting for us," the punk snarled, and lifted his hand to his waist.

Silver glinted like a spark in the light. I jerked my gaze to the others as they moved in to surround me. "I don't want any trouble," I stepped backwards.

I searched the shadows, desperation reaching into the back of my throat. But my gloved lover was long gone. There was only us now. Only me…*and them.*

"*I* didn't want any trouble," the punk mimicked. "I just wanted what was rightfully mine. But your piece of shit, fucking loser of a father went and made me feel like shit."

My fingers skimmed the door behind me.

"You shouldn't have hurt my Skull," a girl said as she stepped from the shadows wearing nothing more than a slip of leather across her crotch and a beaded black leather bikini top. She was ugly, and not in a disproportion of features on her face ugly. She was ugly from the inside. Cruel, piercing eyes. A red slash of a mouth. She gripped a baseball bat, dragging the end along the ground as she walked. "You hurt him…and you hurt all of us."

"What is he, some kind of weakling?" I snarled, the fire inside mingling with a known family trait—*a big fucking mouth.* "Next thing you know, he'll be running to Momma. You gonna cry, *Momma's boy?*"

The bitch girlfriend just smiled and strode toward me, lifting the bat in the air until it rested on her shoulder. "Keep talkin', I can't wait to smash that sorry mouth in."

"The girlfriend's got more balls than you have," I gripped the handle of the door, and gave it a slow shove. "Maybe Momma has those, too?"

But it was locked. Un-fucking-movable. Just my luck.

My panicked thoughts raced, tearing through the door to the men inside, and all of a sudden, venturing out into the darkness without Trouble seemed like a really bad idea.

"Keep talkin', *bitch,*" Nathaniel snarled, and stepped in front of me.

There were too many for me to take on. Five...six... maybe one more skulked in the shadows. Too many for one mouthy Costello.

Should've brought the gun.

The thought filled me as Nathaniel smiled and shook his head. "Maybe *now* we'll get a seat at the table."

"The only table you're *ever* gonna sit at is your momma's, while my dad bends her over the fucking end and takes her from behind. But I'm thinkin' you're gonna like that. Thinking *Nathaniel* is gonna jerk his little cock to that to get to sleep."

The smirk slipped from his face. What? One Momma joke too many? I can go all day...*all fucking d—*

The end of the bat sailed through the air. I caught sight

of it soon enough to duck and shove myself away from the door.

But they were there, closing in around me like a pack of hyenas.

"You gonna scream, *bitch?*" Nathaniel sniggered. "I bet you will. I bet you'll fucking howl."

I clenched my fist, ground my teeth, and lunged, cocked fist sailing through the air. I took him by surprise. My knuckles glanced across his jaw. Not a blow, but it was enough. I stumbled forwards, grabbed his shoulders, and with all the strength I had, I rammed my knee into his balls.

He doubled over with an *oof*. But I wasn't done yet, nails piercing his shirt as I gripped tight and rammed the heel of my Louis Vuitton stiletto through his sneaker and into the bastard's foot.

He roared, and threw his head back, eyes stretched wide, screaming like a goddamn baby.

"Now it's my turn," one of his homeboy's growled, bouncing on his feet, working up his courage to hit an unarmed woman.

But the girlfriend beat him to it. I swung my fist toward her, trying to take down as many as I fucking could. But my blow went wide as I was shoved from the back.

Fists pummeled me, one glancing off my eye, another blow in my stomach doubling me over. Pain tore through me, my stomach and my back screaming as I was hit in the face and knocked to the ground.

"How do you like it, you fucking *bitch?*" Nathaniel screamed.

I tried to shove my hand against the ground, but a boot

stomped down, crushing my hand and five-carat diamond ring under his heel. My scream ripped free, high and piercing, tearing through the alley and into the night.

I lay there in the darkness and the cold. *They're going to kill me.* The thought slipped in.

"Take her out, Skull."

Someone said the words. Female. Scared. Urgent. *"Take her out."*

Something warm slipped into my eye as I tried to lift my head. One breast peeked out from my top. The icy grip of the night was all I felt as the thug loomed above me. I caught a flicker of movement as the girlfriend handed him the baseball bat.

"No," I begged. "Don't do this…my father…*my father.*"

"Your father will what?" he snarled, and took the bat. "He'll pay? Is that what he'll do? I bet he fucking will."

I tasted blood as the warmth slipped down my cheek and crossed my lips. The agony in my head was blinding, casting sparks of white light to hide their faces. "No," I faced the whisper. "Won't cry." I stared into that darkness, gathering every last ounce of my Costello blood and whispered, "He'll kill every last one of you…"

There was a second of silence. And that was there was before the thug raised the bat in his hands…*and swung.*

The steel connected with my head. Sparks moved in, swallowing the pain.

Darkness was all I saw, darkness and cold and emptiness.

I swam in the nothing, until my feet became tangled.

Panic gripped me. I punched and kicked, fighting my way to the surface.

Screams slipped in, faint at first. Calling me. *This way.*

I swam through that nothingness, slicing the air, and slowly surfaced.

A sickening *crunch* came to me as I swam higher. Unmerciful howls of, *I'm sorry...don't do this...don't do this DON'T D—*

And then there was nothing, nothing but the choking scent of blood, and the bitter cold. Footsteps in emptiness. Careful strides toward me as the faint sound of sirens cut through the night.

There was a slide of something, a whisper. Fingers touched me. Icy fingers.

"You're going to be okay," came whispered words so faint I barely caught them.

A whimper tore from my lips as I closed my eyes, and the sound of the sirens came closer. The darkness wasn't done with me, reaching up, trailing its touch along my cheek, and across my lips.

I wrenched open my eyes to red and blue lights spilling into the alley.

Footsteps thundered, a lot of them.

"Ruthy!" Dad screamed. "What the fuck happened here? *Jesus fucking Christ!* Ruthy...*Ruthy!*"

4

B *eep...beep...beep.* The sound of machines woke me. I followed the call all the way to the surface and cracked open my eyes to the blinding white.

A moan echoed in the back of my throat, deep, *burning.* I eased my lids closed as something shifted next to me.

"Ruthy?" Daddy called.

I cracked open my eyes, fighting the glare. I'd fight anything for him, and tried to speak. Fire lashed the back of my throat with the whisper.

"Wait, don't try to speak. Not yet."

The bed dipped to my side. Sparks of white obscured his face. His warm hand gripped mine, the thumb tracing my knuckles as he leaned closer.

"I'm going to call a nurse for you...in just a second. But first I need you to listen to me, Ruthy...*I need to know...*did you do it? Did you do...*those things* in the alley?"

I tried to turn my head toward him, tried to understand what he was saying. *The alley? The alley...* flashes of memory, nothing solid, all sparks...*all screams.*

"I need to know, honey. I can fix this. I can make it all go away. But I need to know if you did that…if you killed all those people?"

Keep talkin', bitch.

The voice slipped in from nowhere. I tried to remember, tried to think. Pain plunged an unseen knife through my skull and into the softer parts of me. But I was close…*I was so fucking close.*

.   The machine fired off next to me as the face slipped into my mind. "The punk."

"Yeah, the punk," Dad whispered and gripped my hand. "You remember what you did to him, right? How you…how you tore his head from his body and smashed it into the wall. How you left his…how you left his people in bits all over the fucking alley like they were parts of a jigsaw?"

His hand trembled, but his voice was rock steady, even when he looked at me. His intense gaze sparkled, fear made the blue brighter. I'd never seen him afraid before, not *truly* afraid. He looked at me like I was a monster… maybe I was.

I closed my eyes to the frantic squeal from the machine beside me. Maybe I was just like him…*a Mafia Monster.* Footsteps rushed forward. Urgent voices telling me to open my eyes, asking if I knew what day it was.

I answered their questions as best I could, but I wasn't there…not really. I was in that alley, lying on the ground. Fragments slipped into place. The sight of the baseball bat sweeping through the air toward me.

I heard a whisper of something, like something sliding against skin.

And cold followed. A frigid touch against my neck, feeling for a pulse.

You're going to be okay, a deep guttural snarl slipped through the past and into the present.

Someone touched me as I lay in the hospital bed. A light shone in my eyes as Dad's hand slipped from mine. I turned toward him, watching the man I'd loved my entire life look at me a little differently now.

Those blue eyes sparkled like never before.

I need to know...did you do it? Did you do...that in the alley?

Did I do it? I closed my eyes and remembered the sickening screams all around me, and the gut-wrenching *squelch* that followed.

Did I do that? *No. No, I didn't...*fear slipped in, finding me in the brightly lit room just as easily as it had found me in that alley.

Someone else had been there. Someone terrifying.

Someone incensed with rage.

And as the doctors poked and prodded, asking me to lean forward while they pressed along my spine, another memory slipped into my mind.

One that had no part in the terror that followed.

A captivating memory.

A perfect kiss...

"No," the whisper slipped from my lips.

The doctor stilled, his hand on the side of my head, touching my temple...*just like in the alley.* But it wasn't the same touch, and it wasn't the same man.

I turned my head to my father. "No, that wasn't me. Someone else was in that alley...someone else did those things."

Relief swallowed him whole.

One nod of his head and a small, careful smile crested his lips. "That's my good girl," he nodded a little harder. "You just focus on getting better now, and leave the rest to me."

He turned then, giving me his back. My gaze followed him as he strode past a guard standing outside the open curtains. As he opened the door, I saw them all waiting.

*Leave the rest to me...*his last words haunted me.

Men waited for his command like soldiers. They'd get them, too. Every last law-breaking, soul-stealing one of them.

They'd obey them all. Every whisper...and every look.

That was the reason he held the seat of power.

But that didn't give me answers, the answers I needed...nor did it ease my pain. I swallowed hard and turned away, feeling the ache bloom along my back.

The alley waited for me in the silence. The kicks. The blows. The sound of flesh tearing and bones snapping. My fingers trembled against the bed...until the tremors turned into shakes.

I clenched my fist to still the tremors, winced at the ache that flared across my knuckles, and willed the memories away. *Think about something else...think about anything else.*

Lips.

Tongue.

Black-leather-gloved fingers against my breast.

Jesus, not that.

But the terror was there, the coldness...the loneliness, it was all waiting for me, waiting for the moment that kiss left my mind, and it'd be back with a vengeance, revealing every gruesome detail.

The door opened and a nurse walked in, eyes bright, spine ramrod straight. But she was new. Trouble's man stepped in front of her, and lifted his hand. "Stop right there."

"*Stop?*" she repeated. "How about *you* move before I jab you with whatever's inside my pocket?"

Trouble's man just eyed her up and down. She was beautiful, in a tough as nails kind of way. Navy-blue scrubs didn't do her justice. High, full breasts and a perfect swell of her hips, whatever weapon she carried, either the needle or her body was enough to make the bodyguard move.

She turned her head, careful eyes finding me, before a smile. But it was a fake smile; a professional smile. I liked her instantly. She lifted a small tablet, stabbed the screen and made her way to the side of the bed. "How's the pain doing?"

"Fine." I answered.

"Lean forward for me," she placed a hand on my shoulder.

I expected her to be rough, and all sharp edges and snarls, nothing like the feather-light touches that followed.

Cold slipped under the opening at the back of my gown as she opened the gap long enough to touch along my back, then tugged the opening closed once more. "Okay, all good."

I eased back, catching my breath with the deep flare of agony as it tore through my side. She stared at me. "Let's do this again, shall we? On a scale of one to ten, how bad is it?"

I wanted to swallow the agony, smile and play it down, until the damn truth slipped free. "About a six."

She gave a nod. "I'll get you something for that."

"Wait," I glanced at the door, finding Trouble's man, and lowered my voice. "How bad is it?"

She stepped closer, and sat on the side of the bed. Careful eyes met mine, then scanned my body before finding my gaze once more. She wanted to know what version to give me, the truth or a watered-down version.

My fingers still trembled, even though I had them clenched tight. The alley waited with all its secrets and teeth, ready to make me weak and afraid. "Please," I met her gaze. "I have to know."

"You have three broken ribs," she started. "A ruptured spleen, a hairline fracture of the skull, and some of the worst bruising I've ever seen. But nothing that requires surgery, although it's *very* important you rest."

She searched my eyes, my face, lingering on the places that ached when I smiled before she reached for my hand. "I wanted to ask what the other guy looked like," she lowered her gaze, her thumb dragging gently across the bruises on my knuckles. "But if the men standing outside your door are any indication of the kind of wrath that's coming to whoever did this, then the worst is yet to come for them."

Tears blurred her face, thickening my throat. I gave a weak smile and a nod, then pulled my hand away.

The worst is yet to come? No. I didn't think so.

Memories waited patiently, with knives wedged between their teeth. They wanted to cut me...they wanted me to bleed.

My throat thickened, the lump so big I could barely breathe. I'd gotten what I wanted, hadn't I?

I'd gotten the truth of how bad this was.

She waited for a second, then rose from the bed. "I'll get you something for that pain."

She came back in a few minutes later, slipping a needle into the port of my cannula. This time, there were no more questions and soon there'd be no more pain.

"Wait," I called as she turned. "I never got your name."

"Charlotte," she gave a wink. "Just like the web."

With a wink, she was gone, stepping around Trouble's man to disappear into the hall once more. *Charlotte...just like the web.* I glanced at the closed doorway. I liked her... more than I expected.

When the door opened minutes later, it was someone else, a doctor who smiled and nodded to Trouble's man.

"How's my patient doing?" he asked, all smiles and teeth.

"Fine," I answered, and turned away.

Silence followed as he fussed and made small talk. I answered with one-word answers, until I closed my eyes and feigned sleep.

Footsteps moved around me. He left seconds later. But I wasn't asleep. I kept the darkness away by focusing on the sounds from outside...the faint cry of a child somewhere in the distance.

Well, looky here rich bitch is waiting for us...

I moaned with the words and clenched my eyes shut...my fists trembling against the bed. But there was no escape, not from the memory of the cold against my skin...or the metallic scene of blood that'd filled my nose.

I need to know...did you do it? Did you do...those things in the alley?

Dad's words came back to me, and something warm slid down my cheek. There had been fear in his eyes, real fear, like for a moment he honestly believed I'd done that...*that I was capable...*

I searched my memories, digging as far back as I could. I hadn't been the happiest kid, hadn't been all smiles and frilly dresses and school recitals. I'd been quiet, keeping to the back of the class. I'd been closed off and careful, but not a monster...not like that.

The girlfriend's got more balls than you have.

Keep talkin', bitch.

I opened my eyes, turned my head, and stared at the machines. *Some of the worse bruising I've ever seen.* Pain waited for me. Pain and memories, until I didn't know which hurt more. I sucked in a breath and clenched my jaw as my fingers found the cold steel of the rail before I pulled, dragging myself upwards.

I couldn't lie here...*I wouldn't lie here.* I wasn't a prisoner, not even of my own mind. I gripped the hard, cotton blanket and threw it from my body. Cold waited for me, trailing along my bare legs as I slid one foot toward the side.

Agony rushed up to greet me, tearing along my back and my side. I froze, grinding my teeth and closing my eyes. My legs trembled, and my will wavered for just a second before I opened my eyes once more.

No more.

No more waiting.

No more feeling like a damn victim.

I wasn't a victim...not even my own. I slid my other

leg toward the side of the bed and grabbed the rail. One small thrust of my hips and I was moving, letting gravity take me until my feet hit the floor.

"Ma'am," Trouble's man stepped closer. "You want me to fetch the doctor?"

Shadow spilled toward me along the floor as he moved, and I was stolen from this hospital room and shoved back into that alley. *He had a shadow...the man who kissed me.* "He had a shadow."

"Who had a shadow, Ms. Costello?"

I jerked my gaze high, finding the brown eyes of my guardian, and remembered where I was. "No one. No one at all." The words were hollow.

"Did you need something?" He glanced toward the door, then back to me. "Want me to get the doctor?"

I shook my head, staring at him. "No...I've met you before, right?"

"Russell, ma'am." He stepped closer.

I had...I remembered it now. The gala last month, he was my primary escort. "I'm sorry, how could I forget."

"It's okay." He took another step closer, and his careful words were softer now. "I asked to be here, to stand guard. Nothing is going to come through those doors without your say-so, Ms. Costello. You're safe here with me."

Safe.

I'd never even thought about the word before. I'd been carefully hidden, dependent on my name. I lifted my gaze to Russell's. Now look at me. "Thank you, Russell. I appreciate that."

"Like I said, I can get the doctor..."

I shook my head as the fresh wave of agony hit,

blinding me. "No…" I shook my head a little too hard and the room swayed. "I just…" I glanced at the machine and the IV. "I just need to move around a little."

I turned, grasping the bedrail, and heard the harsh catch of his breath. Cold swept along my spine.

"Jesus…Jesus Christ," Russell growled.

Fear and sadness welled in his eyes when I turned. He flinched and jerked his gaze to mine. "I've seen some bruises…but nothing like that."

They hurt me…they kicked and punched, until I lost myself in the blows. The words lingered on the tip of my tongue. My breath was a tremble, just a catch of air as I forced a smile and nodded. "I'm alive, and I'm done with lying there…and remembering."

He stared at me for a long while, and slowly nodded. This time when he looked at me, it wasn't sadness in his gaze—it was respect.

"Let me fix that for you," he stepped forward.

Careful hands touched me, adjusting my gown, tightening the ties at my back until the cold no longer slipped in. I was grateful for my panties, at least the thin cotton covered most of my modesty.

"Thank you." I glanced behind me, readied myself, and stepped.

Pain was there, biting and pinching. I ground my teeth and focused on the steps until I reached out and grasped the steel stand of the machine.

The thready pulse in my head was like a hammer, every blow excruciating, until my body trembled with the beat.

I could do this. I clenched one hand around the machine, and the other around the IV pole, and moved.

"You've got it," my cheerleader growled behind me and yanked the plug from the wall. "These things have a battery, but just take it easy, okay?"

I focused on my steps, timing them with the agony, until whatever painkiller the nurse had given me raced through my veins. My knees shook and the bright light in the room blurred.

"Whoa," Russell said, grasping my arm and steadying me. "You sure you should be doing this?"

I held on to the light, gripped it with all I had, and nodded. "I'm sure."

When I stepped forward again, the room stayed still. I gripped the two stands and forced my feet to move. "I'm good," I whispered.

The icy floor chilled my feet as I took two more steps to the end of the bed. But it was the doorway I focused on, forcing myself across the room until the handle was in reach. "If you don't mind."

Heavy steps sounded as he stepped around me and opened the door. The piercing wail I'd been hearing grew louder, cracking the cold armor I held so tightly. My heart clenched with the sound, panicked and terrified. "That's a child."

Concern drove me forward. I pushed the machine and the drip, stepping out into the hallway. My heart pounded, clenching tight with the tiny sound of pain.

"Ma'am." Another one of Trouble's men turned with the opening of the door.

He cut a glare at Russell before I snapped, "This was my idea...need to get out of there."

"We have orders, ma'am," the bodyguard answered carefully.

I stopped and lifted my head. "Are your orders to chain me to the goddamn bed? 'Cause that's what it's going to take. Now you can get the hell out of my way..." the child's cries became louder. "Or you can go and see why that child's crying."

Doctor Smiles lifted his head from the stack of files on the desk and shoved upward from his chair. *"Ms. Costello! Ms. Costello, you shouldn't be out of bed. You need to be resting...the drugs I gave you were heavy sedatives."*

I clenched my jaw, sometimes I really hated the sound of my damn name. But the child's wails called to me, making me feel things I didn't want to feel, pain, anger, *hopelessness*. "The child, what's wrong with her?"

The doctor jerked his head toward the long hallway as though he'd only now registered the sound. "We had to set up a temporary wing for you, if it's the noise, I can—"

I jerked my head toward the asshole. "No, it's not the damn noise, what the hell is wrong with you?"

Wrong with him?

I looked around at the open doors and darkened rooms all along the hall.

What the hell was wrong with him? He wasn't the one who stood all alone in a closed wing bought and paid for by her father.

But that sound...I could feel the burn in my throat with the tiny howl, taste the blood that wasn't mine—*feel* her pain like it was my own. "I want to know what's wrong with her."

"Ms. Costello," the doctor repeated.

"If I hear that name one more fucking time..." My molars crunched.

"The children's wing is overflowing, there's not

enough beds, not enough doctors, there's not enough of anything."

She was in pain. She was hurting. Her parents...*Jesus Christ, her poor parents.* I swallowed the taste of acid in the back of my throat. "Bring them in here...bring them all in here."

"No," the doctor grew a set of balls. "No, we can't... we're not equipped for that—"

I turned my head, met his gaze, and said nothing. There was a second where he glanced at the men behind me, as though they'd somehow rise to his defense and put the woman in her place.

Only he didn't quite know *this* woman.

But the men behind me did.

They said nothing, which should've given him all the advice he needed to hear.

"Do I need to make a call to make that happen?" I asked. "I think I have Samuel Horne's number in my contacts."

The doctor paled with my words. "You have the Chief Executive's number?"

A tiny snuff of laughter tore free. "Doctor, I have *everyone's* number in my contacts. Now...that child," I glanced toward the hallway. "You can start with her."

Muscles flared along his jaw as he swallowed his pride. He jerked his head toward the waiting nurses. I tried to look for Charlotte, but she wasn't there.

They hurried out of the hallway, returning minutes later with an exhausted mom and a wailing daughter. I just stood there in my gaping hospital gown, bruised and broken, but still very much alive.

They rushed more children and parents in, filling the darkened rooms around me in no time.

"Bed now," Russell urged behind me. "You've done what you needed."

I wanted to smile and be content with that. But their tired eyes and their weak movements haunted me. Moms who ran on hardly any sleep nursing little babies and toddlers who screamed with pain.

The doctors and nurses ran from one room to another. I left them in the chaos. Russell placed his hand gently on my arm, guiding me back to the room…and the bed.

My steps were slow, feet heavy, but my heart beat a little easier as I shuffled back to the room, and finally back to bed.

I let Russell fuss…just a little. Let him guide me to the bed once more. Let him pull the hard cotton sheets against my body. I let him stand there, staring down at me, seeing me at my worst.

"I must look like hell," I muttered and closed my eyes.

"Not at all," truth deepened his tone. "You look like a survivor."

The children's cries eased as the minutes slipped by, sending me crashing into emptiness…and my last thought was the children and filled-to-overflowing wards.

I'd do something about that. I didn't know how…but one day I would. I was my father's daughter—I'd make it happen. I exhaled with his words and aching exhaustion carried me down into the darkness where sleep waited. And this time when I closed my eyes, there was no alley waiting for me.

A door closed with a thud. I drifted upwards, to the sound of my breaths and the pounding of my heart. The door. *Something about the door.* I rose higher and shivered. Cold wrapped around me.

"Don't be afraid."

I froze at the voice. I knew that voice. *Don't leave. Not on my account, at least.* A memory surfaced. An alley, boots driving into my body, pain came fast. Blow after blow...after blow. My heart clenched tight with the memory. My eyes snapped open, and I scanned the dark.

"I'm not going to hurt you."

The voice washed over me, warm and smooth like liquid sunlight.

"That's the way. Slower now."

I tried to stare into the darkness. But the shadows claimed that space. My breaths slowed, my frantic thoughts seemed to settle. A tiny shift. Black on black moving with the whisper of fabric. I knew him...knew him...my mind too slow to grasp the words.

I licked dry lips. "What do you want?" My words were warped and strange. *The door...something about the—*

I glanced toward the opening. The guards. *Russell.* Where were the guards?

"I haven't hurt him, if that's what you're worried about," that icy, clipped tone grew colder. *"Is he your lover?"*

I flinched and jerked my gaze to the shadows. "No. *Why?"*

"You seem to...*care."*

48

Panic tried to move in, searching frantically for a way in.

"So, not a lover...*that's good.*"

My heart lunged with the sound.

"You look tired, drowsy."

I sank into the depths with his words, my eyelids grew heavy...*so heavy.* "The alley," mumbled words spilled free. "That was you?"

"You mean the kiss?" he asked.

Shadows moved, blurring. I blinked slowly, fighting the need to close my eyes. I could feel him come closer, the air was different when he moved, pressing in on me. "The barman."

There was a tiny chuckle. "Not quite." Something cool brushed my cheek, lingering on the ache in my jaw. "They paid for this. Every one of them paid. But I'd bring them back in an instant...to make them scream once more."

Cold kissed my lips.

The slide of leather against my lips.

The air pressed down on me once more. I knew when he moved...when he—

His lips touched mine, gentle, *urgent.* I opened my mouth, cold. He was so cold.

A moan came out of nowhere, spooling from the back of my throat. I tilted my head to him, opening my mouth, letting him taste me.

Desire rushed, tearing through me like adrenaline. I wanted more of him.

I needed more...

I opened my eyes to a blurry face. Eyes flickered, steel gray. *Beautiful. God, you're beautiful.*

"As are you," he added. His brow was furrowed with

concern now. "Sleep now. *Sleep. I'll keep watch over you...I'll make sure no one touches you like that ever again.*"

Those words should've filled me with fear.

Should've torn me from the growing darkness in my mind and made me fight him.

Should've done a lot of things.

Instead, I sank into them.

"I'll be right here, Ruth Costello, watching from the shadows."

His voice carried me down once more. I plunged into the darkness...and this time there would be no rising. This time there would be no light. This time there would be only shadows...*and him.*

5

"It's too soon." Dad picked up a piece of freshly cut apple and held it out for me. "You're not healed enough."

"Dad. Look at me."

He shook his head as I took the perfect slice from underneath the edge of the blade. "I'm not..." *ready,* is what he wanted to say.

He wasn't ready to risk the one thing he cared about the most.

He wasn't ready to risk me being beaten and bloody and walking with a wince again.

But I couldn't stay here holed-up in this house like I was some kind of broken animal. I wanted out. I wanted to be alive. My thoughts slipped to the hospital, and the dream I'd had of a man. But the memories were murky, leaving a cold, hollow pit inside me, one I covered over with dogged determination to get back to work. "I'll take Russell, will that make you happy?"

He placed the half-cut apple and the knife on the

counter and closed the distance between us. His blue eyes sparkled as he reached for my face, sliding his thumb down my cheek. "I'll never be happy, not as long as you could be in danger. I'll always be worried, always be terrified. You're my best weapon...but you're also my heart. Someone strikes you, someone hurts you...and they hurt me, too. We only have each other, my Ruthless."

That was our saying, the one we whispered when the *family* wasn't around. I knew he was careful with his brothers, and I had to be, as well.

My Ruthless.

He smiled, until the sparkle died in his eyes and he pulled away from me, turning to hack and cough and slam one hand down on the counter. "Dad?"

I stumbled forward, my hand finding his back. "Dad, you okay?" And my hand touched only bones.

His body jerked and shuddered, wiry muscles straining, as he nodded his head and tried to lift his hand. "I'm okay."

"You're *not* okay," I snarled, sliding my arm around his waist.

He was thin...so goddamn thin, all skin and bone. I jerked my gaze to his eyes. When had that happened? He sucked in a breath, cleared his throat, and dragged his hand from his mouth. When had he grown so *frail*?

Tiny specks of blood shone on his hand. I stared at his fingers as the blood started to slide. "Dad...you're bleeding."

He stilled and slowly lowered his hand, as though to hide it. *To hide it?* "Dad, you knew about this?"

There was a sigh before he turned. "It's nothing, just a damn cold I can't shake. It's nothing, Ruth. *It's nothing.*"

He lied.

I knew he lied. I could tell a lie better than anyone.

"Just need some of your Aunt's horseradish crap and I'll be good as gold."

"No, Daddy." I bent, and made him look me in the eye. "I want you to see a doctor...*today.* No horseradish, no lying. The doctor. Promise me.*"*

Blue eyes sparkled as he took forever to respond. But he could see there was no budging from this. No smiling and patting my hand, no diversion to stop me from seeing the truth. He swallowed, and gave a sigh. "Okay, you win, kid."

"*Today,* Dad."

There was a twitch of a smile. "You're one hard nut to crack, you know that?" *Just like my old man.*

"Promise."

"Yeah, yeah." He shooed me away with the wave of a hand. That was as close as I was going to get the words from a Costello. I'd take it.

"I'm going out. But I want to know the minute you step outside the doctor's office." I leaned close, giving him a kiss on the cheek. "The. Minute. Dad."

There was that sparkle back in his eyes. He both hated it and loved it when I fussed. My stomach clenched as I pulled away, grabbed the last piece of apple, and headed to the door.

There was no *I love you,* no *I'd be lost without you.* There was none of those words in a Costello home. None that I knew of anyway.

We cared when we fought. We loved when we worked, when money we earned was enough to buy the best doctor in the city...*when it was enough to buy a hundred of them*.

Still, worry lingered as I went to the side of the house and to the garage. Sensors picked up my movement the moment I stepped through the door. Lights flickered and buzzed before the overhead lights came to life. Blue sparkled at the end of the massive driveway, hulking and demanding.

The Bentley was Dad's pride and joy, and the most beautiful thing I'd ever driven. My gaze slipped to the Ferrari, Dad's weekend car, then to mine, the simple, silver Audi. I crossed the space and pressed my fingers to the handle, listening for the *clunk* of the locks.

The car was a gift from Dad, as everything was in my life. My house in the city, my weekend chalet up in the hills, where I could drink wine and read books by the fire at night and pretend to be normal—and my job. Transport liaison manager.

It was a bullshit job. I knew it, everyone knew it. But we all played by the rules

Rules that governed our lives.

Everyone had rules.

One's they spoke about, and one's they didn't. Secret rules. Dark, lying *ruthless* rules. I winced and slid into the driver's seat before closing the door.

The rich smell of new leather invaded my body with a deep breath. I reached up, fingers trembling as I hit the button above my head. The garage door rolled upwards behind me, spilling sunlight into the place.

I clenched my fist and tried to still the shaking. One panicked glance at the door, and the voice inside my head came to life. *It's too soon. No one's going to blame you if you need more time.*

It had been two weeks. Two weeks of doctors, two weeks of sitting inside while the world passed me by. *Two weeks of nightmares* and not working. I swallowed and gripped the wheel. I was done waiting. I had meetings to keep and deals to be made. Maybe the most important deal of my career. Goosebumps raced across my arms. I had to do this. I had to find a way to move on.

I reached out, and my finger danced on the button before the engine came to life. I backed out of the garage, listening to the quiet hum of the engine. I lifted my gaze to the imposing mansion with its speckled brick and white-trimmed windows, and looked for movement.

The place was big, too big for just Dad. It'd be too big for a little league baseball team, *and their families*. I turned the wheel and eased forward. I worried about him being out here on his own, and I worried about him even more now that I was going home.

Two weeks of Dad fussing was all I could handle. I needed to be working, to be busy, to be crowded and hungry with not a second to think.

In the silence was when they came.

Memories.

Flashes.

When my heart would race and an unseen hand would slide around my throat and choke me. Now it was time to move, time to work, time to do anything but sit and damn well wait.

I eased the car along the massive drive to the gate, slowing until the sensor picked me up. I lowered my sunglasses, hiding the yellowing bruise along the side of my face, and turned right.

The children came back to me, crying children…sick children. Children that needed more than some cramped, shared hospital wing with sad secondhand toys in a box in the corner of the ward.

Those were kids with cancer, kids whose lives were spent staring at white walls and goddamn vital machines. They deserved more…and I was determined to make it happen.

Two calls were all it had taken, one to the chairman of the board of directors of Crown City Hospital, and one to the Mayor. I wanted a new hospital for those kids, even if I had to buy the damn thing myself.

I turned the wheel and punched the accelerator, heading into the city. But I wasn't headed to the warehouses or the docks—not yet, anyway. Instead, I speared the Audi towards the heart of Crown City, this side of the river.

I wanted answers…I *needed closure.*

Houses gave way to a sprawling shopping mall and scattered businesses that ran all the way to the skyscrapers in the heart of Crown City. But the gleaming shops wasn't where I was heading. I turned after the mall, headed back to the Jewel.

I slowed the car as I neared and pulled up hard against the curb, just far enough away so I could breathe. My eyes drifted to the alley. A shudder tore along my spine. Even sitting here with the engine running, my heart was racing and my mouth was dry. Remnants of the apple sat heavy in my stomach. *Just leave. Just drive away and never come back.*

I clenched my jaw as the words filled me. My hand slipped to the gear shift, foot ready to ease from the brake and take me away from there.

Run, the voice whispered.

But I couldn't. My fingers skimmed the air and rested on the wheel once more. I couldn't run. Not now, and not ever. If I did, I'd be running from something my entire life.

I knew who I was, knew what kind of family I'd been born into. There were no lies in me, nothing but the cold, terrifying truth. I knew with the name and the power would come those who wanted to hurt us...those who wanted to hurt *me.*

I turned the key and killed the engine. Running from this meant I would run from everything for the rest of my life. I shoved open the door and stepped from the car.

The sun was blinding, making me wince even behind the glasses. Still, I felt so damn cold.

Cars whipped past me. I watched the traffic, then cut across the street. Fingers curled into fists, I folded them across my chest as I stepped up onto the sidewalk and stared into the shadows of the alley's mouth.

It had happened in there.

The kiss.

. The brutality.

Everything.

I stopped at the parking meter, knees trembling... heart racing. A flare of agony tore through my chest, but still I couldn't move. I was frozen, terrified, and consumed, staring into the darkened void at the entrance.

I could still smell the blood, still hear the screams. My knees shuddered, clicking into place and folding. I slapped a hand against the meter and held on for dear life. "I can't do this. I thought I could, but I just can't…"

Desire came back to me.

The brush of his lips. His hand down my top, pushing the thin fabric aside, exposing me to the night…*and to him.* My knees stopped shaking, my breaths evened out. That panic gave way to something else now, something that spoke to the very essence of who I was.

A hunter.

I wanted to know him. I wanted to find him. I wanted to…*to do what, Ruth? Pick up where you left off?*

The thought filled my head until it was all I could think of. I straightened my shoulders and brushed my fingers across my slacks. That was what I held onto, the *ache* of not knowing who he was, my mysterious kisser in the dark.

He was human, that was all I cared about. Maybe he'd been the one to run for help? Maybe he'd been…

I licked my lips and jerked from the thought. *Just fucking walk, Ruth.* I lifted my gaze to the rear of the alley, where I'd lain with knees curled to my chest, like a child.

If I had to trick my body into moving, then that's what I'd do. My heels clicked against the pavement as I stepped closer. Darkness reached out from the mouth of the alley, tiny tuffs of green moss grew in the gaps of the paved ground.

I'd forgotten about that, forgotten how it had felt soft under my feet, forgotten the piled trash cans. *Pisa, right?* The word came back to me now as I stepped into the open mouth of the entrance and stared.

My gaze drifted to the spot where I'd cowered, boots driving into my stomach and my back, fists lashing my face. I winced and felt the ache, until the sound of that sickening *snap* of bone gripped me tight. Blood. So much blood.

I tried to breath, tried to feel the warmth of the sun, but cold plunged deep, cutting all the way to my core like I'd never feel warm again.

You're going to be okay...

The deep male voice surged from the darkness. The panicked pounding of my pulse filled my ears. It was him...the one who'd done that...he'd saved me.

He'd *protected me.*

My heart pounded, filling my head with the deafening sound. I wanted to run...wanted to tear away from this place and *never* come back. But I didn't move, not one muscle.

A simple thought nailed me to the spot.

I needed to know who he was.

6

I forced myself to move, to keep to the light until the darkness was all that was left. The door to the Jewel was closed, but new metal gleamed on the outside of the steel door…a handle. One that wasn't there that night, but it was now.

I knew without a doubt why.

One whisper of *she tried to get back in, but she couldn't open the damn door.* That was all it would've taken for the door to be changed. Maybe it was too late to save me, but maybe it'd save another.

Another woman who didn't have a protector in the shadows.

Someone who'd tear limb from limb.

Someone ravenous.

Someone filled with rage.

I'll make sure no one touches you like that ever again. His voice filled me, rising up from that pit I'd tried to ignore.

Something scurried along the top of the trash can at my right. Bottles banged, a can fell from the pile of trash. I flinched at the sound and stepped backwards. My heart was pounding again, punching against my ribs.

I backed out, turned, and hurried, almost running as I tore from the alley, past the parking meters, then ran across the road.

Horns blared, the sun glinting from glass, blinding me.

"I'm sorry." I shoved out a hand and stumbled forward.

A man screamed obscenities from the window and revved the engine of his car as he shot past. One touch, and I yanked the door open, climbing inside to the safety of my car. Tears came, leaving thick wet trails down my cheeks.

I ached as I trembled, folded my arms across my body, and wept.

It was too much. I knew that. But I wasn't myself…not anymore.

I'd been broken in that alley, kicked and punched until I was bruised and ruptured. But it was those screams that shattered something precious inside me.

Those screams of pleading.

Screams of *begging.*

Screams of silence.

I pressed my head against the headrest as the memories flowed through me, until the tears stopped, leaving behind a gaping hole filled with questions.

Who?

Who did that?

More importantly…

Why?

I stabbed the button and started the engine. My hands shook, but I gripped the wheel, pulled out onto the street, and headed for the docks.

What had happened that night was no coincidence, they were not passersby. They'd been there for a reason and my mind slipped to the events of earlier that evening.

There'd been a lot of power at that gathering. A lot of money, and a lot of beasts. Silver eyes flashed inside my head. The Wolves were there, and the Fae…and the *unshadowed*.

I remembered now, remembered how the door opened and darkness entered the room. I remembered the magic and the heat. I remembered feeling heady to point of swimming, and needing to get away from them.

Needing to *hide*.

I turned the wheel, weaving my way back to where the deep blue cut right through the middle of the city, one side east and the other west.

West was where they lived…those monsters in the dark. I slowed the car at the gate and grabbed my ID before I hit the button for the window.

"Ma'am, nice to see you back, Ms. Costello," the guard at the gate tipped his head.

I forced a smile and stared at the holster across his chest and the two gleaming Sig Sauers on display. "Thank you."

Mike. Mark…something like that. Movement drew my focus, two more guards moved inside the hut which operated the boom gate. Two guards? We'd never had more than one before.

I lifted my gaze. "Is there a problem, Mark?"

"No, ma'am, no problem whatsoever," he gushed, his face turning a deep shade of red. "Just…*ah*, training new recruits."

"I can see that," I added. My smile stretched wider. I

gave a nod before I hit the button once more and the window rose as the boom gate lifted. "Training, my ass," I muttered.

I scanned the rest of the managers' buildings, the workers in the distance, and the *Holy Mary* docked at port. They were halfway through unloading the containers, normal schedule. They'd be done by midmorning tomorrow, when the next ship would come in. We ran a lucrative business shipping products all the way to Huntersville and down south to Orion's Gate, it was a huge distance, and we had more people knocking on our door desperate to do business than we knew what to do with.

But there was only one side of the river. One side of the city.

We kept to the rules. We took what was ours.

I glanced into the rear-view mirror and the extra guards on display. Something was changing…and I wanted to know what. I pulled into my parking space and climbed out. It felt strange to be back here, like it'd been months I'd been gone and not days.

I'd had time away before, taking weeks here and there for conferences and working vacations. But returning had never felt as hollow as this. I pinned my ID to the waistband of my pants and hit the remote on the car before I turned.

My office wasn't flashy or perfect. It was a small, paint-flaking, hard-floored room that smelled faintly of dirty socks. But it was where the workers could see me, where they could come, *if they wanted.*

Dad hated me being here. He wanted me at our head office, along with all my cousins, halfway across the city.

But there was no way I was leaving. This was the beating heart of our business, this was our lifeforce, and I wanted to be right where the action happened, every damn day.

I wasn't like him. I couldn't see my purse when I looked at spreadsheets and statistics. All I saw were numbers and figures, all I saw was dollar signs. But this wasn't just a brand new car or a new home in the Hamptons. This was dirt and grime. This was tired faces and calloused hands. This was exhaustion. *This was mine.*

I wanted this.

I worked for this.

I was ready to take the lead.

Engines growled, cranes beeped. The shouting of orders drifted to me in the distance. This was the heart of the Costello operation, and I was right where I needed to be.

I gripped the railing and climbed. Paint flaked in my hand and my heels clattered on the steel rungs of the stairs. I even had a pair of boots and a hard hat in my office for times I went out into the hive of the docks.

But that wasn't today. Today, I'd have invoices to check and work schedules to approve. And guards to investigate, but more importantly, the meeting of my damn career. Nothing was getting in my way to close that deal…and Harlequin Greenholme was my final step to taking over.

Not just this…*but everything.*

I glanced at the hut below me as I climbed. Shadows moved behind the tinted windows. There was something going on there. Something I wasn't part of, and that pissed me off.

It wasn't the first time I'd been muscled out of secret

dealings and company changes. My dear uncle had once forced Dad to step down the entire board of directors without me knowing...*and I was one of those directors.* The last to know, that's how they wanted me. The least to respond. The lowest paid. A second thought, a laughable excuse.

They wanted me out. They'd made that perfectly clear on more than one occasion. The meeting with the Immortals was just one more excuse not to want me around.

They saw me as a liability.

And in their fucking way up the ladder.

They hated that I was Denzel's daughter.

And that they were not his sons.

I clenched the railing as I climbed...but if that was what was happening, *it'd be the goddamn last time.* I strode along the balcony overlooking the water and stopped at the far office door. My fingers moved across the keypad, punching in the code before the door unlocked.

Hot air hit me like a blast. I sucked in the stale air and hit the light switch before grabbing the AC control. The old thing shuddered as it came to life, spewing cold air into the office a few seconds later.

I closed the door, lifted the sunglasses from my face, and slipped them into the neckline of my top before I made my way around the small desk. My paper inbox was full to overflowing ...there was even a nice neat stack beside it with a scrap piece of paper with a scrawled message weighted down by my chunk of amethyst.

Take it slow, boss.
P.S. The 12 o'clock's been cancelled.

Eric

The twelve o'clock? Panic raced through me. The date and time were ingrained into my brain. I bent, hit the button on the desktop, and waited for the computer to boot up. *Like fuck it has.* I sat in my chair and punched in the password, waiting for the calendar to appear.

Greenholme Shipping was the only reason I'd dragged my ass here. It'd been my sole focus since I'd stepped outside that hospital, the only thing that'd made all the tortuous strength training worth it.

And now it was cancelled? *"Fuck!"*

I'd been working on that proposal all goddamn month. I'd gone over logistics, set up costs and overhead for staff, not to mention the millions of dollars that'd grease every damn person in power to make that deal happen.

And now the sonofabitch was stiffing me this close to the line? *I don't fucking think so.*

I glanced at my watch, then opened the folder on the desktop with all the details, before I reached over, snatched the phone receiver, and stabbed Eric's extension.

The phone rang...and rang...*and rang.* Eric was chief production officer, which meant his ass was glued to that desk and his ear to the phone. I disconnected and pressed the button for his secretary, listening as she picked up on the second ring.

"Ms. Costello. I wasn't sure if you'd be in today." Her voice was panicked.

"Yep, I'm here, April. Where's Eric?"

"He's...ah. He's sick today."

Training new guards, and my production officer is sick?

Something stank to high heaven. "That's not good. So, Blane is taking over for him today?"

"Blane is, um, he's not in the office at the moment, Ms. Costello."

"Well, where the hell is he?"

There was silence, awkward silence.

"Thanks, April."

"Sure, Ms. Costello, is there any—" I cut the call and shoved my chair backwards. It was 10 AM, those guys should've been well into the frantic rush that'd see them all the way to the changeover at 4 PM. There was *no way* either of them wouldn't be at their desk, not even if they were dying.

Something was wrong.

I strode around my desk and back outside, slammed the door behind me, and glanced over at the mammoth production sheds. Every other time, I'd be donning the hard hat and the boots, but not today.

I didn't waste a damn second, striding back along the balcony and down the three flights of stairs once more. The coffee-break horn blared across the docks and production stopped right on time. The workers climbed out of cranes and slid out of forklifts, heading in droves for the shade of the production sheds and the breakroom.

"Ms. Costello," some greeted.

"Ma'am," others followed, nodding their heads.

I smiled and answered back, nodding as their steps slowed and their eyes gravitated to my face. *Shit*, my sunglasses. I reached up, plucked them free, and slid them into place.

There was no need to fuel the rumors. I smiled a little

wider, and answered each greeting as I strode toward the three small production offices next to the mess room.

From outside, I could hear the frantic ringing of the production phones. I twisted the handle and opened the door, finding both offices empty. April's panicked voice drifted from her office. I'd get no more answers from there. It was time to go higher.

There were a few of us lowly managers on site. My position was a farce, a few policies to oversee, meetings only if I chose to chase them. But it was nothing compared to those of my cousins.

Judah and Blane were the tip of the iceberg. The two eldest sons of my Uncle Jerry, they were a pain in my fucking ass. I hated them, and that was putting it mildly.

Panic raced as a memory surfaced. I was just eight years old when they both cornered me one day after playing. Eight fucking years old, and they were eleven. They were raised as bullies, seeped with false smiles and rage. I'd never seen that side of them before. But that day I did. I'd felt their strength *and my weakness* as they held me down on the ground away from all the others.

We don't want you around, got that, Ruthy? Don't want you playing with us. We don't want you here.

I reached up, and rubbed my arms. Jesus, all this time and they still had a hold over me, all this time and they still made me feel weak and afraid. They made me feel worthless...*just like a woman should.*

I reached along my arms, still feeling the ache as Judah had held me down. My pulse raced as I remembered how Blane had reached out to flick my hair, then lowered his gaze...right before he put his hand over my nipple.

It was nothing.

Nothing.

I'd had nothing, anyway, just a flat chest, with nipples but not yet any breasts, only seeds not ready to sprout. But he'd known what they were. He'd kept his hand there, scrabbling his fingers until he found my nipple, *then pinched.* Pain flared with the memory, sharp and stinging, puckering the tender flesh under my bra.

I remembered the pain after all these years…and I remembered the way they'd made me feel. *Weak. Vulnerable. Owned.*

And I never wanted to feel that way again.

I kept to the yellow painted line leading from one production shed to the other. There were ten in total. Ten sheds that ran along the river. Ten sheds that ran day in and day out, only closing for six hours on Christmas. Ten sheds that made up sixty percent of our revenue, and I didn't want anything to do with what made up the rest. *Drugs. Guns. Prostitution.*

We weren't the most stand-up family in existence.

But we weren't the worst, either.

We took care of our workers and spent days in the trenches. This was the part of the business I wanted. This was real and honest. This, I was proud of.

"Ma'am," the workers greeted me.

I smiled and nodded. Some I knew by name, some I didn't. I'd fought hard for their respect, working the front lines alongside them. I didn't just breeze in and out whenever I damn well felt like it.

The gleaming midnight blue Maserati was parked sideways, wing doors open, stereo on full blast, belting out some foul beat about whores and whiskey. I winced at the sight and looked for its twin. The red gleaming beast was parked further up, closed and silent. But no less foul just with its presence.

I felt a twitch at the corner of my eye. I had snakes in my family, snakes that lied and cheated, and spent more money than they earned. If they thought I resented their newly appointed positions a step ahead of me on the board of directors, then they were fucking right.

I was pissed, but I was also patient.

One day I'd own it all. *And there wasn't a fucking thing they could do about it.*

They never wanted me to play with them.

They never wanted me to be part of the family.

But I was the sole heir of Denzel Costello. *This was all mine.*

I glanced over my shoulder and cut across to the empty forklifts before I stepped outside of shed two and climbed the stairs. The two executive offices upstairs were kept for meetings on site, but lately they were used as private rooms for Asshole and Jughead. My two least favorite people, whenever they decided to show.

I opened the door and climbed the stairs to the second floor, feeling the cold air-conditioned blast hit me as I stepped out into the foyer.

Loud, brash laughter echoed from the offices at the end of the hall.

"And then I said to her, she better get her fat ass home before I fuck the babysitter instead!"

I swallowed my revulsion, slid the sunglasses from my eyes and plastered a smile on my face. God help me.

The door to the office was cracked open. It wasn't quite secret dealings behind closed doors, but it was close enough.

I doubted they heard my heels on the hard floor, or cared for that matter.

I pushed open the door, and found them face to face with Harlequin Greenholme, the same guy I'd been chasing for months. The same guy who just so happened to have cancelled the twelve o'clock meeting—*with me*.

He jerked his gaze toward me, the laughter dying on his face before he shoved to stand. "Ruth." A panicked flare in his eyes. "We weren't expecting—"

"I can see that." I answered and looked at the two people I hated most in this world, forcing a smile. "You guys needn't have worried. I told everyone I was coming in today."

Judah cast a panicked gaze at Blane. There was movement in the corner of my eye. Harlequin gripped something in his palm, and was edging it toward his pocket. I turned on him, reaching out my hand. "It's so good to see you again, Harlequin. How are Bethany and the kids? Last time we spoke, you were all excited for Alex's first day of school."

A flare of panic followed. He smiled and shoved the nice healthy wad of hundred dollars bills into his pocket. *Spending money,* my cousins called it. But I knew what it was. It was money to spend at one of the many strip clubs my cousins ran. There he'd be well taken care of, only the finest whisky, perkiest tits, and the tightest pussy for him to ride.

"G-good, thank you," he stuttered and grasped my hand. "And you? How are you after your..."

I cut them a glare, so they'd used that against me. Figures. "I'm good, ready to get back to work on closing our deal. I've got so many exciting ideas in mind."

71

The *snap* of a briefcase was a gunshot in the air. But I didn't dare turn my head, didn't look at the one place I wanted to...*at the splayed documents on the desk.* Or the signature, fresh ink, left to dry.

"We thought we'd give you a little breathing space, *Ruthy*," Blane spoke carefully. "We can take over your contacts."

Controlled words, designed to make me feel like that eight-year-old kid all over again. If they thought they could just come in and steal all my—

Blane braced his hands against the desk and leaned over, contempt and danger sparkling in his eyes. "Go home," he commanded. "Let us take care of you."

Harlequin smiled and nodded. All he could see were kindness and compassion. Family taking care of their own.

But he didn't know my fucking family.

It was code for *'let the men take care of business'* and *'you have no place here, you never have.'* I met his stare with my own as Judah reached for the signed papers at the same time as Harlequin did, knocking over a tumbler of the finest whiskey, their *celebratory drinks,* and spilling the alcohol across the desk.

"*Shit!*" Judah lunged as the spill soaked into the corners of the contract.

Harlequin grasped the papers and yanked, knocking over his own drink in the process. Judah had always been a klutz. In that moment, he took the damn crown, stumbling with the papers in one hand, his drink in the other, and smacked into Blane, knocking the open briefcase to the floor.

It was all a damn mess of fumbling buffoons and red-faced glances my way. I just stood inside the doorway and crossed my arms, watching the idiots scramble.

"I've got it!" Blane snapped, yanking his case from Judah' hands. "Just let the damn thing go."

The case snapped shut, the signed contract locked away, without my name as the director. Harlequin turned a bright shade of red as he drained the last dregs of his spilled whiskey and muttered, "Well, it's a pleasure doing business with the Costello family."

Oh, so it was the Costello family now? Not Judah and Blane. I knew what he was trying to do. He was trying to smooth it all over, trying to make it look like a deal with two people was a deal with all of us.

Only I'd been the one doing all the legwork on this, *months* of fucking legwork. Harlequin placed the crystal tumbler onto the desk and grabbed the leatherbound folder before reaching out his hand.

Judah grasped his hand, shaking just a little too hard, before Blane, with a creepy-ass grin, took his hand, hanging on a little too long. The asshole cast a gaze toward me. One more *fuck you* before he let Harlequin's hand go. The guy couldn't get out of there fast enough, lingering at the door to shake my hand.

I shook it, and gave him a comforting smile. "The Costello Corporation will take very good care of you, Harlequin. We're delighted to have you on board."

His shoulders relaxed, the smile a little more settled. "I appreciate it, Ruth, and I look forward to working with you."

I just smiled and nodded as he slipped through the door. He was an idiot if he thought I was taking alpha asshole's sloppy seconds. No, he was in for a world of unanswered phone calls and dropped deals with Judah and Blane in the driver's seat.

Pity, I would've made him more money than he'd be able to spend in a life time. Now all he'd have was shady deals and stale proposals. My cousins wouldn't know progress if it fingered their asses and sucked their balls.

Chairs scraped as they were shoved back, leaving behind dirty tumblers and a half-empty bottle of our finest.

"Ruth," Blane didn't bother to hide his smile as he strode past and out the door, carrying a contract that should've been mine.

He'd get a healthy bonus, six figures at least. But it wasn't about the money. It was all about appearance. They'd see him as more than the piece of shit he was. One day, my father's seat would be vacant, and Blane had just sealed the deal to put him in the running.

My deal.

My running.

My business.

Judah raced past, head down, not bothering to look me in the eye. Slimy bastard.

I stood at the doorway, looking into the office as their footsteps echoed, then faded. They didn't care about this place, nor the work it had taken to build it. If Blane had his way, the shipping business would be shut down for good.

All he cared about was pussy.

Pussy and dust, and money.

As long as he could fuck it, or snort it, or buy either of the two, he didn't care.

And if the board didn't see that, then they were stupid, fucking fools.

I shoved away from the doorway and to the desk, grabbing the dirty glasses and the bottle, tidying as I went, until something silver caught my eye.

A metallic flash drive was tilted on its side, hidden from view. I glanced at the doorway. The briefcase. The fall. My pulse sped...*Blane's.*

I grasped the thumb drive from the floor and slipped it into my pocket. By the time he figured out it was missing, I'd be long gone. I grabbed the glasses and what was left of the whiskey and went out the door.

Anger burned as I strode back along the hallway, stopping long enough to set the glasses in the sink and lock the whiskey away in the cupboard before I headed down the stairs and outside once more.

I traced the outline of the drive in my pocket and pushed open the door. The Maseratis were gone, as was their foul taste in music. I swallow my hate and crossed to the shed. The workers were busy, break now over. It was time to work.

A deep growl echoed from a cracked-open doorway. "She shouldn't be here. It's not safe. You know what they're saying about her, right? That she was the one who slaughtered those assholes."

"Franky, you know as well as I do that Ruth Costello isn't the scary one in the damn family. It's those cousins of hers we need to watch out for. They're gonna take the whole company out from under her just as soon as her old man dies."

I slowed, and stopped outside the door. Eavesdropping

wasn't one of my finest moments, but that terrified part of me needed to know...*I needed to understand.*

"Think what you want. But there's something strange about her. I've said it from the very start. No one talks about her mother, it's like the woman never existed. Don't you find that weird? Come on."

There was a mumble, and then a laugh.

I glanced over my shoulder, making sure no one was watching, and kept walking. My head down, focused on the machinery they were driving and the crates being unloaded. My heels scuffed, the sound a little louder this time. My steps were heavy, my heart pounding, filled with anger and injustice.

But there was no justice with my family.

There never was.

My finger traced the edges as I scanned the buildings up ahead. *He'll be back...for whatever's on this drive. He'll be retracing his steps...he'll find me.*

I lengthened my strides and hurried up the steps to my office, before I stepped inside and shut the door, twisted the lock and closed my eyes. My heart was pounding, slamming against the confines of my chest. I gripped the flimsy locked knob behind me as sucked in a hard breath.

You can do this, Ruth.

You're strong. Stronger than they think.

And stronger than you know.

In a heartbeat, I was snatched from that musty, tiny space and taken back there, to the alley filled with darkness and pain.

And a protector, who'd torn limb from limb to save me.

The memory hunkered in the dark corners of my

mind. It snarled, and bared its teeth—*waiting.* It wanted to consume me, to claim me, and the door handle rattled in my grip. "You're just going to have to wait your turn, aren't you?"

I stepped forward and strode around my desk. I didn't know who was watching my computer, didn't know who was watching the company mainframe, waiting for triggered words.

Not here.

Your laptop at home. The secret one.

The one I had kept away from prying eyes, for a moment such as this.

I hurried, gathered my things, and strode toward the door. The sun was piercing, burning. I winced and slid my sunglasses over my eyes as I hurried for my car. I was desperate to get home now, to see what was on that damn drive. Whatever it was, it was important enough for Blane to carry with him at all times, and if they thought I was ruthless…then that bastard was cunning as a snake.

7

Doors unlocked, and I was inside my car in a heartbeat, starting the engine and backing out of my space. This time, I didn't wave to the guards, didn't wind down my window. They wanted to keep me out of the loop of my own goddamn business? Fuck them.

Fuck them all.

I clenched the wheel and turned toward the city. Not even the river called me today, not the cool breeze, nor the cranes reaching overhead. A bitter taste lingered in the back of my throat. Harlequin would be on his way to meet with the new co-owners of his business and Blane and Judah would show him a damned good time.

I strangled the wheel and speared my way past mechanics and chainlink fences, past stage yards and graffitied mom and pop grocery stores of Crown City, until the landscape changed.

Walls of windows, glittering steel. I shifted my gaze to the middle building, not as tall as some, but standing like a beacon in the heart of the crown. Costello Corporation.

My family. My home...the one place I always thought I'd own.

My fingers slipped on the wheel, just like they were slipping on my future. I tore my gaze from the glinting tower and turned the wheel toward the ancient fig trees and green grass of Justice Park, and slowed.

Houses lined the other side of the street, elegant and gleaming, with manicured lawns and perfect facades. It was quiet, and controlled—*and expensive.* I slowed the Audi as I hit the middle and reached for the remote. It was funny, after five years of living here it still didn't feel like home.

None of this did. Not the tranquil Japanese gardens, nor the award-winning architectural homes in every lot from one end of the street to the other. It was the city that called me, like a pulse inside my head. It never stopped whispering, never stopped breathing life into my soul.

I eased the car into the driveway, and into the garage as the door closed behind me.

Home.

My lonely home.

I shoved open the car and strode to the entrance, my heels clacking loudly on the concrete floor. I didn't look at the set of golf clubs in the corner, still waiting for Alexander, my ex to come and collect them, didn't look at his shirts still hanging in my closet.

I didn't listen to the strained silence he'd left behind.

We could've been happy.

Maybe.

But I wasn't here for that, not now. I crossed into the hallway, then down to the kitchen, yanking open the refrigerator to grab a bottle of water. My heart was pounding as I unscrewed the top, took a gulp, then went to the stairs and climbed.

My heels sank into the plush caramel carpet. I gripped the banister and stepped out onto the landing. One glance toward the master bedroom, and I turned left for the study at the end of the hall.

It was the one room no one else went into, not the cleaner, or even Alexander when he was here. This was my sanctuary, my energy, my soul. This was where I worked until I was bleary-eyed and exhausted, and where all my hopes and dreams came to life.

I shoved my key in and twisted the lock, flicking on the lights as I went. The room was dark, *always dark.* Crowded with shadows, etched with silence—*just how I liked it.*

I took a gulp of the water and lifted my gaze to the blueprint of my life. The journey I'd take to become one of the most powerful women in the country. The wall was littered with business models and contracts, the biggest one being Greenholme Shipping.

I swallowed the ache in the back of my throat and crossed the study. The proposal was ten pages long. I'd painstakingly mapped out every increment I'd take Harlequin on to get to low-to-mid seven figures and blow it sky high.

He knew what I was proposing, and yet he'd gone with Judah and Blane. My way was slow and steady, my way was real growth. Maybe not in the first six months, but there was work involved. There were contracts to negotiate and relationships to build.

My way was harder, and required more time away from his family.

For me, that'd never been a problem. I'd been prepared to move if necessary, prepared to pack up my life and leave Crown City once and for all. I reached up and yanked the stack of papers from the wall before turning to the shredder.

Now, months of my work was nothing more than trash.

The machine snarled and swallowed until the motor fell silent. I reached into my pocket, pulled the flash drive free, and rounded my desk. The black safe sat on the floor in the corner the room. I knelt, punched in the numbers, and waited for the door to pop open.

It felt strange being back here. Or maybe I was the stranger? The one clinging to a dream that was never going to be mine.

I reached inside and pulled out a black laptop, the one device I had that wasn't connected to the mainframe. If Dad knew, he'd have a fit. Everything we did was scrutinized. Every document we scanned, and saved. Every keyword punched into the mainframe was logged and categorized.

This was a ruthless family.

And these were dangerous times.

I gripped the laptop, stood, and took it over to the desk. I had very few friends I could count on, and no one knew me as well as Ace. He was the unlikely friend, the one no one suspected, and the only one I trusted with my life.

We'd started off enemies. He'd tracked me down when I attended Chrisholm University studying for a business degree. He'd spammed my inbox with information about my family, plastered printed hate on my doors. He'd called my unregistered number at all hours of the morning, demanding answers.

Until one day, I gave in.

I met with him in a quiet cafe and let him rant about how we were solely responsible for the poverty and the drugs in Crown City. I let him cast judgment and try his best to rattle my cage, while I figured out exactly who he was. He was a hacker, an activist with a pulsing moral vein. He was, like most keyboard warriors—fucking clueless about the real me. So I let him give me an insight into how the other side saw us—those who were not family.

And as I sipped my chai latte, I felt a tear slide down my face. He stopped ranting. Stopped speaking altogether, and sat.

We'd talked that day, talked and talked and talked. I told him things I'd never told anyone. Private things...*personal things.* I let him in, but not to the family business, that's one thing I'd never reveal.

But I told him about how it was to be the daughter of Denzel Costello. How it was to grow up never feeling the warmth of a mother's love. How it was to be the one woman in a sea of sharks that were always circling.

How my vision was different from theirs, and Chrisholm was one step on my way there. He stopped seeing my name as a reason to attack, and started seeing me as a person.

With hopes and dreams.

With a vision of the future. One that'd take the Costello Corporation far away from the drugs and the guns, one that'd make us different from the Vampires, and the Wolves...and the Fae.

That was the real problem, the never ending fight to be different from those who ruled the dark. My thoughts slipped to them as I opened my laptop and waited for the machine to boot up.

They were savage, and brutal. They were ruthless and unkind.

They were not to be trusted...

Stay if you want. The Alpha's words filled my head. I didn't want to think about the Wolves, or that night. Not the silver glint in his eye as he stared into my soul, or the way he inhaled my scent, marking me in some way.

Beep.

The sound yanked me from the panic. I pressed the button on the flash drive and pushed it in. Lights flickered before a notification popped up.

Flash Drive (E:)

- *Choose what to do with removable drives.*
- *Configure this drive for backup.*
- *Open folder to view files.*
- *Take no action.*

I slid my finger on the trackpad, hovering the cursor over the view file link, and clicked.

Four folders appeared. One titled Circle, the next The Hidden, third was Videos, and the last one, Daddy Dom.

I winced and pulled away from that one, moving the cursor over Videos. If this was some fucked-up sex tape, then I would upload it to the company server, and let the goddamn board deal with it.

My breath welled in my chest as I clicked the folder. There were three videos, and that was all. I clicked on the first one, watching some kind of phone recording of a jumbled mess before the edge of a desk settled into view.

"What if your wife finds out?" a woman mumbled amongst muffled kisses.

"She won't."

I stiffened at the voice and released my pent-up breath as a hand appeared, running along the outside of a milky white thigh.

"But what if she…" the woman's breathless words tapered into a moan. I stared at Harlequin's watch as his face came into frame and pushed between her thighs.

"Fuck me," I muttered, and leaned backwards, watching it all play out on camera.

He was good at eating pussy, I'd give the poor schmuck that. Thick fingers pressing into her thigh as she leaned backwards, her own fingers delving through his hair as he dipped and licked, bringing her to the heights she wanted. The sounds of her pleasure filled the room. My breaths turned shallow and stopped as she let out a shudder and a moan.

My own need rose inside me, before I shoved it away. It was hard not to be affected by this, hard for my thoughts not to drift to the stranger in the alley. I licked my lips. Of all the times I'd had sex, that simple kiss was neon bright.

I clicked off the video as thoughts raced in my head.

The next video was more of the same, only in this one, he impaled her with a nice, thick, lipstick-lined cock.

"Harder, Harlequin," she moaned. "Fuck me harder, baby."

And the stupid fuck obliged, clenching his ass as he

rammed home. She made sure to use his name, made sure to get all the right angles, his face, his watch…his dick.

Laughter crawled through my lips as I shook my head. They'd set him up, the pieces of shit. They'd set the poor fucker up. I didn't know whether to fall to the floor laughing or throw up.

All that fucking work wasted.

All those hours spent in my study while Alexander lay alone in the bedroom. We could've been happy, could've been…*more.* "Yeah, we could've been more, more than strangers who shared a goddamn bed."

I shoved the cursor over the folder called The Circle and clicked.

Password…

"Shit." I clicked once more.

Password…

It was probably nothing. Some creepy goddamn video. My stomach clenched when I looked at the last document as I prepared to open *The Hidden.*

The cursor trembled as it hovered over the file, and remnants of that night slipped back to me.

The laughter.

The drinks…

The Wolves.

And all the while I waited for *them*…those creatures in the dark, the Unshadowed. The beasts they called 'The Hidden'. Only I'd left as the door opened, not wanting to put a face to my nightmares. I wanted nothing to remember them by. There was no more room inside my head for another nightmare. The Wolves and the Fae were bad enough. But for some strange reason,/ they never frightened me, not like…the cold ones.

I pulled the cursor away from the file. I'd survived twenty-two years without knowing them, and I'd survive twenty-two more.

The shredder came to life with a roar. My heart slammed against my chest as I jumped, spilling the open bottle of water. "Shit. *Shit!*" I grabbed the damn thing, catching it as a tiny drip spilled across the laptop trackpad.

And with one fluid motion, I swiped, clicking...and opening the file.

There were documents. *A lot of documents,* and the pissed-off part of me that'd just been shit on by my cousins roared to the surface. I clicked on the first one and opened it.

Costello Corporation's plan for newly appointed member of Congress, Prince Alliard Xuemel.

"What the fuck?" I stared at the document, reading every line, my heart hammering. Since when did we get in bed with the Immortals?

That night...

That fucking night.

Smiles and laughter and drinks all around.

Handshakes and nods.

This wasn't a goddamn discussion about our docks along the river. "It was a fucking alliance. It was a goddamn *fucking* alliance."

The room seemed to spin around me. I grabbed the bottle of water, watching as the liquid splashed the sides, until I gripped it with both hands and raised it to my lips. I couldn't think, couldn't breathe.

The implications of this were...*devastating.*

Sawing breaths filled my ears. I drank until I

spluttered and coughed, placed the empty bottle down, and closed my eyes.

The Costello Corporation was getting into bed with the beasts across the river. Why now? Why…*now?* I opened my eyes and re-read the document once more, before I clicked on the search and typed in *Prince Alliard Xuemel.*

There were three hits. Just three.

The first one was just a small piece in the New York Times. A thank you piece for a hefty donation to a children's charity. "What, no photo?"

I clicked out and tried the next. It was a photo, an old photo. "Fucking old."

The Vampire stood in front of a group, smiling, with pasty skin…I glanced at the description.

Prince Alliard Xuemel, Clan leader of the notorious Sinners, and Region Commander.

"Region Commander?" I muttered and leaned back against the chair. "Like a goddamn army?"

A chill raced through me. I thought of the four of them. Not a whole fucking battalion.

I clicked out once more and went back to the files.

The Circle. There was only one file left I was prepared to open. I sure as shit wasn't going near his porn. I clicked the damn thing once more.

Password?

There was no way I was getting into that. Still, the implications of what was on this drive were massive. The Costello family was getting into bed with the monsters in Crown City, and not in a good way. "Better hope to God this doesn't turn to shit."

But if I couldn't get into the damn file, then I knew

someone who could. I opened my laptop once more and typed in the address: *pekingesetrainingforbeginners.com* and hit enter.

Fluffy smooshed little faces filled the screen, with big brown eyes and long buoyant hair. There were dogs everywhere, the home page filled with information. But it wasn't a dog I was after...*it was a forum.* I moved the cursor over to the top and hit *find a forum,* then scrolled down.

Got a question about your Pekingese? Join Harvey and the Crew.

I hit the link and it took me to a live feed, where questions filled the screen in real time, and answers were given. Only it was all code, and you had to know how to read between the lines.

I was under the account *Anonymous.* I watched the clock, making sure I wasn't connected to the server for long.

I had no idea the kind of information hackers like Ace traded. It was best I didn't know. I clicked on the blinking cursor and typed. *'Hoping you can help me. I have a bone to pick with my current trainer. He's left me in the middle of a training program with my 4-month-old puppy and I don't know what to do.'*

I hit *send* and waited.

I didn't have to wait long.

Bone to pick was one of their 'trigger' phrases. Words they narrowed in on, words that meant something else entirely. Right now, I needed to find him, and with a guy like Ace, this was the only way.

'I have a name and number of someone who can help you. PM for further details.'

"No, no private messages." I dragged my teeth down my top lip and tried again.

'I've heard good things about Horne?'

The cursor blinked.

And blinked.

"Come on. Come on, Ace."

This was no forum for training puppies.

Horne is currently out of the country. I suggest maybe the community notice board, downtown at Paws and Things, 1 AM, sharp.

"Community notice board." I swallowed hard, staring at the clock on the screen. There was a countdown time for interactions just like this. Interactions I didn't want the authorities knowing about. I clicked out of the site, ending the session, and powered off the laptop before stowing it away in the safe once more. But I grabbed the USB and strode from the study to the bedroom.

I wanted to know what was on here more now than ever before. Five PM. I had time to shower, and find my way into the city. There was no way Ace was coming out until dark. I stood and yanked the zipper on the side of my skirt, letting it fall to the floor. This was one of the things I hated about being recognizable in a place like Crown City. Most of the time I didn't think about it, but at moments like this, I had to be careful.

I took my time in the shower, letting the hot water eased that fire inside. Still it never made a lick of difference, not when I stepped out into the steam-filled bathroom or when I watched as slowly the sun sank between the blinds in the bedroom behind me.

I went to the walk-in closet and the pile of folded

sweats. I yanked on pants, a plain t-shirt, and a jacket, before grabbing a cap from the stand and my trainers.

An hour later, I was out the door and staring into the twilight sky. I couldn't take the Bentley, not unless I wanted to be noticed in a heartbeat. So I crossed to my Audi. The sleek silver sedan would blend in a little better amongst the downtown traffic, and I'd park far enough away for it not to be a problem.

I hit the remote and climbed in, then started the engine and pressed the button for the garage door.

A minute later, I was backing out of my driveway, thirty minutes more, and I was searching for a parking spot not too close to where I needed to be. The downtown traffic was still busy for this time of the night. I scanned the crowds, pulled into a vacant space outside an Italian restaurant, and parked. Life crammed the streets, parents with older children spilling out from the open doors of the movie theater after catching a late movie, and a woman running late at night with her German Shepherd beside her.

This was so very different from the empty streets across the river. There was no life there, not unless you were headed for the Hunting Ground. There was no joy, no laughter, no *heartbeat.* That's what this side of the river had…a heartbeat all its own. I grabbed my cap, pushed my hair up into it, yanked it down low, and climbed out of the car.

I felt ridiculous, hiding my identity, sneaking around like I was wanted by the FBI. My hand stilled on the car door as I shoved it closed. I was desperate to hide my identity…and special agent Carina Chase was a pain in my fucking ass. If I didn't think she was watching me every damn second of the day, then I was stupid.

And that was one thing I wasn't. I swallowed hard, kept my eyes down, and slowly turned. I scanned every car pulling into the parking spaces behind me, and the ones across the road. Were they there? Did they have some kind of tracking device? I glanced down to my bag.

I watched Homeland. I knew how those types of assholes operated.

My phone.

I had to ditch it.

I turned, scanning the shops, and headed for the mall. The lights were still on, late night shoppers still in full swing. Perfect. I hurried for the open door, taking every opportunity to watch for movement behind me reflected in the glass, and stepped inside.

My heart thundered, fingers trembling as I delved into my bag and yanked out my phone. I had to get a new one, and fast. I rushed to the electronics store, stepped inside, and headed for the cell phone counter.

"Ma'am, can I help you?" A young male clerk stepped out of nowhere to block my aisle.

He glanced at me up and down, lingering on my t-shirt. "I need a new phone. One to replace this." I fanned the brand new cell around.

"That's top of the line kind of stuff. You sure you want to spend that kind of money? We're got some new brands in that are a fraction of the price."

"No," I shook my head. "Just this one, thanks."

He opened his mouth like he wanted to argue, until I fished out the American Express black card, then his eyes widened. "Yes, ma'am," he added and raced to get me exactly what I wanted.

Five minutes later, I had the new phone in my bag and was turning toward the busy front entrance before I stopped and turned toward the kid once more. "You don't have a back door I can take, do you? I thought I saw my ex-boyfriend."

He jerked his gaze toward the front of the store, his gaze hardening like he wanted to take on the asshole ex all by himself. I softened my voice. "He's a cop, and I just don't want that kind of scene."

That bought the kid's macho illusions crashing down. He winced, then nodded. "Sure, follow me." Then he proceeded to tell me about his asshole boss who told them it was a staff entrance only back here, and they'd be risking their job if they didn't follow the rules.

I fished into my bag, pulling out a fifty-dollar bill and pressing it into his palm as he shoved open a fire door and stepped to the side.

"Thank you," I added. "You've been so kind."

He looked down to the bill, his eyes widening in surprise. But I was already racing out into the night, making my way across the parking lot to head the back way through the mall. My thoughts were turning panicked now. Time was running out.

I cut behind the staff cars and headed for a service entrance. The mall stretched across this end of the block, but it was easy to navigate from one side to the other. I yanked open the glass door and made my way along a dimly lit corridor, stepping to the side as men and women came out of the bathrooms.

A few minutes later, I was in the flow of pedestrians,

then out the other side. Paws and Things was a coffee shop designed for people and their pets. It caused some ·excitement a few years ago, but was now little more than an eclectic meeting place filled with snapping handbag-chihuahuas. I headed across the packed street, then hustled along the parked cars, glancing over my shoulder as I hurried.

I looked at my watch. *Crap. Ten minutes.* I lengthened my side, then picked up pace, moving into a light jog. My body reacted instantly, breaths deepened, eyes focused on what was ahead of me. My bag smacked against my side with each stride, but I raced along the street, then turned.

Lights spilled along the pavement further along the block. The illuminated sign with a big black pawprint in the middle made me push harder. By the time I hit the front steps, I was breathless, but I tried to compose myself as I climbed.

Shadows hugged the interior. I snuck a glance over my shoulder before I stepped inside. There was no movement behind me, no strange cars pulled along the street in either direction. There was just chatter, and darkness… and the faint smell of dog shampoo.

Heads turned my way, critical stares were followed by sneers. How dare I come to a doggy cafe with no damn dog. "I'll give you a fucking dog," I muttered under my breath and forced a smile. "I've been called a bitch more times than I can count."

I made my way to the back of the cafe, to where the notice board was crammed with puppy training notices and puppies for sale. I took a seat opposite and checked my watch as it ticked over to 1 AM. "Come on, Ace."

My knee bounced as I waited. A waitress came closer,

notepad in hand, ready to take my order. I just smiled and shook my head, explaining I was waiting for someone. The moment she had her back turned, I felt the air around me shift.

"Your phone, give it to me."

I flinched at the voice and the young woman who stood at my right. She had shaved purple hair and a t-shirt that exclaimed *All Puppies are Cute.* I swallowed, glanced behind her, then reached into my bag. "I take it you're with Ace?"

She said nothing, just held out her hand, waiting patiently.

"Yeah, you're just like him. I have a new phone, too, just in case there's anything *wrong* with this one." I handed both over to her.

She grabbed both cell phones and was gone in an instant, headed for a door marked *'Bitchs'* as opposed to *'Hounds'*.

Still there was no sign of Ace. There was nothing. My knees jumped and bounced like the stock market after an assassinated politician.

"You wanted to see me?"

Ace slid into the seat opposite and picked up a menu, not bothering to look at me once. I grabbed my bag and prepared to stand before he shook his head. "Stay where you are. Kat's working on your phone now. It was smart to buy a new one."

"I have something I need you to look at," I started, my heart climbing into the back of my throat. "It's a file, encrypted."

"You brought me all this way for a damn file you can't

open? Come on, princess, you should know better than that."

I stilled, anger bursting to the surface. "It's not just *any* file, Ace. It's..." I was lost for words. *What* was *it exactly?* "I don't know what it is, but I have a feeling."

"You have a feeling?"

I closed my hand around the damn thing and pulled it out. "Yeah, I do. My gut tells me there's something important on this drive. Important enough to hide, and I want to know what that is."

He turned his head then, and looked me in the eye. "It's going to cost you."

"How much?"

There was a twitch in his left cheek. "Double."

I rolled my eyes and let out a sigh. "And you say *I'm* the extortionist?"

"Big risk means big payout." He leaned back, smiling. *Asshole.*

"How are you?" I started before he let out a sudden bark of laughter.

"God, I miss the days when you threw shit at me and stormed out. You've gone soft, princess. Soft."

A smile crept across my lips. Ace was the only person who spoke to me like that...the only person I'd let. He gripped the table in front of him and turned, facing me. *He never faced me.*

"You look sad and lonely, lonelier than normal. Your dad?"

I swallowed hard, my smile dying in a heartbeat. "He's...here, barely."

"I'm sorry." There was a small shake of his head before

he leaned forward. "I worry about you…about you being all alone in this."

"I'm not alone," I lied, and forced a smile once more. "I've got you, right?"

"You are alone, and if you're counting me as someone you can call on, then you're even lonelier than I thought."

The sting of his words was brutal, cutting all the way down to my core. I swallowed the bitterness, and the hurt. "You don't need to worry about me." I grabbed my bag and slid along the seat before standing.

The ladies' room door opened and the same punk girl with the sneer walked out and handed me both phones. "I transferred the data from the old one to the new one, and killed the old one. You had a tracer. Basic store-bought shit. I took care of it."

"Not government?"

She shook her head. "Not this one, no. You got yourself some admirers."

My heart pounded with the thought. Someone was watching me, someone other than the feds. I glanced at Ace. "You'll text me the usual address for payment?"

He never nodded, just rose from his seat. I'd forgotten how gorgeous he was, shorter than I liked, but solid, with soft, pouty lips and a hard-ass jaw. He screamed military, but every time I asked, he gave me some bullshit answer. "Let me set up surveillance on your house."

I shook my head. "We've been through this. No. I'm not living my life fucking terrified."

"It's different this time though, right?"

I swallowed the thunder of my heart.

"It's different," he urged.

My hands shook as I stowed the phones into my bag.

"I'm fine," I muttered, and pushed the USB into his hand before I headed for the door.

I didn't look back at him, didn't miss a beat, just hit the door and scurried down the stairs. My senses were screaming by the time I made it back to the car. A light sheen of sweat was cooling with the night air as I slammed the door closed.

Tears blurred the oncoming headlights of a car. I stabbed the button on the Audi and started the engine. It took all my strength not to give in to the emotions, to stem the flow of tears and harden my heart.

You look lonely...lonelier than normal.

The words echoed as I made my way back home and slowed at the entrance to my driveway. I hated those words, and I hated him for saying them. I clenched my jaw and eased the car into the garage before pressing the button and climbing from the car. My feet felt heavy, not anywhere near as heavy as my heart.

I gripped the banister, hauled myself up the stairs, and went to my bedroom. Light spilled across the bottom of the neatly made bed. The place was immaculate, and *empty.* I walked over to the tall set of drawers.

Ace was right. I had no one. Ace and Alexander were the closest thing to a friend. Family? Family betrayed me. Family hid things from me...family made me feel...*insignificant.*

Pain lashed my chest with the thought. My hands trembled as I gripped the handle and pulled open the drawer. The smiles and the laughter of that night came back to me. They all knew they were meeting with the Immortals...every single one of them.

Everyone but me.

I swallowed that bitter pill and reached into the drawer for my pajamas.

My fingers skimmed something smooth, something cold, something that sat on top of my lace panties, and I yanked it free.

A glove? Black leather shone against the light.

A chill crawled along my spine with the sight.

I spun and scanned the bedroom, my heart slamming inside my chest.

It wasn't just any glove.

It was *his* glove.

The stranger from the alley.

And he'd been in my bedroom.

E *ight months later...*

T hey have three rules…those…monsters in the dark.
Bloodsuckers, Dad called them once. Those who steal your money first, then your life. Still, three fucking rules I'd come to know, and as much as I despise those unspoken laws, I can't help but feel a surge of power in knowing who they truly are.

They were not your average *family.*

Nor were they your normal *thugs.*

I cut across the last few steps of the parking lot and stopped in front of my car. It was gleaming black, a beast waiting. It was once my father's car, but like all things in our family, what was his…*was now mine.*

The weak yellow streetlight spilled across the hood. But it wasn't the metallic paint that called me…my gaze slipped higher, and the three rules slipped through my mind once more.

They *will* take your money.

They *will* use your women.

They *will* bleed you dry.

The warning was painted with blood across my windshield.

Pay up, or we take what's ours.

I winced at the words, and my heart sped…just a little. I fought the need to scan the shadows behind me, to run as fast as these stilettos would carry me back to the protection of the warehouse. But that wasn't me. I was a *Costello.*

I didn't run. I stood, sized up my opponent, and took them down.

I am not violent, nor am I malicious.

I'm an end, a result. A *finality* that once you knew it… you knew there was no going back.

The weak streetlight gave me nothing, but I knew they didn't wait for me in the shadows…*those monsters.* They were long gone.

Long enough for the blood to thicken. Long enough to know who it was they were dealing with. Only they'd made one simple mistake. They'd bullied the wrong family.

I'm the one taking over the 'family business'. I'm cleaning up the losers, the hangers-on, the ones who shoot first and ask questions later and do shitty fucking deals that were fated to go to hell.

I'm changing the face of the Costello family business.

One deadbeat at a time.

I'm running a cleaner operation. A streamlined,

entrepreneurial enterprise. Dad laughs when I call it that. But I don't. Out with the old and in with the new. Only *this* new is more ruthless, more determined, more *bitch* than ever before.

I stared at the warning splashed across my windshield written with someone else's blood, and felt that gnawing in my gut.

Those Vampires might run the city west of the river... but the Costello family ran the east, and it was about time they remembered that. I winced at the thought and swallowed hard.

It was about time they *all* remembered it, including my own kin. I reached out, hit the button, and the lights flashed on the sleek Bentley.

Costello, the license plate stated. Everyone who earned a name in this city knew whose car drove down their streets, and after tomorrow, they'd know about the change of the guard.

Lights flashed as the locks disengaged. I yanked open the door and climbed in. I pulled the door closed, stared through the mess on the windshield, and dragged in the faint, foul scent of my father's cigars.

I hated them, hated them more now than ever before. But hate was useless, hate was a waste. I'd use that hate, turn it into something I could use, something that fueled my drive to be the person my family needed now. I reached out, pressed the button, and the growl of the engine filled my ears.

The radio came on in an instant.

"...still reeling from the brutal assassination of the controversial Vampire Senator, Prince Alliard Xuemel, last week. Sources are saying it was a planned attack at his home in

Huntworth, Washington. As you well know, Prince Alliard was the first Immortal to occupy a government seat here in the capital, but after that savage assassination, I'm betting it will be the last."

I ground my teeth and savagely switched the radio off. I tasted acid in the back of my throat as I hit the wipers. But no matter how many times the blades cut across the glass...the writing was still there. The water seemed to stick to the words, waxy and fatty. I could see it as clearly as I saw this whole messy damn end.

We'd gotten into bed with those fanged monsters, and when I saw *we,* I mean the Costello name. We'd pulled back the sheets and slipped underneath, eager to be drained dry...we'd put a Vampire where none had ever gone before. *We'd put that monster in the running for Congress.*

For a few years at least...until the Vampire was slaughtered in his bed.

Still, we'd made a deal. A deal done behind my back, like most deals in my family business—*now that deal has gone south.*

I stared at the words painted on my windshield and felt that seething pit of rage.

Pay up, or we take what's ours.

"Fucking barbarians," I gripped the wheel.

Blood, on my damn car.

And it wasn't even my deal to begin with.

I shoved the car into gear and eased forward, leaving the murky yellow streetlight outside the warehouse behind as I drove out of the parking lot and headed home.

It was late. Too late to wake my father, even if he was sleeping. But these days were sacred, special. I'd grab every second I could. I wound the Bentley through the dark streets of Crown City.

We all wanted it.

All fought for it.

Every jewel and every thorn. I turned, weaving the mighty beast back along the streets that hugged the river. Diamonds sparkled on the surface of the river that stretched wide, carving through the belly of the city, dividing more than the workers—and the money.

It divided territory.

And a battle that my father had fought for the last forty years had been handed down. A battle that I carried in my veins. A battle I was ready for.

I turned my head, staring at the 'other side of the crown' and felt that tug in my belly. They'd sent a message tonight. A message I received loud and clear. But there'd be no giving in, no buckling under to their demands.

If the Vampires wanted their payment, then they could come and fucking get it.

But make no mistake, they'd leave emptyhanded. I'd make sure of that.

I drove past the docks, and the huge ships. My ships carrying my cargo. Guns. People. Those who'd given everything they owned for a bite of the apple, and I was giving it to them.

I'd give them a fighting chance, which is more than they'd get anywhere else.

I leaned forward, pressed the button on the stereo, and felt the deep bass through the speakers as I sped past the cranes that ran on the docks twenty-four hours a day, seven days a week. It was a city of its own here. A city of ships, and workers. A city of money, one that stretched all the way along the six blocks that took up the east side of the Elide River.

And the Costello family owned it all.

Every worker, every Police Superintendent, every union representative.

We had fingers in every pie, and we were swallowing our fair share.

I turned and headed further inland, past the skyscrapers and the brand new district hospital, that, with a little help from me, received its own state-of-the-art children's hospital equipped with three stand-by choppers to retrieve life-saving organs and the best doctors money could buy.

A surge of pride carried me past the gleaming building, and out to the more luxurious part of the city, where old money grew as stale as old blood.

I wove the Bentley through familiar streets until I finally turned into a dead-end street. King Street, named for my father, the Costello King.

I slowed the car and turned the wheel, searching in the distance for the faint sparkle of lights, and glanced at the clock. It was almost midnight. The time when normal people were deep asleep. But if there was one thing my father wasn't…it was normal.

The sensor at the front of the car flashed red before the tall wrought iron gates rolled backwards. I eased the Bentley through the gap.

The long driveway wound around the elegant fountain in the shape of a woman reaching to the moon. Daddy said it reminded him of me, always reaching, always hungry. He said I was born starving, greedily shoving as much as I could into my mouth as soon as I could.

But he was wrong.

I was full. Filled with love, and desperation—I caught the ass end of the cream-colored Rolls and felt the familiar clench in my gut—I was also filled with loathing.

Jerry was here, no doubt whispering in my father's ear. I pulled the car up alongside him, leaving a sliver of a gap between the Bentley and his soap scum on wheels. He'd be pissed when he tried to leave.

I killed the engine and climbed out, walking around the rear of the vehicle to glance at the space between his driver's door and my car. Yeah. There was no way the fat fuck was getting in there.

And in an instant, my steps felt lighter, shoulders a little more relaxed. I turned and headed for the door as one side of the imposing entrance widened. I never slowed, never missed a beat, just stepped inside, hearing that familiar *clack...clack...clack...*against the marble floor.

My gaze drifted higher. In my head, I was staring through the walls of this place, reaching all the way to the bedroom at the top of the balcony, the one specially built for Dad.

"How long has he been here?" I asked as I shrugged off my jacket and handed it to Charlotte.

"Going on four hours now," she said coldly and took my jacket before following my gaze. "Don't worry, your father's in no condition to hold a pen, let alone sign anything."

"It's not his signature I'm worried about," I growled, and met her gaze. "Every minute that slimy, lying piece of shit is here whispering lies in my father's ear, the more he undermines my position."

"Then let's not keep him waiting." She turned her head

and gave a sharp nod to someone standing in the dark. "I'll give him something to whisper about."

In a heartbeat, the house came alive. I turned to Charlotte and smiled. She was a hard woman...a beautiful woman, with her 50's midnight hair slicked over one shoulder, pale skin, ruby red lips, and an hourglass figure that had made many negotiations stop dead in this house while every hot-blooded male, and a few women I might add, stopped and stared.

But she was mine, my confidant, and my friend, even after all these years, and in an instant, I was taken back to that night eight months ago. The night I'd almost died. My back still twinged in the mornings, and on a cold night I sometimes found it hard to breathe.

I could still feel their fists and boots slamming into me, still hear their screams inside that alley as I curled myself into a ball and waited for death to come.

But it wasn't my death that slipped through the darkness...it was the thugs' who'd beaten me senseless.

Charlotte had been my nurse when I woke up in the hospital, and she'd become my friend ever since. And now she was where I needed her to be. My eyes and ears—I reached out and grasped her hand—my friend. She handed my jacket to a young boy standing behind her and adjusted her jacket. The one person I trusted with something more precious than my life.

I trusted her with my father's.

The pin-striped pants suit was her favorite. It tapered in around her breasts, and hugged her ass. I swallowed a flare of jealously and watched as she whipped up the rest of the servants into a frenzy, then turned back to me. "Go get 'em, tiger."

I smiled, and inhaled that surge of power she always gave me.

She fought the same battles…a war that'd last until there was a changing of the guard. Women weren't management material. We were too highly strung, too emotional…too busy lying on our backs while the men of this world fucked their way into our hearts.

But not mine.

No. Mine was already taken.

Dock lights bounced off the midnight water inside my head, sparkling like diamonds, big, fat diamonds. My heart was filled to overflowing…but it wasn't a cock I craved. It was money…*it was power.* And I had it all.

I just had to hold onto it.

I stepped forward, making my way through the foyer, and heard the front door close with a soft *thud.* I made my way through the magnificent entrance, with its Michelangelo statues in the corner, and climbed the three flights of stairs. My heels made no sound on the carpeted runner, the black stilettos sank into the plush as I gripped the banister and climbed.

My thighs flared with an ache. I was tired, running on about five hours of broken sleep a night that was doing shit-all for my frayed nerves. And neither was dealing with shit like this.

The tiny clatter of a tray carried me up the last few steps. I lifted my head to the sitting room we'd turned into a makeshift hospital room, and lowered my gaze to the soft white light spilling from under the closed door.

What were they talking about in there?

What was being said?

I didn't have to strain too hard to figure it out. I curled

my lips, and forced life into my eyes before I gripped the handle and eased the door open.

The *beep...beep...beep* of the machines greeted me as I entered, and the cutting scent of disinfectant followed. Soft murmurs came from the man sitting beside the hospital bed on the side of the room.

He tensed a little, leaned a little closer, spoke hurried words. *Yeah, that's right, you two-faced, backstabbing, lying, still-fucking-warm fresh dog turd.* My uncle turned his head and forced a smile, then rose awkwardly from the seat. "Ruthy."

"Uncle," I forced through gritted teeth, then cast a glance at the man lying in the bed. "How is he?"

"Holding on...holding on for you," he turned to the hollow-cheeked stranger with his eyes closed.

He patted his arm amongst the tubes and wires. "I'll be back tomorrow, you just spend time with your girl now."

Dad's eyes fluttered open, and that same lightning stare found me as I stopped at the foot of the bed. But that part of my father wasn't a stranger, that was the part I knew.

"Take care now, don't worry about a thing," my uncle murmured against his ear.

"What isn't he worrying about, uncle?"

There was no answer, like I hadn't said a word. Instead, he straightened, then turned. There was a flare of the real him in his eyes, a *recoiling of disgust.* He hated me, he denied me. Just like the two others like him.

Two brothers who thought the family business now belonged to *them*, and *their* sniveling, cocaine-crusted, snot-nosed *sons* who liked nothing more than to fuck their way through every call girl this side of the river, then stumble home to whale on their wives.

But I'd heard rumors...rumors that little Jonny and his dumb-as-a-box-of-hammers big brother were venturing across the river in search of a little *'strange'*. Only this strange was rumored to have fangs, and to take more liquid than whatever disease-infected fluid they shot into her.

"Nothing for you to worry your pretty little head about," he finally answered, and stepped closer.

The door opened behind me. With perfect timing as always, Charlotte carried in a tray with a steaming cup of coffee, a light meal, and a fresh IV bag for Dad. I tried to stop the acid from rising in the back of my throat as my uncle waddled forward and patted the back of my hand.

Prick.

Movement caught my eye. Dad lifted a finger, a signal, the only one he had left. I tore my gaze back to my uncle, and as much as I fucking hated playing the game—I did.

I gave a slow, careful nod, followed with sad, puppy-dog eyes, a tiny tremble of my lips. I wrapped my arms around him and pulled him close. "Thank you," I said. "I'm so grateful to have you here. You're a tower of strength, uncle. I'd be lost without you."

I met those sizzling blue eyes from the man on the bed as I hugged Jerry and felt the man stiffen in surprise. He didn't expect me to tremble, didn't expect me to show any cracks at all.

He didn't expect me to play the game...only he didn't realize...*I'd been playing it my entire fucking life.*

"Yes...of course," slack, lifeless hands gripped me tighter.

He felt like a fish. And he stank like one, too.

An oily fish.

The corner of my lips twitched, just a hint of a smile. Just for Dad, before I fell into character and pulled away. I *squeezed* every ounce of emotion into my performance. I dredged up every sad, dead-Bambi's-mom scene I could, and forced a single fucking tear to slip from my eye.

My uncle stiffened at the sight. His eyes widened just a little before he shoved his hand inside his jacket and pulled free a perfectly folded handkerchief. "Oh, honey," he sighed as he pressed the embroidered end into my hand, his hand sliding to my arm.

"I'm right here for you, anything you need, kid, it's yours. All you gotta do is say the word," he gushed, tripping over his words.

I lifted my head, and met his solemn gaze. *How about for you and your entire fucking bloodline to drop dead. Think you can manage that for me?* "Thank you, uncle. I'm so...so lost right now. So very lonely and lost."

There was a catch of his breath. His fingers trembled against my arm, as though he fought to touch me...or he fought himself *not* to touch me.

There was a nod of his head, and a hard swallow. He stepped away, taking one last look at my father before he stammered, "I'll let you two have some time now."

One small nod and a tiny hiccup was all that was needed. I clutched his handkerchief and pressed it to my cheek, watching him hightail it toward the open door, then out into the darkened hall.

Footsteps sounded into the hallway, then the harsh gasp of breath and thunderous *thud...thud...thud* echoed as he stumbled down the stairs.

"I'll leave you for a little while."

I gave a nod and dropped my hand, and the act. Seemed like I hadn't needed Charlotte and her performance after all. Who knew I was a fucking star all on my own?

I dropped the handkerchief and caught the flutter before it hit the floor. It'd be swept up by morning, and taken out with the rest of the trash. Pity they couldn't take the man with it.

My father gave a ghost of a smile as I went toward the still-warm seat next to him. A ghost of everything was all he could give now. Cancer had taken everything else.

*So fast...*eight months to reduce the most powerful man I'd ever known to mere skin and bones. The thought hit me like a punch to my ribs.

Eight months...would he last eight more?

He gave a jerk of his gaze toward the seat. I took my place, and reached for his hand, and the too-thin skin slipped across his knuckles. He was nothing more than skin and bones now. The man...the *mighty* man, all but wasted away.

Except for his eyes. They raged brighter and hungrier than ever before, like he'd pulled back his troops, gathering his strength for one last battle.

His dry, cracked lips moved. A wordless whisper, nothing but air.

"What is that, daddy?" I rose from the seat and leaned over, my ear angled to his lips.

"More tits."

There was a tiny flare of confusion, but that was one thing he'd *never* been. Not confused, not my dad. I straightened and sank into the seat. "You think that's the only way to get to him? Show a little more cleavage?"

He smiled and gave a tiny nod. Clever sonofabitch.

I gave a shrug. "I dunno, I thought the tear worked just as well. I guess I always have that up my sleeve, don't I?"

One more nod, fingers hovering. A tiny pat on the back of my hand. *That's my girl.* He didn't need to say the words. I heard them in my head. Just like I heard all of his words now. Even the ones he'd never say to my face.

I'm sorry.

There was a second for the father, that was all he gave that part of himself before one brow rose.

"It's fine. I just came from the warehouse." I scanned the room and felt that automatic clench in my gut. "I've had meetings with the production people for the *'hospital',* and that's all on schedule. Costs are down, but capital is up. We're winning the battle there." It was code, all code. You never knew who was listening, and I've had the FBI so far up my ass they may as well have given me a damn badge.

But for now, things were quiet...a little *too quiet.* Maybe they were busy with someone else...or maybe they were sitting back, waiting for the machine to give one last beep and fall silent, then they'd see where the cards fell.

They all would. But not me.

I knew *exactly* where they were falling. "I'm gonna make you proud."

"Ruth," the hiss of my name slipped from his lips. I waited. *"Lessss."*

I forced a smile. Daddy always said he'd left the 'less' off the last part of my name. He wanted those who met me to learn for themselves who I was.

Maybe he left it off for me.

Maybe I needed to learn who I was for myself.

I can be the nice, shy, quiet Ruth, the one who'd let her family dictate which seat in the back of the buss she should sit in. Or I could be one of them...a beast—*a monster,* dressed in Gucci and Manolo Blahnik, and drive that motherfucker myself.

Maybe I was just starting to find out who I truly was. "Damn right," I added. "Ruthless to the goddamn core."

Pride swelled in his eyes. I didn't need to flash my tits, not that I had a lot to show. I was all legs, all milky-toned skin. But there was one thing I had that wasn't his...my hair.

His gaze slipped to the top of my head. I lowered my head, letting the vibrant red hair spill across the back of his hand.

I was ninety-five percent Costello. But in that other five percent, I was a mirror of the mother who'd left me behind, just like he's leaving me behind. "Do you think of her?"

I lifted my head, but still his gaze followed the fire of my hair. One small nod. *All the time.*

"Will you...will you tell her I love her?"

Panic flared for a second, a hint of the fighter. He wasn't ready to give up, not yet. Still, he gave a nod.

"They want me out," I growled softly. "I'm just waiting for them to make their play. I'm gonna hold on for as long as I can. I'm trying to put things in motion, trying to make it so they can't get rid of me...not entirely."

"Good," the word was a whisper. "Show them who you are."

The door opened. Charlotte stepped in just as the

machine gave a *beep* and the last trickle of fluid spilled along the tube. I stifled a yawn.

"You want to stay?"

I shook my head. I hadn't slept in this house, not since the diagnosis. I couldn't bring myself to want to. "No, thank you." I turned back to him. "I'll let you rest, be back tomorrow."

He gave a smile and closed his eyes. He was tired all the time now. Too tired to fight. Too tired to demand. "No signing anything without me, okay?"

There was no nod of his head, no ghost of a smile.

But he knew.

They all knew.

I turned from the bed and took a step, lingering at his feet. "Call me if anything changes."

"Always," Charlotte added.

There was a surge of something in her gaze…*desire… drive.* We were more alike than even my flesh and blood, all they were was greedy and weak. Charlotte was the one thing besides me that my uncles hated, and the reason my father kept her around.

I glanced back at him, at the slow rise and fall of his chest. He was a whisper now. A turn of the tide. A shift of the wind. Here one minute and he'd be gone the next.

Then there'd be a battle. Then there'd be a goddamn hurricane.

I stepped through the door and closed it behind me.

I could already feel the winds changing.

Already hear the hiss at my back.

My family weren't saddened. They were fucking vipers.

Just waiting for him to die.

9

My headlights splashed the front door as I started the engine. I hated leaving him, hated how the fallout with the Vampires made me feel divided from my own flesh and blood.

My father was still one of the most powerful men in Crown City, even on his death-bed.

But he was also weak.

Weak to vultures like my uncle, weak to the media and the outside world.

Weak to anyone who thought the Costello family was ripe for the taking, and that was one thing I couldn't afford. I shoved the car into gear and turned the wheel. Dad was safe here, safe with Charlotte and his men. It was the company I worried about.

There were whispers of a divide, whispers that any moment, my claim on the Costello family holdings would be gone. I lifted my gaze to the rear-view mirror, to my home. I couldn't have that, not one second of it, not one thought. I had to find out where those rumors were coming from, and I had to silence the source.

Tires crunched on the asphalt driveway. I slowed at the gate until it caught the sensor and opened. My phone vibrated in my pocket as I eased through and pulled out onto the road. The caller ID splashed on the console as I pulled it out. *Head Office.*

I hit the button and swallowed the flinch. "Ruth Costello."

"Ms. Costello...Ms. Costello, it's James from the night crew. I don't know if you remember me, you gave me your number last year."

"I remember," I answered. "Your daughter goes to Charleston Prep."

"Yes, ma'am, you do remember." Heavy breaths of relief echoed from the speakers. "I'm sorry to call this time of the night, ma'am. But I was on the ground level polishing the floors when they came."

They came? "Who came, James?"

"I don't know who they are, ma'am. Men in suits, and a woman. They look government to me. They had a warrant, Ms. Costello. There was nothing I could do."

The dark road seemed to blur in front of me. My gut clenched tight, spilling the bitter tang of acid into my throat. "That's okay, you did fine, James. Hold tight, okay? I'm on my way."

"Yes, ma'am. I'm real sorry."

"I know you are," my voice was lost to the void as I hit the button and ended the call. "But not half as sorry as they will be."

I grasped my phone and wrestled the wheel, stabbing the first number on speed dial. *Blane Costello.* It rang...and rang...*and rang* until the voice message picked up. "You've reached Blane. If I haven't answered your call, there's a reason. Leave a message...or don't..."

"Nice," I muttered, and waited for the beep. "Blane, it's me. Get your ass to the head office. We have a problem."

I ended the call and pressed the number for his brother, Judah, not that either of them would be any help. Surprise, he wasn't answering either. Probably holed up in one of his many mistress's homes.

My other cousins were useless, even more than Judah and Blane. I stared at the road, and drove my foot against the accelerator. This left me with one choice...one I was loath to call. My finger trembled as I pressed the button, then instantly thought, *what the fuck are you doing? Anyone but him.* I reached out, finger hovering over the end call button as it was answered on the second ring. "Ruth? Are you okay?"

Bed sheets rustled. God, I could almost see him pushing back the covers. White cotton sheets spilling into his lap, his muscles tensing as he reached for the back of his neck with one hand.

"Alexander, I'm sorry to call you like this."

"What's wrong?" His voice was clear and sharp. He was alert in an instant. "Are you okay?"

"Someone's just stormed Head Office. I had a call from the supervisor on the night shift cleaning crew. He said they looked government."

"Shit...*shit.*" His German accent was always stronger when he was pissed.

"Do you know what's going on. Have you heard anything at all?"

"What? No, of course I haven't heard anything. Don't you think I would've given you a heads-up?"

I stared into the city lights as they beckoned, and felt the world rush past.

"How far away are you?" he asked. There was a murmur in the background. *A woman's murmur.*

Guilt and loneliness swallowed me whole. What did I expect? Did I expect him to wallow in self-sabotaging emptiness…like I had? "About twenty minutes."

"Then I'll see you in fifteen," he answered, and hung up.

I knew he'd come. I was counting on it, wasn't I? It was the only reason I called, knowing Alexander would charge in like some white fucking knight. *See you in fifteen.* I strangled the wheel and pressed down on the accelerator. He knew me too damn well.

Streetlights blurred. I turned onto the freeway that'd take me all the way into the heart of the city and I tried to not let my thoughts slip away.

Men in suits, and a woman. They look government to me. They had a warrant, Ms. Costello. There was nothing I could do.

Men in suits…and a woman. My mind raced, flicking through the pages of my life. *A woman…*I stiffened as a memory surfaced.

I'll be watching you, Costello. Bet your goddamn life on that.

My pulse sped as her words surfaced, just another one of my fans. Only this one was different from all the nutters who sent me hate mail and threats—this one carried a badge.

Looks government.

Sweat broke out along the nape of my neck. If she came with a warrant, then she was looking for something in particular, or knew something in particular. *I had an idea what that something was.*

I flicked through the pages of my mind, searching for the moment I pissed this woman off. Carina Chase wasn't someone to forget in a hurry. She was a damn bloodhound, a hard-nosed, laser-driven, stubborn bitch with a hard-on for the Costello name.

My breaths quickened, my hands slipped with sweat against the wheel. "Let it not be her. Let it be anyone but her."

I turned the Bentley off the freeway as the Costello building towered overhead. Like the other members of my family, I had an office here, one I visited twice a week. But my real work was down at the docks. I'd taken a more primary role, moving up into Overseeing Manager. Blane and Judah hadn't seemed to notice, now that they were balls deep in the mess they'd created.

Greenholme Shipping was a sinkhole. One we'd spent close to two million dollars to make work. But the faster we poured money into the project, the worse it became.

Harlequin was now in his second stint in rehab. The guy almost drank himself to death and was hovering on the brink of financial collapse. There was barely any expansion, most of the competitors had moved in to take what they could, until there was nothing left, while Harlequin and his new partners drank and snorted and fucked his company dry.

I could've told him this would happen.

I did tell him it would happen.

But blackmail had a funny way of seeing itself through. And now I wanted to cut my cousins loose.

I nosed the Bentley into the underground garage and stopped at the guardhouse.

"ID," the tired officer muttered.

I reached for my tag and passed it through the window. I didn't come here this time of the night, so he'd have no real reason to know who I was. His eyes widened at the name. He passed the ID back and gave a nod of his head.

A second later, the boom gate rose. "Have a good night, ma'am."

I wouldn't have a good night...not at all.

The driver's door on the midnight Explorer opened as I pulled into the parking space. An ache tore through my chest at the sight. His mousy strawberry-blond hair was messy from sleep, raked from his fingers. He was gorgeous, just as he was always gorgeous. I'd somehow forgotten that fact. But I remembered it now. I killed the engine and shoved open the car door as he rounded the front.

"I made some calls, found out what I could. You're not going to like it." He rubbed the stubble on his chin and stepped close.

It was automatic with Alexander, lean in, warm lips brushed my cheek. "A search warrant in the middle of the night when they knew no one was going to be here? Damn right I won't like it."

"It's Carina. She has some kind of bullshit warrant. I couldn't get much out my guy at the Bureau. All he knew is she has something, Ruth. It's something big."

He tugged down a cream cashmere sweater over gray

linen pants, looking like he just stepped out of a Gucci magazine, while the warmth drained from my body. "She has something big, huh?"

I didn't have time to give a shit what I looked like, didn't have time for anything other than the government officials raiding the building above. I pressed the key and headed for the elevator, his steps comforting behind me. I swiped the card in the elevator's reader, pressed the button, and tapped the ground with my foot. "So, you have no idea what this warrant says?"

He shook his head, strawberry freckles paling under the overhead lights. "He wouldn't say...but if they're here at this time of night—"

"Then they came straight from a damn judge. Who was it? Kinraid? Riley?"

He just shook his head again as the elevator doors opened and we stepped inside. I grabbed my phone. I had half the damn city on speed dial, but to cause a frenzy this early in the proceedings? That was what they wanted. "Fucking Carina. She wants me rattled, doesn't she?" I jerked my gaze to his and saw the answer in his eyes. "Goddamn bitch."

"As your lawyer, I urge you not to say or do anything to stop them. They obviously have something they came for. Let them take it, Ruth. You and I know there's nothing on the drives that can harm you."

I winced. "And if they go for the company server?"

"Let them try." His voice hardened to stone.

He wasn't my lover anymore, he was barely my friend, but Alexander was the best damn lawyer in the city. He was smarter than anyone else I knew, and brutal as fuck when he needed to be, and right now I needed him like never before.

He knew me. Knew my cesspool of a family like no one else did.

So how come we couldn't make it work?

The elevator doors opened on the directors' floor. Movement came from the corner of my eye.

"Ma'am." James stepped forward, wringing his gnarled fingers and worn hands.

"It's okay, James." I stepped close and patted his arm, turning my head toward the Directors' suites. "We're here now. We'll handle it."

Pain lashed the old man's eyes. He just nodded, leaving me to head for the open door. I brushed my fingers along the shattered frame, the brass locks indented from the strain.

Movement came from the middle of the room. FBI Agent Carina Chase marked items off a folder in her hand, and watched her men carry computers from inside the offices.

"You couldn't have called?" I bit my tongue on everything else I wanted to say.

She never lifted her head, not yet, letting me know exactly who's in charge here.

"A copy of the warrant," Alexander said as he held out his hand.

She acknowledged our presence then. *Well,* his, at least. The folded slip of paper hit his palm before she turned to meet my gaze. "You got here fast, I hope you weren't speeding?"

Bait. That's all it was. The glint in her eyes made that acid rise in my throat once more.

"This is very specific, what are you fishing for, Carina?" Alexander waved the warrant in the air. "You and I know this is bullshit and a total waste of my client's time."

"While you're here," she answered, and handed me an envelope.

Alexander just cut her a glare, then reached over and snatched it from my hand.

"Testy...testy." She sniggered and glanced from him to me and back again.

He opened the envelope and scanned the letter with a shake of his head. "A subpoena? You've really hit an all-time low, haven't you? Even for you, this is a little desperate."

"This is bullshit," I said as I turned away, glancing at the open door to my office.

Like my home, it was my domain, a private place for meetings, for discussions. *For sex.* Heat crept into my cheeks as I turned back and looked at Alexander. He glanced at the open door as shadows moved around inside.

Did he remember? Did he remember what we did in there?

Pens and papers fallen to the floor, grunts and groans filling the room. Our sweat. Our bodies. Our desire.

I swallowed hard and turned away, trying to remember every inch of the space when I left it three days ago. Two of them walked out, one carrying the hard drive to my computer.

"Is that all?" Carina strode forward, eyes down on the folders, scanning to see what else the vulture could take from me.

She stepped into my office like she owned the place. Like it was *her* blood, sweat, and fucking tears that created this. How dare she touch it. How dare she touch *any* of it. My hands curled into fists as she disappeared inside and closed the door.

"She can't touch anything." I forced the words through my teeth.

Alexander answered with a touch on my arm, stilling me.

Then the bitch opened my door once more and strode along the hallway. "Wrap it up," she called, and met my gaze. "We're done."

"You are," I answered, cold rage spilling through my body. "You are *very* done."

There was a blink in her gaze, a flicker of what...*fear?*

She should be fucking rattled.

"I want *everything* logged," Alexander ordered as he stepped forward and lifted his hand, pointing to the entrance. "And *you'll* be fixing that goddamn door."

There was no answer, just a twitch at the corner of her thin lips. I hated her. Hated her like I'd never hated anyone as she cut me a gaze. "You have a dead rat nailed to the inside of your door. It's fresh, and still bleeding. Looks like we weren't the only ones sending a message tonight."

With that, she just turned and walked away, leaving echoes of her footsteps behind. I tried to breathe, tried to think, and slowly turned my head to my office. I moved without thought, long strides swallowing the distance.

"Ruth," Alexander called me.

I didn't stop, didn't slow. I was a runaway train hell-bent on coming off the tracks. I strode into my office and yanked the door. The sickening *thump* registered before I looked.

It was there, thick and brown and ugly, Its tiny black eyes open. A knife impaled its body, leaving fresh blood to darken its fur. I slammed my hand across my mouth and stumbled backwards, hitting my desk.

Alexander was behind me, closing the door as he stepped in.

"Jesus," he muttered, closing the door to stare at the thing. "She wasn't kidding. Who the hell would do something like this?"

My mind raced, but it didn't have to go far. I closed my eyes and tried to breathe.

"Ruth?" His voice invaded. "Ruth, talk to me, tell me what's going on?"

He didn't know. How could he? Maybe he did and just didn't want to see the truth. Maybe it was a shallow, one-sided reach of comfort? Maybe I was better on my own? I hugged my body as a shudder rippled from my center. An ache of loneliness drove deep, like a knife cutting all the way to the quick. God, it hurt. God, this fucking void I lived in hurt. "Nothing...*I don't know.*"

The words were a lie. Cold and hard and empty

Still, he bought it.

"This is...this is so fucked up," he answered.

I opened my eyes to look at him. So pure and perfect, even from all the shit he'd done over the years, he was still untainted, *unaffected.*

Unlike me.

"Thank you for coming," *dismissed just like that.*

He flinched and gripped my gaze. Brows furrowed, the crease cutting on both sides. I became aware of him, of the love we'd once shared and the sex we'd once had. It was passionate and intense, and it warmed me from inside...for a little while, at least. "I think I'll stay for a while, and clean up." I glanced at the copy of the warrant. "I might need that to show the rest of the board. I take it you'll be at the courthouse first thing in the morning. We'll need our computers back."

What were they after?

"Sure," he started. "But I can stay—"

One shake of my head ended his words. "We need you fresh and focused in the morning."

Company before everything else. I fought the need to lift my gaze to the rodent nailed to my door. "I'll walk you to the elevator."

I told myself I had to, that at night the elevators only worked with a swipe of the right card. He just gave a nod, then glanced at the mess stabbed into the wood. "It's not safe for you here, not anymore."

Wasn't that the fucking truth.

I just swallowed and nodded. "I know. I'm dealing with it."

"Do you have a gun, at least?" He stepped closer. "For protection."

I could see it in his eyes, the desperation...*the longing.* He had another woman in his bed, waiting for him, and yet here he was, ready to...what exactly was he ready to do? Leave her? Fuck me, right here on this desk? *For old times' sake.*

Heat welled in my chest. Pressure built, tightening like a vise. I exhaled a pent-up breath, and tried to search for a way out of this mess.

In the end, he just nodded. "Call me, okay? For anything, just...*call.*"

If that wasn't a red fucking flag, I didn't know what was. "Okay."

He turned then, slow steps carrying him to the door. I followed, both desperately needing to get out of this place, and yet wanting to see it through. I was stepping out of the darkness here, and into the light, exposing myself...more than I wanted to.

I followed him along the Directors' suites to the broken door, then outside where the hard marble floor shone until he stopped at the elevators once more. The whir of machinery echoed in the distance, a vacuum whined somewhere else. James was here with his crew, loyal and honest, and deserving of the pay raise he'd receive in the morning.

I stepped up behind Alexander, swiped my card on the reader, and pressed the floor. Alexander turned in that moment. His eyes glinted as he met my gaze. My heart thundered, pulse pounding inside my head as he stepped closer, hands moving around my waist, and pulled me close.

His lips met mine, the kiss desperate and passionate, a flicker of a fire igniting between us.

I gave into him, winding my arms around his waist as the *ding* of the elevator sounded.

Broken kisses, sawing breaths. We stepped away, stunned, raw...hopeful.

"Call me," he said once more. Not hopeful now, demanding.

The elevator doors opened. He stepped inside, his gaze

seizing mine like it was the last time it would, until the doors closed, leaving me alone.

Alone with the sound of emptiness...where other people who weren't *us* couldn't reach me.

I turned for the shattered door once more, my thoughts already stepping into my office.

Looks like we weren't the only ones sending a message tonight.

City lights glinted in the darkness as I stepped onto the directors' floor and eased the broken door closed behind me. I lifted my gaze to the wall of windows, and fixed my sight on the darkness outside.

Looks like we weren't the only ones sending a message...

Pay up, or we take what's ours.

What exactly was it they wanted? Fury flowed through my veins. They never said...only demanded—*threatened, more like it.* My family had done a goddamn deal behind my back, now they all wiped their hands when it was broken.

Assassinated, was the word the media used. *Savagely assassinated.*

I turned to my office, steeled my spine, and headed for the door. They wanted to send a message, well, they'd succeeded. My will trembled like a newborn foal as I stepped in and quietly closed my office door.

Blood had dripped from the rat's body down the door, leaving a dark patch on the carpet. The smell unforgivable. And that will inside me quaked and trembled, locking knees desperate to stay strong. I lifted my hands, one around the hilt of the knife, and the other around the tiny beast's neck.

The sickening squelch made me whimper as I yanked

the knife free. My fingers sank into the matted fur, its body cold in my grip.

The Vampires wanted my attention.

Well, they'd damn well gotten it.

Maybe it was about time I had theirs, too.

10

T *hud, thump. Thud, thump. Thud, thump.*
I gripped the steering wheel and fought the need to turn the car around. Lights sparkled stretching west. Different lights. New lights...just like everything this side of the river was new. I turned my head to the docks in the distance and felt my pulse quicken.

How many times had I dreamed of coming to this side of the city? *One hundred? One thousand?* More.

But not like this.

Never like this.

The foul stench of the rat welled in the vehicle. I'd need to get the car cleaned twice after this, shampooed, scrubbed. Set on fire to rid myself of the memory of this damn night. If I survived that long.

*Pay up or we take what's ours...*I could still see the words smeared on the windshield. I had no idea how to reach them. Just an address. An address into the middle of nothing. I stabbed the button on the GPS, backtracking from when I hit the overpass and the bridge. But no matter how maybe buttons I pressed, there was nothing. Just a black hole of nothingness. "Great."

. My phone buzzed, the caller ID flashed on the screen. *Alexander.* I pressed the button, sending the call straight to voicemail.

It'd been an hour since he left. Ten minutes spent securing the door and searching my phone for the one piece of information I had about those monsters. Fifty minutes I'd been sitting in my car, working up the courage to do this.

I was *still* working up the courage to do this.

I hit the turning signal and eased onto the ramp, hugging the river, until I turned right and slipped deeper into the west. This side of the city was for the workers, workshops, and construction lots, closed in by twelve-foot chainlink fences. Rent was cheaper this side of the city. It was the only real draw this place had.

I slowed the Bentley along darkened city streets as truck depots turned to derelict buildings. One touch of the button and the window rolled down low. Shadows clung to the corners and spilled into the streets. Even the streetlights had no claim here, shining onto the pavement like a spotlight until it was swallowed by the dark.

Nothing did.

Unless you were a monster.

I tapped the brakes and stared out the window. Even the air here was different, colder...*heavier.* A dog rushed the fence, barking and snarling, white fangs and dark eyes glistening. My heart slammed against my chest, making me yank the wheel until I pulled back onto the road.

"Jesus..." My fingers shook as I found the button and the window rose. "What the fuck?"

I closed my eyes for a second, then opened them and exhaled. Fingers tapping on the wheel, I strangled the leather to still the shakes. I wanted to pull over. *No.* I wanted to go home, slide into bed, pull the covers over my head and pretend this was all just a bad misunderstanding.

But the smell…

The fucking smell made it all too real.

They'd come for me twice tonight, and both times they'd rattled my cage. "No more," I answered the darkness. "No more."

I turned right, and left again, sinking deeper into the unknown, then stopped the car in the middle of the empty street and grabbed my phone. I hadn't passed a car since I turned off the bridge. Even coming over, there were more heading east than there were heading west. "Figures."

One swipe of my thumb and the screen came alive. I punched in the address and waited for the map to narrow in. The red dot pulsed, picking up my location. A blue marker showed on the street up ahead before the entire screen went dark. "What the fuck!" I pressed the button and tapped the screen, but there was nothing. *Emptiness.* Just like before.

"Great…just great." I tossed the useless device onto the passenger seat and stared straight ahead through the windshield.

The cursor had flashed up ahead before the damn thing went dark. I eased off the brake and let the Bentley roll along the street. Black and red lights flashed up ahead. My stomach tightened. "God, no," I whispered. But the closer I came to the monstrosity, the clearer it became.

The Hunting Ground was a sex club. It had massive black doors and tiny, pulsing white lights. A throbbing beat fought the growl of the engine. "Hunting Ground, huh?" I rolled my eyes and searched for a place to park. "Someone so much as scratches the fucking car, I'll do more than pay up. I'll send you the goddamn bill."

The turning signal was as useless as tits on a bull. Five cars lined the street, but there was not one set of headlights to be seen. But I obeyed the goddamn law and signaled before pulling over.

"I can't believe I'm doing this," I muttered, and killed the engine.

I sat for a while, staring at the closed door, then reached for my phone and the plastic bag. It was three plastic bags, actually…three bags around one paper one. It was all I could find. Still, it didn't mask the stench.

I gripped the damn thing and climbed out of the car before closing the door and hitting the remote. The heavy beat seeped out to pulse in the air. I swallowed, glanced around the darkened street, and stepped up to the sidewalk. It had to be one or close to two in the morning. Standing here, the place looked dead.

Maybe it *was* dead.

Maybe it was immortal?

A hard bark of laughter tore free from my tight throat. I took a deep breath, readied myself, and headed for the door. The pulsing music grew louder the moment I shoved the door wide. I blinked into the darkness, waiting for my eyes to adjust, then stared at the sunken floor of the club.

The place was packed. A long bar was on one side, stretching all the way to the back. I counted five bartenders, *gorgeous* looking bartenders, leaning over to take orders from patrons. Three dancers worked the middle of the room on podiums, shaking their asses and squeezing their breasts.

"You, with the dead rodent stench," came a savage snarl from the shadows.

Silver glinted in his eyes as the massive male stepped forward into the light.

I knew why there were no bouncers standing outside, why they let any unsuspecting mortal step through those doors. Once inside you were at the mercy of the beasts.

"Up against the wall," he commanded.

He was all muscle and long, dirty-blonde hair, striding forward like a hunter.

"No…no fucking way." I muttered.

"You want in? Then you're subjected to a pat down." Full lips curved into a smile as he jerked his head toward a sign above the door.

A search of your person is a condition upon entry.
No weapons or drugs allowed on premises.

God, I didn't want to be here.

"Turn around. Hands up."

I sighed and complied, lifting the bag with the dead rat.

His hands skimmed over my hips and raced upwards to cup my breasts.

"Fuck, I love my job," he breathed into my ear, then stepped away, glancing at the bag. "What's with the rat?"

"None of your business, *that's what,*" I forced through

134

my teeth. "The next time you cop a feel...*will be the last time you fucking feel.* You get me?"

The grabby asshole stilled, elation dying in his eyes.

"Fucking men," I muttered, and strode toward the stairs leading down to the floor. My heels sank into the thick black carpet. The place looked like a damn dive on the outside, but inside...it was breathtaking. Tiny white lights sparkled along the ceiling like stars in a midnight sky.

The carpeted stairs led to long plush banquettes that curved around a small red leather chaise. Three men dressed in suits leaned back and watched a tiny woman straddling and grinding on the damn thing. Her tight breasts jiggled as she moved, dusty pink nipples hardened to peaks as she reached overhead and leaned back, splaying her legs wide.

"Take it all off," one of the men growled as I passed. "I want to see inside that pussy."

I closed my eyes for a heartbeat as desire settled deep. My nipples hardened as memory flared. It'd been a long time since I'd felt the hunger of a man's gaze...and unlike other women, I could pinpoint the exact date and the time.

Leather against my skin, warming with the touch.
The alley.
My lips aching from his mouth. Beautiful lips. God, his lips.
It was nice meeting you, Ruth Costello...very nice indeed.

I was on fire just thinking about it. I needed a second, just one second alone with the memory. An ache flared, *needing...wanting.* Lips on my skin, his tongue in my mouth.

"No, no way. Not here." I shoved the memory from my

mind, opened my eyes, and tried to focus somewhere else...*anywhere else.*

I searched the dancer's wrists and neck for bruises, sure that I'd find some kind of mark. The Wolves were in charge of the women, human women. There had to be some kind of threats, some kind of intimidation, some kind of mark as their own.

They forced them, right? Why would a woman allow herself to be used by the beasts of this world? But I found no bruises or marks of duress. If anything, desire sparkled in her eyes. I swallowed hard. She liked it...like being used like that, being watched, being *looked at.* My pulse sped with the thought.

What would that feel like?

To be both controlled and uncontrolled.

I kept walking, heading for the packed bar, and stood in line behind three of the most stunning women I'd ever seen in my life. Dark, raven hair that shone almost blue under the dimmed lights. Sparkling silver dresses, one even wore a pants suit, the collar of her white buttoned-up shirt open wide, revealing the tops of perfect breasts.

She could be a dancer, but I doubted it.

Dark brown eyes glinted as she scanned the podiums. She looked like any other guy here, desperate to reach that primal, *predatory* trigger. No, she wasn't a dancer, and this wasn't just any bar...

This was a hunting ground.

She looked at me, *eyes, lips, tits, and crotch.* I could see the fantasy playing out inside her head before I looked away. She had no idea who the fuck she was dealing with, none of them did. I wasn't here for the drinks and the entertainment. I was here to settle a damn score.

Her friend ordered for her, leaning across the bar to give their order to the bartender. He was stunning. Muscles. Muscles and strained black t-shirts. A predatory feel…his eyes glinted silver as he met my gaze and turned back to the woman at the bar.

A Wolf.

The last time I saw those monsters, I'd almost been killed. Terror and panic flared, but this wasn't that night, and these Wolves weren't the ones I knew. They weren't the Alphas, just the guys who ran one fragment of their enterprise. Women, right? I looked over my shoulder at the stunning redhead as she traced the line along her pussy, driving the sheer nylon of her panties into the crease.

Heat flared between my thighs. Fuck this place. I felt my body tighten. My own need waited like a beast of its own. I didn't come here to be turned on.

I came here to be fucking *ruthless.*

I scanned the other guys behind the bar. Long hair flowing over heavy muscles, black, brown…*except for one.* One guy who stood toward the back., shorter hair sweeping his shoulders, dark eyes glinting silver as he stared at me.

"What can I get you?"

I flinched at the voice and jerked my gaze to the six-foot-three giant as he braced his hands on the counter and leaned close.

"I want him," I jerked my gaze to the guy standing at the back.

Instinct led the way, taking me down whatever fucking rabbit hole I fell into when I crossed over to this side of the damn city.

"You don't want him, sweetheart," the big barman answered. "That one's trouble. Now, be a nice little lady and order a glass of champagne."

That kick in my gut took the edge off my desire. I held tall, blond and clueless' gaze and smiled. "Trouble is *exactly* why I came." I lifted my hand and plonked the bag with the dead rat inside on the counter.

There was a flinch in his eyes. A carefulness, controlled and dangerous…and *understanding.* "Now," it was my turn to grip the bar and lean close. "Are you going to get me what I asked for?"

He didn't move, never even turned his head, yet the guy in the shadows stepped forward, slowly crossed behind the bar, and headed my way. He was colder than the others, harder…*snarlier.*

"You wanted to see me?" he growled.

"Fuck me, you're beautiful," a desperate snarl came from behind me.

Something hard pressed against my ass…*someone warm.* I jerked my gaze over my shoulder to a guy, red-faced and horny. He swayed as he ground against me, hands on my hips, eyes alight with need.

"Take your fucking hands off me, before I grab my stiletto and drive the heel through your fucking eye."

The guy stopped, stunned, gulping deep breaths, trying to trigger his brain into working. His gaze narrowed for a moment as he just stared. "I know you."

I turned back to the guy now leaning against the bar, arms crossed over his chest, the hint of a smirk on his lips.

"You know who I am?" My pulse spiked, but I kept the mask in place, lifting my foot to the rung of the stool in front of me.

Cold cunt. Ruthless bitch, remember?

"Yeah," he lowered his gaze, captured by the hemline of my skirt as it rode high, revealing my thigh. "I know who you are."

I ran my finger along the line where the fabric met skin, then trailed down, leaning over until the neckline of my shirt gaped. "I don't think so," I urged, reaching to the back of my stiletto, and pulled the midnight blade free.

One step and I had the honed edge pressed against his balls. "Touch me again and I'll slice you so deep you won't even care about your balls…you'll be too concerned with the blood pouring out of you."

"Jesus *Christ,*" he muttered, his skin turning ashen.

"Got it?" I pressed a little harder.

There was a panicked nod before I waited a second and pulled away. My damn hand trembled. But never again would I be helpless. Never again would I let someone hurt me like that. Not from thugs who wanted payback, or from assholes who should know better.

"You wanted to see me." The Wolf strode forward from the end of the bar. "Here I am."

He didn't say more, just shifted his gaze to the bag on the counter.

"Want to know what's in it?" I tried to still the quiver in my voice and lifted my foot back to the stool.

"I know what's fucking in it," he snapped. "I smelled the thing the moment you opened our goddamn door. What I don't know is why it's *in my fucking bar.*"

Anger drove deep, like a spike ramming all the way inside me. I slid the blade along the outside of my heel once more and felt that stony rage consume me. "It was a message. One I received loud and clear. Now, are you going to take me to the assholes who sent it? Or am I going to have to cause a scene?"

There was a twitch at the corner of his lips. His fingers curled against his arm, but he didn't uncross them. He just stood there, eyes boring into mine, until he finally answered, "And which *asshole* do you think sent it?"

"The fucking *Vampires,* that's who," I growled.

His breath stilled, and his brows rose slowly. Muscles with the long blond hair beside him slowly shook his head and stepped away. "Whoa, don't want nothin' to do with this, Arran, or *her.*"

It seemed none of them did. Short-hair just stared into my eyes then he glanced at the bag once more. "They sent you that?"

"Yeah, they sent me this."

He met my gaze. "And you're sure you want to…meet them? The Blood Suckers aren't like us…they aren't this…*friendly.*"

"Oh yeah, I'm feeling the friendliness," I answered. "Now, are you going to tell me how to meet them, or am I going to have to find someone who will?"

There was a hard, brutal bark of laughter from the bartender before he just shook his head and walked away. "Mortal, you've got some balls, I'll give you that. It was nice knowing you. I'll put flowers on your grave."

Warmth slipped from my bones with his words. The words on my windshield. The dead rat impaled on my office door. They wanted me hurt. They wanted me bleeding.

But most of all, they wanted me here, on the other side of the river.

"I'll take you," Arran muttered. "If you're so fucking keen on ending your damn life."

He pushed off the counter and motioned me toward the end of the bar.

"Wait," I shook my head. "I'll take my car."

He stopped and turned his head as one brow rose. "The Bentley? That thing won't make it where we're going."

I swallowed hard. How was I to know he wasn't just going to take me someplace and kill me? I'd called the Vampires out. I'd pissed them off.

"Believe me, if they wanted you dead, you'd *be* dead.," he answered, as though he could read my thoughts.

A memory tried to force its way in. The hospital just after the attack, lying there unable to move. *I'm not going to hurt you,* a whisper floated to the surface. That voice…

"You coming, or what?" Arran watched me like I was a feast and he was ravenous.

No one knew I was on this side of the river. If I turned up dead in an alley, bled dry, with fang marks on my neck, then no one would be any the wiser why I was here.

Alexander would've known…if you'd let him in.

I clenched my fist around the opening of the bag and followed the Wolf through a beaded curtain of fake diamonds…to the room in the back. Moans echoed, and deep, grunting snarls followed by a *slap.* The heady scent of sex and lust hung heavy in the air.

Desire flared as movement came from the edges of my vision. A woman was on her knees, head bent low in a guy's lap. He speared his fingers through her hair, pushing that little bit harder on the descent. Glazed eyes watched me, hungry and desperate as she bobbed harder. God, I needed to get out of there.

Arran turned at the end of the open room and walked along a corridor, heavy footsteps seeming to grow louder as we sank into the dark. My pulse sped, frantic and feeble, flapping like a bird in my chest until he shoved open a door at the end of the hall.

Cold, crisp night air flooded in as I followed, stepping out into an alleyway at the back of the club. He lifted a hand and pointed to a Jeep. "Jump in."

I winced, and rounded to the passenger side, glancing at the open seats and the roll bars. My thin chiffon top and knee-length black skirt weren't an ideal choice. But it was far too late to change, even if I could. Arran just gripped the roll bar and leaped, jumping clean over the driver's door, and slid effortlessly behind the wheel.

The four-wheel drive started with a growl as I yanked open the door, hiked up my skirt, and climbed in any damn way I could. Arran glanced my way as I pulled the door closed behind me and groped for the seatbelt. The Wolf revved the engine and shoved the damn thing in reverse.

Hair flew around my face, covering my eyes, for which I was thankful as the engine whined and screamed. I reached for something to hold on to and found cold steel as we braked, and the front of the Jeep was flung around.

"Jesus Christ," I roared as we lunged forward. "You drive like a goddamn maniac."

All I saw were fangs as he grinned. Yesterday's lunch was dragged to the surface, sloshing around in my stomach. I swallowed, trying to swallow down the bitter acid, and did something that was starting to become very familiar in my life—*a little too familiar.*

My lips moved as I closed my eyes, fingers clenched around the metal bar.

"Are you fucking praying?" Arran barked with laughter. "Fuck, I love mortals!"

Anger flared, driving all the way through my panicked faith. "Fuck you, *Wolf.*"

"Now *that's* the goddamn spirit!" Eyes glinted with the adrenaline high as we sped through the city streets at breakneck speed.

Air buffeted my face, sticking lashes in my eyes. I tried to blink through the blur, tried to get some kind of handle on where we were heading. But it was useless.

Think, Ruth. Come on.

I turned my head, scanning the streets behind us, and caught the sparkle of the bridge lights. We were racing west…further west than I'd anticipated. Darkened windows, guard dogs roaming yards. There was nothing out here, no drug dealers on the corners, no night workers at all. It was a damn morgue.

"Where the hell is everyone?" I jerked my gaze to Arran.

Crown City wasn't as big as LA or New York, but it sure as hell wasn't tiny either. And I knew better than anyone the population here was scattered, west as well as east. We whipped past a lofty apartment building. I mean, sure, it was the early hours of the morning. But where were the night owls? Where were the garbage collectors and the night-shift cleaners?

Locked inside, I was guessing…out of the way of Wolves who drove like death was a fun option. I guessed for them it was. My hold on the bar slipped, slick with sweat. *Lucky for them.*

The Hidden Mountains rose in the distance, looming and haunting. No one came to this part of the valley. It was the one place mortals like us feared. There were no ghost tours, no fang groupies, just smothering darkness, even in the daylight. The trees this far west of the river seemed to grow differently, With gnarled trunks and blackened leaves. They weren't rotting, but *changed.* Some said it was the air here that was different. But I knew better.

It was the Fae.

Dark, Unseelie creatures. Black-haired, blue-eyed beasts. They controlled this place and the magic that hunted in the woods as well as the streets. Magic you couldn't see...but you could feel.

The hairs on my arms stood on end as we left the brown brick buildings behind and slipped further into the darkness, where the silver moonlight refused to glow.

I'd seen satellite images of the forest, and listened to the warnings. I glanced over my shoulder to the city lights slipping away behind us...and wished I could go back home.

11

The Jeep pulled off the pavement, hitting hard gravel and deep ruts. I slammed forward and the seatbelt snapped taut, driving the air from my lungs.

Arran wrenched his gaze my way, but he wasn't smiling now. Instead, he scanned the rear-view mirror and watched the trees at the sides. Looked like even the Wolves didn't like venturing out this far.

I gripped the bar with one hand, my belt with the other, and clenched my jaw as we jolted and jerked. Trees grew closer, crowding in the narrow dirt road. Panic moved in as Arran grew more cautious, tapping the brake and watching the rear-view mirror, then he turned to look at me. "You sure you want to do this? These…Vamps, they're not like the Wolves. They're colder…crueler."

I glanced at the bag in my hand and nodded. "I don't have a choice."

One nod and he turned back to the gravel road. "Your funeral."

The air grew heavy around us and the darkness closed

in, swallowing the Jeep's headlights until there was nothing left—just a void, a *nothingness*. If I thought the empty streets behind us were eerie, then this wall of suffocating night was damn well terrifying.

I opened my mouth, the words *'stop, turn around,'* hovering on the tip of my tongue. If this was what Arran meant, then I'd changed my mind. The frigid air wrapped around me like a fist and plunged deep into my lungs with each breath.

"Fuck," Arran snarled and leaned into the wheel.

He couldn't see. I couldn't see. The Jeep slowed to a crawl, the tiny yellow glow of the headlights dimmed.

"What the hell is happening?" The lights on the dashboard flickered.

And, in an instant, they spluttered out. The headlights were snuffed, like a candle in the wind. Only this wind wasn't anything I'd ever felt before.

Fear crawled along my spine. Fear like I'd never known.

She's here...

The whisper filled my ears. In an instant, the headlights flared back to life, and the dashboard lights flashed, brightening until the glow was back to normal. I could breathe. I plucked the seatbelt from across my chest and sucked in great big gulps of the crisp night air. My face was burning like I couldn't get enough.

"Like I fucking told you, they're not like us Wolves." Arran coughed and spluttered, casting me a glare of *do you believe me now?*

I wanted to go back there, to the strippers and the bar. I'd go anywhere, as long as it wasn't this damn place— until out of the darkness loomed a massive mansion.

Wrought iron gates secured the property, but as we neared, they swung open.

Lights came to life at the entrance of the driveway, soft at first, until we neared. Arran nosed the Jeep into the driveway as the headlights splashed against darkened windows.

"This fucking place, man." Arran muttered, and braked the four-wheel drive to a stop.

The engine died, ticking softly, the only sound in the night. There was no chirp of crickets, no calls of owls, just *silence...*as silent as the damn grave.

Arran shoved open the driver's door and climbed out. I fumbled with the handle on my side, tearing my gaze from the shift of black curtains inside the house. Someone was in there, watching us.

The Wolf looked nervous, glancing behind us and scanning the trees, before he motioned toward the door. "Well, you got what you wanted. Now what are you going to do, Ms. Set the damn world on fire and watch it burn?"

I slid from the seat until my feet hit the gravel. I hadn't really expected I'd get this far. The burning rage that had driven me across the bridge had all but petered out. Now that I was here with the dead rat in my hand, I had no idea what to say. *'I think you left this behind. I found it, stabbed through the heart and pinned to the back of my door—message received, you fucking assholes, so what the hell do you want?'*

Maybe something like that?

I closed the door behind me and stumbled forward. The pointed heels of my Guccis sank into the gravel drive. I staggered, one hand flying out and finding purchase on the hood of the Jeep.

Arran just stood there, arms crossed once more, as I

straightened myself and smoothed down my skirt. I stepped closer, scanning the windows for movement again, and stepped up to the door.

Locks clicked before the door swung open and a guy with the most incredible tattoos stared at me.

"Yeah?" He lifted his gaze and nodded to the Wolf at my back before settling it on me once more. "What are you selling?"

He couldn't have been twenty, with shaved hair around the sides and the top part falling longer over his forehead. A small black tattoo of a cross marred his skin just under his eye. I knew what that meant. He was marked, just like everyone was when they joined the Cutthroat gang.

"I'm here to see *them*." I glanced past him.

"Them?" The kid opened the door wider. He definitely didn't look like he was in a gang now.

His black designer suit was matched with a black shirt and a matte black tie. A silver tiepin was the only change in his midnight attire. He looked well cared for, smart... and every bit as dangerous as he'd been on the street.

"Them?" he repeated, one brow rising to the occasion.

One more glance behind me at the Wolf, and he sighed. "You're not here for a damn autograph, are you?"

In an instant, I found that fire in my belly once more. I stepped closer, gripped the bag, and growled. "Do I look like I'm here for a goddamn autograph? I'm here to see the Vampires, now are you going to let me in?"

He lifted his hands in defeat. "Jeez, okay," he sighed. "Who can I say is calling?"

What the fuck? Breathe, just breathe. "Ruth Costello."

There was a flicker of surprise, before a slow nod of

his head. I lifted the plastic bag with the dead rat inside. "I think they're expecting me."

A deep mumble came from inside. The young thug gripped the door and pulled backwards, turning his head. He seemed to be talking to someone else, someone I couldn't see. One nod of his head, and he turned to me again. He swept his hand, motioning for me to come in.

"You want me to wait?" Gravel crunched under his boots as Arran stepped close.

"No need," the well-dressed street kid said as he looked back at me, then met the Wolf's gaze.

I glanced over my shoulder, fear and determination swirling inside me like a Molotov cocktail, one match and I'd ignite. "Thank you, Arran."

He shifted nervously. "Yeah, well…you know where to find me."

I did, west of the river in a bar filled with sex. A flicker of warmth took flight in that icy heart of mine. Don't tell me I actually liked the guy? He nodded, meeting my gaze, then reached for the roll bar once more. Just like he had before, he gripped the bar and leapt inside, sliding behind the wheel.

I turned back to the doorway as the Jeep started and the headlights splashed my feet.

"This way," the kid motioned. "We don't bite."

I stepped closer, eyeing him as I went. Don't bite, my ass. I knew who he was, and knew where he came from. Memories of that night in the alley surfaced. He was just as pathetic as the ones who'd tried to kill me.

Still, the question surfaced, what the hell was he doing here?

Not now, that voice inside my head urged. *You've got bigger fish to fry.*

I looked around as the kid closed the door. The sound of the Jeep's engine grew distant, and desperation flared. It was too late to call to him now. Too late for anything but to get what I came for…a damn answer.

What do you want? And why the hell are you coming after me to get it?

Whatever deal was made had been done behind my back. I wanted no part of it, not then when I'd found out, and not now. I glanced around at the dark gray slate tiles on the floor to the burgundy drapes across the windows as I walked from the foyer into the living room.

"Which *Vampire* are you looking for exactly?" The kid stepped closer, a smart-ass expression on his face.

"How about the one in charge? How does that sound?" I snapped.

"Then *that* will be me." The clipped growl came from a large, tall-backed black leather chair, sort of a mini-throne.

I didn't just watch him rise. It was more like *come together.* Shadows closed in, sharpening to the outline of a body. He stood, stepping into the faint light, and the most stunning gray eyes shone as they met mine.

My breath caught, my legs stopped working.

"Elithien," the thug muttered. "Didn't see you sitting there."

In a heartbeat, the cloaked male stepped forward. My heart lunged, slamming against my ribs. Tall, broad shoulders and thick thighs strained the tailored black pants. A tremor tore through my body. I wanted to run my fingers along the taut fabric and cup the bulge between his legs. I wanted to see what it felt like to touch someone like him.

The memory from the alley surfaced, almost like a slap. They weren't the same…not anywhere near it. My bartender was real and honest. *Yeah?* a voice whispered. *So why is he still a goddamn memory?*

"I think that's the point," I added, unable to take my eyes from this monster in the dark.

The Vampire stepped closer, barely making a sound, and glanced at the kid, giving a small nod.

"I'll just leave you, then," the young thug muttered, and stepped away.

Footsteps echoed in the hall behind me until they faded away. I forgot why I was here, forgot everything, really…my name…to breathe. For a second, I was weightless, and *nothing,* just standing in front of this *Immortal,* feeling the frantic pounding of my heart.

"My name is…" I tried, but the words refused to come. Instead, I sucked in a breath. The faint scent of deep spices drifted toward me. "Ruth—"

"I know who you are, Ms. Costello."

That voice.

That voice…

He closed the distance and held out his hand. "Elithien Venandi."

A wave of exhaustion swept through me, stealing my panicked thoughts. Tired, God, I was so tired. His shirt gaped as he moved, revealing a smooth, muscled chest. Heat rose between my thighs and that wave of fatigue carried with it a slow burn of hunger. I couldn't look away from him, not his chest, or the corded muscles of his arms, or his fingers, thick, strong fingers with a powerful grip. I ground my teeth, forced a smile, and met his grip with one of my own.

Cool skin met my palm, and a wave of lust hit me. My breaths deepened and my nipples tightened. "I um…" I stuttered.

Get it together.

A moan echoed from an open door. My eyes had adjusted to the light, catching movement from inside the room. A half-naked woman was stretched out across the end of a bed, a tiny trail of blood at her neck. My gaze narrowed and my breath caught, before Elithien cleared his throat and the door was closed instantly, ending the view.

The sight hit me like a cold shower. I'd forgotten for just a second how vulnerable I was. "I'm sorry," I countered. "I didn't mean to intrude."

"Can I offer you something to drink?" Elithien asked.

I jerked my gaze to his mouth, and instantly regretted it.

Perfect blood red lips moved as he spoke. My gaze skimmed his sharp cheekbones, the deep-set eyes. Raven hair shimmered as it caught the light. *Beautiful* was the word that came to mind.

Had he fed from her, the woman lying on the end of the bed? Had he pierced her vein and suckled at her neck? Were there other veins he liked to drink from? I knew there was one along the inside of the thigh…right next to… A muffled moan tore from the room once more. Low, *demanding.* For a heartbeat, I wondered what that must feel like, to be bitten, to be *used.* I swallowed hard and tried to stop the images, fangs and blood, and *sex.* "Thank you."

He released my hand and turned. His tailored pants hugged a gorgeous, tight ass. The thick leather belt caught the overhead light, studded with some kind of midnight jewels.

Leather, I could almost hear the creak as he moved.

Cold and smooth, warming against my skin.

Jesus no...not here...not now.

I clamped my thighs together, stilling that hunger, and glanced around the room. Antique chaise lounges to the tall black leather seats, the furnishings were soft and simple, *refined,* the word came to mind. Polished and perfect, and very...*very* black.

Sheer midnight drapes and granite floors. The soft white overhead lights were too dull for reading. The silver desk lamp was the strongest light in the room. Glasses clinked, a splash of something amber. Scotch, maybe?

"Even though I know who you are, I find myself wondering why you're here?" Long, sure strides closed the space between us.

I fought the need to take a step backwards, to put as much space between us as possible.

Monster and mortal.

My damn hands shook, splashing Scotch against the sides of the glass I held in a death grip as I lifted the rim to my lips. Heat splashed the back of my throat and slid all the way down. I drained the glass in three anxious gulps.

The tall, gorgeous Vampire just watched, bemused. "Another?"

I caught a slight curl of his lips and shook my head. "You asked why I came here and now *I'm* the one who's a little confused." The bag rattled in my hand as I lifted it. "I came because of this."

There was a twitch at the corner of his eye as he glanced at the plastic bag.

"The threats need to *stop*. First my car, then my goddamn office. I don't know how the fuck you got in there. But you wanted my attention, and now you damn well have it."

"Elithien?" A deep growl came from my left.

They moved like the ocean, like a midnight, *powerful* tide surging forward. Three of them, one Vampire in front and two behind. Just as damn tall, just as *dangerous,* as the one I faced now. The first Vampire shifted his gaze toward me. He had thick shoulders and a cold, lethal stare. He moved like a killer...they all did. I'd seen enough of them in my time.

"This is Ms. Costello," Elithien glanced at me and shifted his gaze to the killer in the burgundy suit. "She was about to tell me why she's here."

"That goddamn stench have something to do with it?" one of the Vampires fired from the back.

The words froze on my lips as I stared at the one in the gray suit with a black leather eye patch across one eye. Thin silver scars cut across his face, ending at perfect red lips. He only needed one eye, steel gray, darker and colder than the Vampire's in front of me. He looked like the hitman waiting for you in the alley kind of killer.

The room around me swayed. Powerful strides closed the distance and, before I knew it, they were in front of me, and three powerful Vampires became four.

"Breathe, Ruth. No one here will harm you, I give you my word." Elithien commanded.

I swallowed hard, and the plastic bag rattled in my hand again. "I found this...this *rodent* impaled on the inside of my office door about an hour ago, and earlier tonight there was a message written in blood on my windshield. You got my attention, now just tell me what the fuck you want?"

The one in the midnight blue suit jerked a look of surprise to Elithien. "What the hell is she talking about?"

"I have no idea," Elithien muttered, light gray eyes darkening like an oncoming storm. "I'd like you to tell me everything, Ruth, starting with the message on your windshield."

The way he said it…the way he spoke.

I'll keep watch over you…I'll make sure no one touches you like that ever again.

The voice rose from that dark pit of secrets inside me.

There was something eerily familiar about him. Something I couldn't quite place. It wasn't just the paleness of his skin, or his mesmerizing eyes. Maybe it was both, or maybe it was everything. The deeper I sank into his gaze, the more I lost control.

The blazing anger I'd clung to dulled.

"Justice, you know anything of this?" Elithien glanced at the one with the patch.

"Not a goddamn thing," he swore as he folded his arms across his chest and glanced at the one in blue. "Rule?"

"Not me," the Vampire denied. "Hurrow?"

Burgundy-suit-Vamp just shook his head. He was shorter than the others, stockier, with long pale hair and gray-green eyes. A heaviness settled over me with his stare. A brush of something against my mind, just a whisper before it pulled away. "She's telling the truth."

"Of course I'm telling the truth. Why else would I come all this damn way?" I snapped, and lifted my hand with the rat, my finger pointing at Hurrow. "And stay out of my goddamn head."

His eyes narrowed, one glance at the bag, and he turned. "Just a precaution, don't get your tits in a knot."

I clenched my jaw until my molars practically cracked. "You think this is funny?"

"No one here has threatened you," Elithien claimed as he stepped closer, drawing my gaze, and my fury. "That," he glanced at the bag in my hand, "wasn't us. We don't work that way...we're not that..."

"*Tacky*," the one with the eye patch answered with a snarl. "Tacky is the word he's searching for. If we want you gone, then you're gone. It's as clean and as simple as that."

The tips of white fangs peeked out from under blood red lips. I tried to remember who I was dealing with. These weren't *my* allies. They weren't my friends. "But the deal...you wanted payback after what was done."

"You mean the assassination of one of our Elders?" Elithien's eyes bored into mine. The temperature in the room plunged until I shivered. "Do you know anything about that?"

His attention flared with the words. His breath caught as he searched my gaze.

He wanted to know about the assassination of his Prince, they all did.

But I had the distinct impression that wasn't his main priority here.

I was.

"Nothing," I denied. "Only what's on the news. But you know who I am, right? You know the connections my family pulled to get Prince Xuemel into Congress."

"But *you* weren't responsible for his death." Hurrow stepped forward and folded his arms across his chest. "So why would you think we put the rodent in your office?"

I licked my lips. "Because…" *because…you might've made a deal with my family…but you didn't make a deal with me.*

I lifted my gaze to Elithien. Sparks ignited in his eyes, his blood red lips looked so damn cold…and inviting. The idea shocked me. "You're not my friend."

"Got that right," Rule muttered behind Hurrow, and turned to pour himself a drink.

But it was Elithien I spoke to. "Nor are you my ally. So why should I believe you?"

The commanding Vampire took a step closer. That time, my body moved on its own. My heels clacked on the slate tiles until my back hit the wall.

He was a predator, someone dangerous. My breath caught as he lifted his hand. His fingers curled, reaching for my face before brushing a wayward strand of hair from my cheek. There was a moment where his hand stilled, where I caught something in his eyes, a flicker of desire, like I wasn't the only one who felt this *energy* between us. "Believe me, don't believe me. I don't care. You came here, to *my home,* because you had no one else to turn to, am I right?"

A catch of my breath. My mind raced. There was a brush against my mind, like the touch on my temple, and the memory of cold leather against sensitive skin teased me now, just like the bartender teased me in the alley on the night of my attack.

"You're in trouble, Ruth Costello. And you have *no* friends," he added.

Pain cut deep as the past rose up inside me.

I closed my eyes and pressed my spine against the wall in the Vampire's den, just as I had in that alley. I waited for the touch at my hairline, waited for the slow, seductive kiss, and that desire, that *desperate need* to connect to someone…turned into an ache.

"And because…" he started. *I'll keep watch over you,* the words were resurrected to fill my mind…*I'll make sure no one touches you like that ever again.*

I searched for a flicker of emotion in those storm gray eyes. But this was no knight in shining armor. *No,* this was a beast bathed in blood.

A cold-hearted Vampire.

One I couldn't trust. His lips parted, his icy breath danced across my skin, and that hunger inside me raged. My pulse was frantic in my throat. There was a flicker of emotion before the steel gray in his eyes hardened.

"—because we seem to have common enemies." He pulled his hand away. "I think I want to see that message on your windshield."

"You want to see that message, Elithien?" Rule snarled behind him, staring daggers at the Vampire's skull. "Or is there something else you're interested in seeing?"

"Fuck yes," Hurrow added, never once taking his eyes from me.

Predatory hunger sparked in Elithien's gaze as he lingered close. I could touch him if I wanted to, just shift my body along the wall. Warmth would meet cold, fire and ice. I wondered what he'd feel like under that expensive suit? I wondered if he'd pull away from my touch or if he'd lean in and press me against the wall.

"Is there something else?" Elithien searched my gaze,

and yet I didn't think it was a question aimed at me. "Yes, I think there is."

They weren't afraid of me here. The Costello name carried no weight. I may as well be just a woman on the wrong side of the river. My knees trembled, but I stayed upright. I looked into the eyes of a killer, but it wasn't my death I saw…

It was something darker and more terrifying than danger.

It was desire.

Staring at me.

12

"I can drive." Elithien pulled away, leaving me breathless. "Unless you're scared of being in a car with me?"

"Seems to me she prefers the Wolves," Hurrow muttered. "I could smell them all over her from a mile away."

There was a flinch in his eye as Elithien growled. "We'll see about that."

Mine.

The word swept through my mind, forcing me to swallow. "I don't mind," I forced the words. "You want to see that message on my windshield? Fine. But just so you know, I *have* people in my corner. You're not the only one in this city who's dangerous, *Vampire.*"

Alexander filled my mind as a careful brush flared against the thought once more. I jerked my gaze to the Vampire in the burgundy suit. "I said to stay out of my mind."

There was a shake of his head as he drained his glass. "Not me," he muttered. "Not this time."

I glanced at Elithien.

"We'll take our own ride." Rule moved, heading back the way they'd come, leaving us alone once more.

I took three steps and turned. "Are you coming?"

He was watching me. *Elithien,* his name quaked. *My name is Elithien.* A surge of lust grew stronger.

"That mortal you think about," he questioned as he stepped closer. "The one who's *'in your corner'.* Is he your lover?"

"*That*...that is *none* of your damn business." My cheeks burned as I looked away. This wasn't me. I didn't get rattled. Certainly not about my nonexistent sex life.

"Is that so?" His long strides closed the distance between us. "Let's see how long that lasts, shall we?"

I didn't want to see at all, not the way he moved, or that possessive curl of his lips. I tried to slow the thundering of my heart as he strode past, leaving me to follow.

Simple, gothic, clean. The mansion took my breath away. I strode past masterpieces hanging on the walls and followed the Vampire to a garage that would've made my father envious. Three Rolls, an Aston Martin, and a shimmering midnight Bugatti were the perfect backdrop for the elite. I could've stood in the middle of a million diamonds, and still they'd somehow pale...next to him.

This beast in the darkness.

The Mafia Monster I'd come here to see.

Elithien headed for a shadow-gray four-wheel-drive Explorer, pulled a key from his pocket, and rounded the car. I saw him in the soft white light. He moved like a predator, a cold, controlled predator, with the most immaculate set of manners as he opened the passenger's door and waited.

My heart stuttered. I was like a fly and he was the spider. I knew what he was…knew all about his kind, and still I was helpless to look away.

He turned his head as I stepped into the car and met my gaze. His lips parted, like he wanted to say something, but he closed them again.

Say it.

Just say what you so desperately want to say.

My pulse sped with the thought, until the silence turned strained. I was the one who broke the spell, sliding into the passenger seat before he gently closed the door, then rounded the rear of the car and opened the driver's door.

The car was immaculate, the leather, smooth and soft. It seemed no expense was spared no matter what they touched. *Was it the same with sex?* My mind ran away until I remembered this man had been inside my head.

I jerked away from the thought as the garage door rolled upwards and the engine started with a growl. We rolled out, waiting for a second until the door started its decent.

He wanted to prove a point, wanted me to believe he had nothing to do with the threats. It was futile. Everything pointed to them. So why was I listening…and why was I sitting in a car with him?

We drove in silence, the only sound the tires crunching on the pebbled drive. But this time, there was no smothering darkness, no stuttering engines, or snuffed out headlights. I risked a careful glance beside me. Was he really a monster? A terrifying, bestial animal that cared about one thing...the money he protected for the Vampire Elders?

His hands worked the gears seamlessly. He was like the snow, beautiful, but deadly. *Frigid.* The word played on my mind. That's what they called me, wasn't it?

I pressed my spine against the seat and watched the city lights sparkle in the distance, like fireflies in the night. I hadn't seen Crown City from this side of the river. My breath caught.

"Stunning."

I turned my head, but it wasn't the city he was staring at...it was me. The car hugged the curve, never veering to one side, while heat filled my cheeks. He turned his attention back to the road as we slipped into the city streets.

Headlights flared behind us, filling the interior of the car. I glanced in the side mirror as a midnight Explorer overtook us coming down the mountain. Elithien kept his focus straight ahead as the cool white headlights caught the silver shine of his skin, and in an instant the Explorer had passed.

But the vehicle didn't pull ahead, instead, it kept a safe distance.

"It's the others, isn't it? Justice, Rule and Hurrow."

"Yes," he answered.

"I thought they were in front of us." My words hung in the air.

He'd heard me, I knew he'd heard me. But he didn't bother to answer. I ground my teeth and looked out the window. I couldn't find my footing with him, floundering like a damn fish out of water. I was always the one in control, only with him, I wasn't.

I wanted to say he was rude, but there was nothing rude about him.

He was proper, chivalrous even. But he didn't give me what I wanted.

I was left off-kilter, staring at my footing, searching for cracks in the ground. I was nothing and *everything* around him.

We followed the Explorer as it drove ahead, taking the turns hard, but I barely moved in my seat, just eased to the side. After the third turn, I realized he took the corners which made me lean into him a little harder. Then I caught sight of the Bentley parked outside of the strip club and we slowed, pulling to the other side of the street.

Justice was out of their car first, scanning the street as he strode toward the Bentley. Rule and Hurrow were next. They looked like warriors, thick shoulders moving under tailored suits.

No, they looked like hitmen.

My door opened and the night rushed in. Elithien stepped close and lifted a hand toward me. Fear made me hesitate, but curiosity lifted my hand, taking his.

Cold skin met mine. A shiver raced along my spine as I stepped free of the vehicle.

"The message?" He stared at me with the kind of intensity that took my breath away.

"It was on my windshield."

The others flanked my car, two moving on the far side toward the rear. Hurrow pulled the wipers upwards, peering closely at the glass.

"Elithien," he called.

The Vampire in front of me snapped to attention, leaving my side to cross the road in an instant. They talked in hushed words. I followed, my heels loud in the night. Even the club's music was quieter, a slow heavy beat rippling out from the Hunting Ground's doors...*grinding music.* I didn't need to spend a whole lot of time imagining what was happening on that red leather chaise.

"It's ox blood," Elithien explained as he turned to me, his eyes darkening until the gray matched the vehicle we'd left behind. "Not human."

"The water clings to the fat in the blood, that's why you can still see it. Soap and hot water will wash it off."

I gave a nod. "That's good...that's really good."

"That," Elithien lifted a finger and pointed at the glass, "wasn't us, or any of the others."

"The others?" I glanced at the four of them. "Are there more of you?"

"The Wolves, or the Fae" he answered. "It wasn't an Immortal."

"How do you know?" I shook my head. "If it wasn't you, then it could be anyone?"

"Anyone, yes. But not an Immortal. Trust me."

Hurrow stepped up to the curb behind Elithien, his stony gaze knowing. "That's where you were, weren't you? Before...you went to see them...the Fae?"

"Yes," Elithien answered for them. "And the Wolves have already reached out to us. You can trust me on this. The threats didn't come from us."

"If not you, then who?" A savageness glinted in his eyes, but he was silent. I was a fool, a stupid fool, acting in the heat of the moment, driving all this way with empty threats. I broke his gaze and looked away. "You must think I'm a damn fool."

"Not at all. I'm glad we've had a chance to know each other a little better."

A little better? He meant get to know me *at all*.

I gave a nod and glanced at the others. "Well, I won't make a habit of this. Thank you," and the memory of a woman sprawled almost naked on the bed surfaced. "And I'm sorry for dragging you away from whatever you had planned this evening."

"Nailing rats to office doors and painting windshields with ox blood," Justice mumbled.

I winced at the words.

"It's getting late," Elithien murmured.

Dismissed, just like that. He sounded cold, hard as stone. Maybe we were more alike than I thought. "Right, yes." I dug into my pocket and pulled my keys free. The Vampires converged on the pavement as I unlocked the Bentley.

Ever the gentleman, Elithien strode to the driver's door and held it open. "Stay safe, Ms. Costello. It's was… entertaining, to say the least."

I winced, passing the reaction off as a smile, and climbed inside. I'd come here for answers, and left with more questions. Questions that waited like a cruel whisper for me to start the car and pull away from the curb, swinging the Bentley in front of the Explorers and turned back the way I'd come.

I felt like I'd been here a damn week, but it was only hours. Hours to meet the deadliest beings in the city. I'd probably just added to the list of people who wanted to hurt me, and as I drove, those questions took center stage inside my head.

So, if it wasn't the Vampires, then who was it?

Judah and Blane filled my head. They wouldn't be that stupid, and in any case, what did they have to gain? More money and power and me out of the way for them to take a direct step up to the plate.

There was only one thing stopping them…my dad was still alive.

I leaned forward and hit the button on the stereo, but instead of music, the prompt screen lit up. "Call Charlotte."

Seconds later, the phone rang, and, as always, she answered. "You okay?"

"Yeah, I just want to check on everything there. Is he okay?"

"Sleeping," she answered, concern etched deep in her tone. "Which is where you should be. It's almost three AM"

"I'm heading home now."

"Where are you?" she asked…*she never asked.*

"Coming back from the office."

"At this time of the night?"

"So, he's really okay?"

"He's really okay, Ruth. I don't want you to worry. Drive home safely, okay, Ruth? West of the bridge can be dangerous." She ended the call just like that.

I flinched, and stared at the *Call Ended,* on the display. *What the fuck? How the hell did she know where the hell I was?* My heart beat a little harder. I glanced into the rear-view mirror as I started across the bridge.

She knew I was lying. I didn't know how, maybe it was

my tone. Headlights shone in the distance behind me. But I focused on the road ahead, listening to the *thud...thud...thud...*from the ruts on the bridge, and finally slipped into the turning lane at the end.

Exhaustion closed in as I drove through the city streets. The headlights behind were gone now, leaving me to wind through the suburbs alone. The night was heavy, too heavy. A kiss that shouldn't have happened and a dead rat in my office floated through my mind.

But the Vampires pushed to the front of my mind, one Vampire in particular. *Elithien.* His eyes were stunning, the lightest downy tree in one minute, and like thunderous clouds of a tempest in another.

Headlights splashed the interior of the car as I turned into my street, and for a second, I could've sworn it was an Explorer, dark gray, haunting the night. I tore my gaze from the rear-view mirror, my hand hovering over the remote for the garage door.

Was it him?

Panic filled me. There'd been no car behind me, not since I came over the bridge. *What if he knew where I lived?* I tapped the brakes and watched the car slow and pull over at the entrance of my street.

Do I open the door and pray it wasn't him? Do I keep driving...*yeah, until when? Until you fall asleep and crash the car?*

That voice inside my head was insistent. If there was one thing I knew, a lock on a door wouldn't keep him out. If Elithien wanted to know where I lived, then me driving around all night wouldn't stop that.

I pressed the button and nosed the Bentley into my driveway. Lights lit up the garage. Headlights splashed against the walls, blinding me for an instant. Red flared as I braked and hit the remote once more and, as the garage door lowered, I saw the dark gray Explorer slowly drive past.

He was watching me.

Making sure I was safe.

Sawing breaths claimed me with the thought as I killed the engine and climbed from the car. I made my way upstairs, making sure to check the locks on the doors, and set the alarm for the downstairs.

But somehow none of those things were comforting anymore. *He was...*Elithien. I showered and changed into my pajamas, lingering at the tall wooden dresser against my bedroom wall, remembering years ago when I'd stood there, opened the drawer, and found a glove...

A leather glove.

Wood scraped as I pulled open the drawer and saw the glove. I knew it by touch now.. Steel gray eyes lingered in my mind's eye as my thumb slid across the leather. I pulled the glove out and pushed the drawer closed.

That mortal you think about. Is he your lover?

The Vampire's words haunted me as I pulled down the silk sheets and climbed into bed. I didn't want to think about him...not like this...the cold leather warmed to my touch. I slid the glove across the swell of my breast, and in an instant, I was back there, the bricks cold against my back.

I want you. Jesus Christ, I want you.

My own voice panting and desperate inside my head.

Do you?

That clipped tone echoed as I slid the leather along the valley between my breasts until I pressed it between my

169

legs, rubbing and enticing like I'd done so many nights since.

Tell me...Ruth Costello...how much do you want me?

I wanted him...*I wanted*...I pressed and rubbed. I tasted the leather on a panicked breath, and as the fantasy of that kiss played out in my head, it was another's eyes I saw. Steel gray, blood red lips dancing across mine, his hands delving between my thighs as I climaxed.

Mine, the Vampire's snarl staked its claim...*mine.*

13

"You ready for this?" Alexander lifted his gaze from the file in his hand to capture my stare.

I flinched, jerking myself back into the moment and forced a weak smile. "I was born ready."

He took a step closer and lifted his hand. His fingers brushed my arm, soft and gentle. Energy crackled in the air between us. The kind that set a forest on fire. "You okay?" He murmured. "You seemed a little rattled...I've never seen you like this."

"I'm fine," I answered as the courtroom door opened, but the events of last night pressed in.

The Vampires. The Wolves...all tainted with what I'd done later, in bed. I shoved the image from my mind. I didn't want to think about it. not steel gray fucking eyes, not that seductive smile, or Elithien's voice that echoed as I met Alexander's gaze.

Mine, the Vampire demanded.

"He's ready for you, Alexander." The courtroom clerk

waved us forward. He glanced my way and winced. "Be prepared, he's not in the best of moods."

"Sure," Alex smiled. "Thanks, Indy."

"You got it," the clerk smiled at him and held open the door.

I'd seen Alex in action too many times to count. Once he stepped into the arena, nothing rattled his cage. He was composed, polite, quiet when he was listening, but stating his case, he was a Rottweiler in a suit. I followed him inside, feeling my steps a little slower than usual and my responses a little weak.

I slept hard in the early hours of the morning, plunging headfirst into the darkness with the heady scent of my release slick on my fingers. Now I felt fragile, my steps not hitting as hard as they used to...my gaze a little lower than it should be.

Alex glanced over his shoulder as he pushed through the swinging doors, holding one open, and motioned to the defense table. A woman's voice echoed behind me, sharp and loud, *grating*. I winced at the sound.

Don't do it.

Don't turn your head.

Then laughter followed, a low chortle, filled with smugness and smite.

Fucking bitch.

I stepped through, strode to the seat next to Alexander, and turned to her. Carina Chase looked right at me, the smile still twisting her lips. Her navy-blue suit looked stale, just like she was. Stale for a promotion. Stale for a goddamn purpose.

This was personal for her, a vendetta, and one massive rung up the pathetic agency ladder. Well, I wasn't giving it to her. I forced a smile of my own, dragging all the cold composure I could to the forefront of my mind.

Her smile faltered, giving way to a steely stare. She was here to win, there was no doubt about it. The only problem was, *so was I.*

The door to the judge's chambers opened.

"All rise," the clerk called.

I broke the stare and turned to Judge Galeish as he stepped up and took the seat behind the bench. I'd met Peter a number of times, most of them at charity functions his wife held. I waited for him to lift his head, to meet my gaze and acknowledge who I was. But there was nothing, just a flare of his jaw as he focused on the paperwork before him.

Alex brushed my hand and nodded to my seat as he sat.

"Right, so what's this about, counselor?" He lifted his head and glared at the prosecutor.

"It's all right there, your Honor," the prosecutor muttered, some gangly middle-aged man sporting a cheap and tacky silver suit that was two sizes too small…and short. The pant legs rose up past his black socks as he muttered and shuffled papers in front of him.

"All I see is a bunch of hogwash. What is this? Subpoenas and more subpoenas, based on what?"

Carina leaned forward as the prosecuting attorney rose to his feet. "Your Honor, we think that there is more evidence to be collected."

"At Ms. Costello's home? Where is this evidence? You force your case onto my docket and provide me with what? Mr. Trunkey…*I'm waiting.*"

"We found information on the drives from Ms.

Costello's place of business, your Honor," Trunkey stuttered. "The evidence goes far beyond probably cause. And the government wishes to proceed with a further warrant to search Ms. Costello's home."

What the fuck.

My heart thundered. First they came for my company, and then my home?

It's not your company yet, Ruth.

Dad's voice rose inside my head as my phone waited, the ringer on silent still I'd feel it vibrate.

"Mr. Sewell, your response." Judge Galeish looked at Alexander.

"They can't do that," I glanced at Alexander.

"No, they can't" He reached for the cuff of his crisp white shirt and opened the button. The ends were rolled tightly and pushed midway along his arm before he rose. "Your Honor, this is unjustified and quite frankly, a bullshit attack on my client. The prosecution seems to forget that Ms. Costello here, while wildly attractive and successful in her own right, is only one of many people on the board of directors. Yet they seem to have targeted her, and this request for a search warrant of her home is flimsy, at best. If they have so-called evidence, then where is it? I see nothing about it here in the report."

He's voice seemed to boom, as he gained momentum and power. I felt the entire room shift. All heads turned toward him, he was magnetic, truly magnetic. In that moment, I was reminded of how powerful he really was. All business, that's what he was. A flare of hunger tore through me at the sight.

"No, that's just not good enough, and Mr. Trunkey over there knows it," Alexander declared as he gripped the desk, corded muscles tense. My gaze was drawn across his body. He was commanding in that moment, sucking up all the oxygen in the air until I forgot how to breathe.

"My client, as you well know, is under a great deal of strain. Her father is..." He glanced at me, pain shone through those brown eyes, something glinted...*sadness.* "He's *sick,* your Honor. Frankly, this kind of stunt from the prosecution is lower than low. I request this laughable request be seen for what it is, and be thrown out. When Special Agent Chase and her team come back with something a little more substantial than *'it had to be her',* then we'll do our best to comply with their requests for information, until then...well, they can leave my client alone and stop this harassment."

"And I'm inclined to agree," Judge Galeish growled and leveled his gaze at the prosecutor. "You want a search warrant to Ms. Costello's residence? Then bring me something concrete. And if you try to muscle your way onto my docket again, I'll have your damn license. Do you understand me?"

Trunkey lowered his gaze as Carina clenched her jaw.

"Yes, your Honor," the prosecutor answered.

"Right, request dismissed." The judge glanced my way and gave me the smallest nod before rising.

"All rise," the clerk called.

We went through the motions as Peter Galeish left, and this time, I didn't once look over at the prosecution.

"You ready to get out of here?"

My heart sped at the words as Alexander's gaze drifted over my navy-blue skirt and crossed legs. I sucked in a breath and licked my lips. The question held so much promise. "Do you mean this room?" I answered.

I wanted him to say the words, needed to know exactly where we stood here.

I couldn't become entangled in an affair. I *refused* to be the *'other woman'*. I deserved more. And so did the woman he was dating.

I grabbed my bag and followed him out of the courtroom. Trunkey and Carina Chase lingered outside the courtroom doors while they were closed and locked. Their expressions were grim, locked in defeat. I didn't waste a second more thinking about them.

She'd be back. I knew that for a fact. She was like a dog with a bone, gnawing and savaging until something shattered.

"That was a good outcome." Alexander turned and bent over the stainless steel drinking fountain.

He opened his mouth, catching the steady stream of icy cold water as he pressed the button. I stared at his lips, watching as the water splashed into his mouth. Heat rose in my cheeks. I broke the stare and looked away.

But I was still aware of him, knowing when he straightened and dragged the back of his hand across his lips, knowing when he leveled those beautiful brown eyes my way. "It was very good, thank you."

"It's my job." He stepped close, his free hand reaching toward me.

Mine, that dangerous snarl surfaced once more.

"Ruthy!"

My name was called from the corridor. Chills coursed along my spine.

Blane headed toward me. His expression was grave, lips pressed together, hooded eyes fixed on mine, searching for a hint of weakness. He never came to me... and not like this, all desperate and soft and *caring.*

"It's uncle." He cast a careful glare at Alexander. "He's not good."

The ground seemed to open up, darkness reaching out to swallow me whole.

"Dad?" I shoved my hand into my bag, searching for my phone. "What do you mean, *not good?*"

"Papa called an ambulance. I think you should come with me." His tone was urgent, hard, cruel when he meant it to be soft.

When he meant it to be manipulating.

Chills raced along my spine. I started to shake my head as Alexander stepped closer, his finger skimming my arm. "I can drive you."

It just felt all *wrong.* Anger cracked like a whip as Blane moved closer. They were crowding me, *staring at me.* Expecting me to fall apart. I yanked my phone free and stared at the screen. But my fingers shook.

"We tried to find you," Blane muttered, sucking in deep breaths.

No missed calls. "Where's Charlotte?"

There was a shrug from the corner of my eye. "Never saw her."

Never saw her?

"He stopped breathing. There was no time for anything else. I came as soon as I heard."

So he knew where I was...and what I was battling, and still he refused to step up and be a member of the board. *Only when it suited him, right?* Not now. Not *now.*

The marbled floor and dark, richly lacquered wood of the courthouse bled to white. My heart punched against my ribs. They reached for me, all tender and caring. Whispered words as someone touched my arm before I flinched and pulled away. "No. I'll drive. I'm fine."

I turned from them, standing in the middle of the hallway, and had no idea how to get to my car. My mind was a blank, everything was a blank. My life...*blank.*

And in the middle of the panic, a face filled my mind. Moon-kissed skin, with intense, brooding eyes. The kind of face that made you stop and stare, and that wasn't even the most attractive thing about him. It was his commanding presence, his *demanding* tone. It was him. *A Vampire.* Cool air rushed into my lungs, centering me, anchoring me, like a call that echoed from the darkness inside me.

"Ruthy?" Blane called.

I hated my name on his lips. Hated the way he pretended to be family...*or maybe it was me who was the pretender?* I pulled my keys from my bag. "Where is he?"

Blane's eyes widened in surprise. "They called an ambulance. I'm not sure if they've gotten there already. Let me drive you." He reached for my elbow.

"No," Alexander's snarl stopped him cold.

A look passed between them, one I didn't care for. My mind was spinning. But Blane lowered his hand.

"I'm fine. Thank you." I forced the words and headed for the elevator. Elithien's face lingered in my thoughts as I stabbed the button and scrolled through my phone, hitting the number for Charlotte.

The phone rang, and rang...*and rang.* "So, you keep tabs on me, and I can't even get a hold of you?"

I ended the call and searched for Harmony's number,

trying to remember which of the nurses was on shift today, then stepped inside the elevator as it opened.

The phone vibrated in my hand. *Charlotte* the caller ID cut across the screen. I stabbed the button, feeling the panic rise again. "Are you at home?"

"No, it's Harmony's shift tonight. Why?" Her heavy breaths muffled her voice.

"Something's happened. They've called an ambulance. I don't know."

"He was fine when I left him a few hours ago." Her tone turned hard. "Head straight to Crown Mercy. I'll make some calls and meet you there...and Ruth."

"Yeah?"

"Be careful."

My hands shook as I ended the call. I glanced around the elevator, as though seeing it for the first time, as it jolted to a halt in the basement garage. *Be careful?* Charlotte's words resounded, punctuated by the smack of my heels against the concrete. I searched the growing shadows that clung to the concrete pylons and hurried to my car.

I'd wasted all day at the damn courthouse, waiting for Judge Galeish to throw the damn warrant out on principle. All fucking day...*while my father...*

My knees were shaking. My mind spun. I pressed the button to unlock the Bentley and climbed inside. The engine started with a guttural purr. I shoved it into gear. *Just get to Crown Mercy...that's all I had to do. Just get there.*

I pulled forward as a car tore past at breakneck speed. I slammed my foot against the brake, lurching forward until the seatbelt caught. *"Fucking asshole!"*

Gasping breaths tore moisture from my mouth. I

gripped the steering wheel, my hands shaking so bad the damn thing shuddered. I tried to wet my mouth, tried to breathe, then slowly took my foot off the brake.

The drive was careful, flashes of sparks danced like headlights in my eyes until I finally found my way to the hospital parking lot and parked quickly. *He's going to be fine...he's going to be just fine.* I yanked the handle and shoved open the car door.

Charlotte's black Mazda sat up ahead in the parking lot, the sun's bright glare bouncing off the window to blind me. I lifted my hand, covering my eyes, and searched for her. She wasn't there, not waiting at the doors, or around the car. I lifted my gaze to the front of the multi-storied private hospital. She had to be inside.

I hurried, cutting across the parking lot, and headed for the wide automatic doors of the hospital's lobby. I didn't slow as the doors opened then closed behind me with a *whoosh.*

"May I help you?" the receptionist called, standing from her seat behind the counter as I raced toward the elevators.

My thoughts were filled with panic. Acid welled in the back of my throat. I kept my lips clenched shut and frantically stabbed the elevator buttons as my phone beeped.

I yanked it free, finding a message from Charlotte.

Level 11, turn right out of the elevators. I'm waiting. Hurry, Ruth.

A cry almost wrenched free before I swallowed the sound. *Hurry, Ruth.* I started at those words and jerked my gaze to the stairwell. I could climb faster.

Ding. The stainless steel doors shuddered as they slid

open, and I lunged inside. There were others inside, an older couple and a young woman. They all stared as I stabbed the button for the eleventh floor and slumped back against the mirrored wall.

"Aren't you?" the pretty young thing whispered, her eyes widening as the doors closed. "Ruth Costello?"

All I could do was nod. They treated me like some kind of celebrity. But the fact was, without the name I was no one. *Nothing.* Just a regular woman. If anything, the name only brought me misery and loneliness.

I'd had relationships with those who'd had their sights on the family business, those who thought sleeping with me was the closest thing to fame. My family made them see the light fast enough. No one was good enough.

Except for Alexander.

My stomach twisted as we slowly rose, stopping at level five for the smiling young woman to glance at me one last time before she left, carrying a bunch of flowers and a small pink teddy bear.

The older couple was next, shooting me a look of disgust as they pushed past on their way out. I couldn't win, I was either a celebrity or trash…or maybe I was both? I waited for the doors to close once more, counting the seconds with the booming thunder in my head, until the elevator shuddered to a stop on the eleventh floor.

Turn right. I stepped off, scanning the glaring white waiting room and caught sight of her from the corner of my eye.

Charlotte was pacing, dressed in faded blue jeans and a red top that plunged a little too deep at the neckline.

"There you are," she cried and headed for me, holding

her hands out in front as though to catch me. "Go straight in...they're waiting for you."

"They're waiting for me?" I repeated.

"No, honey. *He's* waiting for you."

He's waiting for me. I let her lead me to the room at the end of the hall. I was so used to the sounds of the machines beeping and whirring by now, I barely registered them at all as I stepped through the door, and felt it close behind me.

"Ruthy," my uncle called, and heaved himself out of the seat beside my father's bed.

There were tubes running from his mouth, from his chest...from his arms. He was tied and tethered to the only things keeping him alive.

"We waited."

I jerked my head up at the words. "Waited? Waited for what?"

"For you to come before we switched off the machines."

I shook my head. This wasn't happening. Not now...*not like this.* "I have my father's power of attorney."

My uncle flinched at the remark, and glanced toward the doctor standing at Dad's bedside. The look said it all. It was the kind of look I'd seen my entire life. *We don't need you. We don't want you. Stay out of this.*

"Leave me," I commanded, my voice turning hard as I gave the doctor a look of my own. "All of you."

They left, shuffling out of the room, and it wasn't until the door closed with a small thud that I moved.

"What happened, Daddy?" I edged around the side of the bed. "You were fine...you were just fine. What the hell happened?"

The noise of the machines answered. I stepped close and lifted my hand, brushing my finger across the loose skin on the back of his hand. His gaunt cheeks were so dark, his parted lips so pale. He was already gone…the words hit like me like a sledgehammer.

He was already gone.

I sank to the seat beside him and lowered my head to my hands. Grief overwhelmed me, smothering, chilling, until I couldn't breathe. My mind went blank. Just a white-wash of terror and fear. Just nothing. Empty.

Gone. The word didn't echo, just drifted in my mind. *Gone.* I shook my head, and waited for the tears to come. But they didn't well in my eyes. Instead, I felt dry, barren, aching, and hollow.

Gone while I sat in a damn courtroom on the other side of town.

The door opened and closed behind me, soft footfalls approached and a hand fell gently on my shoulder. I didn't need to turn my head to know who it was. "Turn it off." I spoke the dreaded words.

Words I'd prayed I'd never utter.

Charlotte left my side for a moment and opened the door, speaking in hushed tones.

The vipers slipped into the room behind her.

Pythons dressed up as family.

Squeezing the life from me.

Just as they'd choked the life from him.

White blurred from the edge of my view. I stood as the doctor neared the machine and reached for the button on the side of the respirator. One press and it was all over. He reached up and unhooked the tube, letting the last breath from my father's lungs escape into the air.

I waited for him to open his eyes, to fight his last fight.

But he didn't move, just lay there, his chest sinking lower…and lower…*and lower….*

I stumbled backwards until I hit something or someone, then lunged for the door.

"Ruth?" Charlotte called behind me.

But I was running. My heels clattered on the hard floor as I tore along the corridors, lost to blank stares and the panic that rushed over me like a storm. I spun as I hit the end and scanned the walls, searching for the elevator.

"Ma'am, are you okay?" A young male clerk approached cautiously.

"Elevator. Where is the goddamn elevator?"

He just lifted a hand and pointed back down the hall. The *crack* of my heels sounded like my shattering resolve. I stumbled forward, frantically searching until I saw the glint of steel in the distance.

I had to get out…*too white. Too close.* Frantically, I punched the button for the elevator. My skin itched, desperate to feel the sting of my nails. I wanted to be free, from this building…from this life. The elevator doors opened and I stepped inside, hitting the button for the ground floor. Seconds felt like hours…minutes like a lifetime.

We waited…

I closed my eyes at the words.

We waited.

The elevator stopped and the doors opened. I shoved forward, cutting through the lobby once more, and headed for the parking lot. Night was closing in, throwing splashes of pinks and purples at the horizon. I'd wasted all day…all *fucking* day while Carina Chase and her pet attorney tried to corner me again, and again.

While my father lay dying.

But no more. No more suffering. No more pain.

Now he was…

I couldn't voice the word, not even in the darkness of my mind. I punched the button to unlock the Bentley and climbed in. Seconds later, I was peeling out of the parking lot, driving anywhere…and nowhere while the night grew bolder, revealing the faint glint of stars in the sky.

I drove until the cars blurred. I drove until lights shone in the harbor. The car knew where it was going, like a horse, I let it take the lead, just turning when something inside me told me to turn.

Come to me, the deep growl echoed inside my head.

I knew exactly who it was. The Vampire.

Elithien…

Come. To. Me.

14

W hite lines blurred. The *thud...thud...thud...*of the wheels against the bridge was oddly soothing. I didn't plan to come here, didn't plan to be anywhere, *except alone.*

My phone rang...the caller ID splashed across the stereo. *Alexander.* I reached out and pressed the button, sending the call to voicemail.

Not now.

Not now.

I knew exactly what would happen if I answered. The whole mess of what would follow played out inside my head. He'd be soft, soothing, whispering all the things I needed to hear. He'd make me tell him where I was...and he'd come find me. He'd drive me home in silence with one hand on my thigh...he'd carry me upstairs. To our room...

To our bed.

And make love to me, soft and gentle. He'd take me to

perfect heights and leave me stranded in misery. I couldn't go back there, not to the numbness of what our life had been before. Not to all his late night meetings with men I'd rather not know. I'd rather be alone. I'd rather be…*what? Dead?* I'd had sweetness with him. I'd had plain, boring sweetness.

But that wasn't what I wanted, *was it?* My thoughts lingered in the darkness and the shadows, and the cold. Leather shone in my mind. The brush of a finger against my cheek before it moved to my temple.

I let myself be taken there, back to that alley before my world turned upside down. The steering wheel turned, and the car followed.

You're in pain. I can help with that.

My throat tightened at the words.

I didn't know why, just the sound of them…the *promise.*

Pain tore through my chest. Could my mystery lover help me now? My chest sank until I thought my ribs would snap. Could he take away the last eight months with a brush of his fingers? I tapped the brakes and pulled the wheel to the left, stopping against the curb.

I wanted him to take me away from all this pain…this misery. I leaned forward, my head against my arms on top of the wheel. My foot bounced on the brake, shuddering and shaking, inching the car forward.

Just drive. Turn at the water…plunge from the bridge. There was only misery now, only fighting and the grappling for control. There was only suffering for me. *For the sake of my family name.*

Knuckles rapped against the side window, making me cry out and jerk my gaze toward the glass. A man peered in, his face *familiar.* "You just gonna park there and scare off the customers?"

Arran. His name came to me. Dark eyes, flashing with silver. One brow rose as he narrowed in on my face. Some kind of emotion flickered in his eyes. *Surprise. Concern?* "You want to come inside?" he called on the other side of the glass. "You look like you could use a drink."

He caught the tremble as I shoved the car into park and killed the engine. I didn't know why I was here...for some reason I didn't care. I was close to where I needed to be, dancing along that feeling of knowing...of *wanting.* I swallowed and grabbed my bag before I climbed out and smoothed my navy skirt down.

My court clothes, smart, all business...*detached.* That's how I looked. That was just how I'd wanted to look. But it wasn't how I felt. I peeled off my shoes as I pressed the button and locked the car.

Arran said nothing, just waited for me on the edge of the sidewalk, then turned and slowly strode to the door. The music was already pumping. It was barely dark, and there were already men here with their business suits and ties. I kept my head down and followed Arran inside.

"What, no rat in a bag this time?" the bouncer muttered, and waited for me to answer.

"Give it a rest, Hugo," Arran growled, and waited for me at the top of the stairs.

I followed, staring at the floor, all meek and mild, not like me at all.

"I have a private lounge in the back. Let me grab a bottle and we can head there."

"I'm not having sex with you."

His steps stuttered, leaving him half a step behind as I

headed for the bar. "Never occurred to me..." he muttered. "Not in the last five seconds, at least."

A smile curled the corner of my lips, even though I didn't feel a thing.

I slowed, letting my toes sink into the plush midnight carpet as he reached the bar. I watched the Wolf as he moved, all corded muscles bunching under his shirt. He moved like he didn't have a care in the world, sauntering toward the barman and nodding toward the bar. The seductive music played in the background. A slow rhythm, the beat hard and driving, drawing my focus to the flare of desire between my legs.

I turned and lifted my gaze to the small round dance floor in the middle of the room. There was a new dancer, with long neon-red hair. A wig, obviously, although I doubted anyone here cared. She was beautiful, long and lithe, with a sheer black bra that barely covered dusky pink nipples and panties to match.

She turned and straightened, her dark brown eyes looked almost black under the dim lights. A surge of heat swept through me as our gazes connected. My breaths turned heavy as I searched her face. *She looked like me.*

The thought made me flinch as she dragged her hand along her stomach, her fingers slipping under the elastic of her panties. Perfect red lips curled in as she dragged her teeth across the flesh.

"Do you see yourself in her, Ruth?" The deep, savage growl behind me was filled with hunger—and it wasn't Arran's.

I spun, staring into inhuman gray eyes. Elithien was there, dressed in black...his lips perfectly poised, steel gray eyes fixed on me, never once looking at the woman on the dance floor. No, that cold, stony gaze was all for me. "All that desire," he searched my eyes for the truth. "No one caring about who she was, only what she was... and the secrets her body holds. Secrets men would pay hundreds of dollars to see...or maybe even touch, kiss...or taste."

"If you're asking me if I've ever wanted to be a stripper...then the answer is no."

"An object then, ripping away all the pretense and the lies." He lowered his gaze slowly. "Leaving you with a kind of savage lust that could last for a lifetime."

The alley roared to life inside my head. My spine against the wall, the stranger's fingers sliding down my chest, shoving aside my top to expose me. His lips on mine. Savage heat. *Unbridled heat.*

Desire tore through me. I swallowed hard as Elithien shifted his gaze to the woman on the dance floor and watched her, not like he wanted to fuck her...*but like he wanted to eat her.*

Until he looked at me once more.

There was a shift. One that roared like a freight train through his eyes. He didn't want to eat me...not unless it was his tongue between my thighs. Lust raged in his gaze when he stared at me. Unbridled lust, purer than any drug known to man. Purer than Heaven...or Hell.

He searched my eyes once more, suddenly lost for words. He knew me, more than any man I'd ever known. He crawled under my skin to find the darkness inside. Darkness he wanted to claim...until the steel doors inside his head slammed down, ending the connection.

"Ruth, I have everything planned," Arran added.

"Don't bother," Elithien ordered.

"What do you want, Elithien?" Arran stepped close.

The Vampire didn't answer, just lifted his hand, fingers extended toward me.

Come with me. The words flittered across my subconscious. The feel of home surfaced, along with that hunger inside me. This was why I'd come here...this man...*no, this Vampire.*

The tremble in my chest took hold as I lowered my gaze to the long, tapered fingers waiting for me.

It's okay. His voice filled me, and carried me away. *You're safe with me, Ruth.*

"She doesn't want to go with you," the Wolf growled, and took a step forward.

"Are you ready to listen now?" Elithien didn't take his eyes from mine. "Are you ready for the answers you seek?"

The temperature in the air plunged. Cold licked my skin as I took his hand.

"Wait," the Wolf's growl held the promise of a fight. Right now, that was the last thing I needed.

"She's made her choice," the Vampire growled.

"Ruth, stay," Arran pleaded. "I won't pressure you, I promise."

I glanced his way. I would've stayed with him, maybe for tonight...maybe longer. He had a way about him, a *casualness* that was inviting. He'd be incredible in bed, powerful and hungry. I would've let him under my skirt... maybe under my skin. But there'd be no ties with him, no promise of anything but a good a time...*for a while.*

And I didn't do casual.

Not once.

Not ever.

I also didn't do Vampire.

Answers. Answers were something I could do. Something more than this empty pit inside my chest, this shotgun hole just waiting to swallow me whole.

"I can protect you," Arran growled, silver eyes flashing to mine.

"From what?" Elithien stepped closer to the Wolf.

I could see them now, see how Arran tried to smother the flinch, and how the Vampire's presence swallowed the room. Even the darkness obeyed him, swirling around the room. He was shadows. *He was night.* The beat from the music grew heavier, sending a shudder through my body with every thready pulse.

"From me?" the Vampire prodded.

The way he said it was a slap in the Wolf's face. Arran's throat worked overtime. I watched the tight muscles clenching as he swallowed. "This bar is Phantom's. You make a problem for me...and you make a problem for—"

"Don't bother finishing that threat," the Vampire warned. "You sound like a little bitch. The next time you touch something that doesn't belong to you, I'll take off your hand...at your goddamn shoulders. Am I clear?"

Movement crowded in. In the corner of my eye, I saw the other three Vampires closing ranks. They'd slaughter this Wolf...and everyone else in this bar, in a heartbeat, and not even blink twice.

They were controlled...utter...rage.

Untapped.

Unleashed, and ready to paint this bar red.

Elithien turned toward me, his voice calm, controlled, not demanding, *hoping.* "The choice is yours, Ruth. You can walk out of here and go back home, or you can come with me. Are you ready?"

Ready for what? I wanted to ask. But my body was not my own. It was a stranger's.

I didn't know this woman who gave a small nod and let him lead her back along the dance floor. I glanced over my shoulder to the whipped look in Arran's eyes. There was a flicker of something...it was the same look Alexander had given me today.

Sorrow.

Helplessness.

The look you gave when you were defeated. I turned my gaze to the man who held my hand. *To the creature who held my hand.* His head was turned my way. I was struck by the utter resolve, the complete concision of those savage stony eyes. He wasn't just immortal, he was as far from human as you could possibly get.

There was no life in the steel gray of his eyes, no kindness, no compassion...he was a blade, an *instrument.* Deadly to everyone else but the person...or Vampire who weilded him.

Was I that person right now?

Was I the hand that gripped the weapon?

I stepped when he did, climbing the stairs to the front doors of the strip club once more. One savage glance to the Wolf at the door and they swung open. I doubt a man like Elithien had ever been slowed or stopped in his entire life.

He was a freight train. A sword on its descent.

He was *terrifying.*

But his hold on my hand was gentle. His fingers

warmed to the touch, and I felt a flutter of something deep inside me, burrowed in the chambers of my heart.

Being here felt like the headlights of an oncoming car, so bright...*so blinding.* I was unable to turn away. Glass crunched under his shoes as he stepped out of the strip club and turned left.

An Explorer idled, the sound a low, savage threat in the night, a sound filled with the promise of darkness and death. Hurrow stepped out of the driver's seat and came around to the passenger's side. My heart sped at the sight of him. Call it panic, or fear...call it anything really—*but what it really was.*

"There's glass." Elithien stepped closer, picking me up like I weighed nothing at all. I tried not to focus on the hard muscles under my hands, or the way his body moved as he carried me toward the passengers door.

I felt protected...*revered. Safe.* I gripped his strong shoulders as the steel wall of pretense inside me trembled.

"My car." I murmured. "I can't."

"Keys." Hurrow lifted a hand as Elithien balanced my weight, his splayed fingers against my ass pressing me against him, and yanked open the door of the Explorer. He gently placed me on the seat.

Numb. Shock. The feel of his hand between my thighs lingered.

"Keys, Ruth." Elithien urged, those steel eyes searching mine.

The damn things jangled as I delved into the pocket at the top of my skirt and handed the keys to the Vampire.

The world stood still for a moment, my life spearing a hard right.

"It's going to be okay" Elithien urged.

My phone buzzed, the ringer set to vibrate.

"Don't answer it." He held my gaze.

Silver shone in his gaze…as hypnotic as the moon. *It was nice meeting you, Ruth Costello…very nice indeed.*

All I saw was his lips…those perfect lips.

All I felt was that overwhelming need to kiss him. To be wanted…*hand on my breast, leather against my skin.* I wrenched myself from the memory and pressed my thighs together.

"I'll meet you there." Hurrow scanned the empty streets. "You want protection?"

"From the Wolves?" Elithien's gaze bored into mine. "I doubt it."

The Vampire was gone in a heartbeat, striding across the street toward the Bentley. Doors unlocked, engine started, and still I didn't look away. Hypnotized, that's how I felt.

"So where do we go from here?" The words came from nowhere. "You came to me asking about Alliard. I want to share with you what I know."

"Why?" A flicker of the woman I once was surged to the surface.

"Why indeed." He leaned, reaching to smooth down the hemline of my skirt.

Electricity raced across my skin with his touch. He was so careful, so controlled, and yet that one brush of his hand, that one flicker of decency, told me so much.

He wants me.

My breath caught with the words.

He wants me in his bed. He wants me by my side. Grey eyes glinted like the honed steel of a blade. *He wants me for good…*

Mine. That word raged in my head. My pulse sped. I knew where it came from now. Where this demand echoed from...it was him...this *Vampire...this*—panic flared, tearing through my veins. Darkness waited, like a cavern inside. I stood on the precipice, and all the answers waited for me down there in the dark and the cold...in the touch of his fingers on my skin.

And the hunger in his eyes.

"I think I should—" I glanced across the street to my car, but it was gone.

How did I miss that?

"Your car is perfectly fine." Elithien took a step away. "As are you. You're free to leave, Ruth, anytime you wish. All you have to do is say the words. No one will harm you, not ever again."

He waited then, standing at the open door. I glanced toward the strip club and felt a twinge of disappointment. I'd almost let myself be dulled by that place, by the lure of sex and the mindlessness of all the alcohol I could drink.

My dad died today.

The words filled me, shattering the resolve. My dad died today and I almost ended up on my back with my skirt shoved around my waist. What I should be doing... what a fucking *Costello* would do, was to hold onto the one damn thing I had left.

My. Fucking. Company.

"I'll stay," I answered. "I'll stay and listen."

Those seductive lips curled at the corners as he gave a nod. "That's my fighter," he murmured and closed the car door.

15

Silence swallowed the space. The car barely made a sound. Just tires on the pavement, background noise really. Elithien was quiet behind the wheel. The silence gave me space to think…and that was never a good idea.

I jerked my gaze from the road ahead to him…for the hundredth time. His chiseled jaw, perfect lips, strong hands swallowing the wheel, taking the corners like he was born to race.

It's was you, wasn't it? The words came out of nowhere to echo in my head. *In the alley…and in the hospital.*

I had his glove…his damn glove that was in my drawer —and in my home.

I'll keep watch over you…I'll make sure no one touches you like that ever again.

I should be terrified, should be out of my mind with fear. I should be anything but this eerie fucking calm.

But I felt none of those things as he handled the Explorer. I felt…calm, *numb.* Thoughts filled my head, none of them made any sense, but right in that moment, I didn't care. This was exactly where I needed to be. Safe and secure, in the company of a Vampire.

If he wanted to hurt me, I doubt there was anything on this earth that could stop him. Not a bullet...not a knife, not a baseball bat. In the dark recesses of my mind, those screams waited, screams from the alley all those months ago.

Screams he'd silenced.

It was you.

I sank back into the seat, my spine cradled against the stitching. *It was you, your fingers against my temple, your lips on mine...your hand reaching under—*

I jerked from the memory, breathless and wanting. I watched him for a second before slowly closing my eyes. The cool air sank deep. The smooth ride carried me away. I could drift away here, let it all slide through my mind, Dad, the FBI, the family—if only for a second.

Let it slide away, like it couldn't touch me, not here... not when I was with...*him.*

We climbed higher and higher, winding around the mountain. My breaths deepened, the pain in the center of my chest just...floated away. The growl of the engine was faint, hungry and urgent. My head lolled to the side. I shifted against the seat, curling against the leather as it warmed under me, until what felt like hours later, the car finally slowed.

Gravel crunched under the tires, the sound wearing away the quiet. I cracked open my eyes, finding faint yellow lights in the darkness, and through the windshield I caught the outline of the midnight mansion. The Bentley was parked in the driveway, with no sign of Hurrow. Clock numbers were neon green on the dashboard...*2:15.*

Two AM? *In the morning?*

"You looked peaceful," Elithien murmured, just sitting behind the wheel. "I didn't want to wake you."

Memories surfaced, memories of what he truly was and what he'd done. I wanted to know, good or bad, I wanted to know all. Tonight, the truth was important. Tonight was *different.*

Grief threatened to consume me. My throat tightened. I swallowed and swallowed, forcing the words. "You killed them, didn't you? Those thugs in the alley. You killed all of them."

He lifted his gaze, steel gray found me in the rear-view mirror. There was no hiding what he was, not anymore. "Yes."

He yanked handle, pushing the door wide. It closed barely a heartbeat later, then he was outside my window, opening the door for me.

I waited for a second, letting it all sink in. He'd done that. He'd killed them.

"Do you want me to apologize for saving your life?" He stepped closer and held out his hand. "Because I won't. I meant what I said, Ruth. I'd kill them a thousand different ways if I had the chance."

Why? That was the burning question. The only question really. Because of a kiss? My breath caught. I reached for his hand as I slid from the car and met those steel gray eyes. I doubted a hard kiss in an alley was enough to rock his world, not someone like Elithien.

The car door closed as movement came from the front

of the house. Hurrow stepped out, his gaze sliding over me. Lips parted, a sudden dream of a breath as he smoothed his tie. "It's all ready."

Only then did he look at Elithien. Raven hair shone, intense eyes glinted. He glanced my way and winked, curling those gorgeous lips into a seductive smile.

Elithien was the leader, the...*Alpha* in this den of Immortals, but I was starting to work out this one was the second-in-command. "What exactly is ready?"

"Answers." Elithien motioned toward the open door of the house. "After all, I am a man of my word."

A Vampire of his word, more like it. I followed him, lowering my gaze as Hurrow turned and closed in behind us. I was shadowed by the most lethal Immortals in Crown City and still I felt safer here than I did at my family home.

Soft amber lights flooded the hallway. The crackling of an open fire greeted me.

"A drink first?" Elithien motioned toward the living room. "I have a feeling you're going to need it."

My steps stuttered, my breath caught. What the hell did that mean? Scotch splashed the bottom of a tumbler before it was held out. "You're safe here," Elithien's gaze searched mine. "I just wanted you to know that...no matter what happens from this moment forward. Anytime you want to reach out to me, my door is always open to you."

My heart thundered, the words on the tip of my tongue. *Why? Why me?* Heat rushed to my cheeks as I took the glass. But for some strange reason, the words didn't come.

It didn't seem like the right place, or the right time. Instead I just took a sip of the alcohol, letting the warmth seep into my bones, "Thank you. I…appreciate that."

A simple nod of the head followed before he glanced at Hurrow standing at the door. "I think we're ready."

I followed them as they headed toward the hallway. I couldn't help but turn my head and glance at the door to the room I'd glimpsed before. The room where a woman had lain seductively across the end of some kind of bed. My steps slowed, the Scotch not the only thing that burned me from the inside.

"You coming?" Hurrow asked.

I jerked my gaze toward him as Elithien disappeared through an open door.

"Sure…of course," I answered a little too quickly, watching as his gaze slipped to the door.

"He told us we were to feed before you arrived…last time you were here."

He did that? "Why?"

"So we didn't come across as ravenous beasts," Hurrow replied, taking a step closer, and my heart gave a tiny stutter.

The Vampire lifted his hand and swept the tips of his fingers across my cheek, tucking the hair behind my ear. "He likes you," Hurrow searched my gaze. "Which is strange, because Elithien rarely likes anyone."

"And you know what they say," a savage growl came from behind me, making me flinch. The one with the eye patch glared at me, his lips twisted into a snarl. "All for one, and one for all."

What the hell was that supposed to mean? I opened my

mouth to say just that as Hurrow stopped at the open door and motioned inside. This place was starting to appear sharper, the edges not so murky as they'd been under the haze of fear. Now I saw it all...and *them,* as well.

I held Hurrow's gaze as I stepped closer, and lifted my glass at the last minute, taking a sip of Scotch. The Vampire just chuckled and slowly shook his head.

"I contacted an old acquaintance," Elithien said as he motioned to a black chesterfield sofa sitting against the wall. "He was able to track down some very enlightening footage. Some I think you'll be *very* interested in."

One nod of his head and Hurrow was striding forward. "Lights," he commanded.

In an instant, the room was plunged into darkness, until a TV screen came to life. The black and white image was clear and precise. The screen was divided into four sections, labelled camera one, camera two, camera three, and camera four. It didn't take me long to register what I was looking at.

A sharp inhale and I jerked my gaze to the Vampire standing in the dark. "Care to explain how the hell you obtained the private security footage of my building?"

"Just watch," he urged, his gaze riveted to the screen.

Heat rushed through my body. On a night like tonight, anger was all I had to hold onto. My staff were like family, I knew each one by name, from the cleaners who worked the night shift, all the way to the board of directors. But *someone* had betrayed me, leaking footage of my own building to anyone who asked for it.

"Are you watching, Ruth?" Elithien chided, as on the screen two men wearing suits strode through the empty floor of offices and stopped outside of mine, then a second later, after fumbling with the lock, they were inside.

I looked at the date, and then the time, remembering that frantic call in an instant...*Ms. Costello...Ms. Costello, it's James from the night crew.*

In the dark Elithien, watched me. But on the screen, my two cousins came out of my office and locked the door again. *Judah and Blane.* Even watching them break into my office wasn't enough. "They could've been in there for any number of reasons."

"Yes, they could have." Elithien just stared into my gaze, then gave the order. "Next,"

And on the TV screen, the next roll of security cameras showed brand new black and white footage, only this time is was the parking lot outside the warehouse.

I shoved up from the sofa and took a slow step forward as they came into view, cutting across the parking lot toward the Bentley sitting underneath the streetlights. My stomach roiled and sank as I watched them pull out a small bag and, with their own fingers, smear the warning onto my windshield.

Pain lashed my chest. Tears pricked my eyes. In an instant, I was that child again, held down by the sheer force of their weight, a hand over my chest. The smothering helplessness filled me all over again.

"Why?" The word tore free as I stared at the screen.

"They threatened you, your own kin threatened your life." Elithien growled as he came closer. "You're not safe there, not even from your own blood."

A harsh, unhinged bark ripped from my lips. "You think I don't know that? There's never been a time I've ever been safe, not in a darkened alley, and not in my home. Monsters and family, family and monsters. To me, they're one and the same."

He flinched at the words, his chiseled jaw bunching as he clenched it. "Hurrow, take Justice and pay Ruth's cousins a little visit. Make sure they understand we're aware of their...*activities*."

"With pleasure," Hurrow snarled, and strode toward the door.

"No." The word was instant. I met the Vampire's steely gaze with my own. "No, don't do this. Not now. My father died tonight."

There was a flinch, a tiny crease at the corner of Elithien's eyes as he bowed his head. "My deepest sympathies. I always found your father...*agreeable*."

Laughter flared inside me, but I swallowed it down. "That's not a word I'd ever associate with him, but I'll take it, and thank you. I told you that, not for your sympathy, but so you'll understand how volatile my family is right now." *That's not something I can cope with.*

He crossed the room, his long strides closing the distance between us until he loomed over me. "They threatened you," he stated, those silver eyes searching mine. "They caused you pain, distress."

"That's what family does, *isn't it?*" I answered.

I was lost in the danger, lost in the cold, cruel savagery of who and what he was. My breath caught, panic flared.

"So I want you to take my number," he added. "And if anything like that happens again, I want you to call me *immediately*. Will you do that?"

"Who are you?" I whispered.

A dangerous smile crossed his lips as he leaned closer.

"I'm the monster in the dark, remember? The beast in the shadows, the hunter in the night."

Power rippled in the room as Hurrow shifted and Justice cleared his throat.

"I mean it, Ruth." Elithien urged. "Let us protect you."

A shiver raced along my spine. In a heartbeat, I was back in that hospital bed with a monster in the shadows, one that whispered promises filled with danger and death, and as I searched those steely eyes, I nodded.

He reached out his hand for my phone. My fingers trembled as I turned it on, ignored the twenty missed calls, most of them from Alex, and handed it over.

Elithien worked fast, tearing his gaze from mine for mere seconds as he pressed the phone into my palm once more. "It's under M, for *Monster.*"

"Really?"

"What do you think?" he asked.

I thought he was unlike anybody I'd ever met before. I thought he was exquisite, and terrifyingly deadly. "I think…my family will be worried where I've been."

A simple nod, and he took a step backwards. "Will you promise me one thing?"

I waited, heart pounding in my ears.

"Be cautious around your family, now more than ever before. Don't trust them."

"Funny," I whispered, and stared at those lips. "That's exactly what they've always said about you."

My phone vibrated in my hand, and a second later, the *beep* of a missed call sounded. "I'd better go, otherwise they'll send out the SWAT team."

He gave a nod before I turned, taking one last look at

the TV screen, then met Hurrow's gaze, and then Justice's, and finally Rule's. "Thank you for being honest."

I walked out of there...the *Vampire's den,* placing my empty glass on a table, and went out the front door. It was late and cold, and mist hung in the air like a blanket, making me shiver as I strode from the house toward my car.

Images from the TV screen flickered through my mind as I yanked open the driver's door and climbed inside. It still smelled of my father, faintly of cigar, and stifling with power. I shivered under the reminder of the man, but there was another scent now, a *new scent.*

I closed the door and grabbed my seatbelt, snapping it in place as I started the engine. Spices, and desire. I turned my head and dragged in that scent from the leather seats. Heat flared through me, desire and need, a need I'd felt before.

One that led me into dark alleys with a dangerous kind.

I swallowed hard, shoved the car into reverse, and drove around the circular driveway. A touch skimmed across my mind as I changed gears and eased forward. There was no fog on the road, no weird thing with the instrument panel or the lights like what had happened with Arran. There was nothing, just a clear, open road.

It's them. I scanned the sides of the road my heart pounding. It made no sense, but somehow, I knew. I gripped the wheel and focused on the road as I headed back toward the bridge that divided my world from theirs.

A world filled with lies and hate.

A world filled with monsters, just the same.

You gonna cry?

Judah's voice filled me, and that same powerlessness came roaring back once more.

You tell no one, got it?

I gripped the wheel as I sped across the bridge. "No, I haven't *'got it'.* Not anymore, you cruel sonofabitch."

Headlights glared at me from oncoming cars. I shifted my gaze to the rear-view mirror and caught the faint flicker of headlights far behind me. I jerked my gaze to the road, then glanced back a second later, and they were gone.

Gone.

An ache filled me as I turned off the bridge and back along the city streets, making my way back home. My phone beeped once more. I glanced at my cell as headlights caught my eyes. Headlights bounced off the rear-view mirror, blinding me for a second as the car behind me took the same turn.

My pulse raced as the car followed as I turned once more, only this time, the car behind me shot past. I hated being so goddamn jumpy. I turned the wheel and eased the car into the driveway as the garage door started to rise. In the rear-view mirror, a steel gray Explorer crept past.

My heart leaped and my hands gripped the wheel as I turned my head, catching the flare of brake lights as the car disappeared from sight. It was him...*Elithien.* "You're just gonna follow me, huh?"

I eased my foot off the brake and rolled the car into the garage. If he wanted to hurt me, he could've done it a thousand times by now. So, if he didn't want to hurt me, then what *did* he want?

The answer waited in the darkness of my mind.

An answer I wasn't ready to explore. I braked and shoved the car into park as I pressed the remote on the visor and the garage door rolled back down.

He was the watcher in the dark.

My silent protector.

My stalker Vampire.

16

The banging on my door was loud and insistent. I rolled over, feet tangled in the covers, and tried to bury my head under the pillow. My phone lay quiet, because after the thirtieth missed call, I'd switched the damn thing off.

Bang...bang...bang...

But this—this I couldn't switch off.

The real world crept closer as I moaned and shoved from the bed, pulling the comforter with me, and stood. The world swayed as I stepped forward and kicked the empty whiskey bottle, sending it bouncing into the wall with a *thud.*

Bang...bang...bang... "I know you're in there!"

A groan rumbled from the back of my throat as I trudged down the stairs and braced my hand against the wall, taking two deep breaths as I pressed my finger to the keypad and heard the front door lock *click.*

I yanked the door open and blinked into the glare. Alex just stood there, arm braced on the wall as he leaned against the frame. Anger darkened his eyes and carved a line between his brows. He took one look at me, and his gaze softened. "You look like hell."

"Thanks." I muttered, and turned. "Nice to see you, too."

"You know that thing that buzzes and rings? That thing you carry around with you, it's called a cell phone. You answer it when someone tries to call you, you understand that, right?"

I heaved my foot onto the first stair and grasped the banister as the door closed behind me.

"I was scared half to death, Ruth. You understand that, right?"

His hate and anger swirled around me, but it was nothing compared to the tornado of pain that waited inside, the pain of betrayal, and of grief.

"The funeral's today."

I froze, my hand trembling on the banister as I closed my eyes. A small bark of laughter tore free. "That was fast. Who was it? Who made the call?"

"I did."

Pain plunged like a knife. I kept on walking, kept on climbing all the way to the top of the stairs and turned toward my bedroom.

"You left me no choice when you didn't answer my calls or my damn messages." He stopped at the doorway and picked up the empty bottle. "Your uncle was pressuring me, telling me it was better to move fast, for the good of the company."

"For the good of the company," I repeated, the words like poison.

"I tried to reach you," he added.

I just nodded and let the comforter fall to the floor.

"Ruth." My name was a groan on his lips.

I turned my head, finding his stare on my body as I stood in panties and a bra. His lips parted, eyes working their way down along all the places he knew…or used to know. Yeah, the places that were once his to explore, and to bite and to tease and to hunger for—but not anymore.

Not anymore.

"I'm going to shower now. I have to get ready," I whispered. "Can you text me the time? I know the address, unless you've changed all that, as well?"

"What?" He jerked his gaze higher, meeting mine.

"The funeral," I answered. "My father's funeral at La Madre Maria Funeral Parlor, unless you changed that, too?"

He flinched as though I'd slapped him. "No, no I didn't change anything else."

I just nodded, that was all I had the strength to do. "Then I'm going to shower, and I'll see you there."

He just lifted the empty bottle of whiskey and set it on the nightstand. *His* nightstand, the one he used to use for his watches and his wallet, before he decided I wasn't enough.

I reached around and undid the clasp of my bra and stepped into the bathroom and closing the door. Guilt and anger made me nauseous. I let my bra fall, listening to him in my bedroom and the soft thud of his steps drifted away.

The hard *slam* of my front door made me jump. My fingers trembled as I shoved my panties down and hit the lever for the shower. I had nothing left to give him, no more love, no more agony over what could have been. I

211

had nothing but this empty hole I my chest, this dark lonely hole.

Not even the heat of the water touched me as I stepped under the spray and dropped my head backwards. I washed and shampooed, running conditioner through the strands of my hair and shaved my legs. But I stepped out just as dirty as I'd been when I stepped in.

I was filthy with anger, choked with remorse and regret. I toweled my body dry, lifted my gaze to the heated mirror, and stared into the eyes of someone all alone in the world.

My hands shook, elbows trembled as I leaned forward. "All alone, in a family of hyenas."

Tears threatened to fall, until I bit the inside of my mouth hard enough to draw blood. The sweet tang filled my mouth. It was all I needed, just enough to push myself back from the edge. I straightened, and stared at myself. "Time to get ready, Dad. Time to put you in the ground."

I strode from the bathroom. My comforter was placed on the bed, the ends smoothed out, the top edge folded over, the top corners pulled down low, like he used to do, one side for me, and the other for him.

I stood there naked and stared at that corner on what once was his side of the bed. A scream tore free, violent and piercing, rebounding through the room, as I lunged and ripped the comforter free.

How fucking dare he...*how fucking dare he!* "You left *me*, you sonofabitch. *You left me, remember?*" White tore through the room as I swung the bedding, hurling it over the banister, and stumbled back into the door to my room. "You *fucking left me.*"

Tears came, cruel stinging tears that burned like acid. I swiped away the mess and stumbled to the walk-in closet. Cream, red, and black filled my half of the small room. I made for the high-necked, knee-length lace dress and eased it free from the others.

It was new, brand new. I'd bought it on the same day of Dad's diagnosis, two hours before, actually. It was like I'd already known what was coming, like I wanted to be prepared. Calmness swallowed me, the quiet in the wake of the storm. Tears dried on my cheeks as I carried the dress to the bed and laid it down.

I strode to the dresser and yanked open the top drawer, taking out black lace panties and a matching bra. Leather kissed my fingers. I pulled the glove free and stared at the it.

Memories of last night came back to me in a rush. His hands on my body, curling me into a muscled chest, my fingers splayed over his shoulders as he carried me. That look of dominance, that look of hunger.

I'll keep watch over you...I'll make sure no one touches you like that ever again.

The words filled me as the memory of those headlights outside my home returned. He'd followed me...the Vampire, *Elithien.* All the way to my home.

He hadn't left me. He hadn't strayed.

He'd kept his promise.

My heart thundered as I shoved the glove back inside and turned from the drawer. Panic eased inside me, there was a purpose to my fear now, a driving motion rushing me into someplace I'd never been.

I slipped my underwear on and returned to the bathroom, moisturizing my skin with cream and sprayed perfume, then grasped my dress from the bed. My hands didn't shake as I drew the dress on, then plucked my silent phone from the nightstand and switched it on.

Forty missed calls and as many messages. I scrolled to the end of Alex's frantic texts to the time for my father's funeral. Four PM.

At 4 PM, I'd say goodbye to the one constant man in my life. The *only* man I'd trusted. The only man who'd never left me, never betrayed me, never *hurt* me.

I glanced at the clock and moaned. It was almost 2 PM. I'd slept away the morning in a deep, ravenous sleep, stained with the touch of whiskey and kissed with fading dreams. Two hours. That's all I had. Two hours until I needed to be the epitome of a class; cold, withdrawn... where nothing could touch me—not even this.

I squeezed drops in my eyes and waited for the sting to fade then applied makeup and fixed my hair. Heels, that's all that waited. I strode from the bathroom to slip my feet into Guccis and checked myself in the full-length mirror at the end of the closet. I looked perfect on the outside, not even a hint of the mess I'd been before.

It was amazing what makeup could do, hiding the pain and the bruises, and make you brand new...all over again. I grabbed my bag and made my way downstairs, hit the arming code for the security system, and headed into the garage.

The Bentley was waiting, a reminder of the drive last night.

Come. To. Me.

The memory of that call throbbed, mingling with my pulse. I took a tentative step and reached out. I don't know why the car made me think of the Vampire instead of my father. I opened the driver's door and slipped inside.

It was Hurrow, that's who waited for me in here.

Dark, dangerous spices and chilling seduction.

I clamped my thighs together and yanked the door closed. I wasn't going to think about them, not today...not when everyone was watching.

I gripped the steering wheel and leaned my forehead against the cool leather. "Just get through this, then we'll take the next hurdle, okay? Just get through this."

My fingers trembled as I stabbed the engine button and the Bentley roared to life. One press of the remote and I was backing out of my driveway and turning the wheel. The garage door rolled downwards and I was driving, letting instinct take me and trying not to watch the clock. Deep inside, I knew where I was headed, well before I turned the last corner and slowed the car to a crawl. The same parking space was empty across the street, as though the divine had intervened on my behalf.

I eased the Bentley into the space and let the engine idle as I stared at the alley behind the Jewel. It was the place it had happened, that night...that beautiful and terrifying night.

What would've happened if it had been just a bartender...just a mortal man?

Would he have saved me? Or run...

I waited for the panic to push in, to sweep me away and take me down that dark alley, kicking and screaming once more. But there was nothing, nothing but the detached knowing that it wasn't just a man who'd come back for me that night.

That it was a Vampire.

Elithien.

The violence. I'd never heard terror like it. Their screams would forever haunt me. But so would my own. It's a beast eat beast world, isn't it? *And I was the one left standing.*

I shoved the car into gear once more.

Yeah, I was the one left standing. I was the one alive.

Protected.

I made my way toward La Madre Maria. *Mother Mary.* It was the place Dad had chosen months ago, when we knew it would be time soon. Everything was as he wanted it. The casket, the flowers, the wake at Uncle Jerry's after the service beside the casket.

It was the service I thought of. The service I had to prepare for.

Soaring city buildings slipped into my rear-view mirror as I drove through the heart of Crown City and headed to the perfect green valley of La Madre Maria. It was beautiful out here, with lofty pine trees in the distance and manicured lawns.

We held a sixty-percent share in this company, and death was always lucrative. I rolled the Bentley through the tall iron gates and headed for the brick reception building. The place was half gothic and half colonial, with wrought iron trellises and worn, brick buildings. The place kinda gave me the creeps.

Every space in the parking lot was taken, except for one near the front. They were double-parked along the streets outside the gates, triple-parked along the grassy areas at the front of the reception building.

I nosed the Bentley in beside my uncle's Rolls Royce. It seemed he'd left the flashy Lamborghini at home. I glanced at the clock. It was after three. I killed the engine and just sat there, in the quiet and the cool, staring at the place where my father would finally be put to rest.

I tried to remember the events of yesterday. The courtroom, the *almost*-kiss with Alexander, and the panicked footsteps of Blane. His face, that's what I remembered the most. His face.

It was so calm, no wide eyes of panic, no shine of sweat on his forehead. Just calm. I guess everyone dealt with grief in their own way. It wasn't like we hadn't known this was coming.

A white van crept along the drive and stopped at the back of my car. The doors opened and a camera crew climbed out. *Goddamn paparazzi.*

"You," a massive male in a black suit and thick black sunglasses strode toward them. "Get back in the van and fuck off, this is private property."

The camera guy heaved the camera onto his shoulder, ready to take every shot he could and make a fortune. I could see the headlines now. *Crime Boss, Denzel Costello has died at age 65.*

But the bodyguard just shoved the camera from his shoulder and all but heaved the guy back into the van. Tires spun, leaving thick black marks in their wake as the vehicle roared out the driveway and was gone.

"It's okay now, Ms. Costello." The bodyguard scanned the area as he stepped toward my door.

He lowered those thick black rims, and familiar eyes stared down at me.

"Russell?" I called.

"Yes, ma'am," he answered with a hint of a smile. "You're safe now."

I yanked the door handle and he reached to pull the door open. "Thank you."

"Just doing my job, Ms—"

"Ruth, remember?" I reached for his hand, letting him help me from the car and closed the door behind me.

"Are they all here?" I asked, scanning the building just like he had seconds before.

"Yes, they are…and they're waiting."

17

T*hud.*

Cold, clumped earth smacked the casket.

Red roses peeked out of the dirt like blood. Blood all around me, driving through my veins with every painful *boom* of my heart.

They all looked at me, sneaking glances, or flat out staring, searching my face for a flicker of emotion. Sobs surrounded me, wails and weeping. Tears shimmered like diamonds on perfect make-up. But they weren't my tears, and they weren't my wails. They were theatrics. A play put on for everyone around them...everyone who they thought mattered, at least.

They were all there, monsters...beasts, *and the Wolves and Fae, too.*

I stared at the glistening midnight shine on the wood and waited for the damn thing to open. My dad was in there. Hiding like he used to, crouching around corners, sneaking up behind me.

Boo!

I waited for his roar, waited for the dirt to slide and the roses to fall. I waited to see his face, the secret smile he had just for me. *It's okay, Ruthy,* his voice was blindingly clear in my head. I turned my head and looked behind me.

Smiles. Red lipstick stretched until it cracked. I caught Charlotte's sad smile, and echoed it with my own as I turned back. Alex stood beside me, a careful hand resting on my waist, curled fingers giving the illusion of steely strength. I swallowed the revulsion and stepped away, shucking off the unwelcome touch, but drawing every gaze a heartbeat before the priest ended the sermon.

"Amen," Father Ignatius finished.

"Amen," the entire congregation repeated.

My stilettos stuck in the grass. They were my trusted heels...my *hidden weapon* heels. I'd sworn to myself I'd never be vulnerable again, and yet here I was, chest open, heart exposed to every word or every look. I all but ran toward the Bentley as a dark blur stepped out from behind a black Chrysler.

I blinked away tears as Russell stepped closer. "Will you let me drive you?"

Grief swallowed me, sending a tremor through my body. I nodded, not trusting my voice. The bodyguard seemed to know instantly what I needed. He strode to the passenger's side and opened the door. Flashes of memories came back to me, of doors opened, only by another man...*no,* not a man—a Vampire.

I stepped into the car, my skirt sliding on the leather seat. The lingering scent of Hurrow swept through me as the passenger-side door was closed gently. But the

Vampire's cologne was fainter now as Russell opened the driver's door and slipped behind the wheel.

The Bentley's engine started with a growl. I couldn't move, not to pull the seatbelt over me, or to lift my gaze to those who remained huddled around my father's casket.

"Here," Russell reached across.

He was careful not to touch me, careful and kind to grasp the seatbelt and click it into place. "You want to just drive?"

I nodded as he eased back. "Please."

We were backing out of the parking space a heartbeat later. The man could drive, steady, sure, taking the dip at the bottom of the drive with the finesse of a NASCAR driver as the roar of the engine filled my ears. I was pushed back with the motion, careful hands on the wheel, silence...beautiful, peaceful silence.

We drove, taking corners a little faster as time ticked on, until the needle on the tachometer was trembling and my breath blew hot and furious from my lips.

But still I wanted more.

I stared straight ahead, watching the white lines blur, until he braked, pulling us into a dirt parking lot next to an old, beat-up diner. Dust billowed up around the sleek midnight machine as Russell put the car in park and growled, "Wait right here."

He stepped out of the car and closed the door behind him, striding up the ramp to disappeared into the diner. Adrenaline slipped away from me, leaving the pain to close in before he was back again, shoving the door to the diner open with his hip as he carried two drink cups back down the ramp and toward the car.

He seemed to forget how to balance the two drinks when he got here, finally setting one on the roof as he open the driver's door and passed a drink over. "Here, and don't judge."

I took the cup from his hand with perfectly manicured nails and stared at the burned mess of goo inside.

"Try it, better than sex," he growled without thinking, as he stiffened and turned a bright shade of red. "Sorry."

Laughter spilled from my belly as he clamped his lips around the straw and sucked. I wasn't useless, although the stuff did look like it needed a fire extinguisher and 911. But when I dragged the goo into my mouth, warmth hit me, followed by a blast of delicious malted cold.

A moan tore free. I gripped the cup a little tighter and reached for the straw, lifting it to puncture the burned mess once more.

"Good, right?" he urged.

"Oh my God, what the hell is this?" I sucked harder, tasting browned marshmallows and some kind of delicious flavor underneath.

"They call it Campfire Delight. Best drink there is in the city in my opinion, and I should know, I've had my fair share."

He patted his belly and sucked until his cheeks bowed and the *slurp* came from the bottom of his cup. "Roasted marshmallows on top of caramel, then malted milkshake."

I eased back against the seat and drank until my belly bowed with the cold mess, then handed it over. "I can't finish it. You have the rest."

"You sure?" Hope sparkled in those eyes.

He made me smile, like *really* smile. I can't remember how long it'd been since I felt that. *A long time.* "I'm sure.

That was the most delicious thing I've tasted in, like forever. Lucky Dad isn't here...he'd pitch a fit at the thought of that in his Bentley."

"Lucky he's not here then, isn't it?" Russell took the last of the shake and drained it just as fast as he had his own.

"Yeah," sadness stole my smile. "Lucky."

We sat there with the motor running for a second. "You're gonna be okay, you know that, right? Whatever happens from this moment, you're gonna be okay."

I turned my head, meeting his hard stare. He was ex-military, a former Navy SEAL or something, a walking, talking, breathing weapon. I lowered my gaze to his hands and wondered how many lives he'd taken. "You think so?"

He shifted on the seat, turning that muscled body my way. "I *know* so. Your father was a smart man...Ruth. He knew this day was coming."

"But family is family, right?" I answered, as my uncle's face moved into my mind...him and his sadistic fucking sons.

"They ain't shit against fancy lawyers, just you wait and see. You're already protected."

I forced a smile and reached out to pat his hand. "Why couldn't I have been born into a regal family? I might've ended up with someone as sweet and innocent as you."

It was his turn to laugh as he shook his head. "Hey, don't let the shake fool ya, underneath this is a tyrant." He pressed the button and the window rolled down as he shoved the car into gear and rolled us forward, just enough for him to toss the empty cups into the bin before the window rose and we backed out.

My lips were sticky and sweet. I licked the mess and

pulled my visor down to check my lipstick. "They should've made a bodyguard trying to cheer you up on the day of your father's funeral long lasting lipstick."

"I hope to God there's not a call for that kind of thing. After all, there's only one of me to go around and I don't share my favorite drink with just anyone." He gave me a smile and a wink.

I reached out without thinking and placed my hand on his thigh, and hard muscle flexed under my fingers. Desire flared...gray eyes, cold lips that filled me with heat. "Oh God, I'm so sorry," I snatched my hand away.

The energy in the car changed. No longer playful, it was tainted with an edge of seriousness. "It's okay, really...it's okay."

But it wasn't, not with him. He was sweet and caring, and totally not who I wanted...*or who I needed.* A touch skimmed across my mind, darkness and seduction. The presence was gone practically when I registered it.

"Look," Russell stared at the road straight ahead. "Don't get me wrong, I'm flattered, like beyond flattered. Shoot me in the chest and I'll still be sitting here dumbstruck that you'd even touch me, let alone think of me. But your father was buried today, Ruth."

"I know."

He glanced my way. "You might feel different in the future, you might not. If you still want to pursue this later, then we'll make plans for me to resign. The last thing I want is for you to be hurt, and being romantically involved with your bodyguard isn't something your family would take lightly."

"Fuck my family," I growled.

He drove, slower this time...more *carefully.* "I agree,

fuck your family. But family is family, and I don't need their lawyers using this as a way to tear you to shreds. I care more about you than to let that happen."

God, this was a mess, a full-blown mess. "Can we forget this happened? Can we start from the end of the drink, can you do that?"

"I can one hundred percent do that." He smiled at me, but the smile didn't quite reach his eyes.

In my mind, it hadn't been *his* thigh I'd reached for…or his hand on the wheel I saw, or him taking care of me. *Elithien.* His voice echoed through my soul as Russell slowed the car and turned into the drive.

My gut tightened, my hand went to the armrest, and the nails into the stitching of the leather. It was an opulent brown brick colonial, with open dark shutters and rolling green lawns. I hated this place, even now, years later…I'd burn this place to the ground if I could.

The car crept along the drive, waiting as women hurried across, giving us a smile and wave as they went. I didn't want to be here. I didn't want to be anywhere near here.

I glanced along the cars and found the blue Maserati and the cherry red Lamborghini parked along the drive. All of a sudden, that marshmallow shake didn't sit well. I swallowed and nodded. "Here's fine, Russell." I reached for the door handle, making my bodyguard pull up sharply.

"But—" he started.

I was fumbling with my belt and shoving the door open wide as I climbed from the car and crossed the driveway. Memories crowded in as I climbed the front steps and strode through the open door into the house.

Heads turned, watching me, some I knew...some I didn't. The heads of boards, directors of multi-million-dollar corporations, Senators, and even the Vice President, Orlan Powell. He smiled and nodded as I entered, blue eyes searching mine as he spoke to someone in the corner of the room.

I didn't care, not about him...not about this entire fucking charade.

I went straight to the fully stocked bar. "Bowmore, make it a double."

The bartender didn't blink, just grabbed a clean glass and reached for the ice. "Neat."

A nod of the head and he poured. I didn't feel a thing, not even the burn, as I downed the amber liquid and set the glass back down. "Again."

Amber spilled into the bottom as I turned, carrying the glass with me. I knew I was neglecting the duties of a dutiful daughter. I was supposed to be the one smiling, taking the time to thank everyone for coming. I was supposed to stand there and listen to their story of the Great Denzel Costello, the most upstanding man there ever was.

Only that's not how my family was.

Not when your back was turned, or fresh dirt was on your grave.

I sipped the Scotch this time and strode to the rear of the house, where the women gathered in the kitchen and gossiped.

"The Vampire deal hurt them, it really did. The company...well, Jerry said it's not doing too well. And no one is criticizing the man, God rest his soul, but Denny was reckless, and left us to scramble and pick up the pieces."

I froze just outside the door, listening...*to their lies.*

Their carefully constructed lies.

I bet they'd had the battle plan set in motion the minute my father took his last breath.

"They are such monsters," one of the other women gasped.

"They are," my aunt agreed. "Vile, savage monsters. Jerry is afraid the city will turn against him."

"It wasn't his fault," the stupid bitch cooed, falling right into the trap.

My gut told me she was as fake as she was plastic. All the nips and tucks in the world couldn't hide her greed and shallowness. "No, it wasn't, it was Denzel's fault, and that daughter of his," my aunt whispered.

I stepped out of the doorway, feeling the burn of the whiskey all the way into my belly.

"*Ruth,*" my aunt called.

Her dirty blonde hair was caught in a tumble of waves down the plunging neckline of her too tight black dress. Her eyes sparkled as she saw me, summoning a fake smile as I walked straight past the cancer cluster and out the back door.

So the smear campaign had started. The *cancer* had bloomed. A stage three cluster of lies and half-truths, all for a deal that hadn't been our idea to begin with.

A deal that lined every single pocket of Costello Corporation, everyone's but ours.

Dad never took a cent of the Vampire money, not for himself.

It was a bad deal, he said. A deal made in a desperate

fight for survival against a side they couldn't defeat. A deal the mortal world wasn't ready for—they weren't ready to see the true monsters of the world.

I had a feeling he wasn't talking about the Immortals.

The cancer would spread. Words, and whispers. By the time the wake for my father had finished, everyone would've been fed the lies until in their eyes, it was the truth.

The afternoon sun hit my eyes, yellow and cold, the sting not anywhere near what it had been. I drank and made my way down the back stairs. The smell of a BBQ filled the air. The men, gathering around with stories and drunken laughter. It didn't take long for them to notice me.

"Ruth, come over here," Jerry called as he stood with the men.

I wanted to stab the bastard in the gut and watch him bleed to death.

I was done with being the joke.

Done with doing what they wanted.

Done with calling them *family.*

Couldn't I take my company and kick them all out? Untangle the many greedy fingers all licking the cream from the pie. *My pie. My company.*

Acid spilled into the back of my throat as Jerry came toward me. "Ruthy, you okay, sweetheart?"

I would not cry. I would not cry.

I would not cry.

I hurried, swallowing that burn, and left them far behind, making my way along the path to the rear of the property that curled around the now empty stables and stopped.

You gonna cry?

The concrete was still the same, the path hidden by the hedges, out of view from the house.

Go on...cry.

I was a kid again, my spine pressed against the cold hard concrete, my wrist trapped against the edge, his hold crushing. One heavy hand over my chest, fingers finding the nipple.

Tell no one...got it?

Dark eyes staring right through me as he pinched and touched. His head turning, finding my bare thigh as my dress rode high. Hunger filled his gaze, cruelty, too. The way he looked at me stole all my strength.

Pay up, or we take what's ours.

That's what they said, right? That's what they wanted me to do...roll over, take what their filthy hands offered. Say nothing. I couldn't, not anymore.

Too silent...for far too fucking long.

"Elithien." His name spilled free.

I'm right here, the growl answered.

"There she is," came a voice behind me.

My heart hammered, punching into the back of my throat as I turned. Judah and Blane strode toward me, dressed in black and blue and purple like polyester princes.

"Dad told us to come and find you," Judah lowered his gaze to where I stood. "I see you found our spot."

Fire flared with the panic, and Elithien's growl filled my head. I tried to fight the memories, tried to keep him from seeing.

A savage, brutal snarl echoed deeper as the memory

came to life once more. *Tell no one...got it?* Judah's words echoed.

If he touches you, he'll answer to me, the Vampire warned. *I'll tear him apart, and this time I'll leave nothing behind.*

I swallowed hard as the warning echoed through my head. "I'm fine."

Blane lowered his gaze, taking in the black lace dress, lingering at my breasts. My skin crawled. "If I'd known how gorgeous you'd become, cousin or no cousin..."

"You'd *what*? Force yourself on me sooner? Go all the way and rape me next time?" The words were a croak.

Yet they didn't flinch. There was no rattling someone who'd already thought of all the possibilities...*over and over again.*

"Now...you listen here," Judah snarled. He smothered that rage, tucked it inside his glinting eyes as he adjusted his jacket. "We'd never hurt you, Ruthy," he forced the words through his teeth. "Never in a million years."

I'd never spoken about it, not what they'd done to me that day when I was just a child.

But it lingered between us *unspoken,* like a beast lurking in the shadows.

If it was just about the assault, I'd live with the terror of that day. But it wasn't just about my body, or about the innocence they'd replaced with fear. This was about the threat they'd painted on my windshield, and the rat they'd nailed to my door.

This was about stealing the biggest deal in my career, and ruining a man to get more than their share of the pie. This was about a line that'd been crossed...maybe not their line...*but mine.* "I know about the USB," I warned.

Panic moved in, wild-eyed and feral, tearing at the

seams, screaming until it was hoarse and still it was *here*, like blood in my veins and grit under my nails. "I know all about what you did."

The smile slipped from Judah's face. Blane's dark eyes hardened, glassy and cold.

Ruth, no. Elithien moaned. *Ruth...*

"You thought you could get away with it," I whispered as Judah took a step forward, dangerous and cold, like a killer. "You just made a bad—"

"*Ruth!* Here you are." Alexander came around the hedge carrying two glasses.

He took it all in. Judah towering over me, a menacing look in his eyes, and me, fists curled, ready to fight.

"Everything okay here?" the lawyer questioned, oblivious.

"Yeah," Blane grasped his brother's arm.

But Judah wasn't budging. His dark eyes bored into mine, promising terror. "You be careful now, Ruthy...you be *very* careful. I heard about the rat in your office...it'd be a shame if it was something else."

Something else. He meant me...

I'd lived with their threats all my life.

What was one more?

Until Judah let his brother pull him away. His lips curled as he glanced at Alexander then me once more, before striding away.

"What the hell was all that about?" Alex handed me a drink.

I watched them leave and lifted my glass with a shaking hand and swallowed.

"Hey," Alexander asked, handing me another, "you okay?"

A waitress wandered around the end of the hedge, trying to hide, most likely. I lifted my empty glass to her as one of the male guests came out after her, yanking his zipper up. A Congressman, I think. I turned away from the sight, waiting as she took my glass and forced a smile, the edge of her lipstick smudged. I was sure I'd find it around the base of the old guy's cock.

Am I okay? How about no. How about I still carried the pain you left me with…and *this…what the fuck was this?* My whole life was a game of cat and mouse, to anyone who wanted a piece of it…and there was a long fucking line.

"I'm fine," I lied, as revulsion filled me.

I'm right here, Elithien whispered inside my head. *I'm right here.*

This daylight world felt tainted now, filled with dirty old men who took advantage of anyone they could, cousins who wanted to be rapists, family who were waiting with knives drawn.

I knew what they waited for…*the reading of the will.*

I didn't want to be here anymore. I wanted to sink into the shadows and disappear into another world, one where monsters didn't hide behind a mask. In the center of that world was a Vampire…*no,* a den of them. Elithien, Hurrow…Justice, and Rule. I wanted them, that was the truth. I wanted to find out how much of a monster they really were. Call it a need of self-destruction, call it lust…I didn't give a fuck anymore. I was past the point of caring.

I wanted to be that woman in the room…I wanted to be the one they fucked.

"Ruth, have you heard a word I said?"

I jerked from the image and stared at Alexander. The

sun had dipped lower, shadows crept out of the cracks to spill across the ground. Slow, careful breaths.

"Where were you just now?" Alexander tilted his head, trying to catch my gaze.

I lowered my gaze to the drink in my hand and whispered, "I can't be here anymore. I'm leaving."

I handed him back the drink he'd brought, turned, and walked along the footpath, only this time, I avoided the house and everyone in it. I wanted to be home...I wanted to be alone.

No. Not alone.

I wanted to be with *them...*

My Mafia Monsters.

18

I stepped outside and lifted my gaze to the deepening purple on the horizon, then to my bodyguard hunched over the front tire of his car. I expected to see the Bentley waiting for me. I expected Russell to be long gone...I didn't expect this.

"Everything okay?" I asked as I came closer.

He muttered and cursed under his breath, words I didn't quite catch. Someone like Russell, I knew I wasn't meant to.

The trunk of the Chrysler was open, the jack lodged under the car where he knelt. He gripped the spare tire in his hands, thick, corded muscles along his back strained under his white shirt and black holster. The tire on the ground beside him was a mess, the sides had been slashed, gouges carved deep.

"I was gone five minutes," Russell snarled and fiddled with the nuts on the wheel. "Five goddamn minutes to use the bathroom and I came back to this."

Rage plunged deep, cold and cruel. I scanned the cars,

knowing exactly what I'd find. There was an empty space between cars further down, a space large enough for two ugly-ass Italian sports cars.

"Can you believe this?" He jerked his gaze to mine.

His gaze was sharp, sweat beaded along his brow. I'd never seen him rattled like this before.

"It was my fault." I answered. "I'm sorry. I'll have the tire replaced."

He bore down on the cross bar, tightening each nut, and rose from the ground. "You think I care about the tire, Ruth?" He closed the distance and glanced at the sprawling mansion behind me. "Are you okay? Did something happen in there?"

I barked a laugh. The sound was raw and unhinged. My hands were still shaking. *I* was still shaking. Gone was the pissed-off anger in his eyes, now it turned to something else. Something darker...*something dangerous.*

"Did they hurt you in there?" he asked.

God, he was like Elithien, pulling me under...making me weak. I wanted to give in to them, to be consumed by them...to be cared for by them. My heart beat frantically, like a bird trapped in my chest.

"I..." I sank into his gaze. "I...just want to go home."

He wasn't buying it, not for a fucking second. That careful gaze took in every inch of my body as he searched my face, then my hands and legs. But it wasn't my breasts he wanted to look at...he was searching for marks on my body...he was looking for a reason to hurt them.

God, I wanted to give him a reason.

I wanted to give them *all* a reason.

But these were my demons to battle...

"Please," I whispered. "Please, Russell, take me home."

Those words jolted him into action. He met my stare. On the surface, his gaze softened...*for me.* But underneath that shimmer of warmth lay something as terrifying as any savage Vampire—*honor, courage...and the ability to go to the end.*

"Always," he declared. "Just let me get the jack out of the way."

I smiled as, in an instant, he turned into that awkward guy once more. He turned, strode over to the jack, and lowered the front corner of the Chrysler to the ground.

Judah or Blane had done that, a retaliation for the things I said. I knew all their dirty little tricks now, and now they knew I knew it.

Russell grabbed the slashed tire from the ground, carrying it like it was nothing, and heaved it into the open trunk. The tools were packed away in an instant, the trunk closed, and the perfect black suit jacket was snatched from the roof of the car.

He shoved his arm in the sleeve and hurried to the passenger-side door. But I wasn't waiting for him to be a gentleman, I was catching the uncomfortable flare in his eyes as he dragged on the jacket over the sweaty patches of his shirt.

"Don't," I placed a hand on his arm, stopping him. "Don't worry about the jacket."

He was armed...*to the teeth.* The gun sat strapped off-center on his chest. He wore another on his hip, alongside a couple of loaded magazines. I'd never seen the weapons on him before...never even knew he carried them, not by the way he moved.

"You sure you don't mind?" he asked. "I can cover up."

I shook my head and forced a smile. "No, I don't mind at all."

I needed to get out of here.

To get as far from *these* people as possible.

I needed...*I needed.* I closed my eyes as that soft brush came across my mind once more.

I needed something else.

He was there, under my skin...in my head, *waiting.* Predatory eyes, cold, lethal precision.

The Vampire.

There were no lies with him or any of them.

No pretense.

No fear.

They were who they said they were—beasts...*monsters.*

I slid into the car as Russell opened my door and closed it behind me. Movement in the rear-view mirror made me lift my gaze. Alexander stepped out the front door and stood under the soft lights, watching me as Russell climbed into the driver's seat and started the engine.

We pulled away, careful not to dig up my uncle's perfectly manicured lawn, and eased over the concrete edging to climb back onto the driveway once more.

Headlights splashed against the ostentatious entrance to my uncle's property. My whole body was shaking as I gripped the seatbelt and Russell drove toward the city.

He took the highway, and I lost myself to the hum of the car's engine and the sparkle of the lights. The world moved on, just like I knew it would. It survived and it breathed, without a second thought for the great Denzel Costello, or for me.

I didn't know what I'd expected. Not this spiral, this

unravelling at the edges. Certainly not *them,* the four Vampires that waited for me in the dark. Russell hit the turning signal and exited off the ramp.

Ruth, Elithien growled.

I waited for him to whisper *come to me...*I ached for it. I burned to dive headlong into his dark, Immortal world. God, the feel of male was all around me, the scent of Russell's body crammed down my throat, the hunger for Elithien's touch. I closed my eyes, fighting the desperate urge to go to them. Maybe this time I wouldn't leave?

Maybe this time I'd give in...

Heat burned between my thighs as headlights flared behind us. I swallowed, my breaths hard and fast as Russell took the turns. Was Elithien behind us? Following us once more...like the predator he was.

Was he jealous? Watching our every move?

That fire between my thighs grew bolder.

"Ruth, you okay?" Russell inquired.

I kept my eyes closed. "Yes, fine."

"You moaned...I wasn't sure."

Jesus fucking Christ.

I opened my eyes and focused on the houses as we turned once more and this time, the bright lights behind us didn't follow.

I felt nauseous by the time Russell swung into my street. "Just out front is fine."

God, please don't let him want to come inside.

"You sure?" he double-checked.

That baritone rumble in his chest did all kinds of things to me. "Mmmhhmmm." I grabbed my bag and clawed the handle of the door as he pulled up outside.

"Ruth, I'm worried—" he started as I shoved the door open.

"I'm fine," I barked a little louder than I'd intended. "Just a headache."

The flare of headlights splashed along the street. I lifted my gaze as the car came closer...a big car...*a gray Explorer.*

I hurried along as I drove my hand into my bag and hit the garage remote. The door moved instantly, sliding up as I hurried down the drive and slipped inside. I hit the button once more, waiting with my heart clawing its way into the back of my throat as the door came to rest.

Those lips. Those perfect lips...

It was nice meeting you, Ruth Costello...very nice indeed.

The words resounded as I strode into the house and climbed the stairs. Desire spread through me, tightening my nipples until they rubbed against the lace of my bra.

I hit the light switch in my bedroom, kicked my heels off at the door, and clawed the zipper of my dress, tearing the damn thing over my head. Headlights shone from a car in the darkened street outside my house. I dropped my dress into a pile and stepped closer to the window in my panties and bra. He was out there, watching me, waiting for a chance to slip inside my house...to do things with me I'd never wanted—*before.*

But I wanted them now.

Oh God, I wanted them now.

I wanted those cold lips on my body. I wanted those fangs on my skin. The memory of that night I went to them stayed with me, the woman's moans as she lay draped across the bed in that room, that hidden room, closed off from the world. Were they biting her? *Were they fucking her?*

I thought of that...his teeth against my neck. His cock thrusting between my thighs. I closed my eyes and gripped the dresser as a wave of desire hit me. He was always there, lurking in the shadows...and in my mind.

I opened my eyes and yanked the drawer open. Leather shone against the light.

*Take the glove...*Elithien murmured. *Then go to the bed.*

My breaths deepened as I took the glove and switched off the bedroom lights. I did what he said...helpless to fight, and stepped to the side of my neatly made bed.

Moonlight spilled in through my window. I heard every creak in the house, *felt* every gust of wind. My cleaner had made everything new again, no empty bottles of Scotch, no thrown bedsheets from a fit of rage. Just perfect. Just *precise.*

"Like you, right, *Elithien?*" I whispered and sank to the mattress.

His deep chuckle was so clear as it slipped through my mind.

It was like he was here...in the room...*in my bed...*

Close your eyes, Ruth, he urged.

Panic sped my heart, goosebumps raced across my skin.

Then he was there, in my mind, brushing over me like a cool breeze, pressing against my body, making me yield to him...making me *hunger.*

I did as he commanded.

You want to pick up where we left off in the alley? he whispered. *The glove...*

Cool brushed my lips, once...twice, delving inside as I

opened my mouth. I lifted my hand, the rich smell of leather tantalized me. This was more than a dream, more than a fantasy.

This was him.

Phantom hands skimmed down my body. Cool air kissed my breasts, just like his touch.

I arched my spine as another touch brushed my mind, only this time, the energy was harder, *rougher.* Fingers skimmed my collarbone and grasped my throat.

"What?" I whispered. "What are you doing?" The scent of dark spices bloomed inside me as I breathed deep. *"Hurrow?"*

Princess, Hurrow growled, and clenched his grip around my throat just enough to speed my pulse.

He was darkness, and danger. He was the hunter you feared in the shadows.

The one you crossed the street to avoid.

Ruth, Elithien whispered my name, and kissed me. "Let us take care of you."

Calloused fingers travelled over my breasts, *Hurrow's fingers,* brushing over my nipple, as another delved between my thighs. I dragged the glove along the swell of my breast and trembled, that hunger burning deeper.

I shuddered under their touch, my body slick with need, hurrying and desperate. They were all I could think of...all I wanted. I pushed my hips into the air and parted my thighs. "I...*I want you.*"

Energy coursed with a brush between my thighs. I was wet, panting. I wanted more. I slid the glove down, pressing it against my core. "I *need you,*" I growled.

And you have us, Elithien promised.

That lick of searing heat moved deeper as I rubbed the

glove between my legs, the friction taking me higher...*higher.* Climbing to that point of no return.

Hurrow's grip around my throat softened as he pressed his lips against the hollow of my neck and growled *I'm going to fuck you, princess...and then I'm going to bite you.*

Shudders tore through me as warmth spilled...until my phone chimed *beep!* Wrenching me from the fantasy.

Stay with us, Elithien growled, his lips traveling down my stomach, as he slipped a hand between my thighs. *Stay right here.*

But the sound of the phone made my heart thunder, dragging me back to reality.

In the wake of my father's funeral.

And the attack from my family.

My own family.

Ruthy, you okay, sweetheart? My uncle's voice ripped through my mind.

I opened my eyes, and the spell broke. Sadness moved in as their touches turned faint, then disappeared. All the delusions in the world couldn't change my reality. *I was alone.*

I was utterly...and helplessly alone.

Ruth, Elithien whispered.

"Just go," I forced the words around the lump in my throat. "Please. I just want to sleep."

I dragged my feet higher and lifted the covers. Tears slipped down my face as I curled on one side of my lonely bed. I wasn't made for this savage world, not meant for their cruelty and their lies. Not tonight anyway. Tomorrow I'd be stronger...tomorrow I'd be *ruthless*...just not tonight. Not tonight.

Sleep moved in, cruel sleep that cut like a knife, severing my thoughts in one dark incision, and as I drifted into the nothingness, a thought tore free of the ether and drifted into the abyss.

The security never beeped, and I set it before I left.

The cleaner? The thought skimmed across my mind.

No. Not once had she left the house unarmed.

Someone else had been in my house.

Someone else had—

19

The reading of the will wasn't going to be a simple process. Nothing about my dad had ever been easy, so why the hell start now, right? They'd had months to prepare, and still it wasn't enough.

One more week to tell me what I already knew...*that the company was mine for as long as I could hold onto it.*

I woke up late the morning after the wake and lay in my bed staring at the single glove near my pillow. I could stay at home, even take some leave and maybe jump on a plane. Bali sounded nice, somewhere tropical and very...*very* far away.

But running away wouldn't solve a damn thing.

Monsters were coming, stalking with sharpened claws and blood on their snouts. A tremor cut through my body. These were precarious times...

I rolled out of bed and dropped my feet to the floor. *What do I do now?*

I had no anchor, no guiding light...no guidance.

My uncle wanted to whisper lies about my father.

He wanted a call to war.

Show them, kid. Dad's voice echoed. *Show them what kind of Costello you are.*

I once *had* a purpose…remember? I had a plan.

I was going to take my father's company and clean house. I shoved up from the bed and strode to the bathroom. I was going to take Costello Corporation out of the gutter and into the light.

Purpose filled me with each step, remnants of last night drifting to the surface as I lifted my gaze. A blush raced across my cheeks as I lifted my hand, fingers tracing my neck. I swallowed, remembering how Hurrow's grip had felt around my throat, demanding comforting, protecting.

Mine, the grip had demanded.

I hardly knew the Vampire…hardly knew him at all.

But he knew me, knew what made my knees weak… knew what made my heart thunder.

I turned away from the sight of my cheeks burning and undressed and stepped into the shower. Hot water ran down my shoulders as I washed and rinsed, taking my time with my hair, then stilled. *The security system…*I jerked my gaze upwards and turned, hitting the tap and ending the spray.

Fear crept in as I hurried, drying quickly and yanked on a robe. I raced down the stairs, stopping at the codepad. *Unarmed.* The lights blinked. I picked up the phone and dialed security.

"Hunter Security, how may I help you."

"My name is Ruth Costello my address is 1278 Palace Parade and my ID number is 181197. I'd like the information of the arming and disarming codes for the last 48 hours please."

"Yes, ma'am, just verifying your details, Ms. Costello. Please stand by."

I waited, for what felt like hours while they followed protocol. Every creak in the house was a potential footstep, and every car slowly driving by was them...*whoever they were* coming back for me, until finally the operator came back on the line.

"Ms. Costello we can verify there have been ten instances of a code accessing your security, six times you accessed it with your code, twice by the cleaner and twice more by an unverified code."

"Unverified...what does that mean?"

"It's a code our system doesn't recognize, ma'am."

Fear crept along my spine. "How...how does that happen?"

"Sometimes, Ms. Costello, a technician is contracted who doesn't work for us to add a code into the system. Have you authorized any such code to be added, ma'am?"

"No, I haven't."

"We can send someone around to remove any codes that haven't been authorized to you—"

"Yes, do it." The words sounded distant and cold.

"But unfortunately, due to the Public Holiday we won't be able to get there until next week. Is there someone who can stay with you, or somewhere else you can stay until our technician can get there?"

I was already lowering the phone from my ear, my heart thundering...until in a blinding moment of clarity, I wrenched the phone high one more. "This, *unverified code*, can you tell me when it was added?"

"Yes, ma'am. It was added last week, on Thursday, ma'am."

My hands shook as I licked dried lips. Last week, while I was busy elsewhere. I lowered the phone, ending the call, and cutting off the operator midsentence.

My home was no longer my fortress.

My home was no longer safe.

I turned and lifted my gaze up the stairs to the closed door of my study. I placed the phone back on the cradle, and climbed. My pulse was frantic, beating in my temples, making me feel nauseous and lightheaded. At the top of the stairs ,I turned to my bedroom and slowly knelt, grasping my stiletto from the ground and sliding the three inch steel blade free from the heel.

The hilt of the blade was a wide flat handle curving in two places. Just big enough for my fingers. I clenched my grip around the end, leaving the sharp blade sticking out between my fingers before I turned to the study door.

It was quiet…quiet in my head, and quiet in my home. The eerie silence made my knees tremble, still I lifted my gaze to my study door and felt that deep-seated rage spill through. How fucking *dare* they come to my home. How fucking dare…

I gripped the knife and walked toward the study door, and reached out.

The soft brush came across my mind, urgent…*insistent. Ruth,* Elithien's faded voice invaded.

But like last night, I shoved that feeling aside, and slammed steel doors down inside my mind—cutting them off from my thoughts and my emotions.

I'd let myself become swept away in their world…and become a predator for my own family in return.

They saw me as weak. They saw me as wounded.

Even with the death of my father, I was neither of those things.

I reached for the door handle, the blade between my fingers aimed high as I barged in. *"What do you want from me!"*

But the room was empty. I moved in and swung the door closed, searching for another dead rat nailed to the inside of my door, and turned away when I found none. Shadows slashed from the drawn dark blinds around the room.

I glanced at the desk, and tried to remember the last thing I had there.

The laptop.

I shifted my gaze to the safe and swallowed hard. There was no way they could know about my private connection to the company's mainframe. I lowered my fist with the knife and rounded my desk.

One scan of the room and I placed the knife down and crouched in front of the safe's keypad and pressed the combination. No one knew the sequence, not Alexander, not even Ace. I opened the safe door and reached inside.

The laptop was right where I left it. So was the money and a folder with my personal documents. So who had come into my house? I lifted the laptop free and turned. It took me a second to yank my chair aside and lift the computer to my desk. The hairs rose on the back of my neck, first they threatened…and now…*they what?*

I waited for the screen to come alive and punched in the codes to access the company drive. *Beep. Access denied.* "What the fuck?"

I tried again, making sure I entered the correct code.

Beep. Access denied.

My heart was racing, making me shake. Access denied, what did that mean? I tried again, and again…my heart racing as a *ding* sounded. Only it wasn't the computer. I reached my head upwards as the sound came once more.

Ding. Ding. Ding…DingDingDing. The front door chime blasted until I ground my teeth and shoved to stand. I glanced at the laptop and stepped around the desk.

"I know you're in there!" Charlotte called.

I stilled in surprise and walked to the door.

"I'm not leaving until you open the door, Ruth!"

"Fuck." I whispered and glanced at the laptop once more, then strode out of the study and closed the door behind me.

I tightened the sash on my robe and made my way down to the front door. Locks clicked as I turned the lever on the deadbolt and opened the door. Charlotte stood on my porch wearing a low-cut top just like she had on the day Dad died.

The day Dad died…

The words echoed in my mind as I forced a smile. "What are you doing here? I didn't know you even knew where I lived."

"Oh, I knew where you lived all along," she forced a smile. "I just never thought you'd make me have to drag my ass all the way out here to check on you."

A chuckle rumbled in the back of my throat as I shook my head.

"You gonna invite me in, or leave me standing out here like some hooker?"

"We don't call them hookers in this part of the city," I

muttered and stepped aside. "They're escorts, and make a damn fine living doing it, as well."

"I bet they do," she stepped in, and stopped, wrapping her arms around me. "Good to see you, kid."

"Good to see you, too." I whispered, and exhaled.

It was like I'd been holding my breath for the past three days, ever since the morning of the court hearing. Now...now I breathed. She strode in all sass and vibrancy and looked around the place, stopping at the doorway to the one place I never visited—not since Alex left—the sunken lounge.

"Got coffee in this place?" she scanned the kitchen.

I lifted my gaze to the closed study door. "Sure, let me start the coffee machine."

So this wasn't a drop in and say *'Hi'* kind of visit. There was more. I swallowed the urge to groan and turned to the kitchen. There was nothing between us now, no dad to discus, or worry about. What were we? Former employer and employee.

I strode into the bare kitchen and stopped in front of the Goliath of a coffee machine and tried to remember how to use the damn thing.

"Wow, that is one hell of a coffee machine." Charlotte muttered behind me.

I shook my head and smiled turning to her. "I don't suppose you know how to use it?"

Her brows furrowed as she looked at me and laughed, then pushed up her sleeves and walked past me. "Don't even know how to use your own coffee machine. Things are pretty dire for you, aren't they, Ruth?"

She said it as a joke, or maybe she didn't. Maybe she

was fishing for more information. Silence was all the answer she needed.

"How about I make us a nice flat white and you put on some clothes. We can chat, woman to woman."

I wasn't used to being ordered around. But with Charlotte, it was different. I was still that woman nursing fractured bones and bruising, holding on to my last thread of sanity. She had taken care of me when I needed her, and then she'd taken care of my dad. But she was more than that, she was my confidant—she was my eyes and ears.

We'd never spoken about our relationship, nor had we spoken about all the things she witnessed and heard tending to my father in the last months of his life. She'd become family, more family than my own flesh and blood. So for her, I did as I was told, climbing the stairs and making my way to my closet, where I yanked on sweat shorts and an oversized shirt Alex had left in his rush to leave.

"Is this better?" Charlotte eyed me as I walked into the kitchen.

She slid the steaming coffee toward me and lifted her own, taking a sip as she winced. "It's too hot."

"Want to sit in the living room?" I picked mine up and waited for her to follow.

Two steps down from the doorway, and the grand living room opened up. The fireplace sat unused, the thick, luxurious sofas sat empty. It was one of the reasons why I'd bought the place, and yet, since Alex left, I hadn't stepped foot in here.

"This place is just stunning," she sighed.

The paintings, the high-end furniture…the hand-made

chandeliers, all the grandeur of this place and still, it never felt like home. Maybe it wasn't bricks and mortar I needed, maybe it was *someone.*

My thoughts turned to Alex, and that old pain stabbed into my chest. "Why did you come all this way to see me, Charlotte?"

She turned and pierced me with that look of exhaustion as she sank into a chair. "You really gotta ask me that?"

I sipped my coffee and sat on the end of one of the sofas. "I guess I don't."

"There's talk, kid, even if I am on the outside now. I still listen, and it's not good."

I took another sip, letting the heat slide down the back of my throat. "Let me guess, the deal with the Vampires has crippled the company, and it was all Dad's fault."

One eyebrow rose. "So you heard about that. What else?"

"Nothing," I said, and sipped my coffee. "Yet."

She made a low growl. "If your father was still alive, he'd have them executed for treason."

I laughed, if only because he'd have said the same damn thing. "Maybe not go that far."

"A long walk off a short plank," she muttered, "wearing concrete boots."

My smile eased the tension, even if it was a fantasy.

"You know they'll go after the company, don't you?"

I lifted my head, meeting her stony gaze. "Yes, and if they do, there's not a lot I can do about that. I have Alex. He has his ear to the ground."

"You think you can still trust him?"

I thought of all the heartache and the longing, all the

soft brushes of my hand and the times we'd spent together. "Yes, I can trust him."

She gave a nod and drained the last of her coffee. "I'm worried about you. Worried about this…Vampire thing you seem to be caught up with."

Drive home safely, okay, Ruth? West of the bridge can be dangerous. Her words slipped into my mind and that deep flare of surprise filled me once more. She'd known I'd been to see the Vampires, known exactly where I was.

"They're dangerous, Ruth." She leaned closer and reached out to touch my knee. "And I worry about you being all alone. Maybe if you want, you can come and stay with me for a while?"

Stay with her? I searched her gaze as the thought of that settled deep. I hadn't run in my entire life, and I wasn't about to start now. "Thank you for the offer, but I'm going to fight with everything I have."

"You'll lose," she glanced away for a heartbeat. Fear darkened her eyes when she looked at me once more. "I don't think you realize how dangerous your uncle truly is."

Anger flared with the words. She didn't think I could do it. Just like the others, she saw me as weak. I swallowed the pain and forced a smile. "Yeah, well, you haven't seen me fight, have you?"

She sat back and looked at her empty cup. "Maybe with the reading of the will it'll be different, give everyone a little time to process everything. Calm everyone down. I'm sure it's nothing."

She smiled and leaned back in the seat, looking around the room. "I really do like this place, Ruth, but it's a little lifeless, don't you think? It's not really you."

"No? Then where do I belong?" I waited for her to say my family home.

But she didn't, just gave a shrug. "I don't know, maybe somewhere else. A different city, a different life."

Somewhere where I wasn't the mob boss's daughter, that's what she meant. Turning my back on my family meant I'd be turning my back on me. I hadn't been bullied and threatened to turn away now.

"Well, thank you for the coffee. I'm not sorry for turning up on your doorstep. I was worried about you and I knew you'd just blow off my calls." She rose from the chair and took a step toward me, drawing me into a hug. "Stay in contact with me, okay? I worry about you."

I wrapped my arms around her and for a moment, let myself sink into her hug, before she pulled away.

"Right," she exhaled hard. "I guess that's all I came to say."

Apprehension slowed her steps as she climbed the stairs and made her way into the kitchen. The cup was rinsed and upended in silence, then she turned and gave me a soft, sad smile. "Take care of yourself, kiddo. My door is always open to you, day or night, and treat that bad boy well," she said, jerking her head toward the coffee machine.

She left, giving me a squeeze on the arm and headed for the door. I waved goodbye, watching her walk the path to the curb where her blue Mazda waited.

An uneasiness sat in my gut. I wasn't sure if it was what she'd said, or how she'd said it. Leaving everything I was behind for a different kind of life was like tearing out my heart because it wanted a different body. My hopes, my dreams, my blood were in this name and this company.

I couldn't just walk away.

Not now.

Not after all I'd been through.

I walked back to the kitchen and rinsed my cup before stacking them both in the dishwasher. There was something nagging me about being denied access to the company's drive, something that didn't sit right. I thought of calling Ace, but he'd had that USB I stole from Judah and Blane for over eight months now…and not a damn word.

How long did it take to break a damn code?

Too fucking long…

The study called as I looked at the clock. It was getting late, later than I expected. I'd go to the shipping yard, where no one would be expecting me.

I'd be in and out before anyone knew.

Knowing all the dirty little secrets my family had in store for me.

One last look at the front door, and I made for the stairs.

Dirty secrets and lies.

Maybe I'd find it all.

Maybe I'd expose them for what they really were.

Lying, filthy scum.

20

The sun was already dimming by the time I showered, dressed, and climbed into the Bentley. Time had no meaning for me now, not like it used to.

Death made the seconds slip away into the black hole of shock, and that empty void inside my chest was still growing, eating the minutes and the hours until the days were a blur of pain.

I licked my lips, fighting the urge to drive to the nearest bar and drown my sorrows.

Blue skies bled into purple as I backed out of my driveway and waited for the garage door to close. I looked at the place, with its slick steel and concrete facade, shoved the car into gear and turned the wheel.

I didn't belong. Not to the house or to this street.

I knew that...I'd *always* known that. I'd felt it my entire life, always one step out of rhythm, always one flicker of warmth from the cold. I swallowed hard and punched the accelerator, letting the hum of the engine fill the car. But I didn't lose myself in the deep, throaty purr. The magic wasn't there today.

There was only silence. Cold, hard emptiness, that made me want to shift in my seat and swallow hard. I hit the turning signal and turned onto the freeway, not bothering with the winding streets where I cruised in the Bentley.

The night was approaching fast. I hurried, climbing onto the entrance ramp and merging with the cars heading into the city. Everything felt strange for me now. This car, this city, like I was already being pushed aside… for someone new.

I clenched the steering wheel and lifted my gaze to the faint flicker of lights on the water in the distance. This river was everything to me, the lifeblood that ran through my veins…*my goddamn legacy.* I pressed the accelerator harder, and the needle on the speedometer rose.

Night had come by the time I turned onto the off ramp and nosed the car under the overpass, heading to the shipping yard. Bright lights glinted across the water, the cranes were in full swing, offloading a container ship docked at the port.

Business never slowed, not even for the death of my father. It didn't matter what was happening in the world, there was always money to made—*somehow.*

I nosed the Bentley down the backstreets that led to the gatehouse and tapped the brakes, rolling my window down as the door to the guardhouse opened and one of the security guards stepped out.

Dark, beady eyes and pock-marked skin. I didn't know him, and I knew everyone who worked here. I watched him give the car a once-over as he stepped up to the window and fixed that deadpan stare on me. "ID"

"What, no, *please?*" I muttered, and handed over my card.

He didn't reply, just grabbed the ID and stared at the image. There was something about the way he acted, cold, detached. "I haven't seen you here before. When did you start?"

He didn't answer, just handed the card back and met my gaze with a stony stare. "You're free to go through, *Ms. Costello.*"

Cold slithered along my spine with his words, stealing the heat of anger. I took my card and rolled up the window, watching him as I shoved the car into gear and rolled beneath the lifting boom gate. The night shift was in full swing, the docks humming with the skeleton crew, which suited me just fine. There were no managers' cars parked in the spaces when I pulled up. I killed the engine and stepped out, glancing behind me toward the guardhouse as I closed the door.

Lights flared as I pressed the button to lock the door. My heels rang out against the stairs as I climbed, making my way to the small office. It felt like forever since I'd stepped into the space. Smelled like it, too. I winced as I opened the door and the musty smell filled my nose. The lights blinked and buzzed as they brightened the space. The glare was too bright, almost neon out here in the dark. I killed the glare, then stepped inside and closed the door.

I headed for the desk, stepped around, and pressed the power button, waiting until the computer booted up. Seconds felt like hours and that seed of doubt bloomed. I wanted to call Alex, wanted to find out what he knew. My family were pushing me out and taking over. But it was too early to pull the trigger on the only gun I had left. Once the bullet was fired, then there'd be no going back.

Password?

I punched in the details and waited while the screen loaded. Seconds later, I was in, accessing the drive like I'd always done. Relief swept through me. I exhaled hard, and shook my head. I was imagining things...out of my mind with grief. I clicked on the folders, were exactly the same as mine. I clicked on HR and checked the latest folders...*New Recruits.* There were a lot of them, pages and pages of new employees...all hired in the last week, *with immediate start.*

A scrape came from somewhere outside. I lifted my gaze, but my focus was on the folders.

Cleaners.

Security.

Office personnel.

"That's not right." I clicked on the folders for our current staff. *Empty.* "No way..."

Blood drained from my face as I opened up the search and tried my PA, Denise Pree—employment terminated. Chief of Security, Gabe Stevens—employment terminated.

Supervisor, Night Crew Cleaning, James Joyce—employment terminated. "No, not James."

They couldn't do this! They couldn't even suspend anyone without going through the board...*and I was the fucking board.*

The scrape came once more from outside, only this time, it was closer. A click made my pulse stutter. My senses fired as I stabbed the button for the monitor, throwing the room into darkness.

No one knew I was here, only the guards at the gate…

I blinked, adjusting to the dark, and caught a shadow outside the window. Panic punched through, sending a chill along my arms as I glanced at the door…unlocked. The chair gave a squeal as I stood. Fear drove me now, as I stepped around the desk and rushed to the door. The handle rattled as I turned the lock. I froze, watching the mechanism catch and hold. The handle turned once more, and rattled again.

My blood ran cold. I stepped backwards, unable to take my gaze from the window. "Who's there?" My voice sounded shaky. But there was no answer, no call from the guards on their rounds, no reassurance from any of the workers outside. I swallowed hard and backed toward the desk, reaching out without looking away from the door as the handle rattled once more.

My fingers shook as they danced across the screen of my phone, calling the only person who came to mind.

"Ruth?" Elithien's growl was soft and seductive.

"Please tell me that's you outside the door." I whispered.

He snapped to attention in an instant. "No, I'm at a meeting…"

The door handle rattled again, drawing a whimper from my lips. "Someone's trying to get in, someone is…."

"Fucking Christ, are you at home?" he snapped.

"I'm at the office…at the dock."

"Stay right there. Is the door locked?"

"Yes, but, Elithien." I closed my eyes, fear was a knife to

my chest. "They're all gone. Everyone I knew…I'm all alone here."

Heavy footfalls sounded at a run. "You stay right there, Ruth. I'm sending someone now. Ruth…*Ruth. You there, baby?*"

The door rattled again. Only this time, there was a scrape against the lock, like something slid inside. "They're almost in, Elithien. They're—" I dropped the phone as the lock turned.

Fear gave way to desperation. I lunged, slamming my body against the door as it cracked open. My hands trembled as I grasped the handle, gripped it tight, and pushed, flicking the lock once more.

"Give it up," a male snarled through the door. "You're done here, *rich bitch.*"

I held on as he banged against the door. The wood shuddered, but the lock held. My heart thundered, booming in my ears as I leaned hard against the door. *Fight.* The need raged inside. *Fight them!*

In an instant I was back there, in that dark alley once more. "No…*no, I won't accept that. I won't.*"

One heel tore free as I pushed against the floor and gripped the handle. It turned in my grip, burning the skin on my palm.

"Ruth!" Elithien's voice was so faint now, coming from the phone on the floor.

The door shoved inwards, jerking my hold loose. Panic roared through my veins as I stumbled backwards. He stood in the doorway, the guard from the gate.

"Get out," I tried to keep the tremor from my voice.

"Now, is that any way to talk to an employee…*Ms. Costello?*" He stepped into the office.

I backed up until I hit the wall. Anger and fear were a dangerous cocktail. I glanced at my phone on the floor. "My PA knows I'm here."

He just smiled and shook his head. "No, she doesn't."

"How do you know I didn't just call her on my cell?"

That sinister smile only grew wider as he stepped further into the room. "I think I'll take that chance."

I glanced behind him at the doorway and lunged. But he was fast, and big, his bulky frame closing me in.

"Get the *fuck* out, now!" I roared.

He moved fast, striding forward to grip me around the throat. "You shouldn't have come back here, Ruth. You should've been the good little, brokenhearted daughter and stayed away."

The words were a fist to my gut. "Who the fuck are you working for?"

He stilled for a heartbeat. Hate and rage mingled in my blood. I swung my hand and slapped him hard across the cheek. His head snapped to the side, and he froze for a second. Rage glistened in his eyes as he turned back.

I was done now, I knew that. They'd find me bleeding in a ditch somewhere tomorrow…or worse…dead.

His knuckles turned white as he clenched his fist. "Say goodbye," he sneered, and drove it through the air.

I closed my eyes as a deep, savage voice came from somewhere in the room. "Goodbye."

A brutal *crunch* came instead of the blow I expected, followed by a howl of pain so raw and horrifying it made my stomach roll.

I opened my eyes to see Justice standing there, his fist closed around the guard's hand.

One eye patch and a menacing snarl. He towered over

the security guard, his powerful frame swallowing the space like a jaguar ready to strike. Justice was the perfect Vampire, possessive and dangerous, a terrifying villain. Only this time, he'd come to save me.

The pathetic piece of shit buckled, falling to his knees.

"You okay?" Justice searched my gaze, one fast scan of my clothes was all business as he searched for torn clothes…or blood.

I'd never been so glad to see someone. I closed my eyes for a second and took a shuddering breath before answering. "I'm okay. Thank God…I'm okay."

Justice lifted his other hand and I caught sight of the cell phone. "She's okay." He listened to the voice on the other end of the phone while the guard howled with agony.

"Get the fuck *off* me!" the guard cried.

But Justice paid him no mind, instead, he squeezed a little harder when he turned and handed the phone to me. "He wants to talk to you."

My shaking fingers grazed his as I took the phone. I had to hold it with both hands. The sight of that only pissed Justice off more. Long fangs peeked out below his lip as I lifted the phone to my ear. "I'm here," I gasped.

"Thank *fuck*," Elithien snarled. "Did that piece of shit hurt you?"

"I'm okay," I whispered. *"I'm okay."*

"You're safe now. You stay with Justice. I'm on my way, and Ruth…"

"Yeah?"

"I think it's time you consider a permanent bodyguard, or maybe…a change of address." His cold tone said there would be no room for discussion.

The growl of a gunning engine echoed through the phone. The sound of urgency belied the gentleness in his tone.

"I'll think about it."

"See you soon," he growled and hung up the call.

I lowered the phone and met Justice's gaze. "He's on his way."

There was a nod from the Vampire as he turned to the guard. "You and I are going to have a little chat."

"Fucking *bitch*," the asshole snarled my way.

Snap. Bone splintered in Justice's grip and a fresh howl of agony ripped free.

"You don't fucking speak to her, *you got me?* You don't *look* at her, you don't even *breathe* in her general fucking direction."

A chill raced along my spine as Justice leaned close to him. "Your life hangs in the balance of your every fucking move. There's nothing I love more than to turn scum like you into an oozing pile of flesh."

I swear his fangs grew even longer.

The piece of shit just whimpered, then nodded. My pulse raced, the booming sound filled my ears. But it wasn't the guard I looked at...it was *him,* Justice, as my phone gave a *beep* to signal a message.

I stepped to the side, unable to take my eyes off the Vampire, and bent and grabbed my phone.

"The lady's shoe...pick it up," Justice commanded, and another howl of agony followed.

The pathetic excuse for a man fumbled, slapping the floor as he found my heel and lifted it into the air with a shaking hand.

I took it from him, and lifted my foot to put it on.

"Now the other one." Justice glared at him. "Before I realize how being pissed off actually makes me fucking hungry."

The guard gave a half whimper half groan and lunged for the other heel. He clawed the floor before he grabbed the shoe and shoved it toward me. "P-please…d-don't," he stuttered.

"Please *don't?*" Justice grabbed his hand and dragged him up from the floor.

Bones crunched and blood trickled through the gaps of Justice's fingers.

"Please *don't?*" Justice repeated. "You come in here, terrify a woman in her own fucking office, threaten her, try to beat her, and you're telling me, *please don't?*"

Cold plunged into the room. The chilling drop in temperature made me hold still. My senses were screaming, urging me to *run*. My breaths deepened, my nerves fired. My gaze flittered around the room. This Vampire scared me more with one snarl than the asshole had charging in here in the dark.

"Let me go," the guard whimpered as he cringed and stared up at Justice. "I'll tell you everything you need to know."

Justice smiled a murderous smile, but then, in an instant, the smile disappeared. He straightened, his gaze moving to the door. "Oh, you'll be telling us everything, alright. But it won't be me you'll be answering to…it'll be him."

I turned as shadows spilled into my office. Elithien moved without a sound. His gaze finding me, searching my eyes, then my body, as long white fangs slid from his

265

perfect lips. He was ferocious and feral, pure power sheathed in a massive form.

He said nothing…and yet he didn't need to. The guard jerked his gaze toward him, and shuddered.

Hurrow was behind him, cold and menacing, those terrifying eyes narrowed in on me as he crossed the room. He lifted a hand and brushed some strands of hair from my face. "You okay?"

I jumped at the touch. I didn't know why. Hurrow didn't care about my attacker, not yet…all he focused on was me.

"Do you know who I am?" Elithien asked the guard.

His voice was so careful, so controlled, like glass, one crack and it'd slice you open.

The guard just lowered his head. One nod from Elithien, and Justice dropped the asshole's mangled hand. Justice looked at the blood, and curled his lip and reached for guard's pocket.

"Who sent you?" Elithien inquired.

The guard stayed still, head down, spine curling until his head almost touched the floor. But Elithien didn't move. He was cold, hard…stone. "Tell me who it was."

A wounded sound came from the guard as he rocked back and forth. "My hand," he moaned, and gripped his wrist. "I need to go to the ER."

"The name."

The guard stopped moving, shaking his head. "I can't…"

"The. Name."

The guard wrenched his head up, tears shining against his cheeks as he screamed, *"He'll kill me! Don't you get that?"*

I winced with the shrill sound as Elithien carefully

knelt in front of him. "No, I don't get it. You're already a dead man."

The phone in the guard's pocket brightened, gleaming through the navy blue. A second later, it went dark, then brightened again, drawing Elithien's gaze. "Your phone, give it to me."

The asshole made a move, trying to shove upwards. Justice was there in a blur, driving out a massive size thirteen boot to pin his arm against the floor. "Ah ah, don't even think about it."

The phone screen brightened once more as Elithien reached out and shoved his hand in the guard's pocket, pulling out his phone. One press of the button, and he growled. "Passcode."

Silence followed, until Elithien lifted his head. "Passcode or Justice, here, will do more than break your damn fingers."

"Five-five-seven-two."

Something silver shone from the edge of his pocket. Elithien pulled it free as the guard tried to shove against Justice's foot to get away.

A sickening sound came from Elithien blood-thirsty and inhuman. My throat tightened, and my gut clenched.

Steel sparkled in the predator's eyes as Elithien glanced at the guard. Then he moved in an instant, faster than I could track.

Snap.

The guard's head swiveled as it flopped sideways, shattered bone poking out of the side of his neck...and Elithien rose slowly, watching the life slip from the guard's eyes. "You don't deserve to live."

I retched with the sight. My knees were shaking as I

lowered my gaze to the phone in Elithien's hand, then to that small square packet on the floor. *A condom.* New, ready to be used...*ready to be used...*the thought hit me like a blow. I lifted my gaze, finding that menacing stare.

The truth shone brighter than any neon light. "He was going to rape me...wasn't he?"

There was no answer from the Vampire, just a flicker of...*fear?*

My knees gave way...strong arms caught me before I had a chance to fall.

"I got you," Hurrow was beside me, his arm wound around my shoulders, pinning me to his body.

But Elithien...Elithien just stood there, watching me with a detached look.

"Who?" I snarled, and gripped Hurrow, forcing myself to stand on my own. "Who sent him? I want to know *WHO THE FUCK SENT HIM!*"

"It's an unknown number. But I can guess."

Judah and Blane.

Their faces filled my mind as I trembled and shook, rage mingling with terror. "I'm going to kill them...I'm going to fucking kill them."

"You won't have to," Elithien growled. "I'll do it for you."

21

Headlights from the oncoming cars nearly blinded me. But I didn't turn from the glare. I stared into it until my eyes watered and the washed out stain lasted well into the dark.

But it didn't blur that tiny silver packet from my mind.

The condom...*meant for me...*

Rage coiled in my belly, cold and dangerous.

"Are you okay?" Elithien asked me for the fifth time in as many minutes as he gripped the steering wheel.

"You shouldn't have killed him." I looked out the window. "Not like that."

"He was *never* going to live, Ruth. I would not allow it. Not someone like that."

"No, I mean I wanted him to hurt." The words chilled me to the bone, but I was past the point of caring. "He should've felt naked. He should've felt fear," my voice trailed into the dark. "He should've felt..."

Elithien glanced at the road, then back at me once more.

You gonna cry? The cruel voice of a boy slithered from the cracks of my past.

I closed my eyes. "Bone raw," my voice turned husky. "So terrified that the feeling becomes you, another you, stains your soul for the rest of your life."

You tell no one, got it?

"What he received was too easy." I winced and glanced away. "Far too easy."

"Don't you worry," Elithien's voice was steel cold rage. "I'm saving myself for the piece of fucking filth who paid him."

He drove the Explorer hard, riding the brakes into the corners, only to gun the engine as we flew out. Headlights flared in the side mirror. Hurrow, Rule, and Justice were behind us, driving just as fast as we raced across Crown City to the quiet suburbs.

Soaring apartment buildings turned into neat brownstones before they became bigger and more expensive. Trees blurred between them, manicured lawns and long driveways blurred in the headlights.

I searched my memory for Judah's place. The huge white monstrosity he shared with his brother...*the fuck palace...that's right* and lifted my gaze as we turned the familiar corner. "That's it over there."

Elithien downshifted, slowing the Explorer as he turned into the driveway.

The sickening sound of snapping bones echoed in my head.

I slipped out of my skin, returning to that small,

terrified girl as she lay pinned to the concrete path behind her uncle's house.

Headlights splashed against the front door as we braked to a stop. The Explorer's engine died and the driver's door opened.

They were shadows in the night. A blur of menace and fury sweeping the front of the house as lights came on and my cousin, Judah stepped out from the front door. My body didn't work, not like it should. My hand trembled reaching for the handle as I opened the passenger's door and climbed out.

Judah tore his panicked gaze from Elithien's to mine as I climbed the stairs. "Want to tell me what the fuck this is about?"

I lifted my hand, my fingers shaking as I pressed the keypad on my phone.

"911, what is your emergency?"

"Yes, hello," I answered, my voice eerily calm. "I'm at 777 Crown City Way and I'd like to report an assault."

"Ma'am—" the operator started.

My cousin's eyes widened as I lowered my hand, ended the call, and tossed the phone through the open door of the Explorer. He glanced toward the phone, then back to the Vampire as Elithien stepped further up the stairs, forcing my cousin backwards. "Yes, she *is* unharmed, *no thanks to you.*"

Judah flinched, glancing to the three other Vampires as they flanked Elithien on either side.

"You think you could get *anywhere* near her?" Hurrow growled.

"I should fucking kill you right here," Rule added.

Justice stepped closer. "Just like we did the piece of shit you sent after her."

"Whoa, wait," Judah was panicking now. "What the fuck are you talking about? What *piece of shit?*"

I stepped closer, hearing Blane's voice from inside the house as the front door opened further.

"Judah," Blane's voice was stony as he stepped out.

But Judah didn't look at his brother, just remained focused on the four Vampires as they stepped closer. "What's going on?" Blane demanded.

"They've come to…" Judah started. "They've…"

Judah broke his stare and stumbled backwards. Elithien moved faster than I could track. He had Judah around the throat in an instant. Judah's feet tap-danced in the air as the Vampire lifted him off the floor. My stomach rolled, fear weighed like a stone.

Silver glinted in the headlights' glare as Blane leveled the muzzle of a gun at Elithien's face.

"Put him down, Vampire. Don't make me blow your fucking brains all over the damn landing."

The ferocious sound that came from Hurrow chilled me to the bone. But the sight of that gun aimed at Elithien brought me undone. "Put the gun down, Blane…or I'll kill you my damn self."

There was a flinch as he turned to meet my gaze. The hiss of tires echoed in the distance and the faint splash of headlights lit up the stairs. "Threatening me was one thing…*but rape?*"

Justice snarled. "Weak-ass cocksucker. You like to threaten women?"

My pulse surged at the sound of his voice. I took a step

as the sound of a car came closer. In the distance, I swore I caught the faint sound of sirens.

"You're going to jail," Elithien stated. "Both of you. Just make sure you don't sleep…you never know what kind of monsters will be waiting in the dark."

A car pulled up, skidding as it stopped.

"Ruth?" Alexander called as a door opened and closed. "What the hell's going on?"

I fought the need to turn away and find him. But I was riveted by that gun. "We have the phone and the messages," I stepped closer. "Pushing me out of the company was one thing, but sending one of your bullies to threaten and rape me was beyond anything I thought you were capable of."

Blane jerked his gaze to mine, his eyes widening. But the muzzle dropped, aiming at Elithien's chest. *Jesus… please, don't shoot…I'll do anything, just don't shoot.*

"I have no idea what the fuck you're talking about," Blane answered as police cars screamed up the drive and pulled to a stop.

"Put the gun down!" a male officer roared.

"Ma'am," a female called. "Did you call in an assault?"

"I did," I turned.

"I'm not going to tell you again, *put down the gun now!"* The officer roared.

"Okay…*okay,"* Blane sank to the ground, and lay down the gun. "It's down…*okay, it's fucking down."*

I met Alexander's gaze, then the female officer's as her partner mounted stairs and kicked the weapon toward her.

"These two men sent a man to assault and rape me."

She stilled, her gaze narrowing. Alexander gave a small shake of his head and glared at Blane. "They did *what?*"

My Vampires were there, standing between me and the two men who'd never really been family. My heart swelled at the sight of them…my protectors, my avenging angels, dressed in cold skin and tailored suits.

"You'll find all the evidence you need here," Elithien turned and lifted his hand with the phone as Blane was grabbed by the officer and spun.

"Hands against the wall!" The officer roared and took the weapon from his hand.

"I have a permit—" Blane started.

"If you don't take him away, officer, you'll find that permit rolled into a tight ball and shoved up his ass," Justice warned.

The cop just turned and stared at the Vampire. White fangs glowed in the night. They would've killed them… torn them apart in an instant. An ache settled in my chest, and pride and desire swirled around me.

I was safe with them…for the first time in my life, I was truly safe.

"This is a fucking low way to get back your seat on the board. It's not over, you can be guaranteed of that."

I folded my arms across my chest, covering the shudder that tore through me.

"The phone," the female officer demanded, holding out her hand.

"Five-five-seven-two," Elithien answered as he gave it to her, watching as Blane was pushed past Alexander to the police car.

"Jesus," the female officer muttered and lifted her gaze from the phone. She shook her head, yanked a bag from her pocket and shoved the phone inside. "Hands behind your back."

Handcuffs were yanked from her belt and snapped around Judah's wrists in an instant. "You're a tough guy, huh? Like to threaten a woman with rape?"

"I didn't fucking do it." My cousin thrashed hard enough to meet my gaze. "So this is payback after all those years, is it? You always were the weakest of the family... now you can play the victim all over again."

The shudder burned like a coal sliding down my center. I dropped my hands and strode forward, climbing the stairs with a clatter of my heels. I acted on instinct, the *need* to lash out, wrenched my hand back and drove it through the air to slap his face.

His head cracked sideways, hair lashed his temple and stayed there, messy and disheveled. There was a second where I inhaled hard before he was shoved forward.

"Move," the female officer growled. "Ms. Costello," she gave me a slow nod.

Doors were opened and closed in the police vehicle as I lifted my gaze, meeting the steel gray of my Vampire. Elithien said nothing, just held the stare. Something passed between us. I wanted to speak, to tell him why I'd called the police and not allowed him to handle it the way he wanted.

"Ruth," Alexander called.

I turned away, finding the man I couldn't escape. A hand slid around my neck, the grip firm, sliding up to cup my chin as Elithien turned me back to him and, in a thunderous heartbeat, kissed me.

The world stopped still, dark, day...I had no idea where I was. All I felt was that possessive grip around my neck and the hungry taking of my mouth. He kissed me deeply, moving against me, and in my mind, I was back in that alley, pressed against the mossy bricks with his hand down my top.

But that wasn't where he stayed, was it?

No, that wasn't where any of them stayed.

Elithien broke the kiss, moving away just an inch to stare into my eyes. I knew then...knew there wasn't a damn thing he wouldn't do for me. Life, death...it was all inconsequential in that moment.

"My turn," Justice murmured.

Massive hands wrapped around my waist, lifting me. I was once again in his arms, pressed against his body.

"Ruth, for fuck's sake...*no*." Alexander called behind me as the police car started.

The siren blared for a second before it fell silent. Red and blue lights flared, the colors splashing against the leather patch on his eye as Justice lowered his head and kissed me.

He was so soft, so gentle, taking only as much as I'd give him. I reached up and wrapped my arms around his neck, pulling him harder against me. There was no fear with them, no terror, only a sense of power, one I'd found amongst these Immortals.

My Immortals.

"And me," Rule neared.

Justice held me as Rule reached up, sliding his finger down my cheek and breaking our kiss. "You belong to us, Ruth," he whispered and leaned closer, kissing me hard, stealing my breath.

A car door opened and closed. I was stolen from his stony lips with a ravenous growl. My lips burned as Rule broke away. It was a good burn, an *aching* burn. Heavy footsteps echoed, coming near. I turned my head as Justice lowered me until my feet hit the floor.

"I told you before, we share, but not everyone."

"Not anyone," Elithien added. Surprise surged inside me as I met his gaze. "Only you, Ruth...only you."

Hurrow lowered his head, his breath tickling the hollow of my neck. The kiss over my vein made my knees tremble. I closed my eyes, loosing myself as Hurrow countered, "We can't let you go now, Ruth. I just can't risk it." He lifted his head and stared into my eyes. "I can't think about anything else but you."

My heart thundered, and for a second, I almost gave in, almost let myself sink into their world completely, until reality crashed back down. "My company."

"Fuck the company." Elithien growled. "Let it all go under. You want money? We have enough money you couldn't spend in a thousand lifetimes."

"It's not the money."

"Then what is it?"

Hate swirled around me. I was eight years old once more, being held down. Hands on my skin...over my chest. Blane's sneer was sinister and cruel, knowing exactly what he was doing. The pain at my nipple, and even after all these years, it still roared back to life like a freight train. His fingers skimmed the smooth swell of my nipple, the tender skin multiplying the pain as he pinched and twisted.

I could feel the weight of my rage, low and heavy in my gut. Not liquid like acid. It was hard and heavy...cold and unforgiving. Savage. Honed. Steel. I lifted my gaze to the glint in the Vampire's eyes. "I want what's mine."

"This can't happen again," Hurrow urged. "What if next time—"

"There won't be a next time. I'll have protection, I promise."

"Every second of the day," Elithien urged, his brow furrowing as he came closer. "No compromises."

"Every second," I repeated.

Justice just gave a snarl of disapproval. The sound made me warm inside. I reached out, taking his hand in mine. "I promise, Russell is good at what he does."

"He'd better be, or he'll have to answer to me." the big, dominating Vampire answered.

No one came close to them, not in their protection, or in their aggressiveness. But I had meetings to attend...*day meetings,* and I had to learn how to juggle this.

I was falling for them, hard...and fast, falling head over heels, until I was swallowed by their deadly aura. A shudder coursed through me. My teeth barely began to chatter as Elithien strode forward, shrugging out of his jacket to drape it over my shoulders.

The way he looked at me...the way *they all looked at me.*

Dangerous.

Intense.

Obsessed.

I felt it all. Every burning need that lingered between us...and the *consuming* ache in my chest. I wanted them, more than I wanted air to breathe...more than I wanted anything at all.

Even the Costello Corporation.

22

"We're all ready?" Constance Purdy questioned, staring over her thick, tortoise-shell glasses frames.

"Yes," Alexander answered coldly. "We are, now just get on with it."

I sat on one side of the room, Alexander and my uncle to the middle, and my cousins to the other side. Judah was sporting a neat black eye. One he hadn't had climbing into the police car. I clenched my jaw, knowing what sick, depraved lengths he'd have gone to to keep me from this moment.

I wanted to hit him, to scratch his eyes out, to rage and scream at not just him but his father sitting on one side and his brother on the other. But I did neither. I sat here, cold and quiet, while inside a tornado brewed...one that'd been coming in the weeks since my father died.

None of them looked at me, especially Alexander.

I'd tried to speak to him, Tried calling his attention as he stepped out of the elevator and strode past. But there was no turn of the head, not even a polite smile...no kind of acknowledgement.

Ruth...no. His words reverberated inside my head.

"Right," Constance muttered, and shuffled the papers in front of her on her desk. "Well, with that, let's get started."

"Finally," Jerry snarled with a sneer.

I watched them, the way they leaned forward, eyes trained on the files in her hand, desperate to find a mention of their name...*hoping it was somewhere at the top.*

"This is a reading of the Last Will and Testament of Denzel Hargraves Costello. First of all, I want to say that family has always been the most important thing for me. I know I haven't always been the most upstanding leader of our family. But if I can't do the right thing while I was alive, I want to make sure I do it in my passing. So this is what I leave behind...first, to my brother Jerry...'"

My breath caught. Here it was, everything I'd waited for, everything that both terrified me and filled me with hope, and yet...as I sat here with the world standing still, I didn't think about my dad. I didn't even hear the words, just saw the look of rage crowd my uncle's eyes as he got not what he deserved...but a small portion of a fortune.

Constance talked, and the more her lips moved, the less I heard. All I could see was storm filled silver eyes, and feel the brush of Elithien's hand along my cheek.

I gripped the armrest of the leather chair, digging my nails into the cushioning, then shoved to stand.

"What the fuck do you mean, a million dollars?" Blane growled as he jerked his head toward me. "Is that it? Read it again."

"Mr. Costello, I can assure you, I've read this more

times than I can count and it's a nominal sum, one point five million each to you and your bother Judah."

"That is fucking bullshit," Blane howled.

But I was already walking, stepping around the leather chair and heading for the door as Constance continued. "And the rest of my estate, with a sum total of five billion dollars in stocks, bonds, and real estate, including the sole ownership and position as head of the board of directors of Costello Corporation, goes to my daughter, my Ruth. Give them hell, kiddo."

My hand was already on the door handle, turning it and pulling the door open as I stepped out and closed it behind me.

My heels clattered on the tiled floor, but I felt nothing, just an aching emptiness…the silence a kind I'd never felt before.

Footsteps fell in sync one step behind me, only these were the heavy sure *thud* of boots. I didn't need to turn my head to know who it was…

"Ms. Costello!" Constance called behind me as I reached out and stabbed the button for the elevator. "Ms. Costello, you haven't heard it all!"

"So, did you win?"

You tell no one, got it? My cousin's snarl echoed back to me from all those years ago. I remembered how it had felt then…how that small, helpless child lay there, blinking away tears, powerless to fight them…and powerless to run. Next time, I vowed to save myself. Next time, I vowed I'd win.

"Yeah, I did." I answered as the elevator gave a *ding* and the doors opened.

I lifted my gaze to Russell's reflection in the elevator as

we strode inside. He turned and pressed the button for the garage.

"Hold the fucking door!" Blane growled from the other side as I turned.

He tried to step in, until Russell lifted a hand, blocking his way. "This one is full."

My cousin lifted a savage glare to my bodyguard. His lips curled as Judah stepped up behind him. Hate raged in his eyes as he met mine, but he said nothing, not even as the doors closed and we were alone.

Blessed silence...blessed, bitter silence.

The truth hit harder than words ever could. I wanted it all...*well,* I'd thought I did. But now that I had it...well, it felt...*empty.* My future waited just as empty as my life. Desperation and duty welled inside me like a poison. The pain of it carved across my chest. I winced and lifted my hand, pressing the heel against my breast.

"Ruth, you okay?" Russell stepped closer.

I just gave him a nod. My breath came in short, sharp pants. All day I'd waited...all damn day I'd paced the hallway of my home...all day I felt the walls closing in and I couldn't wait to breathe. "If I asked you to take tonight off, would you?"

"Well, seeing as how you're the boss, I wouldn't have much say in the matter. But I'd have to advise you against it. Advise very strongly, in fact."

"I need to be alone." I barked, then lifted my eyes to him. In the reflection, they were wide and hollowed. "I just need quiet and to think."

"Why don't I just hang back? Drive you to your home, then give you a little space. But I'll be there in case anything goes down."

Anything goes down...
He meant repercussions.

The elevator came to a shuddering stop and the doors opened. My heart leaped as Russell stepped out first and scanned the garage. The events of last night hit me harder than I'd thought. My pulse was thundering, filling my head with a roar as Russell turned toward me and lifted a hand, motioning me forward.

I left the world behind, left the trauma and the noise, as I strode toward my father's car. Russell lifted the remote and pressed the button as he opened the passenger-side door and waited, scanning the garage as I slipped inside.

Moments later, he was climbing into the driver's seat and starting the engine. I secured my seatbelt and pressed my head against the headrest, waiting to feel something other than numb.

Movement came from the elevators as we backed out of the parking space and eased forward. I caught Blane lifting his gaze as we shot past, and then we were gone. I looked ahead as Russell drove me back through the city and headed home. I glanced at the clock, it was already four in the afternoon.

Sleepless nights and confined walls. I crossed my arms, and rubbed my bare arms. I turned my head, searching for the tall trees and glinting warmth of the afternoon sun, but they were just shapes. Just light. Just everything but real. Nothing was real. Not in my world, not with all the money and power in the world.

A shudder tore through my chest as I stared at the flicking glare of the sun. All I wanted was the dark...the perfect, *consuming* night. Russell tapped the brakes and nosed the car into the driveway. I hadn't even noticed we'd driven halfway across the city.

Numb.

A volcano brewing under the surface. I reached for the handle of the door. "Thank you, Russell. I need to be alone now."

He said nothing, just killed the engine, as I strode around to the connecting door to the house. I tossed my bag onto the counter in the kitchen. My phone, wallet, and a lipstick slipped out. I grabbed the mess and shoved it back inside. My phone came alive, an unread message from Ace waiting in the notifications.

My fingers trembled at the sight. I couldn't look...not now. I closed my eyes and turned away. That storm inside me grew violent, lashing my insides with savage blows. I opened my eyes and stared at the stocked alcohol cabinet. My feet were moving before I realized. I yanked open the door and grabbed the bottle of Scotch and a glass from the drawer underneath.

Through the closed door, I heard the garage door roll down and come to a stop. I kicked off my heels and padded barefoot up the stairs, my thoughts a whirlwind. Faded sunlight spilled along the landing as I hit the last stair and turned to my room.

Neat. Perfect. *Empty.*

I crossed the floor and stopped at the dresser. My hands shook so bad the glass danced on the surface as I let the damn thing go. Desperation roared as I cracked the lid and poured. Amber splashed the bottom. I watched it through blurred tears, grabbed the glass once more and downed the contents in one gulp.

The burn was perfect, searing along my insides. The

only thing I felt…was the phantom touch on my cheek. A touch from a man I wanted…from the *Vampires* I wanted.

They were here with me, lingering in my mind, just waiting. Elithien. Hurrow. Justice, with his mammoth arms wrapped around me, protecting me, and Rule. Rule, with his vicious stare. I poured once more, filling my glass just a little more.

My hands didn't shake as much this time as I lifted the glass to my lips and swallowed. I filled the glass again, then left the bottle on the dresser and yanked open the drawer. Black leather shone. I grabbed the glove and lifted it to my cheek. Smooth and cold, it warmed to my touch. .

The room spun a little as I turned and carried my glass and the glove to the bathroom. The afternoon sun was fading, turning yellow to dark purple. Haunted eyes met mine as my feet hit the cold tiles. "Five billion dollars."

The words were flat and cold…*haunting.*

"Five billion dollars, and it's all mine," I whispered, and lifted the glass, watching myself in the mirror. My fingers clenched around the leather and that storm inside me grew a little too close, lashing and clawing, hurling a lifetime of memories at me.

Cruel memories.

Lonely memories.

All the laughter at my expense, all the sly smiles and the pats on the ass. All the times where I was alone. *"So fucking alone. You never really stood up for me, did you, Dad? You never were the white fucking knight."*

But…five billion dollars, and the seat at the head of the table.

It was all I'd wanted…*so why wasn't I happy?* I drained my glass and turned away from the mirror, making my way back to the bottle once more. The room was darkening, turning bruised and dangerous. My heart sped at the sight.

I lifted the glove and closed my eyes, inhaling the traces of his scent. My white knight had come, just not in the way I'd expected, and he'd brought with him a coven of steely-eyed killers. I opened my eyes and poured.

I didn't want to be alone.

I wanted to be with them...I wanted their lips on my body. I wanted the promise of Hurrow's kiss along my neck to go one step further. I wanted to be *alive*. To be wanted, to be *seen*...

I drank down the glass and poured again. I reached up with numb fingers and worked the buttons on my blouse, and unzipped my skirt. I let the clothes fall to the floor, including my underwear, and opened the drawer once more.

Black, thin, lacy...heat moved from my belly to lick between my thighs. I dressed carefully, clipping and smoothing, pink skin peeking through the soft lace of my bra. The panties were French-cut, barely riding the curve of my ass.

I wanted to be sexual. I wanted sex. I wanted to be drowned in them. The memory of Elithien's hand around my throat roared to the surface, forceful, *unyielding*. I wanted to be owned by them, to be more than the name and the face. I wanted them to know me...*the real me*.

The one hidden under the surface, the one waiting in the eye of the storm. My steps were a little slower, the colors a little brighter, as I made my way into my closet. I stepped past the safe black pencil skirts and business suits and headed toward the end of the rack—where I never went.

Red shone brighter, floor length, the slit open at the thigh, showing far too much leg. I'd bought the dress off the runway in a spurt of daring excitement, and had never worn it. I curled my fingers as I lifted my hand, then forced them to unfurl.

My heart thundered as I worked it off the hanger and slipped it over my body.

It fit perfectly…a little too perfect. I spun, looking at myself in the mirror. A toned, long thigh, high breasts, the glimpse of my black bra peeking out from the top as I bent over.

I turned before reality could force its way in and make me change into something safer, and went back to the bathroom. I took my time, drinking and applying makeup, striding into the bedroom to put on music…the loud, heavy beat swallowed the room before I returned.

I was taken back to the Wolf's club…and the stripper. The way she danced. The way she was watched. They didn't care about her name…they didn't care about her money. They only care about her body, and the way she made them feel.

I wanted that.

I wanted Elithien to look at me the way those men had.

I wanted Hurrow…

And Rule…

"Oh God," I groaned as I reached out and gripped the counter. "And Justice." *Justice, with the black patch over his eye.*

Justice, who towered over me. I still felt his hands on

my body, still felt the intensity of him as he'd gripped the guard. His gaze roaming over me. *You okay?* That guttural snarl wormed its way into my head.

I opened my eyes and stared at my reflection. Dark, glittering eyes, just like his. Deep, blood red lipstick. My hair pulled high, revealing the long line of my neck with just enough hair untangled to soften the style.

I sprayed my favorite perfume into the air and walked through. Dark and seductive, it was me in a bottle. By the time I stepped into my heels, it was after eight. I'd spent almost four hours drinking and dressing, fantasizing about them.

I grabbed a small clutch and went into the hall. My steps were a little unsteady, enough that I grabbed the railing and took a deep breath as I tackled the stairs. But the room barely spun now. I was sobering, and that wasn't a good thing, not on a day like today.

*Ruth...*Elithien's voice drifted in.

I didn't answer. Instead, I opened that connection we shared. Flickers drifted through my mind. My hand caressing my breast as I adjusted my bra, the sight of my panties cut high over my ass. The touch of the dress, and the glimpse of my bare thigh peeking out from the slit.

A growl echoed through my mind. They were all there...*every one of them.*

Jesus fucking Christ, Rule whispered.

My lips curled at the savagery.

I let one more image give way, the tangle of my hair, long wisps of hair falling away to brush my neck.

Desire drove through me. I swayed under the need, reaching out to grasp the counter in the kitchen.

What the fuck are you doing? Hurrow asked. *Trying to kill us here?*

"Don't you know seduction when you see it?" I whispered to the empty kitchen.

Fuck me...

My lips curled a little wider as heat moved through me, burning hotter than any alcohol could. That was the point...the whole, undeniable, suggestive point.

Their hunger swallowed me, dangerous and calculating. I grabbed my cards and slipped them into the clutch and went to the door. I punched the buttons, arming the system, as I yanked open the door.

I felt the Vampires inside my head, smiling in a savage, dangerous way. They were ready to play the game...the game that hopefully ended up with us in bed. My body hummed with the thought as headlights came on, parked three spaces away. The sleek, black Chrysler pulled out and Russell pulled up along the curb.

"Changed your mind about staying in I see." He looked at me through the open window as I yanked open the door.

His breath caught as I stepped in, hands clenched around the steering wheel. But he said nothing, just turned his head and stared respectfully straight ahead as I closed the door behind me.

"Say it," I muttered, elation and desire dying a little inside me. "It's too much, isn't it?"

"No." The answer came hard, and fast, his growl a little huskier than normal. "No, it isn't too much at all. It's just perfect, actually...*more than perfect.*"

Pain and desire raged in his eyes as he turned and

forced a smile. "He's a lucky bastard, that's all I'm going to say."

The smile came back hard and fast. "What makes you think I'm dressing for someone else?"

"No one dresses like that for themselves, Ruth. I don't even want to think about the sonofabitch who kisses you tonight. I'm here to protect you, and keep you safe…"

An ache cut through my chest at his words. The sad smile fell for a second. "Right, where are we headed first?"

He was such a good guy, so perfectly professional, and caring. Any woman would be beyond lucky to meet someone like him. So what did that say about me…that I didn't feel that same burning desire as I did when I thought about my Vampires? "How about some food? Care to join me for dinner?"

He chuckled. "I think that would be a disaster. All you'd see is me dropping food into my lap every time you looked at me, and it'd be setting the very wrong tone for the paparazzi combing the streets, desperate for a glimpse of you."

"Then somewhere dark and quiet," I answered. "Where I can eat alone."

He gave a small nod and turned back to the street, glancing into the side mirror. I let him drive, taking me through the back streets to a small, hidden restaurant I'd tried and fallen in love with twelve months before.

"You remembered?" I asked as he pulled up.

"Always," he answered, and shoved open the driver's door, making his way around the back of the car to open my door.

"At least let me buy you a meal, even if you sit a table over."

He just chuckled and slowly nodded his head. "Sure, only because their steak is the best in the city."

We walked in, him half a step ahead, scanning the darkened corners as he held the door open for me. I had no reservation, and no need. The maître d' lifted his head from the booking sheet. His eyes widened when he met my gaze.

"M-Ms. Costello, what an honor."

I forced a smile. "I hope I'm not imposing. But do you have two tables? One for me, and one for my bodyguard?"

"For you?" He lifted his hand, snapping his fingers. "Immediately."

Waiters scurried at the movement. They rushed forward, taking us to two small tables toward the back of the restaurant shrouded by shadows and the soft amber glow of a fire. It was perfect.

Heads turned as I walked through. Men and women stared, but tonight I didn't care.

Not what they thought of me.

Not what they heard.

I sat as the young waiter pulled out my chair. I glanced over, watching Russell take the opposite seat on the table next to me. I faced the wall...he faced the entry.

"I'm happy to order, if that's okay." I added, placing my order, and adding some of their best Scotch.

Russell spoke after, ordering a simple steak and sides.

We waited in awkward silence, me sitting back and trying to ignore the whispers as the drone in the restaurant became that little bit louder now I was here.

The drink came fast, the food not long after. I ate seared salmon cooked to perfection, taking my time, and drank more. By the time we were finished, it was over an hour later.

Dark, dangerous energy swallowed me. They were waiting for me...waiting to make a move...waiting for me to give them what they wanted.

A nightclub slipped into my mind. One my family owned, dark and seductive, the perfect stage for what I had in mind.

You sure you don't want to come to this side of the river? Elithien growled.

I chuckled and whispered, "I come to that side of the river and there's only one place I'll end up."

That such a bad thing? It's happening either way, Ruth.

"Cocky much?"

When it comes to you...yeah, I am.

I let the connection slip, taking another drink as Russell finished up his second dessert for the evening. I didn't turn my head, just let him enjoy his meal in peace as he wiped the corner of his mouth and placed his napkin down, satisfied.

I raised my hand, signaling the hovering waiter, and lifted my glass. I took my time, sipping the alcohol now that I had a little food in my stomach. *Five billion dollars.* I swirled my glass. *Five billion dollars and more power than I could ever imagine.*

I couldn't process it all, even sitting here drinking my Scotch and staring at the wall. It was too much, too everything.

My third glass came, the waiter bending low. "I hope all is satisfactory, Ms. Costello?"

"Yes, thank you. I'd like the bill please, for me and my bodyguard."

"At once, ma'am."

He bowed a little lower, rushed a little faster. Memories slipped in, my father at his most powerful...all heads turned when he entered the room. I understood now. It wasn't just about money and power. It was the image of who he was, just like right now, it was all about me. Russell drank the last of his soda and waited. I swallowed the contents of the glass and rose, making my way to the front of the restaurant once more.

They all watched me, taking in my dress, my body... my face. I kept my focus straight ahead, the alcohol settling into my bones. If there was anything I'd learned to be good at, it was holding my liquor.

I paid the bill, not even looking at the amount, then Russell held open the door for me. Cameras flashed as I stepped out. I lowered my head, making my way for the passenger's door.

"Ms. Costello!" they chanted, calling me left and right.

The loud drone only muffled when I slipped into the passenger's side of the car and Russell closed the door. I reached up and pressed the lock as they swarmed the side of the car, holding their lenses to the tinted window and snapping.

The driver's door opened and closed a second later. The engine started, and we were pulling away, leaving the chaos behind.

Russell handled the car with precision, pulling out of the restaurant parking lot and onto the road.

"Unredeemable," I murmured. "If that's okay."

"You sure?" he asked, overstepping for a second before he turned back. "Of course."

He steered the car through the streets, heading for the

darkened night club. It was time, time to quiet this storm building inside me, time for me to take what I wanted, to seduce and destroy all in a swirling tornado of lust.

Russell turned the car, pulling into the lane and parking in a reserved spot at the rear of the building. I'd been here a few times, once with Alexander and twice on my own, but both ended in disaster, leaving me to go home alone.

But not tonight.

Tonight was different.

I was different.

I opened the door and got out, needing the freedom of being on my own for a second. He scrambled to catch up, shoving the door closed and pressing the lock before his ground-eating strides made him surge ahead of me in no time.

The air throbbed with a heavy beat, sending the pulse along my skin as Russell opened the rear door to the nightclub, nodded to the guard standing inside and waited for me to step through.

The guard knew who I was in an instant. His eyes widened, then smiled. "Ms. Costello."

Soft lights did their best to show the way through darkened hallways. I sucked in a breath and felt that fist inside my chest loosen and followed my bodyguard. A waitress made her way toward me carrying a tray of empty glasses, dressed in scanty panties over fishnet stockings and high heels with a shimmery silver top.

She lifted her head and smiled as she passed.

It didn't matter if she knew who I was, didn't matter if the lights dulled my face. It didn't matter if I lost Russell in the crowd as I stepped out onto the dance floor. I scanned faces, plunging deep into that desperate storm inside.

They were here...

I could feel them, their hunger carving through the warm, swaying bodies. My gaze gravitated to the bar. Steel eyes flashed for a second as someone moved through the crowded lines. I stepped around two young lovers, his hands on her hips, pulling her hard against him as he stared into her eyes.

A familiar face came through the crowd before it was gone, but it wasn't one of my hunters. I thought for a second it was…

Someone bumped into me. I spun, finding a male smiling, looking down at me. He was gorgeous, dark eyes, and a wicked smile that dimpled his chin.

"Hot damn," he muttered. "You are fucking stunning."

He had his hands on my waist, moving closer like a lion for the kill. I grabbed his wrists and shoved, tearing his hands from my body. "I don't think so."

There was a flicker of disappointment in his eyes, as muscles tensed in his jaw. The air plunged in temp as a possessive growl cut through my mind.

Someone reached around, grabbed my hand, and spun me hard.

"What the *fuck* are you doing?" Alexander barked, moving far too close.

I tried to take a step back, which gave him the wrong impression, as well as the handsy asshole behind me.

"Who the fuck are you?" came the growl at my back.

"I'm her *boyfriend*, who the fuck are you, *asshole?*" Alexander snapped.

Alcohol was pungent on his breath. His tie was loose,

his hair disheveled, and there was an unhinged look of fury in his gaze.

"Ex-boyfriend," I added, meeting Alexander's cruel gaze.

Power surged inside me, explosive and lethal. I lifted my head, finding Elithien across the dance floor. He searched my gaze, then shifted his gaze to Alexander. Hurrow was at his side...and the dangerous stab of jealousy came from somewhere to my left.

My heart thundered as I stared at Alexander, who had moved far too close. He was one word...and one touch, away from being savaged by four of the most dangerous Immortals I'd ever met.

Alexander's grip tightened on my wrist. "You didn't answer me," he growled. "What are you doing here, Ruth?"

"Firstly," I snapped, and looked down. "You're hurting me." I jerked my hand away, breaking his hold. "Secondly, it's none of your business."

But he wasn't listening, pressing closer, eyes flashing, unhinged and wild. For a second, I wondered why I'd hurt for so long after he betrayed me. What was it about him I'd needed so bad? I couldn't see it now, couldn't feel it. He was no longer my need. I searched for a different high now...*a darker high.*

"What the fuck is going on with you lately?"

I shifted my gaze to the spot where Elithien had stood moments before. Alexander caught the shift and glanced over his shoulder, searching the crowd at the edge of the dance floor.

But my Vampire wasn't there.

When Alex turned to me once more, there was a cruelty in his eyes, one I'd never seen before. "You don't answer my calls," he said as he lifted a hand and dragged it through his hair. "You disappear for hours at a time. You're not careful anymore, out like this in a fucking bar with strangers." He lowered his gaze to the neckline of my dress.

I could feel his need, palpable and choking. His breaths deepened, tongue peeking out to skim his lips as he undressed me in his mind. "It's like I don't know you anymore." He lifted his gaze and stared into my eyes.

"If you don't know me?" I answered and curled my top lip, hating how I was the one made to feel cheap and afraid. "Then maybe it's *you* who needs to be careful."

I took a step backwards, not caring anymore. "Maybe you need to run back to your girlfriend, Alex…and stop lusting after me."

Shadows closed in on all sides. Elithien stalked through the crowd like the predator he was. Those on the dance floor moved aside, unconsciously knowing danger prowled close. Alexander turned at that moment, and the life died in his eyes. "I see," he answered.

Hurrow closed in on the other side, and behind us, massive and menacing, came Justice, turning his head at the last moment to glare at the handsy asshole. A snarl rumbled in his chest and spilled from his lips, making the male shrink.

I was surrounded by a wall of formidable males.

"I'm glad you do," Elithien stared at Alexander. "Because I'd hate to be the one to upset her. But let me make this perfectly clear, Ruth belongs with us. I'd appreciate you respecting that…or you and I are going to have a problem, one I'll be only too happy to deal with."

Under the strobing nightclub lights, my former boyfriend paled.

Hurrow took half a step closer to Alexander. "We *all* will."

My heart lunged at the words. It took him a second, but Alexander gave a slow nod, then stepped backwards before he turned and left, shoving his way through the staring crowd, leaving us alone.

Stormy gray eyes found mine as Elithien murmured, "I'll give you one thing, Ruth Costello...you're never dull. Now...you said something about seduction?"

2 3

The heady beat throbbed inside me as I stared up at my Vampires. This wasn't what I had planned. There was nothing seductive about this, not the jealous ex-lover or the remnant of Scotch on my lips. Gyrating lovers seemed to sweep around us, like we stood inside a void of awkwardness.

"I…I wanted," I started.

"You wanted what?" Hurrow lowered his gaze, taking in the dress.

The tips of his fangs peeked out from his perfect lips. Pain mingled with the alcohol. I shook my head, hating the way everyone was staring. "Maybe this was a mistake."

"I don't think so." Elithien stepped closer, blocking my retreat. His fingers skimmed my hip as his gaze took in my body. "You came all this way," Elithien said, splaying his other hand over my ribs.

Hurrow moved closer, his hard chest pressed against my spine. "For us," he finished. "You did *come* for us, didn't you, Ruth?"

Images filled my head. Me on the bed, the leather glove fisted between my thighs. The sounds of my own panting release heavy in my ears.

My breath quickened.

I closed my eyes for a heartbeat...*it wasn't fair.*

"Who said we played fair?" Hurrow growled, and lowered his lips to the back of my neck.

The sound was carnal and suggestive, dragging my hunger to the surface.

Shivers raced along my spine...I turned my head to Justice. The huge male watched me with one glinting eye from across the room...the past rushed to the surface. He'd saved me that night in my office, he'd protected me.

That's how I felt now...

Protected.

Guarded.

Justice pushed off the bar, and everyone hurried out of his way. The male moved like all that *predatory power* wanted only two things, blood...and sex.

My heart stuttered at the sight. My breath caught.

Elithien just chuckled. "He likes you."

I flinched at the words and jerked my gaze to him.

"We *all* like you, Ruth," Elithien finished.

"Dance," Justice ordered, pressing against my side. I closed my eyes at the feel of his knuckles grazing down my spine. "For us."

They crowded in until all I could feel was them... Hurrow's lips on the back of my neck, Elithien's hand sliding down my hip, and Justice's touch lingering at the small of my back. He pressed against me, making me move. Elithien gripped my hip, moving with me.

"God, I want you…" Hurrow croaked.

The words hit me like a bolt of lightning.

Heat flared at the words. "Tell me…tell me how much you want me."

"I want you so much I'd murder everyone on this dance floor…just so I could take you to the floor," Hurrow growled. "I want you so much I can barely control myself when I'm around you."

"And we'd help him," Justice added.

In a fucking heartbeat. Rule's voice filled my head as he cut through the crowd, heading toward us.

Elithien's touch was still there, searing into my body. "This dress," he said as he dragged his fingers toward the long slit on my thigh. "Did you wear this for us?"

My pulse jerked in my chest as I answered. "No."

He chuckled as Rule just smiled and shook his head. Silver eyes glinted under the strobing lights as Rule took in every curve of my body.

"I bet you did," Hurrow disagreed as he moved his body with the music.

"Oh, I *know* she did," Elithien pressed in close.

One hand rose, his fingers dancing at the edge of my jaw as he slipped his other hand through the slit of my dress. My panties were thin…so thin, I felt every brush of his agile fingers…

"It's all about you, Ruth," Elithien whispered. "You can say no at any time."

No? The word hadn't crossed my mind.

But it was all about me with them. Every look…and every promise.

Breathless urgency swept through me. Strobing lights

splashed against my face as I tilted my head to his. His lips parted, the points of his fangs glinted, waiting. It was the alley all over again...*only so much more.*

I saw him now...saw him without the shadows, and without the lies.

I saw the hunger, the brutal strength of his passion.

His finger slipped under the edge of my panties. My hands trembled as I fisted his shirt and he slid his finger all the way along my crease. I burned for him, trembled for him...*I yearned for him.*

"Let go," Hurrow whispered against my ear as he dragged my scent in deep. "Let go, Ruth. Let go for us."

I wanted to...*I ached to.* "Wait," I forced the words.

I couldn't give in...not this easily. *I wasn't this easy.* I wanted to make them work for it. To be as desperate for me as I was for them. I stared into Elithien's eyes, then turned my head to Rule, and then Justice...I wanted the desperation to be a battleground between us.

The tip of Elithien's finger danced across my clit. I swallowed hard and dragged him closer. That animal lust raged in his eyes.

But others crowded in, the lights, the sounds...the *exposure.*

"Take me out of here." My words were a breathless whisper. "Please, take me out of here *now.*"

There was a flicker of desperation as Elithien slid his hand from under my panties.

One nod was all I needed. Elithien skimmed his gaze along my body and reached out, adjusting my dress. "Hurrow."

The Vampire at my back eased away and reached for

my hand. Cold fingers found mine as he gripped me tightly. "You ready?"

Ready for them? That's what he was asking.

I met his stare and gave a nod. "Yes."

I was ready for more…but the question was, *were they?*

We pushed past the young lovers on the dance floor and made our way to the front of the club.

The bouncer took one look at me and stepped forward, opening the door. "Ms. Costello."

The cold night air hit me as I stepped out. A crowd blocked the sidewalk, the young men looked me up and down, their eyes widening. I tore my hand from Hurrow's and stepped around them. Cat calls and wolf whistles filled my ears as a gust of air caught my dress, lifting it higher.

Hurrow jerked his gaze toward the young men and gave a threatening snarl, slowing half a step. The calls and cheers ended in an instant. Eyes widened as they stared at Hurrow…and shifted their gazes to Elithien, and Rule following close behind. But it was Justice that made them stumble backwards.

"We didn't mean…" one muttered.

The menacing growl from Justice made them turn and run. They wanted no part of that…

My *coven* of Vampires.

I shoved my dress down and turned, finding the darkness of the alley. My heels scraped against uneven asphalt. I shoved out my hand and stumbled. *Get control of yourself…please get control—*

"Ruth," the deep growl came from beside me. I pressed my palms against the wall of the club and moved into the darkness of the alley.

"I won't touch you without permission," Hurrow growled in my ear. "I need to hear you say it. Say *'I want you to touch me, Hurrow'.*"

"I want you to touch me, Hurrow." The words spilled free without a thought as I pressed my body closer to the wall.

The heavy beat from the nightclub bled through the bricks and into my hands. Hurrow moved closer, running his hand along my side, finding the opening of my dress.

His breath was a cool rush against my neck. I craned my head to the side, catching movement at the end of the alley. Elithien stepped closer, Justice and Rule on either side…watching us as Hurrow slipped his hand between my thighs.

I was wet, slick and ready, moaning as his other hand slid over my breast.

"Jesus fucking Christ, I want you," he growled.

I leaned forward, dislodging his hand as he traced my slit. His hand moved so fast, sliding from my breast to grip my throat. He was all beast…all hungry and ravenous.

He never once hurt me, never once made me scared. If anything, I wanted him more.

"Stop fucking with me."

He lowered his forehead to my back. I pressed my body against the wall and he moved with me, grinding his cock against my ass. I hated that I wanted him…hated that my knees trembled.

Hated that I had to crack before I allowed his hands on my body.

Gone was my family.

Gone was my life.

Hadn't I fallen far enough already?

Hurrow reached around, grabbed my hip with a cruel grip, and yanked my hips from the wall as he thrust his cock forward, shoving it against that aching part of me.

I braced my body against the wall as he slid the back of my dress aside. There was no more teasing, no more seduction, as he dragged his fingers along my crease and delved under the elastic of my panties.

Slick, he thrust his fingers inside.

"Fuck me, you're so ready," he moaned, low and throaty.

I shuddered, curling my own fingers, and rocked against his hand. His fingers slipped deeper before he pulled them free.

"There's only one thing I love more than the taste of blood," he growled in my ear.

The salty scent of my own desire filled my nose as he slipped his finger into his mouth. He stilled as his fangs grew longer, glaring white and lethal in the shadows.

I knew why Elithien waited at the front of the alley, knew why they all did. They wanted to watch us...*He wanted to watch us.*

"I warned you," Hurrow muttered.

The slow side of a zipper filled my ears. I became aware of everything about him, the weight of his hand, the slow slide of his finger. My heel skimmed asphalt as I widened my legs. I wanted this...*needed this.*

The brutal invasion of his cock stole my breath. I clenched my fingers as he drove deeper, making my knees buckle. He was there, holding me steady, as he slid free and thrust deeper once more.

His hand slid over mine braced against the wall. My

clenched fingers were trapped under his just like I was trapped by him...his hard length ramming inside me, stealing my thoughts as he caught my thigh and lifted my leg higher.

I told you before, we share, the memory of Hurrow's words surfaced, his voice mingled with Elithien's. *Only you, Ruth...only you.*

"Only me," the words tore free.

"Only you," Hurrow breathed against my ear, his arm lay against mine as he thrust once more.

Heat roared through me. The exposure. The filthy alley...the invasion. I closed my eyes as my climax bore down on me like a runaway train.

"Ours," he demanded.

The claim brought me undone. I shuddered, reaching up to grasp his hand as a whimper slipped free. But Hurrow wasn't done, slamming home over and over again until there were no more sounds, just the delicious, brutal invasion.

"I want you," I cried. "I want all of you."

"That's *good*," Hurrow grunted and stilled, hilt-deep inside. His cock twitched, filling me as he breathed hard. "That's real good, 'cause we're planning on taking you." He eased back enough to press his forehead against my shoulder. "Over and over again."

My legs shuddered and trembled, my breath came hard and fast. I skimmed my tongue along my arid lips as Hurrow pulled out. I felt the ache, the hollowness of where we'd met.

The feeling turned to sadness as he smoothed his hand down my back and slipped it between the cheeks of my ass, adjusting the French-cut panties I'd picked out on purpose, then smoothed the fabric of my dress.

Headlights blinded me for a second as Hurrow grasped my hand. The shadow-gray Explorer pulled up, and Hurrow moved to the passenger-side door, not once letting go of my hand, and yanked the handle.

I stared into the darkness, the soft green lights of the dashboard illuminating Elithien's face. Hurrow waited, the door open.

"You want me to go with you?" I whispered, trying to catch my breath.

"You didn't think we were done, did you?" Elithien questioned from behind the wheel. "That was just a teaser."

Hurrow gave a cocky smile, waiting patiently.

I prayed my knees would hold and stepped toward the open door, slipping inside the vehicle. The door closed behind me and we were alone. Elithien and me…with the scent of Hurrow's seed warm between my thighs.

"Did you enjoy him?"

My heart punched against my ribs. "Yes."

I waited for the jealousy, for the cruel slap across the face. I waited for the rejection…but none came.

"Good," Elithien shoved the gear into drive. "We're not like your former lovers, Ruth. You'll find no jealousy with us…as long as it is just *us*."

A shudder tore through me. "You mean Alexander?"

"I don't like him…I want you to be careful, always stay with your bodyguard through the day…or if you prefer, I can have one of the Wolves—"

"No," I answered remembering how Arran wanted more than friendship. "Russell…"

"Has been taken care of…and by taken care of, I meant instructed to retire for the evening. You won't be needing him tonight…or tomorrow."

Or tomorrow?

My heartbeat throbbed at the base of my throat. I swallowed hard as Elithien pulled the Explorer into the street. Headlights flared in the side mirror behind us.

I just fucked a Vampire in an alley. I breathed deep as the realization set in. All the makeup, all the perfect planning…all the pretense.

"You okay?" Elithien asked.

"I can't believe I just did that."

"Had sex?" He chuckled and glanced my way. "From where I was standing, you seemed to be enjoying it very much."

"This isn't me." I shook my head. "I don't do this kind of thing."

He reached over and grasped my hand, pulling it gently until he kissed my knuckles. "You are an amazing, vibrant…intensely fucking sexy woman, Ruth Costello. You deserve someone who is prepared to show you that, or in your case, four someones. I hope you're ready."

A shudder danced along my spine, catching my breath. In an instant, he'd stolen my doubts and humiliation and turned them into something seductive. He held my hand the entire trip, driving with one hand with the kind of smoothness that lulled me deeper than any alcohol could. "Why me?"

He glanced my way, punching the accelerator as we crested the upcoming ramp and hit the freeway.

"That night…in the alley. Why did you stay…with me?"

He was silent for a second, then he whispered, "Because of purpose…"

"The deal?"

"At first…and then I met you. You were so full of fire, blazing brighter than the damn sun, and I'd been cold for so damn long." He turned his head, meeting my gaze.

Something fluttered in my chest. Something so perfectly imperfect.

"But the kiss…" he stole a glance at the road and turned to me again. "Jesus, that kiss consumed me."

The Explorer surged that little bit faster, moving in and out of the traffic as we sped toward the bridge. I wanted him more than ever. I wanted to belong to all of them, to feel their cold touches warm against my body, to find out how far this could go.

And if it was nothing…*then I'd go back home.*

Just like nothing had happened.

But tonight.

Tonight was for Mafia Monsters…both mortal and Immortal.

We surged off the freeway and nosed toward the bridge that took us to the other side of the city. My thoughts blurred with the alcohol, and the brain-to-mouth filter refused to engage. "The money…that you move in the freight trucks, where does it go?"

There was a sly smile. "So you know about that, hunh?"

"I know everything. I thought you knew that already."

A chuckle spilled from between his perfect lips as the Explorer rose. The familiar *thud…thud…thud…*of the tires hitting the bridge carried through the cab. Headlights flared in the side mirror. That fluttering in my chest only grew stronger.

*I want you...*the words hovered on my lips. I wanted to break down the walls inside me for the first time in my life. I wanted to reach out and take something other than the next business deal. I wanted love.

I deserved love.

Didn't I?

I deserved someone special I could go home to. I deserved something more than the empty space that waited for me at home. I wanted something more than memories.

In that moment, I allowed myself to sink into the fantasy that this was somehow destiny.

Thud...thud...thud...

I stared at the hard line of his jaw and felt the strength in his grip as we shot off the bridge.

"You keep looking at me like that, and we're not going to make it home."

My heart sped with the promise. His lips curled as we tore off the bridge and into the darkness. I lost track of where we were, speeding through quiet streets this side of the city. He hadn't answered me about the money...he hadn't answered me about many things.

But we had time, didn't we?

Yeah, we had a lifetime.

The tires hit asphalt before I knew it. Still, Elithien didn't slow, spearing the car toward the shadowed mansion as the headlights splashed against the darkened windows. My palms turned sweaty as panic raced through my veins.

Sex.

Good sex.

What if I wasn't enough for them? What if I wasn't…

"You are," Elithien said as he tapped the brakes, pulling the Explorer up along the front of the sprawling house. "You're more than enough, Ruth, and tonight isn't about us. It's about you. *Always you.*"

He shoved the gear into park and killed the engine. Headlights swept through the interior of the cab as the midnight Explorer parked beside us. Hurrow climbed out of the driver's side and Justice from the passenger's, as the rear door opened and Rule emerged.

I trembled as Hurrow opened my door and held out his hand. Gray eyes glittered in the glow of the moon. My hand slipped from Elithien's hold as I stepped out.

Justice was there, reaching for my other hand.

Hurrow forced a smile, making him look younger. How old were they, anyway?

Questions crowded my mind as Justice led me to the front door. I waited for the tattooed Goth punk to open the door and smirk. But there was nothing, just a simple, quiet, relaxed entrance as Rule opened the door and held it open for me.

Warmth hit me like a furnace the moment I stepped inside, taking my breath.

"Too warm?" Justice growled, shaking his head in frustration. "I told them not to turn it up too high, but they don't listen to me."

I lifted my gaze to his furrowed brow. He really was upset. "It's fine, really…it'll just take me a second to get used to the sudden change."

He led me into the living room, the same room where I'd met Elithien with such an improper introduction. God, I felt ridiculous now, remembering how I'd stormed in here wielding a plastic bag with a dead rat like a madwoman, when it'd been Blane and Judah all along.

"You okay?" Justice asked.

I forced a smile and nodded. "Just thinking how I'm glad this is all over."

"Then, a cause for celebration?"

I gave a small chuckle. "Yes, I think so."

I let him lead the way, but this was familiar territory now. *Very familiar.* I glanced at the closed door as Justice made for the liquor cabinet. The last time I was here, moans had come from behind that door...and now I wanted to know why.

Glasses clinked as the front door closed. But I still carried the last traces of Scotch in my system, and the courage that went with it. I turned and strode toward that door.

Silence filled the room behind me. I felt the moment Justice turned to watch me as I reached out and grabbed the handle.

My breath caught as I turned and shoved the door open. Darkness filled the space, but underneath it was the scent of sex...I knew hunger and desire when I smelled it.

"Ruth," Elithien called as I reached in and found the light switch.

One *flick* and dimmed lights came on from far back against the wall.

"We weren't expecting you that night," Elithien protested gently behind me. "You have to believe that."

I didn't answer, just stepped inside. The room was filled with black and midnight blue. An obsidian colored bench seat was built in, running along the far wall to where the dark blue light splashed against the wall.

I caught the shine of steel at the foot of the seat. Leather straps were buckled and tucked neatly in place. There was a bed in the middle of the room. The end stuck out far enough I'd have been able to see it with the door open.

This was it...this was where the woman had been, almost naked. Heat raced to my cheeks. I wasn't stupid. Four Vampires and a lifetime of need. I swallowed hard and stepped inside, making my way around the bed to the seat.

"Say something," Elithien requested.

Tiny white lights glittered from the edges of the floor, reminding me of the strip club the Wolves owned, The Hunting Ground.

That's what this room was...a replica almost, but this was all private.

"You loved watching her, didn't you?" Elithien moved closer, knowing exactly what I was thinking of. "The dancer at the bar. You remember how every man was captivated by her. How she was wanted...*desired for what she was...not* who *she was.*" He dragged the back of his finger down my spine, finding the bare flesh of my lower back. "That's what you want, isn't it? You want to seduce and be seduced. You want someone to watch you, to *hunger* for you. To burn the image of your body into a memory they'll never forget. Then dance, Ruth...dance for us."

I flinched and took half a step forward and turned to meet his gaze. "What?"

Stars sparkled in his steely gaze. He was serious...*dead serious.*

"Dance, Ruth." He captured my hand and led me into the room. *"Dance..."*

24

ance...

I hadn't had enough to drink. Ice clinked against a glass as it was shoved toward me. Justice just stared at me, those perfect lips parted in anticipation. I looked down at the Scotch, then back to the Vampire's gaze.

"There's more where that came from...if you need it," he offered.

A tiny shake of my head. "I can't dance. I..."

"Have no music?" Rule asked as he stepped around us to a stereo against the wall.

My stomach tightened. I didn't want to dance, especially not in a room like this. Not one used for...*used for...sex with other women.*

"I promise you on my excruciatingly long and empty life that another woman will never come in this room after you. Not for sex...or for *feeding,* if you stay...if you give yourself to us."

Feeding. The idea hit me like a blast of hot air. I met

315

Elithien's gaze, fully understanding what he was asking. He wanted more than sex. He wanted my blood. I shifted my gaze to all of them. Need echoed in every single one of them. I couldn't possibly.

"We'll take it in turns, and take just enough to stay connected. We can find strength from other sources. But I promise you here and now, none of it will involve sex, not again."

He wasn't asking for something casual here. He wasn't expecting *'no strings attached'*. He wanted it all, my body and my blood. "What, no ring?" I joked.

"You want a ring?" Seriousness deepened his tone. "I'll buy you a fucking diamond mine...how's that? You give yourself to us and I'll give you the goddamn world, Ruth Costello."

"We all will," Hurrow growled.

"Every one of us," Justice added.

That monstrous black chasm waited inside me, a remnant from when Alexander left. I'd tried to fill it with work, tried to drown it with alcohol. But nothing had worked. It was too big, too monstrous. Too big for a Vampire to fill...

But four of them?
Four Vampires filling up my world.
Four Vampires to love, and to love me.

I lifted the glass to my lips and took a deep swallow, draining the contents. "Another," I demanded as I handed Justice the glass once more and I reached up, finding the zipper at the small of my back. "And someone said something about music?"

Heavy steps echoed before I even knew he'd moved. Justice tore from the room, clattering the glasses outside the room, and a heartbeat later, Rule moved to the stereo and pressed a button.

Soulful and husky...the voice of James Arthur filled the room, crooning about lies and sadness...and empty spaces.

"I brought the bottle," Justice's gaze gravitated to the open zipper at the curve of my ass. "Just in case."

I grabbed the bottle from his hand and rose up on my toes, meeting his lips. A ravenous sound rumbled in his chest as he kissed me. His large hand engulfed the side of my face as he cradled my cheek, deepening the motion of his mouth and pulled away.

"Take it off, Ruth," he commanded. "Take it all off for us."

I pulled away, feeling the weight of every stare in the room...well aware I was a mortal standing in the middle of a Vampire's den. But they wouldn't hurt me. That was the one thing I was sure of.

I slowly strode around the room, my gaze skimming the shining leather.

Just like the glove.

I could still feel it...still smell the richness. "Your gloves," I commanded, knowing Elithien knew exactly what I meant. "Get them for me."

The blur of movement came in the corner of my eye. He was gone and back in a heartbeat, striding toward me, and neatly folded in his hand was a perfect pair.

"You're not going to ruin them, are you?" One perfect brow rose. "They're brand new. I seemed to have lost a glove from my last pair. Pity. They were my favorites, too."

My lips curled into a smile as I took them from his hand.

"What, no kiss?" he whispered.

I moved closer, falling into him...and my heart kept going, surging to be closer to him. I kissed him hard and slow, pinching his lower lip with my teeth before I pulled away.

"Ouch," he ran his tongue along the lip, and smiled. "God, you drive me crazy, Ruth Costello."

I stiffened at the words. But there wasn't a hint of awkwardness in his gaze. Just pure purpose.

The kind I could get used to...very quickly.

"Sit," I jerked my head toward the sofa.

One throaty chuckle and he was striding forward, cutting across the room to take a seat and neatly cross his legs. The rest of them followed, all four sitting along the bench seat, watching me like I was their favorite meal... which, by the way their eyes glittered, I was.

I took another swallow of courage and bent, placing the open bottle in the middle of the room as I dragged the zipper at my back a little lower. I closed my eyes, leaving my body for a second to be one with the music.

Memories slipped in...

The way the dancer had looked as she'd stretched her arms over her head, pink nipples hardened.

Desire rushed in, licking between my thighs.

Cold moved in, kissing the top of my ass as I reached for the clasp at the back of my neck and twisted the clip. Satin skimmed my skin, running like hands over my body. There was a hiss of breath as the garment crumpled to my feet, leaving me standing in the black French-cut panties and bra.

I opened my eyes and stepped out, turning to find my Vampires mesmerized. I felt sexy…felt wanted.

Felt consumed by their need.

I dragged my teeth along my lip and reached for my hair. My fingers touched the clip. One twist and the strands fell, falling around my face. The black bra was see-through, with velvet edges and mesh cups. They saw it all. My nipples hardened as I stepped away from them, crossing to the opposite side of the room.

Spread your legs. The man's words returned to me from the Wolves' club. They wanted to see the dancer…to see *all* of her. I turned, giving my Vampires my back, and took another drink, swallowing hard and set the bottle on the seat. My trembling fingers slid along my hips, catching the elastic edges of my panties. I'd given my power away once before, and this was about getting it back. Getting all of it back.

My life.

My company.

My desire…

There was silence under the music. Cold, *chilling* silence. Panic filled me as I bent slowly, inching my panties all the way to the floor. I risked a glance, catching the glint of polished boots.

They were still there…was I that bad? I straightened, heat rushing to my face as I turned. Stony gazes were fixed on me…there was a glint in their eyes, a hunger I'd never seen before.

I was dancing in front of four of the deadliest creatures I knew…

Power hummed through my veins as Elithien

swallowed hard. I reached around, and unclasped the hook of my bra.

Movement came toward me in a dark blur. I was grasped, lifted. I opened my legs as Elithien dragged me close and locked my ankles around his waist.

Cool hands warmed on my back as he dragged me closer with one hand and speared his fingers into my hair with the other.

"I thought you wanted me to dance?" I taunted.

"Oh, you will, don't you worry." His deep voice was guttural.

Fear shivered around my body for a second as desire swept through me like a summer squall.

He pressed his hand against the back of my head, pulling me toward him. The kiss was everything I remembered...*and then some.*

Firm lips took what they wanted. The brush of a fang sent my pulse fluttering. I moaned into his mouth, giving myself into him. Fingers brushed my arms, a breath on the back of my neck. There were too many to keep track of.

Lips.

Fangs.

Growls of desire.

The strap of my bra slipped over my shoulder and the hooks at the back sprang free. Cold breath hit my nipples, turning them hard in an instant. Fear and excitement made me shudder. The feel of their touches stayed with me as Elithien strode forward and knelt, laying me along the leather couch. I looked up at them, all four looming Vampires.

"Fuck me, you're beautiful," Justice growled.

I clutched hold of the leather gloves. My breasts bounced as I hit the sofa. Stilettos dug into the leather as I pulled my knees higher. Elithien reached out, took the gloves from my hand, and slowly pulled them on, one finger at a time.

My lips parted, my breath caught. This was everything I'd wanted...everything I'd dreamed of. Elithien lowered his body to the sofa beside me. his gaze lingering on my eyes, slowly taking in my bare skin. He reached out, painstakingly slowly, and trailed a finger down my collarbone and over the rise of my breast.

I shivered under his touch as he circled the tip of his finger around that puckering flesh. His eyes glittered with hunger as his finger moved lower. Leather skimmed over my ribs and trailed down my stomach, then my abdomen.

He moved with precision, slipping his finger along my slit, then slid inside.

My hand slipped, palm slapping the sofa hard.

I parted my thighs, widening them until the tendons strained along my groin. Justice watched Elithien's hand with predatory attention as his finger moved deeper and slid out.

Silence surrounded me.

Chilling silence.

They made no move to take from Elithien...made no demands...only stood there watching as Elithien gently thrust his finger inside and out. Hurrow kissed me, running his hands over my breasts.

Elithien fumbled with his shirt. It was gone in an instant. There was only his pants next. The button was sent flying across the room with the grind of the zipper.

"This..." he growled, patting my opened thighs,

splaying me wide for his gaze. "Will be the start of your new life, Ruth. *Only the start...*"

He growled again and leaned forward, curling his spine. He was all I felt...all I smelled...I was absorbed by the feel of him as his hips surged forward.

A cry tore from my lips as he breached my defenses and rammed deep.

A snarl rumbled in my ear. Leather warmed against my skin as his hands snaked around my wrists and wrenched my arms upwards. He pinned me against that sofa, both with his hold on my hands and his thrusts as he drove his hips further.

I arched my back, meeting his delicious *unmerciful* blows. I grazed my teeth along my lip, smothering the cries in the back of my throat.

I tried to hold on as desire swept me away, taking me back into the darkness with him.

But I didn't think I'd ever really left.

He was an expert, quickening the strokes inside me until my body trembled with need and the heady scent of sweat filled the air. He turned his head, his cool breath a blast against my neck.

The end was coming, barreling down on me, but still I knew what he wanted.

I turned my head away from him, thrusting my neck against his lips. "Do it," I cried. "For sweet Christ, *do it!*"

And for one terrifying moment, my Vampire stilled, *then struck.*

Fangs pierced my vein, then shock and pain.

My orgasm...

My body jerked and trembled as he plunged his cock deep once more, taking me over the edge.

He was hilt-deep between my thighs as he sucked on my neck, taking a slow, careful draw of my blood…before he released me.

Heavy breaths between us, the sound deafening in my ears.

I lay there like that, my pussy pulsing…my thoughts cyclonic inside me. Elithien leaned close and licked my neck. The sensation sent a shock wave coursing through me.

"Ruth?" Fear crowded his voice. His grip eased around my wrists and pulled away. "Ruth…did I—" *hurt you…*

The words hung heavy in the air. I tried to catch my breath…tried to calm my swirling thoughts, and turned my head carefully toward him. "That…"

His gaze narrowed. There was a flinch of terror as he waited for me to continue.

"That…was the best sex I've ever had." The words slipped from my lips. "Jesus fucking Christ."

A twitch came at the corner of his lips as he eased away. "You scared the shit out of me for a second. I thought—"

I lifted my trembling hand and carefully felt the side of my neck. There was nothing, no puncture wound…no pain. I remembered the piercing flinch…the shock. "Do…" I stared. "Do I taste okay?"

His brow furrowed, the blush of my blood still in the corners of his lips. One slow slide of his tongue, and he captured the remnant. "You taste incredible," he answered. "Better than I've had in…*forever.*"

A ravenous sound rumbled in Justice's chest as Elithien moved away. Cool air spilled between us, licking between my thighs.

I lifted my gaze to Justice, knowing this was where I was meant to be, with him...*with all of them.*

But the Vampire just forced a smile. "There's going to be plenty of time, Ruth. Don't you worry about that. I like to take my time...like to play with my prey. Just a little, anyway."

A chuckle tickled my throat, and the room swayed. Too much alcohol and not enough food. "In that case, I'm starving. What does a girl need to do to get a meal around here?"

Justice's smiled widened as I lifted my hand toward him. "Now you're talking. Food is what I do best."

I glanced at the others. Rule crossed the floor and grasped the bottle of Scotch from the floor and turned toward me. "You've never had an omelet until you've had one of Justice's."

Elithien leaned close, pressing his body against mine as he kissed me. "God, you're perfect."

Justice grasped my hand as Elithien kissed me, and I knew then. Knew why this here was just us. This was fate...and not an ending, but a beginning.

Elithien pulled away, grasped my waist once more, and lifted. Justice was there, as was Rule. One holding me steady as I kicked off my heels, the other working the buttons of his shirt as he moved close to slip it over my arms. They fussed. They smiled.

They touched me, and in that moment, I felt more at home than I'd ever felt before.

Maybe Charlotte was right, maybe that empty house wasn't my home...

And maybe these Vampires were?

"Don't plan on returning," Rule demanded, holding the

Scotch with one hand while his deft fingers worked the buttons of his shirt. "You belong on this side of the river, Ruth."

"Maybe I always have?" I ventured.

He smiled, lips stretching with his grin as he leaned down and kissed me.

25

"You okay?" Elithien inquired.

I blinked in the darkness and lifted my head. My hair was a mess…my body hummed. There was a tingling in the valley of my groin, a remnant from pointed fangs. I blushed with the memory of what we'd done. I was still naked…*very* naked, lying in the middle of a Vampire's den. "No, I don't think I am," I answered. "I feel like I'm having an out-of-body experience."

He just chuckled and, in the soft pale glow of a light on the other side of the room, I caught him shaking his head.

"Did you just shake your head at me?"

He froze for an instant. Steel eyes glinted as they found mine sparkling with amusement. "What would you say if I did?"

"I'd bust your balls," I answered with the last trace of energy I could find.

Which wasn't much.

"Tomorrow," I finished. "Tomorrow I'd bust them."

I'd lost count of the times I'd been pulled back to bed.

The same bed I lay in now…I flopped back down, curling one arm under the pillow. A moan turned into a snarl on the other side of me. A hand reached out, and a calloused thumb danced across my nipple. My body came alive in an instant, those low, steady embers of desire flaring with the touch.

"Again?" I whispered, and rolled toward him.

Hurrow's lips curled in a cheeky smile. "If you prefer I don't…" he slid his hand from my stomach. Embers turned into a flame…that burned brighter than any need.

"Don't you dare," I warned. "You can't ask for something and then take it back."

He shoved upwards, sleep driven away in an instant by a ravenous gaze. "What makes you think I was taking it back?"

He rose up on his elbows, and the black silk sheet slipped, pooling around his waist with the movement, before he pounced. He manhandled me, gripping my waist with careful hands and dragging me underneath his body.

My breath caught with the movement. God, he was fast…*and strong.* So unbelievably strong. Heat burned inside me, flaring to life with his touch. White fangs peeked out from his lips as he stared down at me. "There's no taking it back, Ruth…I warned you, there's no escaping us."

No escaping.

I swallowed hard as butterflies filled me. There was a tiny part of me that was terrified at the thought of that. That part of me struggled, bonds of destruction wound tight…as tight as his wrists around mine as he stretched out on top of me and pressed his cock between my thighs.

"Does that frighten you?" Hurrow whispered as he lowered his head.

I closed my eyes, taking in everything about him, from the musty scent of our bodies, to the way his fingers traced the veins of my wrists. I waited for it to frighten me...enough to pull me out of this spiral. But it didn't...if anything, it turned me on.

"No," I whispered, and opened my eyes, meeting his gaze. "It doesn't."

He drove his hips forward in a slow thrust, then lowered his lips to the tight peak of my breast. "Good," he breathed against the tightening flesh.

Fangs scraped across the tight nub, making me shiver. I closed my eyes once more, feeling the bed shift beside me as Elithien rose.

We'd made love for hours...or days, I wasn't sure anymore. Rule and Justice stayed in the beginning, but then disappeared sometime later. But here in the darkness...in the pit of the den, we were all alone.

It was a room deep in the house, with electronic locks and key switches that couldn't be overridden. Here they slept...*or tried to...*Hurrow made a low sound of pleasure as he licked my puckering pink flesh. I widened my legs with the sensation, ready for him once more.

Footsteps sounded near the bed. I stilled and my senses came alive, searching for Elithien.

"He's fine, checking the cameras and making sure you're safe. Are you safe, Ruth?" Hurrow questioned, and rocked his hips forward.

His cock pressed against my slit, dragging my focus to his grip around my wrists and his knees pressed against the inside of mine, opening me wide. My breath caught. I was ready for him...*Dear God, I was ready.* I rocked my hips forward as he slid all the way inside. A moan tore free.

"Fuck, I love the sound of that...*do it again."* he urged, pulling out before he thrust back in.

The movement had the desired effect, tearing another moan free from me. He chuckled with the sound and thrust once more, bring me back to that brink in an instant. My breath sped, I was panting now as he rode my body.

"You're mine, Ruth Costello. So help me God, you're mine."

He branded the words into my soul, stitched them into the very fabric of who I was, and I was made better because of them...*I was made whole.*

"You belong to all of us," Elithien declared beside the bed.

He watched...*he liked that.* I focused on him, biting my lower lip, and gave myself into them. My climax came at a rush, biting deep with its own set of fangs. I bucked underneath Hurrow, hands trying to punch through the mattress. But he held me down carefully, using his hold as an anchor to bring himself undone.

A low, guttural sound rumbled in the back of his throat, bestial and raw, until he stilled and the sound ended, leaving only the heavy gasps of our breaths behind.

I lay like that, slick and wet under him, until he dropped his body to the side and rolled. "Okay...that's enough...for now."

I licked dry lips as they stuck to my teeth, and answered. "You said that last time."

"This time I really mean it."

"It's almost time, anyway," Elithien announced. "Ten minutes and we're free."

Free from the vault in the middle of the house. Free to leave.

The thought had pushed in before, in moments like this, when I was too far gone to stop the worry. I had to leave. I knew that. My life waited...my company waited. Only this bed felt so damn good.

"Stay if you want, stay as long as you want. Hell, if I had my way, you'd stay here forever," Elithien sighed.

"And what? Become a full-time Vampire mistress?"

"Mistress?" Elithien shifted in the darkness, standing over the bed to stare at me. "I was thinking more like a wife."

A wife? I rolled, pushing upwards on shaking limbs. "You're kidding, right?"

He leaned down, gripping the mattress to advance like a predator. "There's one thing about me, Ruth. I *never* kid."

He was cold. Chilling...and utterly seductive.

The idea that he wanted me around was kinda...*hot.*

I smiled and stretched out, my hand searching for his as he fisted the mattress. "Ask me again...later."

It wasn't a no...nor was it a yes. Elithien just shook his head and chuckled. "Only you would make me beg, Ruth. Only you."

He straightened as Hurrow rolled out of bed on the other side. Noises came from behind the vaulted door. I lifted my head as the bathroom light clicked on and seconds later, the sound of a shower spilled into the room.

"When you're ready to leave, I'll have Justice drive you home. But the bodyguard, Ruth. He has to stick with you, especially when we're not with you."

I shoved the silk sheets aside and scooted to the end of the bed as Elithien turned to the door. The locks gave way with a loud *thunk!* Then the door was opening, letting the air from the house spill in.

Justice was waiting, and strode into the room. He glanced at me and the rumpled bed, the corners of his lips curling. "Someone had a busy day."

"Beats boardroom meetings, that's for sure," I answered. "How did you…sleep?"

"Restlessly," he answered, looking me dead in the eye.

The thought of that made me smile. Heat followed, the simmering scald of excitement. I raised my gaze, taking in his mammoth six-foot-four frame and his powerful chest. He was bigger than the others. More dangerous, too. An apex predator…among a coven of beasts.

"You want to shower, and I'll take you home?"

I jerked out of the fantasy and gave a nod. "Give me ten and I'm yours."

"You've always been mine, Ruth. I've just been waiting for you to catch up to that," he declared, and turned for the door.

Possessive. *Dangerous.*

Staying with these Vampires was going to take a lot to get used to. I strode into the bathroom as Hurrow ran fingers through his sodden hair and stepped out of the shower. "All yours."

The shower was massive, one glass divider in the middle of the room and four overhead jets that rained down. Hurrow grabbed me, pulling me close as I went to step in. One hand found the small of my back, the other my shoulder. He kissed me, slow and hard, and stepping away. "Have a nice shower. We'll be in the house."

331

He left then, striding from me with trickles of water running like veins down his muscled back. God, that ass was perfection, tensing as he reached for a towel. I tore my focus from him and stepped under the warm spray, tilting my head while the warmth slipped over my skin.

I washed and shampooed, used a creamy lotion that smelled divine, and emerged ten minutes later with a towel wrapped around my body. There were clothes laid out on the bed. Casual sweats...and my dress from last night draped neatly next to them.

I could get used to this. I felt myself tripping, stumbling into the kind of emotion I'd searched for my entire life. I wanted to be the first one someone thought of. I wanted to be the center of their universe. I wanted to be their sun. I lifted my gaze to the open door. The faint sound of voices comforted me. I dressed, tugging on a soft cotton shirt and baggy shorts before grabbing the dress and heels and walking through the door.

The smell of bacon wafted along the corridor. My belly clenched tight, snarling and ravenous, as I made my way to the kitchen.

Justice looked up at me as he stood by the counter and stared at a plate.

A plate that was piled high with everything imaginable. Fluffy pancakes sat to the side, a thick curl of butter melting in a drizzle of syrup. Bacon was next to them, stiff and crispy, creamy and fluffy eggs in a small pile, and beside it...hulled strawberries.

"I wasn't sure what you liked," the Vampire muttered, then frowned as he looked at the mountain of food. "So I made everything."

"I can see that." I stared at the huge breakfast. "It all looks amazing."

He jerked his gaze to mine, as a brow arched high. "Really?"

"Really," I laughed, and strode forward, plucking a strawberry from the plate and popping it into my mouth. "And I'm damn near starving."

He beamed, grinning ear to ear like a fool. But I'd never felt so alive, so hungry and free, and cared for. "The fact that you took the time to do all this for me makes me the luckiest damn woman on this earth right now."

Something bloomed in his gaze. Something primal, something lethal. He inhaled hard, chest pushing out as I chewed and swallowed. He dragged his teeth along his lower lip as I reached for more. "Will you let me feed you?"

I stopped, my hand at the rim of the plate, reaching for another berry. "As in…"

"From my hand, let me feed you."

I pulled away, fighting the instant reaction to say I was big enough to feed myself. I wasn't used to this kind of attention, not like this. "Yes, if you want."

He grasped the plate and my hand, and led me to the expansive dining table in the middle of the room. It was neat and sparse, with a black glass top and high-backed leather chairs that looked expensive.

He set the plate down and pulled out the chair, waiting. I swallowed, then sat, expecting him to sit next to me, but he didn't. He picked up a strawberry, swirled it through the mess of butter and syrup, then reached around to capture my jaw. "Open."

The command was cold and hard…*and terrifying.*

A tremor cut through me as he focused on my lips when they opened. Buttery sweetness hit me, and the perfect taste of the berry followed, crisp and juicy. A rumble echoed in his chest at the sight. I chewed and swallowed, licking my lips. "More."

He swallowed hard. "More?"

I nodded, starting to understand him. Pride ignited in his eyes as he searched the plate, finding the most perfect piece of bacon. I opened for him, waiting as he slid his fingers along my lip, then slipped the crisp morsel inside.

I moaned as the perfect salty taste replaced the sweetness from the berry. God, I'd never tasted anything so good, not in the hundreds of Michelin-starred restaurants I'd eaten at. This was by far the best.

"You keep making sounds like that, mortal, and I'm going to have to rethink my whole slow seduction stance."

"You keep making food like that, *Vampire,* and I'm going to have to seduce you my damn self."

He roared with laughter, throwing his head backwards, letting the sound spill through the house. His hand slipped from my jaw as he stepped backwards and fixed me with a look of pure delight. "I think I'd like that."

He left me then, chuckling, and went to the study. I ate slowly, taking my time with the food, until my belly was contented and I became drowsy. I could see myself here, see myself happy. But I couldn't give up what I'd worked for. My company, and my name, it was ingrained in me.

I rose from the table, carried the plate still with some food into the kitchen, and scraped it into the trash before rinsing it.

"You ready to go?"

I turned, finding Rule in the doorway. "Chef Justice is

busy this morning, so I'm stepping in as chauffeur."

"Perfect," I smiled at him.

There was a cheekiness with Rule I hadn't felt with the others. He slouched against the doorway, arms crossed, watching me as I grabbed my dress, heels, and bag from the counter.

Voices came from the back of the house. I wanted to stay goodbye, and maybe make plans for later, but the whole idea of that sounded tacky…and a little desperate. So I followed Rule out the front door into the cool evening air.

"Wow, time really does slip away from you in there, doesn't it?"

"Time is different for us than it is for you, but we're still always chasing the moon. Just like you chase the sun."

I was going to have to get used to this change of work 'day', to schedule meetings and take calls around my Vampires. It was either that, or be permanently exhausted. I was going to have to spend a fortune on under-eye concealer. Rule unlocked the Explorer and opened the door, waiting for me as I climbed in.

Barely a heartbeat later, he was sliding into the driver's seat and starting the engine. "Hurrow called ahead, your bodyguard is waiting at your place."

I jerked my gaze toward him. "Really?"

He just smiled. "Don't worry, he was careful not to step on your toes, just giving him a heads-up you might be coming home."

"Step on my toes, hunh?" I muttered. I could see this was going to be a thing with them. Possessive and guarded. I like it, even if it was going to be a pain in the ass to deal with.

I relaxed back in the seat, letting Rule's skill behind the wheel lull me.

"I was sorry to hear about your dad. I liked him, even for a mortal."

I flinched at the words and turned to look at him. "You knew him…my dad?"

"Yeah, met him a number of times, actually. He used to come out to the warehouse. He liked to see the green, as he used to say."

The green. "Sounds like him, alright."

"He liked Elithien, too. Liked the way he was ruthless…that's how he said it. *Ruth-less.*"

Pain cut deep. I could still hear him saying my name. *Give 'em hell, Ruthless.* God, I missed him. "He liked Elithien, huh?"

"Said he reminded him of his daughter, crazy when you think about it. That night, the meeting…the chances that you and Elithien would meet. He almost backed out of it, you know. But your father was one insistent stubborn old mortal."

Not taking no for an answer, Ruthy. You're coming, that's final. I got some special people coming…I think you're gonna like them.

Goddamn.

It hit me hard. It was a setup…*I'd been set up.* "That old snake in the fucking grass…"

Rule glanced my way and grinned. "I was wondering when you were going to figure it out. Seemed like your old man still had a few tricks up his sleeve."

"I'd tear him a new one if he were alive," I muttered.

Maybe not. Maybe I'd hug the shit out of him, but I'd think about it long and hard. He'd set us up. That night in the alley...that's how this had all started. I thought about that, about fate and loyalty.

My Vampires were more loyal than I'd thought.

I settled back in the seat, knowing that, and reached out to grasp Rule's hand.

He drove like that, fingers entwined with mine, as we passed over the bridge and into the other side of Crown City. The mortal half...the *strange* half.

I'd thought it was 'us' and 'them'.

Mortals on one side of the river, and beasts on the other.

Only, the lines had blurred in the months since the night of that meeting at the Jewel. Family had stepped up and proven themselves monsters. I was glad it was over, glad I had nothing to do with Judah and Blane anymore.

I squeezed Rule's hand and he lifted it, pressing my knuckles to his lips.

I didn't want the drive to end. Each of my Vampires was different. Each brought their own energy and personality. Elithien was colder, and quiet...*calculating* my father would have called it. Hurrow was all drive, all raw power, and Justice...Justice was downright scary, so huge, and when he looked at me...I felt invincible.

But Rule, he was more like a mortal, purposeful and accurate, and utterly gorgeous.

He glanced my way. Those seductive lips curled as he stared at me. I was caught in the shine of silver, trapped like prey. Only this target wouldn't fight...she wouldn't even flinch.

She'd hold onto him, onto all of them, and take all she could.

Forever...

26

"What was all that about?" I asked, turning to Russell as headlights splashed along the driveway while the Explorer backed out.

"Oh, nothing," he answered, his tone rock fucking steady. "Just getting to know each other is all…you know, man to Vamp."

I followed him as he turned away, locking the door behind us. I'd been home less than five minutes, and already my world was changed. But if they thought I was going to roll over while they turned my world upside down, they had another damn think coming.

"Well?" I dogged the bodyguard's every step as he went to the kitchen and busied himself opening drawers and grasping cups.

I didn't give in, dumping my bag, clothes, and heels onto the counter and watching him. "Well?"

"He was…*very detailed* in his expectations of my performance, let's put it that way."

"Goddammit." I jerked my gaze to the door. "Listen, I'm sorry ab—"

"Don't." Russell lifted his gaze to mine. "You think I wasn't prepared for this? They care...*he cares,* that's all."

He crossed the kitchen in the blink of an eye, moving soundlessly to stalk toward me. For a second, my heart thundered, the urgency in my head said, *step back...*But I held my ground, watching him stop in front of me.

"Nothing's getting past me, Ruth. I'm not about to let anyone hurt you. Not your sick-as-fuck cousins, or anyone else."

So that's what the private talk was about...

I winced at the words as he reached out and touched my arm. "You're safe with me...well, mostly safe. I make pretty crappy coffee." He slid his hand from my arm and gave a shrug.

"Makes two of us," I muttered. "Doesn't matter, anyway. I was going to go into the head office and get some work done."

"Then we can grab some on the way." He smiled. "See, worked out perfect after all."

I shook my head, unable to stop from grinning. "You know, this might be the best relationship that I've had in about eight years."

"Why, 'cause we both can't cook for shit?" he called.

I laughed, and grabbed my stuff from the counter and headed for the stairs. It felt weird and kinda casual having Russell here in my home, almost like it had life once more and not the half-filled existence I'd given it.

I went into the bedroom and closed the door behind me. My body still buzzed with desire. I licked my lips and lifted my hand, probing the hollow of my throat. I could still feel him there, biting deep, drawing my blood into his mouth.

I shuddered with the sensation. The heat inside me was instant, flushed and desperate, even after last night. I should be exhausted…I should be in a damn coma. My smile stretched wider as I cast my bag and clothes onto the bed. My phone fell free, the screen black…the battery now dead.

I sighed, then reached over and picked up the charger on the bedside table and plugging it in. A red light blinked, and blinked…and *blinked.* "Damn thing."

I needed clothes, appropriate clothes and not a Vampire's sweats. I went into the bathroom, took one long look at myself in the mirror, and smiled. "Okay, not as bad as I thought."

I grabbed my brush and dragged it through my long strands before tying them up in a high ponytail, then yanked the shirt off over my head. My bra was next, then the sweat shorts.

I was bare underneath…thanks to Elithien and his fangs. "You betch your ass I'll make you buy new panties, too…and I'll make damn sure they're expensive."

My heart raced at the thought.

It didn't matter how much they cost, they wouldn't last long.

I strode back into the bedroom and went to the drawer, yanking it open and selecting a comfortable set. I couldn't sleep anyway, not after lying in bed all day, not that I'd had a lot of sleep.

Sounds of movement from the kitchen drew me out of the memory. I put on my underwear, then went into the closet and pulled on slacks and a soft silver cashmere sweater. My phone was still blinking, only this time the screen came alive when I pressed the button.

Five percent charge.

I sighed, glanced at the door, and grabbed it from the charger, this time taking the lead with me. Nice sensible heels, and I strode around the bed and opened the door. Russell was waiting for me as I headed downstairs. I smiled and held up my phone. "Dead, can I charge it on the way?"

"Absolutely," he said and headed for the front door.

I waited for him to hold it open, but instead, he stepped through, slowing enough to check the street. I pulled the door closed and twisted the lock. He had a remote for the garage, and anyway, I doubted we'd be returning until the early hours of the morning.

No doubt my inbox would be filled with messages… and there was the rather large issue of firing all my damn staff to deal with. Orange lights flared as the locks disengaged. Russell was at my side, opening the door and waiting for me to slip inside.

A second was all it took to plug in the charger and wait for him to start the car. I clicked on the seatbelt, watching as the screen came to life.

Six percent.

"We good?" Russell asked.

"Yep," I jerked my gaze to his.

He started the car and the pulled out onto the road. I tried to sit back, but the phone got the better of me. I checked it again.

Eight percent.

The phone beeped, taking me by surprise. I pressed

the button and saw thirteen missed calls…all from Alexander. But there was only one single message.

Ruth. Call me when you get this message. It's urgent.

"Shit."

"Everything okay?" Russell glanced toward me.

I just nodded, pressing the button and lifting it to my ear. The phone rang three times before it was picked up.

"Oh, thank God. I've been trying to reach you all day," Alexander growled. "Where the hell are you?"

"I'm in the car heading to the head office."

"We have a problem at the docks, a *very* big problem. I suggest you get down here, wharf five."

"What is it? What's going on?"

"I'll explain it when you get here, and Ruth, don't turn your phone off again."

I flinched and pulled the phone from my ear as Alexander ended the call. "Okay, then. Jesus."

"You alright?" Concern bled into Russell's voice.

I forced a smile, and looked up at him. "Sure, change of plans. Can you take me to the yard? Wharf five, apparently."

"Sure, what's going on there?"

I glanced into the night and mumbled. "Not too sure on that."

He didn't push, just turned the wheel and steered us toward the river and not the city. I sat back against the seat, turning to stare out at the city lights.

"Don't turn off your phone, who the fuck does he think he is?" I muttered.

The more I thought about the words, the more pissed off I became. He was acting like an asshole. Memories from last night came slipping back to me, memories that had hidden under the haze of too much Scotch.

Alexander grabbing my arm and yanking me close.

I reached up and rubbed my arm.

You don't answer my calls, Alex's voice crowded in. *You disappear for hours at a time. You're not careful anymore, out like this in a fucking bar with strangers. It's like I don't know you anymore.*

God, had he really said that?

If you don't know me, my own voice was savage in my head, *then maybe it's you who needs to be careful?*

Tension pulsed in the back of my neck as I glanced at my phone. Maybe I should call Elithien, just to check in? *And now you're sounding clingy and desperate...no one likes a desperate girlfriend, especially not a Vampire.*

I exhaled and thought about everything other than the shitstorm I was about to walk into.

Obviously, Alex was pissed, and maybe a little humiliated.

I'd apologize. *Yeah,* first up, I'd apologize, *even if I'd done nothing wrong.* Goddamn, I hated working with men sometimes.

I thought about Elithien as the first sparkle from the river shone in the distance. He wasn't like that, not desperate or cruel. He was dangerous and possessive, but one word from me and he'd walk away. I knew that with every nerve in my body.

I lifted my gaze to the open dock gates in the distance and steeled myself for a moody and pissed-off ex-lover.

"Okay, I can do this." I reached forward, unplugged my phone from the charger, and noticed the waiting message from Ace. He'd messaged, *that's right.* "Shit."

We drove through the open gates and swung around to the empty yard. The small guardhouse was still plunged in darkness. I felt frustration rise...until I caught sight of a car in the middle of the open yard. A dark blue Toyota, one that was faintly familiar. I glanced at the plate as the driver's door opened and a woman climbed out.

"Isn't that your nurse?" Russell asked.

Headlights from the Chrysler splashed over Charlotte. She winced and turned her head away, but not bothering to shield her eyes. "Yeah, it is."

The yellow dock light barely reached her, leaving the rest of wharf five plunged in darkness. I was already reaching for the door handle as Russell pulled up behind her.

"Is she broken down?" my guard wondered.

The hood of the car wasn't up. There was no real reason for her to be here. I didn't even think she knew this place existed. "I don't know..."

I shoved the door open and climbed out. "Charlotte, you okay?"

She didn't answer, didn't even move as I closed the door behind me and walked around the front of the car.

"Are you hurt?" Russell asked as he climbed out of the car.

I was already cutting behind her car as she lifted her gaze, her brown eyes cold and stony as she lifted her hand. "I'm sorry, Ruth, I really am."

Silver glinted from the muzzle of the gun, the shine almost gold in the light. My heart thundered, punching against my ribs as, in an instant, she shifted her stance and fired.

Boom.

Boom...

BOOM!

I stood there, frozen, just a shell. The glint of the gun was blinding as Charlotte shifted her gaze to mine. There was no panic in her eyes, just determination. The panicked rush of my pulse churned like an undertow inside my head. The roar was all I could hear, until a gasp came from behind me. I moved achingly slowly and turned my gaze.

Russell was slumped against the car, staring at her. Blood sprayed into the air as he coughed.

Blood bloomed across the upper part of his shirt. But there was nothing in the center. *A vest...he was wearing a vest.*

He reached and dragged his gun free, desperation widening his eyes as he looked at me. "Ruth...*run.*"

Crack. Crack. Crack!

The side mirror of the Toyota shattered as he opened fired. The sound of breaking glass tore into me, cleaving through my terror.

"RUTH, MOVE!" Russell roared as he stumbled backwards.

Shots rang out again. I lunged, driving my body around the Chrysler as silence descended.

My ears rang. A sickening bitter stench clung in the air. I dragged it in until I gagged. Acid spilled into my mouth as I peeked over the hood of the Chrysler.

Silence. Cold chilling silence. "Russell?"

I jerked my gaze to the side of the Toyota, then stumbled to the rear of the vehicle. He was slumped on the ground, his back against the driver's door, blood pouring out of a wound in his neck. There was blood...*so much blood.*

"Don't..." He jerked his gaze to me. His eyes were wide, the whites blinding. "I got her...but I don't know..."

Panic pushed in, making my knees tremble. I braced against the car and lifted my gaze along the side of the Toyota. She wasn't there. Blood was smeared along the window. I walked forward, and glanced down. Brass shell casings were scattered on the ground, but there was no more blood, no Charlotte. I stumbled forward and dropped to kneel at his side.

Blood gushed, pulsing from his neck. "Jesus, Russell," I slammed my hand against his neck.

"Don't bother...it's okay," he whispered, his skin so pale in the dim light. Dark circles welled under his eyes. They weren't there before. "Take my gun." He tried to lift his hand, but his arm shook. "Ruth...take my damn gun."

A sob tore free as my fingers slipped in his blood. "No, *Russell, no.*"

"That's a good idea," came from right behind me. "I'll take that, Ruth."

I spun at the sound of Alex's voice. He stepped close and bent down fast, tearing the gun from Russell's hand. Blood glistened on the gun.

"Alex?" I cried, tears welling in my eyes. "What the *fuck* is going on?"

"You?" Russell whispered.

But Alex didn't answer, just glanced at the Toyota and reached around his back, pulling out a set of handcuffs.

"Now, you're not going to cause me any trouble, are you?" he growled as he bent low.

Russell gave a savage snarl and shoved forward, knocking into me. *"You fucking piece of shit!"*

I shoved against the ground and stumbled backwards.

"Now that's not very nice," Alex snarled and lifted the gun, the muzzle trained pointblank at Russell's head.

"No!" My scream ripped free.

I lunged, slamming into him and knocking the gun from his hand. It hit the ground with a *thud.* Arms and legs entangled as I fell into Russell. The stench of blood filled my nose until my hair was yanked hard, and my head snapped back.

"You think I'm fucking playing here?" Alex roared, his eyes glinting with rage.

My vision blurred as he dragged me backwards. One savage snarl, and he kicked the gun aside and grasped my hand. The cuff snapped tight around my wrist. Metal ground against bone and agony followed.

"You really are a stupid fucking bitch, you know that?" He yanked my arm behind my body and reached for the other.

"A-Alex…Alex, what's going on h-here?" I tried to keep the terror from my voice.

Steel teeth bit deep, ratcheting to a close. I shoved away, falling and rolling, fighting to get upright.

"Don't…" Russell groaned, and tried to push upwards. Blood flowed as he moved. "Don't hurt her. We can talk about this. We can…"

"Shut the fuck UP!" Spittle flew from his mouth as Alex screamed.

That wasn't the man I knew. That wasn't the man I thought I'd been in love with.

"We can talk about this." I closed my eyes and tried to

stop the world from spinning. "Alex, whatever this is, we can talk about it."

He barked a hard laugh. I opened my eyes to the manic gleam in his.

He bent and grabbed the gun from the ground. "You see, Ruth, at first it was about the company. I wanted it for *us*. I would've done anything to get it. I had it all set up, offshore bank accounts, a whole new crew of employees waiting in the wings to obey only me."

Cold moved in, chilling me to the bone. "That was you?"

"Judah was an easy mark to take the blame. The guard was only supposed to frighten you, to make you come running to me like you always did. But you didn't, did you, Ruth? You didn't come running at all."

He took a step toward me, his movements slow and calculated. "I saw you…last night with them in the alley. I *watched* you."

Terror plunged deep like a knife, carving all the way to my soul. "What did you say?"

He didn't answer, just glanced at Russell and strode forward. I flinched and fell backwards, kicking my heels against the ground until one shoe tore free.

"No," I pleaded as he bore down on me. "No, *Alexander no!*"

He grasped my wrists and yanked, bowing my arms behind me until agony roared. I had no choice but to climb to my feet and stumble, leaving my heel behind. "Please Alexander, don't do this."

Russell shoved his hand out toward me. But there were no more words from my bodyguard…only a fragile stare.

Tears blurred as Alexander yanked me backwards, dragging and heaving me.

"No!" I screamed.

Russell blurred under a sheen of my tears. Pain lashed my foot as I stumbled. Lights shimmered against the inky black. Water slapped the moors, the sound filling me with panic.

I struggled, thrashing my body and shoving. But he was stronger, yanking me around to face him.

His first lashed out. The blow cracked my nose. My head snapped backwards, agony radiating through my face. Stars sparkled, blinding me. I moved without thinking, dazed and disorientated, as warmth slid from my nose and trickled over my lips.

"Please..." the word was feeble and pathetic. "Alexander."

"I was going to take you with me," he grunted, dragging me closer to the shimmering lights. "But when I saw what they did to you, I knew that could no longer be part of my plan."

He shoved me forwards. My steps unsteady, my knees gave way. I fell facefirst and hit the ground hard, the sting along my cheek instant.

Ruth? Elithien's voice bloomed in my head.

Chains snapped around my ankles, drawing them together.

Ruth!

"Please," I whimpered. "Don't do this."

Links clanked as Alexander rose. There was nothing good left in him now. No remnant of the man I once loved. There was just an animal...*just a beast.*

"I'd like to say we had some good times, Ruth. But you ruined it…you ruined it all."

Ruth, I'm coming! my Vampire roared in my head.

But even I knew it was far too late to save me. Alexander bent and yanked me upwards by the cuffs around my wrists, then he hauled a heavy concrete block to his waist. One shove and I was stumbling toward the end.

Cold wind cut through me, making me shudder. I shoved toward him, driving my body forward. It was like hitting a wall. He shoved me backwards, making me stumble until my bare foot found the edge.

"I'm sorry it had to be this way, Ruth. We could've been incredible together."

With one savage push, I flew backwards.

Only this time, there was no ground to catch my fall…

There was only the water…

Only the cold.

2 7

H is face blurred as I fell. A loud *splash* followed, filling my view with the rush of white.

The concrete block sank fast, diving past me until the chains snapped taut around my feet and pulled me under. I tried to thrash, tried to kick, and scream…but there was nothing.

No give in the steel.

No flare of hope.

I was gone now, fading into the murky depths as Alexander lingered at the water's edge, then turned and walked away. Desperation burst free, tearing bubbles from my mouth and my nose to the surface. Pain followed. Pulsing and quivering, filling my head with a deafening roar.

I tried to think, tried to feel.

Tried to do anything but sink down…down…*down.*

Goddamn it, RUTH! Elithien's roar punched through. *Fight!*

Lights shimmered above. The weak glow was fading

into the darkness. I bucked as my Vampire screamed, and tried to lift my feet. But they were so heavy...so very heavy.

Pressure built inside my chest, punishing and burning. I shuddered as the icy depths wrapped around me tight. It was so dark here...so cold and dark, *and lonely.*

*It's okay, kid...*a voice slipped through the emptiness of my mind. *Dad's here.*

A bubble burst free at the sound of his voice. I blinked into the darkness, my heart beating like a thousand drums. *You're going to be okay, Ruthy. I'm right here.*

I didn't want to see him. Not yet. Not when I had...*them.*

My Vampires, my hope. My Mafia Monsters.

Ruth, Hurrow's voice. *Ruth, hold on, baby. Ruth, hold on!*

It's okay. I tried to speak the words, but my lips would no longer move.

I wanted to cry, to really cry.

To feel and love, and hate and rage.

I wanted to touch them...once more.

The burn in my chest turned to fire. I tried to hold on...tried to fight for them. But my thought faded...like I was forgetting.

Forgetting how to live.

Forgetting how to breathe.

Ruth, Elithien begged, *Ruth, please.*

Energy pulsed through me. I felt them...felt them come for me.

Splash. Splash. Splash. Splash.

I wanted it all. But what I really wanted was them...*always them.*

Only, I watched my kingdom fall.

Something blurred in the darkness. My eyes were burning now, catching shapes in the murkiness. Hands gripped me as I finally opened my mouth and breathed.

Water rushed in, slipping down into my belly, weighing me down. I felt myself slip now, leaving the sheath of the body behind as I was jerked and driven higher. Higher still…

So high I could touch the sky.

"Ruth!" someone screamed. *"RUTH, breathe!"*

Someone punched my chest. Lips pressed against mine.

It's okay, I wanted to whisper. *It's all going to be okay.*

"No, don't you do this to me!"

Kid.

I turned as Dad called my name. I saw him now, just as perfect and fierce as he'd always been, blue eyes shining with his cheeky grin. *Dad?*

He made no move toward me, just stood there… hovering at the edge of the light.

It's not your time yet, honey, he said with a shake of his head. *You need to go back.*

Go back?

I turned my gaze, seeing four men kneeling over a body, long chains at her feet.

You've got things to do, kid.

I glanced at Dad, *I do?*

Yeah, Ruthy, you do.

A jolt came at my chest. A heaviness at my lips. I lifted my hand, fingers pressed against my lips.

"Breathe, baby, *please breathe.*" One of the men pleaded.

I took a step toward them and the woman lying on the ground. Her skin was so pale…deathly white.

"I'm going to kill them," one of the men snarled as he pushed to his feet.

He was massive, built like a bull. He clenched his fists as he turned toward me. White fangs punched out between his blood red lips. "I'm going to fucking kill them all."

Go, Dad growled behind me. *Go!*

I was shoved from behind, slammed back into that cold, lifeless body with a savage jolt.

Fire lashed through my lungs, tearing out and through my lips as a cough tore free.

"Ruth! Jesus Christ, *Ruth!"* Elithien screamed.

I blinked and rolled, coughing and heaving. Water spilled from my lips, cold and fetid as I clung to life. They held me, holding me close. I sank against them and closed my eyes as the faint voice of my father slipped through.

Give them hell, Ruthless...give them hell...

"It's okay," Elithien whispered in my ear as he pressed me close. "You're going to be okay."

I lifted my head to him, to the sodden strands of his hair, and the wet clothes stuck against his skin, and growled, "I want him dead, Elithien...I want them all dead. But first, I want you to save someone, turn them into a Vampire if you have to."

My Vampires looked at me...with murder in their eyes, and asked, "Who?"

I was their payment on a debt...and they were my salvation.
Click here to get your copy of Vampire's Sin.

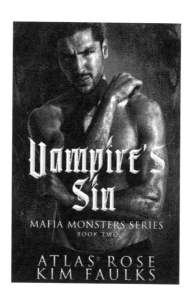

RELEASES IN TWO WEEKS!

Click here to grab your copy

I was their payment on a debt...and they were my salvation.

My Vampires dragged me from the river and brought me back to life, and in turn I saved the one man who gave his life for me...my bodyguard, Russell.

Only to save him will be to turn him into the monster he despises.

With Unseelie Fae blood in his veins he locks himself away until danger comes for me once more.

I vowed revenge on those who tried to destroy us.

I'll make them pay with five *merciless* Immortals at my side.

Because to them, I'm not a possession...to them I am *forever.*

I'm starting to think they're my forever too...

WHO IS ATLAS?

Gothic Paranormal Romance Author
- Chosen by the Vampire Series
- Loves black cats
- Eats all the black jellybeans
- Book hoarder

Connect with me on Facebook and Instagram

Printed in Great Britain
by Amazon